A BLIS

Her imaginary man was there. Sky sensed him before she saw him and allowed his essence to wash over her with a strength that took her breath away, even as his spirit drew her to him. Concentrating, she shut his image out of her mind, then opened her eyes. He remained, walking slowly, determinedly, toward her. Confused, she watched him approach. She could not see his face, but she began to walk toward him, the pull something she could no longer resist.

Then he was there in front of her, but his face was still hazy, blurred, not unusual in a creation of her mind. She reached out one hand to touch his face and immediately a current of desire, passion, need, flowed between them. She concentrated again on making him disappear. Instead he took her hand and brought it to his lips, then pulled her closer until they were pressed tightly together. Sky brushed her fingertips against his jaw, tracing a somehow familiar path to his mouth. When she focused on individual aspects of his face, he became clearer. Before she could think, his mouth had covered hers and branded a tantalizing kiss into her, his tongue touching hers slightly, asking entrance that she freely gave.

Sky felt a languidness passing over her, a hot, sultry heaviness flood through her veins and pool down low inside of her. She opened her mouth to his and he delved deeper, his hands moving over her body, lulling her into a sweet, sweet peace.

To Touch The Stars

Tess Mallory

LOVE SPELL BOOKS   NEW YORK CITY

*For Jan Miller, and the golden days of T.C. and Jan,
sweet memories that will never be forgotten or ever
replaced.*

Live long, my friend, and Prosper.

LOVE SPELL®

March 1998

Published by

Dorchester Publishing Co., Inc.
276 Fifth Avenue
New York, NY 10001

ISBN 0-505-52253-5

The name "Love Spell" and its logo are trademarks of Dorchester
Publishing Co., Inc.

Printed in the United States of America.

ACKNOWLEDGMENTS

To the Underground Rebel Alliance: a group of talented writers destined for great things, who make me laugh and cry, who cheer for me—and give me a good "smack" when I need it! Thanks to my Lovely UGLy (sic) Rebs: Jentle Jane "La Segunda" Appelt, Sally "La Torquemada" Walker, Lorraine "LOLly" Stephens, Linda "Spock" Opdyke, Debra "Troutie" Brown, Sherri "Sherrilicious" Erwin, Sara V. "Brook, li'l sis" Olds, Jo Anne "Jypsy Jo" Dreyfus, Carolyn "Caromia" Rogers, Sara "Sarafin" Reyes, Kerri-Leigh "Lady Enigma" Grady, Ron "Stormy" White, Janet "Laine" Gocke, Lisa "Pearls" Coleman, Jennifer "Miss Jennypenny" Licata, Deanna "Didji" Padilla, Anne "Aussie Anne" Clarke, Leanne "Finlea" Ellis, Susan "Suzie Q" Stevenson, Denise "Deli" Agnew, Lynn "Lynnfin" Whitney, Beverly "Calico" Haynes, Sherry "Sherabim" Davis, April "Red" Redmon, Nina "9-uh" Rowan, Jennifer "Jeff" Wilkins, Ruth "Sugar" Kerce, Judi "Judicious" Phillips, Claudia "Hugs" Yates, Ellen "Elinowy" Hestand, Carmel "Nila" Vivier, and Mary Lou "ML" Frank. UGLY REBS UNTIE (sic)! Much, much love from your La Jefa, Testy M.

Thanks also to Flo Moyer (Hayley Gardner for Silhouette), honorary Reb, for her advice and support, as well as the Ladies of Leisure, and the San Antonio Romance Authors (SARA).

Special blessings on my friends at Books to Share in Kerrville—Barbara, Jack, Mark, Gloria and Don, and to Cindy, Debbie and Debbie at Hastings.

A special thanks to C. K. Dexter Havens for his support and understanding. And always, to my children and family, just for being who they are.

To Touch the Stars

Prologue

Flames soared above their heads, and his men shouted at him to leave before the palace ceiling collapsed, but he would not listen. The stench of the dead and dying permeated the smell of smoke, and the heat closed in around him, sucking the air from his lungs, replacing it with fire. And yet he would not leave. Not yet. He stood, one foot on either side of the woman's body, staring down at her. She was dying, and for a brief moment he was struck by the fact that even as life ebbed out of her, her beauty remained. Beauty she would never let him touch, never let him experience. Silver-blond hair spread beneath her. Lavender eyes gazed up at him with such reproach, and such great sadness, that he could barely stand to watch her die. He swallowed and closed his eyes as some deep, forgotten sense of conscience shuddered through him. The unfamiliar emotion passed, and when he opened his eyes again, she had passed as well, her eyes now glassy, as devoid of life as the crystal around her neck, resting against the hollow of her throat.

"Commander! Commander Zarn!" The shout came from behind. He turned and saw his leader of the ground troops signaling him desperately. "The roof! The roof is about to go!"

He glanced up, then bent over the woman's corpse and, with one sharp tug, wrenched the necklace free. Letting it dangle from his fingers in front of his eyes, he threw back his head and laughed, loud and long.

"And so I win after all, Aletha," he said, as the sweat danced against his forehead and the heat burned through the bottom of his boots. "You may have hidden

9

your daughter from me this day, but never doubt that I will find her, and when I do—" He clutched the crystal tightly, lifting his fist above his head, feeling drunk with the blood he had spilled this day. He lowered the crystal, bringing it to his lips, pressing it to him as she had never allowed him to press her sweet flesh.

"I will take her power . . . and end her worthless life."

The ceiling above him crumbled, embers falling, flames surging downward. Zarn turned and ran, making it out of the fiery furnace just in time, his laughter echoing through the smoke as the inferno utterly consumed the House of Cezan.

Chapter One

"I am not prepared to be merciful. Plasma-blasters will be issued to every member of the crew."

Skyra Cezan heard her voice tremble, and she stiffened as two of her officers glanced up from the map spread across the table in the briefing room. The rest of her senior officers began murmuring either at her startling announcement or the emotion she had inadvertently revealed. The plasma-blasters, illegal weapons banned in half the galaxy, had been stolen over a year ago. They had yet to use them, for Skyra had pronounced the risks too high. Until now.

P'ton, security chief, and T'varr, helmsman and communications officer, looked first at each other, then back at their commander.

"Captain," P'ton began, "with all due respect, if we use the plasma-blasters—which propel a highly inaccurate ball of energy—we could end up killing or harming the children." He stabbed one finger down toward the map. "Station One is essentially a world of domes. Each contains an atmosphere of artificial oxygen. The natural atmosphere is unbreathable. If we start using the plasma-blasters, we could accidentally dissolve the domes."

Lieutenant P'ton was short, barely five foot six, but had a dense body composition and huge knotted muscles that gave him the appearance of a strong animal not to be treated lightly. Sky had chosen him to head up her security team because of that strength as well as his single-minded fixation on obeying orders. So far his loyalty had been unwavering, both to the late Redar and to his new

11

captain. She turned her attention back to his concerns.

"Can we isolate the children?"

He spread his hands apart. "There's no way of knowing where they will be at any given time. According to our sources, their schedules vary randomly from day to day for security reasons."

Sky closed her eyes briefly, feeling a wave of dizziness sweep over her. Although she had only recently become the captain of the *Defiant*, she was getting used to making the life-and-death decisions that affected the twenty people making up her crew. Still, she always listened to her senior officers and took their opinions into consideration. That was part of the reason she had been able to maintain the standard her predecessor, Redar, had set before he died, and why her crew of rebels had still been able to wreak havoc on Zarn's forces across the quadrant without getting caught when others had been long ago sent to penal worlds.

She was a good captain because she listened, because she knew she was fallible and still had a lot to learn, and wasn't ashamed to admit it. Whatever gave her crew a better chance to come away from their mission alive— that was the course of action she always pursued. But this time it was different.

Sky bowed her head for a moment, gathering her strength, then snapped herself erect, the muscles in her back, arms, and neck taut. She moved away from the table, hands clasped behind her back, aware that she presented an odd figure in the silver tynarium droid suit she wore. The form-fitting heavy suit in no way hid the fact that she was a woman, but the helmet deposited at her feet would hide her face and her identity when they landed on Station One.

"This is the situation, harsh as it may sound: There is one child whose safety we are concerned about and one child alone: the heir to the throne of Andromeda, my sister, Mayla Cezan." *It wasn't true.* She wanted to shout the words. She was stricken with concern for the other children, but there was nothing she could do about it. She had to save her sister.

The sound of a throat being cleared made her pause in her circling of the briefing room and she turned, nodding at the tall, blue-skinned man standing in one corner of the room. He was an Altairian, a race once known for their rage and love of war, whose culture had only recently found the peace of logic. Not for the first time, Sky felt grateful for the presence of her first officer. He always backed her up—at least in front of the crew.

"Yes, Kell? You wanted to say something?"

"I was merely going to suggest that it may not be necessary to actually use the plasma-blasters. If you let the Guardian and his men know you have this power and will not hesitate to use it, you may be able to bluff them into surrendering."

"Excellent idea," Sky said after a moment's thought. "P'ton, arm everyone with a regular phaser as well as a plasma-blaster. When we land, we'll fire the plasma-blasters at something that will make a good but harmless target for our power." She pointed at a diagram on the map and her people moved closer to the table. "Here. This is some sort of decorative tower next to their landing port. As soon as we land, we'll hit it with the plasma."

"Of course they will have already experienced the power of the plasma," Kell reminded her, "because you will use it to punch a hole in the planetary shielding."

She nodded. "Yes, but I want something they can taste. P'ton, you take ten people and blow the tower, secure the landing port. The rest of us will transport from the ship to the outside of the main building. We'll give the Guardian another little dose of plasma; then we'll switch to phasers." She pushed away from the table. "Any questions? Very well. Battle stations."

Sky wearily watched her officers leave. When the door slid shut she let her shoulders sag and released her pent-up breath in a long sigh. Twisting her long hair back into a knot at the nape of her neck, she sank down into a chair, allowing herself one moment, just one, before she began her own preparations.

The soft *shoosh* of the cabin door opening sent her to her feet and back into her customary stiff pose of authority as she turned to face the intruder. Her shoulders sagged again as she saw it was Kell. His pale blue face and brilliant blue eyes should have been a welcome sight to her. In all the universe there was not a more loyal friend, a better comrade, but she turned away knowing all too well what he was about to say, too tired to hear it said again.

"You're going to wear yourself out." His normally soft voice was even softer than usual, reflecting his concern. He crossed to her side and after giving her face a searching glance, led her to a chair beside the oval table occupying center stage in the small room. "Have you eaten today?" He pushed her down into the cushioned chair and knelt beside her. "Did you sleep last night?"

Skyra sighed, then groaned as the Altairian took one of her hands in his own and began kneading her palm in slow, relaxing circles. She was too tired even to feel surprise at Kell's actions. Usually he avoided contact with others at all costs, but sometimes, once in a great while, he would bend a little. This was the first time in a very long time, however, that he had touched her. She always sensed Kell keeping a part of himself sealed away from her, locked away with his emotions. Perhaps as a new student of logic, he did not trust himself to keep the strong feelings he had for her at bay. And she knew he had feelings for her. It was impossible for her not to be aware of it, even though he had struggled ever since she came aboard to hide how much he cared.

"That feels wonderful." She let her head fall back against the top of the chair and allowed her spine to curve in an uncharacteristic slump.

"Why don't you take off this contraption and go lie down for a while?" he said, gesturing to the silver droid suit she wore.

She shook her head, eyes closed. "No. I've got to be ready the moment we get there." The droid suit was heavy, no doubt about it, but she needed the strength she would gain from the tynarium studded throughout the skin-tight silver uniform. The connecting circuits were presently left undone down the front of her suit, but once snapped together, the tynarium would pulsate into her own muscles and increase her strength by one hundred percent. It was illegal and dangerous, but in this scenario she needed every advantage.

"You know this thing can backfire on you—people have used them and never regained their own strength afterward."

"Shut up, Kell."

He fell silent. Sky counted to ten and smiled when right on cue he began to speak again.

"Have you eaten?" he persisted, moving to the other hand and continuing his ministrations there. She smiled down at him, affectionately brushing one lock of his dark blue hair back from his forehead.

"No, I haven't eaten and I haven't slept," she admitted. "Please, Kell, don't start this again. I'm not hungry. I can't sleep. How can I when I don't know what's happening to her?" She sat up abruptly, jerking her hand from his grasp, and sprang to her feet to pace again. "How long until we reach Station One?" she demanded.

"Not long." Kell caught her by one arm and brought her to a standstill, then quickly dropped his hand back to his side. "Sky, you have got to stop this or you won't be in any shape to help Mayla when we get there."

"I know, I know. All right, I'll eat something."

"You know it doesn't do her any good to beat yourself up about this. It wasn't your fault."

Sky muttered an eloquent curse she'd learned on Candor 7 and was rewarded by the sight of the implacable Kell raising one blue brow. "The hell it wasn't," she amended. "I should have never left her with him."

"It was just for a few hours. How could you have known? He was one of us."

She tossed her long hair back from her shoulder and shook her head in disbelief. "It's my job to know, Kell, or have you forgotten my father gave Mayla into my care ten years ago, put her under my protection before he was murdered?"

"Quite a responsibility for a sixteen-year-old, giving

her a three-year-old child and then disappearing into the galaxy."

"He didn't disappear—he was murdered by Zarn and his Dominion Forces."

Kell folded his arms across his chest. "You don't know that for a fact," he reminded her. "Your father simply never came back for you and Mayla."

Sky moved around the room, shoving chairs against the table distractedly, her head aching with the thought of what might be happening to her sister even now as they hurried to rescue her. "He would have come back if he'd been alive," she whispered. "I know he would have."

"You need to believe that, Sky, but it is not necessarily true."

She spun on the man with clenched fists, and he took an involuntary step backward. "Damn your Altairian logic!" she shouted. "My father loved my sister too much to just abandon her and disappear to save his own skin!"

Kell lifted one brow again. "Did I suggest such a thing?"

"It's what you're thinking—it's what you're always thinking."

"I asked you to stay out of my thoughts, *Captain*," Kell admonished. "I thought we had an agreement on that."

Sky blushed but lifted honest eyes to meet his. "I—I was speaking from an emotional viewpoint, of course. I haven't been reading your mind, Kell. I gave you my word on that long ago. Besides, I can't read anyone's mind as long as I'm wearing this." Her fingers touched the silver band around her forehead.

A slight smile curved his thin lips. "Of course. Then I take it that it is still working well for you?"

"It's wonderful. I can't tell you the freedom I feel now. I mean, the first prototype Redar invented stopped the thoughts of others equally well, but it was heavy and awkward. This is like—" she spread her arms apart. "Like being given wings."

"I'm glad for you, Sky. Have you always had this problem? Did you never have natural shielding in your mind?"

She frowned. "I have a limited ability. It was never a problem on Andromeda. I never experienced the mental assault of other minds until I went to Bezanti. I can only assume that my parents protected me somehow and did not realize I had no ability to protect myself, as their other children did."

"You are fortunate then to have this device."

"I'll never stop being thankful for Redar's genius. I only wish—" She hugged her arms around herself suddenly and turned away. Kell turned her back to face him, his hand gentle on her shoulder.

"He's dead, Sky. You must accept this and go on. Redar abhorred grief in any form."

Sky nodded, letting her hands fall back to her sides. "I know," she said, feeling again the ache that always accompanied any thoughts of Redar. "But I can't help it. I miss him." She glanced back at her first officer. "He saved me, Kell. If he hadn't come along when he had, I don't know what I would have done. Mayla's help in keeping the thoughts of others from my mind was draining even her power. I truly think I would have gone insane if Redar hadn't traced my thought-aura and offered to help me."

It was Kell who turned away this time. "Never forget that the helmet, and the band, came with a price," he said, his voice muted. "And never paint our departed leader as a hero. Redar never gave anyone anything without expecting something in return."

"How can you say that?" Sky asked, hands on her hips, aware her tone was arrogant but unwilling to let the slight to the dead man pass. "He was fighting for Andromeda just like the rest of us. If he had to be ruthless, even to some of his own people in order to hurt Zarn, it was worth it. Besides, it's take or be taken, isn't it? Kill or be killed. And the fact that I used my . . . abilities to help Redar in his raids was simply my way of paying him back for giving me peace the rest of the time. I thought it an extremely fair trade."

17

Kell didn't answer, and Sky began pacing again, her booted feet hitting the deck in a hard staccato.

"Are you sure our intelligence reports are accurate?" she asked, fighting down the panic threatening to overwhelm her from moment to moment. Mayla was in Zarn's hands. The thought of little Mayla at the mercy of the man who had massacred the rest of their family made Sky almost choke with fury and fear.

Even at a young age, the children of the Cezans had had a part in governmental affairs. Sky had been only fourteen years old when she arrived on the peaceful world of Bezanti as an ambassador of goodwill. The invasion of Andromeda had come soon after and she had never returned to her homeworld. Two years later, her father appeared to give her the terrible news that her mother and brothers and sisters were all dead, all except for Mayla. He entrusted her with her little sister, then three years old, before disappearing back into the Bezantian night. She never saw him again. Sky bit back the sob throbbing in her throat and forced the memory away, spinning around to meet Kell's solemn gaze.

"Well?" she demanded. "Are they? Are we sure Mayla is being held on Station One—on that monster's private hellhole for children?"

"Yes," Kell reassured her. "Our agents have determined she was seen being loaded onto one of the Dominion's freighters and its destination was listed as Station One."

"If I took off this band I'd know for certain she was there," Sky fumed. "Perhaps for just a moment—"

Kell's hand stilled her own and she looked up at him in frustration.

"If you take that off, you won't be in any condition to help her when we find her, Sky."

She spun away from his hands, clenching her own in impotent rage. "I know." Tension snaked up her back, tightening her spine until she thought it would snap. When she spoke again, her voice was a whisper. "How long until we get there, Kell? How long?" Desperation curled inside her like a serpent, biting at her insides, bringing tears to her eyes. She blinked them back as she

18

slapped both hands down against the table, fighting for control.

"I'll find out," he said softly. As the doors slid open, then closed again behind him, Sky sank down into one of the conference chairs and leaned her elbow on the edge of the smooth tabletop, her forehead resting against her palm. Her eyes closed as she considered the monumental task she and her crew were about to undertake.

Two months she and her crew had been in space searching for Mayla. Two months since Sky had hurried home after a mission and found she had been betrayed by a man she had trusted with her life—and her sister's life. A member of the rebellion, a man Mayla had healed, practically brought back from the dead, he had been staying with them, going on a few raids, but mostly still recuperating. Sky had stupidly left Mayla behind with him while she set out on a new mission to Aldeburon. She had returned to find he had disappeared, and her sister had been taken by Dominion soldiers.

She stopped pacing and lifted one hand to her temple, tilting her head to one side as she tried to ease the tension there. Her fingertips came in contact with the cold, smooth band of silver encircling her forehead. Kell was right, of course. Removing the band would only bring more pain, pain even she couldn't heal. While she had the telepathic power of the Cezans, she had somehow been born without the innate ability to shield her sensitive mind from the thoughts of others. After she had reached the fullness of her powers when she was thirteen, her life had become a living hell. A nervous tension seized her again. Mayla would soon be thirteen.

Redar had developed the new, thin band only a few months before his death. She could never forget that he had saved her life, for surely if the cacophony of a thousand thoughts had continued to permeate her mind every waking moment, she would have been driven mad and taken her own life. A sadness touched her soul. How she wished she could have saved Redar. But her healing powers were limited, and he had been struck down during a mission, with Mayla far away on Bezanti. His death had

19

been unexpected and there was still a hollow place inside her where his friendship had warmed her for so many years.

Her fingers smoothed the silver band around her forehead. If only Redar were alive, he would know what to do. She dismissed the sentimental thought. She knew what her old teacher would do, and that's what she was doing. He had trained her well, teaching her how to harden the natural woman's softness in her heart, teaching her how to kill before she was killed.

She tangled her fingers into her long hair before jerking her hand impatiently away. Soft silver-blond strands clung to her fingers, bringing a lump to her throat and a sense of panic back to her innermost being. Mayla's hair was the same unusual color. The mark of the Cezans. That, combined with Mayla's pale lavender eyes and her telepathic and healing powers, told the world and the universe of her aristocracy, her right to rule. Sky sank down in a chair in front of the large oval table in the center of the room, pressing her fingers against her closed eyelids. As a child she had been jealous that she had not been chosen by the Creator to be heir. That had been long before Mayla was even born. But now she found herself wishing it again—this time for unselfish reasons. If she had been the heir, Mayla would not be in this danger.

Quelling the turmoil inside her, Sky forced her thoughts to the job at hand. She stood and checked the instrumentation on the silver droid suit she wore, making sure the power bands were ready to be connected whenever she needed the strength of the illegal garment. She smiled as she finished the check. Thank the Seekers Redar had taught her well how to plunder Zarn's weapons dumps scattered across the galaxy. The remote facilities were filled with items seized during his many conquests, most of them now declared illegal by his government.

The complement of her ship, the *Defiant*, was composed of twenty men and women, some of the toughest fighters in the galaxy, handpicked by Redar to form the fledgling underground resistance group. Redar had organized them, planning one day to raise up an entire army and openly strike back at Zarn, freeing Andromeda. But their leader's life had ended prematurely, cut down in one of their raids by Dominion soldiers. Another reason to hate Zarn. It was that hatred, coupled with her own fear of failure, that had led Sky to decide to use the plasma-blasters on Station One.

She shuddered at the thought, then scolded herself silently for her timidity. This was war, after all, and all was fair, even using illegal weapons that left their victims writhing in unfathomable pain. Besides, she had no doubt the Guardian of the station would order his men to lay down their weapons and surrender. Well, perhaps she had a little doubt. If they didn't surrender, of course, she was prepared to fight. But her crew was nervous about the new weapons. She'd heard their whispered concerns.

What if they couldn't control the plasma? It was said that if you didn't handle the guns properly, you could end up with plasma burns yourself. What if Zarn's forces outnumbered them and they were caught with the contraband? A slow, torturous death was the penalty for possessing plasma-blasters. Just for a moment, Sky faltered as she thought of the possible casualties this action could produce. Then the memory of her sister's face when last she'd seen her, happy, whole, safe, pushed her fears for her crew and herself completely under.

The door to the briefing room slid open, and Sky jerked her head up to meet Kell's placid gaze.

"We have arrived, Captain," he said formally. "Station One. Any new orders?"

Sky stood, snapping together the outer flaps of the silver suit. She felt the tynarium energy surge against her skin and picked up the helmet at her feet.

"Give the word," she said, wondering at the cold lack of emotion she felt. "We'll give the bastards down there a chance, but if they don't throw down immediately and surrender—" she paused and met Kell's blue eyes with a dead calm that rivaled his own—"kill them."

* * *

Eagle looked up through the curved plasticene window jutting out from his office wall. The stars twinkled above Station One like the eyes of some ethereal goddess, calling him with a siren's allure, and for the hundredth time that day he wished he could be up amidst the sparkling orbs instead of staying planet bound. He walked unhurried, up and down in front of the view, hands clasped behind his back. His outward expression of nonchalance was deceptive, much like the calm appearance of the world he now surveyed, a world with its own hidden secrets. Underneath his complacent mask an anger was growing, increasing each and every day he had to stay on this chunk of rock some people deigned to call a planet.

The sun in the remote system was too far away to lend any warmth or light to the moonlike world the Kalimar had chosen for Station One, for his prison of children, and so all light and heat was manufactured, as well as the oxygen. Artificial life support for an artificial life. Eagle shook the thought away, striving to focus on the beauty of the stars. But his thoughts, along with his glance, could not avoid what lay below the stars, not for long anyway. His office occupied the highest point on Station One and gave him visual access to most of his domain.

Scattered across the planet surface, dozens of giant domes curved like translucent bubbles, covering this portion of the otherwise empty world, leaving little exposed of the dead, dry planet between their pristine surfaces. Connected by smaller corridor domes, the oxygen-laced semicircles housed the educational buildings and the dorms for the ten thousand or more students occupying the facilities in any given year. There was also an infirmary, the "canteen" for Forces officers working on the station, and the cafeteria.

Eagle's gaze traveled beyond the domes below him, toward the distant dark side of the planet where two single domes lay. The indoctrination cells were situated well away from the rest of the station's dwellings, in darkness as befit their dark purpose, and could only be reached by air-skimmer. Personnel used one of the small crafts to pilot students to their daily or weekly sessions in the Kalimar's mind-probing, personality-altering machines housed there. The Stations were how Zarn, the Kalimar of Rigel, and now ruler of half the quadrant, kept the people of Andromeda, and other worlds, under his control. Children were required by law to live on one of the four Stations, from the age of two to the age of seventeen. Then, the young men and women began a mandatory five-year service in the Forces division of the Dominion—Zarn's name for his vast kingdom that spanned half the quadrant. Any parents who resisted sending their children were summarily killed, or their children were killed in front of them.

Eagle turned his mind away from the sickening thought and for the countless time since he'd arrived at Station One, tried to figure out what he was doing there. He'd made the mistake of commenting to his father that he was sick of fighting, sick of war, sick of watching different cultures—even Andromedan cultures—be systematically destroyed. He was sick of watching comrades die, of watching friends die. He grimaced, pushing the thoughts threatening to flood into his mind away from him. He could avoid thinking about it when he was awake, but when he slept, it was another story.

Ever since Alpha Centauri, since Telles' death, he'd been dreaming—strange dreams, terrible dreams. Amazingly enough, it had been the mention of the dreams that had gotten him sentenced to Station One. His father, usually a very logical man, had grown very upset when Eagle told him about the dreams. Not long after that, he'd sent him to his new assignment. Of course there'd also been a few other little things like failure to obey orders.

So this was his punishment: to be the Guardian of Station One. If Zarn left him here much longer, he might find this particular attempt at chastisement backfiring—for if he was stuck on Station One, he was going to start making major changes, beginning with the elimination of the mind-probes.

He had witnessed a mind-probing the first day he arrived on the station and had begun to shake so badly he'd bolted from the room like a child. It had terrified him, and the fact that he had been unable to force himself to return had frightened him even more. Frightened him, Eagle, son of Garnos Zarn the Kalimar, conqueror of Andromeda, ruler of Rigel and a dozen other systems. He couldn't ever remember being afraid before in his life. His courage was as well known in the Forces as his nickname—Eagle.

His father had given him the name when he was but a child. The family story went that his father had shown him a picture of one of the strange legendary creatures of Terra and his son's first word had been "fly," his second, "eagle." Forgotten was his given name of Benjakar, and forever after he was Eagle. The name seemed almost a prediction of his future, for from the time he could walk, talk, and think cognitively, Eagle had yearned to fly. When he reached the age of seventeen, he had eagerly joined the Forces against his father's protest, and he became the youngest pilot ever to graduate from the Forces Academy. It was at the Academy that he had met Telles.

For a moment Eagle allowed himself to dwell on those days, when he and Telles had been like brothers, when they had fought side by side. The pain threatened to slip free and he beat it back, locked it down, until it disappeared. He took a deep breath. Like his namesake, he was the predator, not the prey. Nothing frightened him. He'd seen it all, done it all. War was his life—or had been for the last ten years.

Then why had the sight of a child strapped into one of his father's mind-probing machines sent the insides of his stomach rushing to his throat and drenched him in sweat?

Eagle cursed under his breath as he stared at the stars, unseeing. Sometimes he thought of just leaving, of taking on a new identity and finding a remote world far from the fighting where he could live in peace. He would not—could not—continue to be the one responsible for the mind-probing of children. A new child had arrived only an hour ago, twelve years old. He hated greeting the new ones, especially those that had been hidden away and only recently discovered. Invariably they cried or screamed, and many had to be sedated.

His gaze shifted, and suddenly his own reflection in the window came into focus. He wore his dark hair a little longer than most Dominion soldiers, and he noted he was due for a trim. His hair had a tendency to curl when it grew past his jawline as it had now. He tucked one long lock back behind his ear, resolving to trim it the first chance he got, then brushed a speck of dust from the black uniform he wore. The insignia of a Rigelian citizen, red circle edged in black, was the only spot of color except for one tiny decoration he wore on his right pocket—the small silver star he'd received after attaining his pilot's standing in the Forces. Only officers of the inner circle of Zarn were allowed to wear the black uniform. Others wore a standard brown garb.

The inner circle. If he kept opposing his father, he might soon find himself summarily booted out of that sacred inner circle. Two steady green eyes, trained to reveal nothing, devoid of any emotion save complacency, continued to stare back at him. He closed them, briefly, and resisted the urge to lean his forehead against the glass.

A soft trill sounded behind him, and Eagle spun away from the window, striding over to the large black desk occupying center stage in the starkly furnished room. Two curved, matching black chairs sat in front of the oval-shaped monstrosity, which housed the planet's records and daily reports. Another slightly larger chair sat behind it. Eagle flung himself down in that one, hooking one foot over his knee as he pressed two fingers into the top of the desk. A thin viewscreen rose from a recessed notch and flickered to life.

Eagle stiffened as the face of a man appeared. Two green eyes, so much like his own, stared back at him. The Kalimar of Rigel was a handsome man, square-jawed, dark-browed below a mass of salt-and-pepper hair of which he was vastly proud. He looked younger than his sixty-one years and was still in great physical shape. In fact, sometimes Eagle found himself hard put to keep up with his father. His nose was large but not bulbous, his mouth—well, Eagle had often heard female members of the Forces sighing over the Kalimar's "sensuous lips." He was a charmer, there was no doubt of that. Right now, however, Eagle could see his father was in no mood to charm anyone, least of all his rebellious son. That sensual mouth looked grim and angry despite the fact that his lips were curved into the semblance of a smile.

Eagle decided to go on the offensive right from the start. He leaned back in his chair and propped his boots on the desk, crossing them practically under the Kalimar's nose.

"Well, well, so the great Zarn finally decided to return his son's messages."

Anger flared in the older man's eyes, and just as quickly was brought back under control.

"Hello, son," Zarn said, his deep voice pleasant and calm. Eagle knew better than to trust how his father sounded. "I do regret I've been unable to speak with you before now, but I am a busy man, as you know."

"Sure." Eagle brought his feet down to the floor with a thud. "Just tell me one thing, Garnos." His father's brows lifted. He hated it when Eagle called him by his first name. "Why have I been sent to this little piece of hell? I said I was tired. I didn't say I was dead."

Zarn chuckled, but there was no humor in his gaze. "Why, Eagle, my boy, I thought Station One was exactly what you needed right now. You seem a little distracted lately. You really haven't been yourself since your friend died. I'm not sure I understand why this was so devastating since his loyalty was under question at the time. He's actually lucky he died in battle, and so are you. If he'd been brought before a military court, you'd have been called upon to testify."

A muscle in Eagle's jaw tightened as his mind flashed back to a day six months before. Under the two moons of Alpha Centauri 7, he had held his best friend Telles in his arms as the blood pumped from the man's chest.

Helpless he had held him, helpless he had watched him die. And Telles hadn't even wanted to be there. In recent months his friend had begun to crack under the strain of the incessant fighting and had told Eagle and anyone else who would listen that he was going to join the rebellion. Eagle had tried to shut him up, had passed it off as a joke whenever he could, but Zarn's intelligence agents were always around. They always knew.

He took a deep breath and released it slowly. Zarn was right. He hadn't been himself since Telles's death. Two months ago he had refused, point-blank, to lead the Forces on a totally uncalled-for attack on a small world in the Delta Five system. Zarn had ranted and raved but Eagle would not relent. He was sick of the needless killing and the needless dying. It was one thing to defend themselves against invasion, but quite another to go out looking for blood. Had he really ever thought it was all right? Had he ever really believed all the propaganda his father and his ministers dished out to the Forces? Apparently he had.

He recovered quickly, but knew for once he had not been able to hide his pain from his father. He forced a smile back to his lips. One point for Zarn.

"No, I haven't been myself. And you of course thought watching little kids get their brains flushed would be my idea of a real relaxing time, no doubt."

Zarn's own facade slipped for a moment as he slapped one palm down on the console in front of him. One point for Eagle.

"There is much to learn before you step into the new responsibilities in my hierarchy that I have planned for you. The Cabinet members have been making noises lately about your escapades. They say they won't agree to you officially being named heir unless I can convince them you still place your Rigelian heritage above all else."

"Just stick them in one of your mind-probes and I'll wager they'll do anything you tell them to," Eagle said, feigning a yawn.

Another, tighter smile slid over Zarn's lips. "Even a

27

monarch needs advisers, Eagle, advisers who still have their wits about them."

"I don't understand what this is all about anyway. I am Rigelian. I am your son. What's the problem? I've been the heir since I was born, haven't I?"

"But you are not officially the heir until you have reached your thirtieth year, and that is coming up in a matter of months."

"You're telling me." Eagle stood and shoved his chair backward, rubbing the knotted muscles in the back of his neck with one hand. "And lately I've been feeling every year. Tell me, isn't there any other way to keep the Andromedans in line? I mean, requiring them to live in the Stations from the ages of two to seventeen and then mandatory service in the Forces should be enough. Do you have to alter their minds?"

"The mind-probe is essential for controlling the rabble in the systems where we cannot afford to leave behind much of a provisional government."

Eagle snorted. "Yeah. Right. So what's your excuse for Andromeda? Your freaking military headquarters is stationed there."

Zarn shook his head, a look of utmost patience on his lined face. "I will not argue the point with you. The conquest of Andromeda came as a result of their aggression against us. We do not control the thinking of the Andromedans. We adjust the thinking of their children in order to give them a chance to grow up without the barbaric influences of their parents and their twisted views on what caused the war between us."

"Father," he said softly, "you don't even let them keep their own names."

He hadn't known that until he'd come to Station One. Children from conquered planets weren't allowed to retain their names, or any other personal information or memory that might draw them back to their heritage. To do so would be dangerous, would plant seeds that might one day grow into rebellion.

His father seemed confused by Eagle's concern. "Well,

of course not. I want their allegiance to be to me—not to their barbaric parents. And I allow them to choose their new names, don't I"

Zarn's face was flushed, and Eagle was glad to see he had finally hit a nerve. Sometimes he wondered if his father had any nerves at all—or any heart. The question between them echoed through his mind, as though he were hearing it for the first time:

"What name do you choose for yourself?"

A chill rippled down his spine and he sat down again, his muscles stiff against the curved back of the chair. He laced his hands together on the desktop in front of him.

"You do know, don't you, that the Andromedans are refusing to have more children?"

Zarn waved one hand as though tossing away the ridiculous notion. "Pah, they believe too deeply in their God to stop procreation. It is one of the fundamentals of their creed."

"Still, it's the truth. One of my old pals in Intelligence told me so just a few months ago." He leaned forward, his hands flat on the desktop, his voice intense. "You're losing control of all of these worlds—or you will, eventually—if you don't change the way you rule them."

Dark brows collided over green eyes that turned as hard and cold as glass in the space of a moment. "And I suppose you know exactly how they should be ruled—you with all of your years of experience?"

Eagle shook his head. "No, I don't have the answers, but I could make some suggestions. How about a little forbearance? A little freedom? And a little mercy wouldn't kill you."

"It might!" Zarn snapped. "I warn you, Eagle, if this kind of talk gets back to the Cabinet, you can kiss your inheritance good-bye. Great Kikimir, you sound like some of the rebel scum we've hunted down. What is the matter with you? None of this ever bothered you before."

Eagle sighed and ran one hand over his face wearily. He leaned back in his chair, his anger leaving him all at once, his hands dangling over the sides.

"You're right. And I don't know what the hell is the matter with me."

The tension in Zarn's face faded. He smiled, the lines around his mouth deepening in a familiar, somehow comforting way. "You're just tired, boy, that's all. Your friend's death hit you pretty hard, and after you complete this mission for me, I want you to take some time off—as long as you need."

"Mission? You mean there's another reason for my being on this god-forsaken planet besides getting my hand slapped by Daddy?"

"Amusing. Yes, there is a very important reason. Haven't you learned by now that I never do anything without a reason?" His shoulders hunched forward and he lowered his voice in a conspiratorial tone. "A child arrived there today, a little girl."

Eagle raised both brows. "You keep up with that?"

"This time I do. This is no ordinary student for the Station. She should not have been brought to the station at all and she will not remain. I want you to leave today and bring her to me on Rigel."

"You're on Rigel?" Eagle frowned. He could count on one hand the number of times his father had returned to Rigel in the last ten years. He was usually too busy leading his military endeavors. "What's going on?"

"I will explain when you arrive. Do this, and I assure you the Cabinet will have no basis for turning you down as my heir."

"Is she going to be probed first?" Eagle asked cautiously. "I have to tell you, I can't be a part of that. I hate it."

"We'll speak of this more thoroughly when you arrive." A thin line furrowed the middle of Zarn's forehead. "She will not be probed. I daresay she cannot be probed. Just bring her to Rigel immediately."

"All right, I will. But you have to do something for me in return."

A gleam appeared in Zarn's eyes. "You are a soldier in the Forces, my boy. You obey orders; you do not negotiate for rewards for doing so."

Eagle shrugged. "I don't have to be in the Forces, you know. In fact, lately I've been considering giving it all up and becoming a trader."

Zarn laughed out loud, his teeth flashing white and even. "I can see you now with some broken-down old freighter, peddling your wares among the outcasts of space." He chuckled again. "But never let it be said that I turned a deaf ear to my son. What do you want?"

"If I bring the kid to you, you take me off this post. Transfer me."

"To where?"

Eagle opened his mouth, then closed it, pressing his lips together unconsciously. To where? He didn't know.

"I'll have to think about it."

"Of course," his father conceded. "And I agree, within reason. Now, I must go. The Cabinet is meeting and I want to give them the good news. Good-bye, Eagle." His gaze softened. "Be a good boy."

Eagle laughed, the sound sharp and bitter. "If I do that, Kalimar, I won't be able to do any of your dirty work for you. Eagle out."

The screen darkened and lowered back into the desk. He brushed one hand against his eyes. Damn, he was tired. He never got tired in space. He rubbed his eyes again before leaning over and punching into the com unit.

"Security," he ordered the automatic linking connection.

The voice of his security chief crackled back to him. "Millon here."

"Millon, bring the new arrival up to my office right away."

"Will do."

He brought up the records on the child out of curiosity. The girl's name was Mayla, no surname given. She had lived with a relative—the report was vague here, no names listed—in the Delta Quadrant on a remote world called Bezanti. A neighbor had reported suspicious actions, citing large sums of money changing hands and strange loads being carried in and out of the large shed at the back of the property. Long known as an area where pirates preyed on Zarn's ships, a squad had been sent to scope out the situation. They had found only an Andromedan child. Obeying usual procedure, the child had been processed by the officer in charge and sent on the first freighter to Station One. Now Eagle would be taking her to Rigel. But why?

Eagle rose from his chair suddenly and moved back to the window, staring up again at the stars. He didn't know and right now, he just didn't give a damn. So he'd take the kid to Rigel, and then . . . then maybe he'd just disappear for a while. He leaned his hands against the narrow sill at the base of the window for support. No matter what, he knew he wasn't coming back to Station One.

"Hello, Eagle."

Eagle whirled, startled to find a man standing inside his office. The intruder leaned against the wall near the door, one hand behind his back, his handsome face tilted slightly to one side. Eagle realized with alarm that the force-field protecting his office had been deactivated.

"How the hell did you—" Eagle broke off as the knowledge of who the man was hit him with the force of an afterburner. "Merciful Creator," he said softly, feeling numb inside as he gazed at the man he'd once considered his brother in arms, the man he'd left for dead a year ago, on a bloody battlefield. He staggered backward against the window, shaking his head, his voice a whisper.

"Telles. But—*you're dead*."

Eagle let his gaze travel over the man. He was younger than Eagle by a couple of years, and although they were both tall, Eagle had an inch or two on him, always had from the time they were children. Their physical builds and strength were still just about equal, just as they had been back before the battle for Alpha Centauri where Telles had died, slaughtered with the other brave fallen men of the Forces. But he hadn't died. He was standing right here in front of him, and he looked just the same as he had a year ago, except that now instead of the neat Forces haircut, he wore his golden blond hair past his shoulders, adorned with braids and twisted pieces of bright material.

They'd been told once, years before, that they could pass for brothers with their square jaws, aquiline noses, and long-lashed eyes. Telles's were blue-gray, Eagle's green. He'd always thought they were like two sides of the same coin; he, dark and reckless, Telles, golden and steady. He had known Telles all of his life and they had been partners, comrades. Why then was the man standing there staring at him as though he'd never seen him before?

Eagle took a quick step toward him and Telles just as quickly unfolded from the wall, bringing his hand from behind his back to reveal he held a phaser. Eagle stopped in his tracks, feeling the confusion tighten around his brain.

"Telles, I don't understand. What's this all about? How did you get here? What happened on Alpha Centauri? I thought—" A quick rush of pain flooded through Eagle's well-controlled facade and choked him. "My God, man, I held you in my arms until you stopped breathing. Then they started pulling us out. There was no time to get the wounded, let alone the dead. How—"

Telles held up one hand to stop his words. Eagle snapped his mouth shut and used the chance to pull himself together. Something was wrong. Something was very, very wrong.

Telles took a step toward him. "Sorry to drop in on you like this, but things have changed a little since the last time we saw each other. And you're right. I died in your arms." A shadow crossed his face. "You were a good friend, Eagle."

"How can this be?" Eagle demanded, his hands flexing into fists, his heart pounding so hard in his chest it seemed to echo into his brain. "I watched you die! I saw you take your last breath!"

"Think I'm a ghost?" He smiled, then quickly sobered. "Sorry. You have no way of knowing what's happened to me—nor what's happened to you. I was dead, my friend, but I was raised from the dead, and in my new life, I'm

33

no longer the man you once knew, so in that regard, I suppose Telles—the Telles you knew—is still dead."

He gestured toward the desk and Eagle started backing toward it.

"Stop talking in riddles. What do you mean, raised from the dead? Why are you waving that thing in my face? Put it away."

" 'Fraid not. Sit down, Eagle." He pulled the chair out from behind the desk. "We have a lot to talk about."

"How did you get past the sensors?"

Telles smiled again and Eagle felt his heart turn over. How many times had he seen that cocky grin on his best friend's face? He'd never thought he'd see it again.

"Wouldn't you like to know?"

"Telles," he said, feeling strangely awkward, "I'm—I'm glad you're alive."

The smile disappeared and Telles's tawny brows knit together over stormy blue-gray eyes. "You may not be when you learn why I'm here. There's someone I want you to meet." He kept the weapon carefully trained on Eagle as he tilted his head toward the doorway. "Mayla, honey, come on in." Telles cocked one dark brow. "Your security chief was kind enough to save me the trouble of searching for her. In fact, he was bringing her here when I, er, talked him out of accompanying us."

"You didn't kill him, did you?" Eagle asked casually, rising from his chair and leaning one thigh across his desktop. "I like that old man."

"He'll have a bad headache tomorrow, but he'll be all right."

Somewhat relieved, Eagle turned to the doorway, his mind racing as he watched the young girl walk in through the deactivated entrance. Was Telles crazy? Sometimes trauma did that to a person. If he had been left for dead and then somehow recovered, could that have driven him insane?

The girl looked to be about eleven or twelve years old, but seemed much older. There was a gravity, a maturity about her that was in stark contrast to her childlike appearance. Short, silver-blond hair curled around her oval-shaped face. Her skin was pale ivory. The long-lashed lavender eyes—a peculiar color—were round, yet tilted up at the corners. She gazed up at him, steady, unafraid. A buttonish nose and two pale pink lips were her most childish features—that and her tiny frame beneath the brown, shapeless tunic she wore. Around her neck was a chain that disappeared beneath her clothing. Some kind of jewelry. That was odd. Children sent to the station had all personal items taken from them.

Eagle frowned. Something about this child bothered him. Her gaze turned from him to Telles and he knew what it was. She was too damn calm. Most kids her age brought to Station One, wrenched from their families, were dragged in half-hysterical. This girl had a poise that, given the circumstances, was incredible. Eagle felt something tighten around his heart. There was something else about her, something that had nothing to do with her calmness. When he walked closer to her, he felt as though he were drawing near a warm fire, a soothing heat. The closer he came to her, the more intense the sensation became until he could feel it flowing out from her, wrapping itself around him, easing itself over his tired muscles and aching limbs. He stood within the phenomenon for a moment as if mesmerized.

"She's special, Eagle."

Telles's voice brought him back to himself, and with an effort Eagle jerked himself away, backing toward the desk. Shaken to the core, he tried to hide his confusion by speaking the first thing that came to mind.

"Why do people think they can hide them? It only delays the inevitable, and it's so much harder at this age."

"You don't even know who she is, do you?" Telles asked. "You feel it, but you don't know. The great son of Zarn doesn't know."

"Who is she?" Eagle snapped. "And what do you want with her?"

"She is Mayla, the heir to the Andromedan throne. Mayla Cezan. Does that ring a bell?"

Eagle felt as though the air had been kicked from his lungs. Mayla Cezan. The youngest child of the Cezans,

35

the decadent ruling family who had started the escalation of the power struggle between Rigel and Andromeda all those years ago. When Zarn conquered Andromeda, the Cezans had ringed their palace with the last of their soldiers. Strangely enough, it had been the Andromedans themselves who had stormed the castle and killed the royal family, blaming them for the defeat of their world by Zarn. All had perished, except for one child. She had been but a baby, not even christened, and had somehow been spirited out of the castle before the attack began. Zarn had been looking for her for the last ten years of his life, for it was said that the Cezans had bizarre and dangerous powers. He feared a Cezan would return to Andromeda and use her powers to convince the people to revolt.

"She's the heir?" Eagle whispered the words. "She's the one?"

"Yes. And you're going to help me get her out of here."

His words were like a cold dash of water in the face. Eagle laughed.

"Help you take the child my father has sought for years off of Station One?" He shook his head. "I don't think so." Once again the barrel of the blaster was thrust against the side of his face. "C'mon, Telles," he said, gauging the distance between the two men as well as the grip his captor had on the weapon. He wasn't sure he could take him, but it appeared he might have to try. "You know I can't do that."

"You don't understand, Eagle. She healed me. She's the one who brought me back."

Eagle heard the information but it took a full minute for it to reach his brain. He frowned, sure he had heard wrong. "She did what? She brought you back—from where?"

Telles sighed, lowering the blaster slightly, his golden hair sending shadows across his face. "From the darkness, from death."

Eagle leaned toward him, his voice fervent. "The only darkness I care about is the darkness you're going to see when Zarn tosses you into a solitary confinement cell.

Damn it, man, you're a Forces soldier! If she really is the heir to the throne, you know what it will mean if you take her out of here."

"I'm not with the Forces anymore."

"So who are you with?" He knew the answer even as the man opened his mouth to reply. He groaned aloud and cut him off. "Aw, hell, Telles, don't tell me you finally did it. Don't tell me you finally joined those damned rebels you were always talking about."

"Why, Colonel, if I didn't know better, I'd swear you could read minds." Telles turned the setting knob on the side of the phaser he held with two fingers, keeping his gaze on the other man. Eagle tensed, watching for his chance to attack.

The explosion came without warning, throwing the two men to the floor. The child sprawled nearby, but still did not utter a word as the two men grappled for the weapon that had been knocked from Telles's hand. They fought each other, rolling over the smooth surface, fists flailing, legs flying. Eagle almost had the weapon, when another explosion rocked the office and the phaser spun out of his reach. Telles picked it up and stumbled to his feet, grabbing the little girl by the arm.

"This isn't over, Eagle," he said as another explosion ripped the air. "There's more you have to know!" He hesitated another instant, then lifted a communicator to his lips and said something. The air around them shimmered, sizzled, and he and the child simply disappeared.

"Transporter," Eagle whispered, then jumped to his feet and made it to the com unit before another quake shook the ground. "Report!" he shouted. "Anyone! What's happening?"

The unit crackled and spewed and finally a voice came back to him, confirming what he already knew.

"Colonel!" Millon cried. "We are under attack!"

Chapter Two

"Calm down, Millon Just tell me what the hell happened."
Eagle purposely calmed his own voice but his muscles
were taut, prepared for battle.

"Spacecraft attacking, Colonel," Millon said, his voice
more even. "They just came out of nowhere and ordered
us to lower our shields or be blasted by plasma-ray. Before I could even contact you they started firing. That's
why we're being rocked, but so far our shields are holding."

"We're just feeling the resonance," Eagle mused, rubbing the back of his neck. "They're probably still too far
away to punch holes."

"Yes, sir, but they're coming closer fast!"

"Who the hell are they? Are they out of their minds?"

"They're signaling again. Should I—" The unit suddenly went dead.

Eagle whirled from the device and headed for the
weapons locker in the corner of the office. He deactivated
the lock and took out a fully charged phaser rifle. As an
afterthought, he shoved three thermal grenades into his
jacket pocket. He turned in time to see ten forms materialize outside the curved observation window.

Cursing roundly, he ran back to the com and snapped
it on. "All officers, we've been invaded, repeat, we have
invaders. Battle stations, I repeat—"

The explosion that blew his door into a million frag-
ments caught him from behind, sending him flying
across the room and skidding flat on his back for several
feet before coming to a stop against the weapons locker.
The sound of booted feet thundering into his office made

it through his stunned senses, and he managed to lift himself to his elbows only to be thrust back again suddenly, the breath knocked from him as a heavy weight descended on his chest. Cold metal pressed against his temple, then slid across his cheek, turning his face toward the man sitting on top of him. No, not a man, a droid, studded with what looked to be tynarium pellets. Illegal. Had they come with Telles? Most likely. They were mercenaries or privateers, but what in hell did they think they were doing attacking one of the Kalimar's strongholds? They must be insane.

The droid on top of him leaned forward and Eagle blinked, realizing all at once that the creature had the body of a female. Clad in silver, the droid had been fashioned to resemble a woman from the neck down. The head was a typical helmetlike apparatus whose frontpiece mimicked a human's face. But why the female body? Eagle tensed. It was possible they weren't outlaws but Psyks, a group of certifiably crazy renegades who killed for the love of killing and feared no man, not even Lord Zarn, ruler of a dozen systems, undisputed dictator of Andromeda. Eagle felt his throat go suddenly dry. The children. If they were Psyks and they reached the children . . . He ran his tongue over his dry lips and tried to speak.

"Silence," the droid said, its voice toneless. "You will not speak. You will listen and if you do not obey you will be destroyed, you and all of this despicable planet."

Eagle frowned. It sounded like a droid but its choice of words was rather emotional for a machine. He cleared his throat and opened his mouth again only to have the muzzle of the weapon the thing held thrust between his lips and halfway down his throat.

"I said be silent."

Eagle nodded his understanding and almost gagged before the droid finally removed the weapon. He lay gasping for breath beneath the heavy mechanism, wishing he could just get one good lungful of air before he died.

"Where is she?"

He stopped worrying about breathing and started worrying about answering. They were here for Zarn's prize. "You told me to be silent," he said. "Make up your mind."

The hand of the droid lifted and Eagle winced as it came crashing down. There was no way to avoid the backhanded blow across the side of his face, and his neck snapped to one side.

"We will not waste time with you, *Guardian*, or should we call you *murderer—mindstealer—defiler of children*?"

Eagle shook the hair back from his brow and tried to get a better look at his assailant, ignoring the pain throbbing through his right jaw and the jagged cut the edge of one metallic finger had gouged in his cheek. Droids did not speak like this. His gaze raked over the female body, the helmet, and belatedly he realized he was likely looking at a human garbed in a tynarium suit. Also illegal. His suspicion he was dealing with Psyks grew by the moment.

"What do you want?" he managed to gasp.

"We want the child brought to you by the demon Zarn. We want her now."

"What for?"

He was rewarded for his question by another blow, this one catching him across the mouth. Blood poured down his throat from his busted lower lip and almost choked him. He rocked upward, hoping to dislodge the weight on his chest, but the droid pushed him back down.

"To sacrifice to the gods for all you care. Give her to us or not a man will leave this planet alive!"

Someone walked up beside the droid-woman at that moment and Eagle blinked, trying to clear his vision. It was a man, tall, thin, with the blue skin and hair of an Altairian. He didn't have the look of a Psyk, but you never could tell. He bent down and whispered something to the droid-woman and instantly it/she stood, relieving the pressure from his chest. Eagle drank in great lungfuls of air, then gasped as a pain laced through his side. A broken rib? Probably. He started to wrap his arms around his middle, but tucked down the natural reaction of his body. If they knew where he was hurt, they would likely try to reinjure that spot to make him talk.

"Manak!" The droid-woman flung the curse skyward and spun back around to stab one long silver finger at him, her bland metal features belying the fierceness suddenly empowering the droning voice coming out of the helmet. "May the god of light damn you to an eternal torture!" Without warning, the droid-woman unsnapped several fasteners at the neck of her suit. Lifting both hands, she wrenched the helmet upward, pulling it off and tossing it savagely aside. It hit the wall with a dull thud, but Eagle was not watching its fall. His gaze was locked on the sight before him.

Silver-blond hair cascaded around the features of the woman glaring down at him, dark brows arching in contrast above two slanted, catlike turquoise blue eyes, intelligent, presently filled with fire, edged with long, dark lashes. A silver band encircled her forehead. Quickly Eagle reevaluated his captor. Human, no doubt about that. Probably Andromedan. One square-jawed face with a determined, stubborn chin. High, sculptured cheekbones. One nose, straight, aristocratic. Full, beautifully shaped lips drawn back in an angry line.

"Hell," Eagle breathed softly. "What kind of Psyks are you?"

The woman crossed back to him and, leaning down, grabbed him by the uniform just under his chin. She lifted him from the floor in one smooth movement, heaving him above her until his feet were dangling in the air. His bruised ribs complained loudly, and he couldn't help groaning aloud.

"She's gone, you son of a bitch!" she shouted, shaking him with her metallic fist. "A ship left orbit just after we landed. Where is she, space-boy? You'd better start talking if you want to save the rest of this stinking world."

"Aren't they with you?" he asked groggily, even as understanding rippled through him.

Telles! He'd taken the child and used the diversion of the invaders to get away. He hadn't been part of this band of renegades at all.

Eagle hung helplessly above her, suspended by her super strength. Dazed, he stared down into two beautiful eyes, so angry, so passionate, and wondered how a woman like her had become a Psyk. She didn't really seem crazy—just furious.

"Where is she?" she demanded again, giving him a shake.

"I don't know," he said at last. Blood dripped from the gash in his face and his lip and splattered on her chest.

With a curse she let him fall to the floor. He hit the surface with a grunt, rolling to his feet, wincing as he staggered upright. Instantly he was surrounded by the rest of the invaders. They were a well-groomed bunch, all wearing nondescript uniforms of a dirty green color. They were from a variety of cultures, he reasoned, noting a few extra ears here and there and variations of skin tones. All biped homo sapiens though, so they were from this galaxy. They didn't have the look of Psyks, now that he saw them all. Psyks were raving maniacs whose trademarks included savage body piercings and brightly painted skin. So if they weren't Psyks—who were they? And why did they want the girl—unless they knew she was the heir to the throne? Of course. Why else would they be here? Obviously the woman was the leader, and from the glint of determination in her eyes, he assessed she was not one to be taken lightly. Still, if she wasn't insane, maybe he could negotiate with her.

"Listen, I—"

He saw her nod to the man beside him but didn't have time to prepare for the stunning blow of the phaser blast that caught him in the back of the neck and sent him spiraling down toward unconsciousness.

"You won't find her without me," he had the sense to whisper just before the light disappeared. Her voice was the last sound he heard.

"Then, space-boy, get ready for the ride of your life."

"He's Lord Zarn's what?"

Sky spun around and stared at her head security officer, hands on her hips. Kell stood silently next to him.

"His son, Captain," P'ton said, giving her a second salute to accent his deep-throated words.

"Why the hell didn't our intelligence people tell us that before we hit the Station? We could have eliminated the future of Zarn's empire right then and there!"

Kell raised one brow. "I've yet to see you kill someone in cold blood."

"There's always a first time. Well, this is just great," she muttered.

"I would say it is a gift from the gods, if you believe in such things," Kell said. "Depending on how attached the commander is to his son, we may be able to negotiate a trade—Mayla for the colonel." Kell stood near the closed door, his arms folded over his chest.

Sky laughed, the sound harsh and mocking. "Are you out of your mind? Zarn thinks we have Mayla. He will follow us and blast us out of the sky for having the effrontery to take both his son and his prize!" She shook her head, lifting her hand unconsciously to the silver band at her temples. "We've got to make the colonel tell us where she's been taken before Zarn gets word we've attacked the station."

Kell crossed to her side. "May I speak to you in private, Captain?"

Sky pressed her lips together. As much as she hated leaving her security chief out of the loop, right now he, along with the rest of the crew, was on a need-to-know basis. She trusted P'ton, but the rest of this conversation was better held without him.

"Thank you for your report, P'ton," she said, turning and giving him a grim smile. "You've shed some much needed light on this dark day. Any other data you may remember may be directly submitted into my computer site. You are dismissed."

The man saluted her sharply and she returned the gesture, fist to her chest then hand thrust outward on a level even with her shoulders, palm down, fingers together. He turned on his heel and headed out of the room, pausing only long enough for the automatic doors to open in front of him.

"He's a good man." Sky shot Kell a reprimanding look.

"Don't you think the head of my security should be in on this?"

"Not yet." He gestured toward a chair. "Let's sit down, shall we? You've got some tough decisions to make, and I have some recommendations to make concerning them." He lifted one blue brow. "That is, if you are interested in hearing them."

His terse manner made Sky realize she had once again let her tendency to command everyone and everything around her get the upper hand. Kell was her best friend, and she valued his opinion above all others.

"I'm sorry, Kell," she said softly, sinking down into the chair opposite his. "Of course I want to hear your recommendations. I'm just so worried about Mayla." She broke off as her throat closed convulsively around the name. Tears brimmed against her lashes and she reached up to brush them away, laughing apologetically. "I hope none of the crew walks in on me when I'm having one of these crying jags. It wouldn't do much for morale for them to see their tough, cynical captain boo-hooing over her little sister."

Kell reached inside his jacket and brought out a soft cloth. He handed it to her and his stern lips eased into a smile as she blew her nose loudly.

"Don't worry about the crew. They understand more than you realize. Mayla is more than your little sister, she's almost your own child. After all, you've raised her since she was three years old." He lifted her chin and tilted her head upward. His smile grew even softer and Sky felt a slight pang at the concern she saw reflected in his blue eyes. She knew Kell's feelings for her were more than friendship, much as he tried to deny it, but she also knew he had accepted that what she felt for him could never be more. "Don't beat yourself up for having emotions, Sky," he said. "Most humans do."

"Even you?" she teased, taking his hand from her chin and squeezing it slightly.

The brow arched upward again. "Just because I have chosen to live my life in a logical way, never suppose I don't have feelings. I control my feelings. That does not mean I don't choose to use them from time to time."

Sky grinned at him wholeheartedly then. "I'd love to tell the crew what a softie you really are. They all think you're a cold-blooded—"

"I know exactly what they think of me," he said, rising from his chair. "And I am not unaware of the prejudices that exist against me on board."

"Prejudices?" Sky laughed but the sound was hesitant. She had somehow wandered onto dangerous ground now and she knew it. Kell might claim to have complete control over his emotions, but she knew the subtle slights behind his back did not go unnoticed. "You're the most respected man on the ship," she insisted.

"Thank you, Captain." The sudden tension in his pale blue face faded as he smiled down at her. "Now, what shall we do about the prisoner?"

Sky stood and felt the mantle of command settling firmly around her shoulders once again, her fears for Mayla's safety necessarily pushed to the back of her mind as she considered her next move.

"Have him stripped and taken to the lower cargo hold," she said, her voice suddenly hard. "Get one of the tables we use for emergency surgeries from sickbay and set it up down there. Strap him to it. Bring up that equipment we liberated from one of Zarn's outposts."

Kell stared at her without answering for a moment and she allowed anger, brief but potent, to touch her gaze. "Well, Lieutenant?" she demanded.

"Are you sure that—"

"Set it up and report back to me. I'll be in my quarters." She stalked toward the doorway. "And find out if news of the attack on Station One has reached Andromeda yet." The doors parted.

"Captain—" The exasperation in her first officer's voice stopped her and she turned back, noting the open disapproval on his face. "What in the world are you planning to do to this man?"

She hesitated before squaring her shoulders and hardening her gaze. "Whatever it takes," she said softly. "Whatever in hell that it takes."

45

* * *

Eagle came back to consciousness slowly, one piece of his brain at a time, as he tried to ascertain where he might be. He couldn't see—sight was always one of the last senses to return after a blast from a phaser set on stun—along with the ability to move. He doubted there had been time to reach another world, but then, how did he really know how long he'd been unconscious? The pain returned next, his cracked or broken ribs reminding him of his ordeal with the droid-woman. He tried to breathe shallowly as his vision at last began to clear, but he was still quite literally left in the dark.

After a moment his eyes adjusted to the dimly lit room and he could make out large shadowy objects. He squinted upward and saw what appeared to be the riveted surface of a bulkhead similar to others he'd seen in cargo ships. So he was most likely in a cruiser of some kind and in space—but headed where? He tried to sit up but couldn't. For a moment he thought his muscles just wouldn't yet respond, but glancing down he made out the shimmering outlines of energy shackles around his wrists and ankles. They were invisible to the naked eye, but in darkness a thin aura could be detected. And speaking of naked . . .

Eagle tightened his hands into fists. The invaders had stripped him, shackled him to what appeared to be a laboratory table, flat, cold, and hard, and had left him in the blackness. For what purpose? To intimidate and humiliate him, no doubt. Taking the protection of clothing from a prisoner had an immediate effect, creating a vulnerability an interrogator could use to his best advantage. Eagle had used the ploy himself as an officer in Zarn's Intelligence Division of the Forces. He had despised himself for it, but it had been effective. Was that when he had first begun to question the ways of his father? In Intelligence? Maybe so. It had just taken Telles's death—or what he believed was his death—to push it to the forefront.

Telles was alive. He wanted to shout with the joy of it but at the same time he knew it wasn't Telles at all. Something had been done to him. He'd always had tendencies, and in the last few years had openly talked against Zarn, something that had strained their relationship at times. But Eagle had felt Telles was just blowing off steam like a lot of men who worked in the more harrowing divisions of the Forces did periodically. It had even gotten to be sort of a game between them, Telles pointing out what was wrong with his father's regime, Eagle countering with what was right. He closed his eyes. It wasn't a game any more. Telles had done the unforgivable this time, and when Zarn caught up with him, his death would be real and completely final.

He turned his mind away from the thought. He couldn't deal with this now. Didn't have to deal with it now. Right now he needed to focus on getting the hell out of here. These renegades were playing for keeps. They wanted the girl and they wanted her badly. They had to know she was the heir, but how? She'd been taken on a backwater world on the edge of nowhere. And what if she was? What use was she to renegades? Did they think to use her to negotiate with Zarn for some kind of pardon? If they thought that would happen, they were stupider than he suspected. Were they being paid by someone to steal the girl?

He couldn't think of any amount of money that would make even the toughest outlaws take the kind of risks these people had taken. To attack one of Zarn's stations was in itself asking to be evaporated off the face of the universe, but to abduct the heir to Andromeda, the child he'd searched for for so long—and then kidnap his son—was asking for slow, terrible torture. If they were Psyks, it would make sense because of its senselessness. But these weren't crazies. In spite of her anger, the woman who had attacked him was perfectly rational. She was on a quest to find the child and he had no doubt she would stop at nothing until she reached her goal. He had seen it in her eyes. So there was only one possibility left: They were rebels. But if that were true, why had Telles run away from them?

He looked around the room restlessly. How long would

they leave him here before the interrogation began? he wondered. His vision had adjusted to the darkness completely now, and he could see square and cylindrical containers stacked around the walls, coming to within several feet of him. He glanced at a tall, rectangular object only a foot away from the table he lay upon and went suddenly cold, his breath leaving him, his throat tightening, almost closing altogether. A mind-probe. One of the new, experimental models. He'd never seen one in person but his father had sent him schematics of the devices over the years, and this one had crossed his screen only a few weeks ago. It was portable and lightweight. Only recently one had been stolen by renegades from a remote outpost where it was being tested.

It had come to the Kalimar's attention in the last year that his mind-probing devices were not always as effective as he had supposed; often children taken to indoctrination returned without having their minds and personalities completely stripped from them. He had immediately begun to rectify the situation and ordered his scientists to develop a new machine, one capable of probing even the most resistant mind.

Eagle swallowed hard, willing the saliva back into his mouth to counter the dryness there. Although he had been a soldier since he turned seventeen, had fought in some desperate battles and been captured several times, he had never been subjected to a mind-probe. Until he was assigned to Station One, he had never even seen one. But after seeing the children on Station One go through it, he knew he wasn't going to like it. Still, since he had no idea where Telles might have taken Mayla, the probing would tell the renegades nothing, except who had taken her. Even Zarn's best devices couldn't read what wasn't there. He wasn't worried about what they might find inside his mind. He was worried about how little they might leave behind.

"Nervous, Colonel?"

A light snapped on and a familiar female voice swept over him, harsh, knowing. For a moment panic seized him by the throat, but he quickly brought himself back under control. She came into view, moving from the head of the table to his side. She no longer wore the droid suit, but was clad in a uniform that hugged her figure in a most disconcerting way. The blue of the material made her turquoise eyes seem even darker as they moved over his naked form in a calculated, unemotional manner. Her silver hair was pulled back severely from her sculptured face, tied at the nape of her neck. The blue-skinned man stood beside her, his gaze likewise dispassionate.

"Should I be?" he said, the sound rasping and weak. He cleared his throat and tried again, inclining his head first toward his naked torso and then toward Kell. "Is this how your kind gets their kicks?" he asked, summoning a cocky grin. "If you take off the shackles it could be a lot more fun, though it's been awhile since I've shared a woman."

"Shut up." The command was accompanied by a sharp blow to his already injured ribcage. Eagle winced but didn't make a sound. "Give your name, rank, Forces number, and current assignment."

Eagle tried to breathe shallowly to still the pain in his side. "Zarn, Benjakar, Colonel, Forces number 5943750, Guardian of Stations One through Four, Andromedan system."

"But don't they call you something else, something . . . stupid like Bear or Canthar or Bluebird or something?"

Her lips curved up in a smirk and Eagle longed to wipe the gesture from her porcelain features. He didn't answer.

"All right, then, we'll just go with *Guardian*. Listen, scumbag, and listen well. If you answer my questions I might let you live—with your brain still intact. Where is the child? Where has your ship taken her?"

Eagle met her imperious gaze unflinchingly. "First of all, it wasn't my ship. Second of all, I've been beaten up, stunned, stripped, shackled, and I don't even know what the hell all of this is about. If you want some answers, sweetie, you'd better tell me who you are and what you want with that little kid."

The woman lifted her hand and Eagle braced himself

for the blow. Her fist hovered over him for a moment, then fell back to her side, her eyes glinting with suppressed fury. He could tell she was fighting for control. He'd been there too often himself not to recognize her tension. She glanced up at the man beside her and he seemed to nod slightly in her direction.

"We will have our answers—space-boy—whether we deign to tell you who we are or not." She began to walk slowly beside him, letting her fingertips lightly touch his sweat-soaked skin as she moved toward the end of the table. She stopped, glanced back at him, then started walking back up the length of his body, fingers trailing across his skin.

The cargo hold was stuffy and oppressive and he could see fine beads of sweat across her forehead, beneath the silver band she wore. He tried to disconnect himself from her touch. What was presently a gentle, teasing stroke up the side of one leg could quickly change to pain, as he knew from experience. He'd been captured a number of times during his service in the Forces, and torture was a common occurrence. Still, he shivered unconsciously as her fingers continued to trace a line up his calf, over his knee, across his thigh, and up to his hipbone. She rested two fingers on the pelvic bone protruding slightly beneath his flesh and for a moment their eyes locked, Eagle's daring her to do her worst, the woman's promising him she could if she chose to do so. He expected her to touch him intimately, for that was another way to humiliate a prisoner—violate him—though he had never used those tactics himself. But her probing fingers moved upward, across the flat of his belly to his chest, where she stroked the dark hair curling there for what appeared to be an absentminded moment.

Eagle knew better. She was playing with him, letting him know who was in charge, who was the master. Her fingers flattened against his chest before moving to explore his side. He didn't move as she touched the places that had plagued him since her attack, schooling his features not to reflect his pain. She smiled, obviously aware of his struggle. Gently she touched the side of his jaw, rough with a day's growth of beard. Her fingers moved against his lips, then slid upward to his temple and into his hair. Eagle refused to close his eyes and instead tried to fix her with his burning gaze, a gaze he hoped conveyed to her exactly what he intended to do if he ever got free. The blue-skinned man cleared his throat and the woman hesitated, then, in one last gesture of control, combed her fingers through his slightly wavy hair before dropping her hand back to her side.

"Is he all there?" the man asked, his voice edged with a taut sarcasm.

"Hook him up," she ordered. She leaned over him, placing both hands palm down on Eagle's chest. He could feel the warmth of her breath, could feel the soft crush of her breasts beneath her uniform, could feel her heart beating against his.

"I'm going to find her," she whispered, her mouth scant inches away from his own. Her fingers threaded through his hair at the temples, and tightened against his scalp. "If I have to tear your mind apart and leave you a thrashing, helpless vegetable to do so—I will find her. Do you understand, *space-boy*? I don't care whose son you are or how pretty you are—you are completely expendable."

She pulled away from him and, turning on her heel, left the room. Eagle closed his eyes, mustering courage for what lay ahead.

Sky stalked out of the cargo hold and didn't stop until she reached her quarters three decks above. It was foolish to go so far when she would only have to return in a matter of minutes, but she had to get away and bring her raging anger under control. She stormed into the room, wishing she had a good old-fashioned hinged door like back on Bezanti that she could slam to vent her fury. In its lieu, she picked up the small figurine depicting an ancient Terran cat Kell had given her for her last birthday, and lifted her arm to throw it across the room. Her fingers inadvertently caressed the smooth surface of the object and slowly she lowered her hand, replacing the little cat on top of her desk where it stood guard over her computer. Sky crossed to her bunk and sank down upon its hard surface. Closing her eyes, she forced herself to take deep, calming breaths. For several moments she did nothing else as she cleared her mind, focusing only on the air moving in and out of her lungs. When she opened her eyes again, her temper was under control, leaving her to face the always appalling aftermath of her volatile emotions.

She had wanted to hurt the man as he lay helpless and naked before her, had wanted to torture and maim him, and the intensity of those feelings had shaken her to the core. As a daughter of a Cezan she had been raised to be gentle, forgiving, and at all times to follow the peaceful teachings of her father and mother's religion. But after her exile to Bezanti everything had changed. She had changed in order to survive in the new world in which she found herself. No longer was there a mother and father and brothers and sisters to watch over her, as well as guards and palace attendants. For the first time in her life she had been alone, on her own, with a three-year-old to protect at all costs.

She stood and moved aimlessly about her cabin. There was little there to reflect its occupant. The bunk was narrow, hard, the covering a dull olive green. There were no pictures on the walls, no personal items at all except for the figurine Kell had given her and a two-foot-high clay statue she had taken with her to Bezanti. She had sculpted the statue the season before her journey to the distant world, and when she'd learned she was to go there, she had sneaked her fledgling attempt at art into her trunk. Perhaps she had felt, even then, that she would need something of herself to hang onto in the days to come.

Sky moved to the statue sitting on the small table next to her bunk and touched it with a loving caress. About two feet high, the statue represented a woman clad in a long dress, her hair, part of it braided, twisting in disarray almost to her feet, one hand lifted to her heart, her eyes staring straight ahead, bold, clear, as if she could see into the future. Her lips curved up in a half-smile and

Sky touched the side of the statue's face. She had thought of her mother as she sculpted the image, and it resembled her slightly. What would her mother think of her now if she could see her from the Afterworld?

Sky turned away from the statue, clasping her arms about herself and moving to look out of the fairly large porthole she'd had installed—one of the few luxuries she allowed herself as the ship's captain. She pressed her lips together tightly and stared unseeing at the stars in their silent ageless beauty.

She feared her mother would not be pleased if she could see what her daughter had become. There was a hardness inside her that extended into every area of her life, except her love for Mayla. She had not realized until now how immune she had become to the possibility of inflicting pain on another human being. Over the years it had become almost second nature for her to fight—first in self-defense, later as a means to whatever end was on the day's agenda. Her morals, her religion, her beliefs, had all been swept aside, pushed away, forgotten in her quest to survive and to make sure her sister survived. It had been necessary, for how could she have continued as privateer, renegade, and soldier, and still adhered to her parents' teachings? She could not, and so she had changed, focusing her life on protecting Mayla, sacrificing her own feelings and beliefs in the process. It had taken its toll upon her as a woman, as a person, as an Andromedan.

Now this man who deserved death had somehow pulled from the depths of her being such feelings of rage and anger she feared she would kill him before the interrogation could even begin. That was only part of her frantic need to get away from him. She had thought to taunt him by touching him, had hoped to make him fear what she might do next. But as her fingers collided with his warm, damp skin, her senses had quickened and something had stirred inside her, warring with the violence she kept under tenuous control. She had wanted him. It was as simple as that. No, maybe not that simple. For it had been more than a desire for his body—although the feel of his taut muscles under her hands had sent a quick thrust of need through the depths of her body—but she had felt something else besides desire. She had felt compassion.

Compassion. She sneered the word in her mind. Compassion for the barbarian who had helped steal her sister from her. Compassion for the demon Zarn's son. She must be slipping, must need a rest, a break, a drink. How could such an emotion have ever entered her mind, let alone the desire to bed the man? A sudden nervous thrill ran through her veins, and she turned away from the porthole.

Zarn's main area of expertise had always been mind control. It was how he had gained the trust of the Seekers and used that trust to gain admittance to the palace of the Cezans. After the conquest, it was how he maintained control for a time before he hit upon his plan to use the children as virtual hostages. It was common knowledge his scientists had continued their quest to perfect mind-probing and mental manipulation. He had never been known to use a telepath in his probings, but there was always a first time. Could his son be a telepath? Was he using his powers to sway her, to cause her to feel such an emotion for the son of the man she hated? She shuddered at the thought of her mind being invaded by Zarn or his son, then calmed and raised her hand to touch the silver band around her forehead.

Nothing could penetrate the protection Redar had given her before he died, at least nothing had been able to so far. She chose to believe nothing would. To entertain any other possibility would leave herself open to a kind of speculation that could easily undermine her mission. The compassion she felt for the man in the hold was just a leftover emotion from her past, from the days when she had the luxury of such feelings. Nothing more.

A soft buzzing sound filled the room, and Sky leaned one knee into the middle of her bunk, reaching to answer the com unit attached to the wall near the head of it.

"Yes?"

"We're waiting for you, Captain." Kell's voice was as

calm as an android's, and the steady cadence of his words sent a soothing balm around Sky's raw emotions.

"On my way," she said. She strode toward the doorway but paused in front of the waist-high, built-in dresser in the wall of her cabin, which held sundry items of clothing. She pressed a button on the side of it and a mirror, the width of the dresser, rose from its recesses. Staring at her reflection, she took rapid stock. The turquoise eyes reflected her confusion, while narrow lines of fatigue and strain were etched into her forehead and around her mouth. She looked weary, fearful almost. This would never do. The prisoner must never suspect anything he had done or could do would ever shake her. She must be in control at all times.

Sky took a deep breath and turned inward, finding the center of her mind, the place from which her telepathic power emanated, as well as received thought, when left unshackled. The center was like a soft blue-green light, flickering there, calling her to its core of tranquility and strength. She saw herself inside her mind, riding the dark gray waves of confusion and anger into the vortex, down into the deepest part of her mental being. The blue-green light encompassed her, drew her inside, folded her in the warmth and calm. Once there, encased in the power, it was a simple matter to reach out and mentally release the tendrils of disorientation and hostility from their energy-sucking attachment. She watched them snap, hover a second, then dissolve into nothingness. When Captain Sky Cezan emerged from her almost trancelike state, the form staring back at her from the mirror had changed. The lines of strain in her face had disappeared and her eyes revealed only control and strength. She smiled, once again filled with the surety of her own power. The smile faded and in its place, a grim line of determination appeared. It was time to question the enemy.

Eagle fought down the fear welling up inside him as the man called Kell began attaching a conglomeration of wires and tubes to his flesh. Suctionized ends clung with deceptive lightness to his head, chest, stomach, groin, and legs. He tensed as the man raised a hypodermic needle and flicked his fingers against the clear tube. Eagle ran his tongue across his lips as he noted that the needle was connected to the machine standing next to the table on which he lay.

The helplessness hit him all at once, spread through his veins with a shuddering flow he could not prevent.

How would it work? Would drugs be injected into his system to help the process? The hypodermic seemed to be connected to the machine—was that in order to monitor the dosage? He had been trained on the machines on Station One, but this one was different. The one on the station hadn't used needles and, in fact, the hypodermics were an archaic holdover from a bygone era. No one used them anymore. Was there some reason they were necessary for the new mind-probing device, or was it just his father's way of adding more terror to an already horrific device? Eagle closed his eyes against the thought. He wouldn't think about his father's political tactics to keep power, not now.

The blue-skinned man reached behind the apparatus at that moment and took something out from the back of the cylindrical machine. A mind-probe helmet. That he knew from Station One. The man approached him.

"Damn," Eagle whispered as he felt the helmet slide over his head and face. Plunged into darkness, a terrible panic seized him. He tried to subdue it, used every relaxation technique he knew, to no avail. Sweat poured suddenly from his pores and his heart began to pound.

"Is he ready?"

The woman's voice, clear and cold, pierced the stillness beneath Eagle's helmet and he felt hatred—dark and overwhelming—roll over him. When he escaped from these pirates, he would make this woman pay for the violations of his body and mind.

"Why haven't you injected him yet?"

He stiffened at the words and awaited the answer, holding his breath, willing his heart to stop beating so loudly.

"I thought you would want to do the honors yourself," he heard the blue man answer. "After all, Captain, this is your affair."

"Damn you to Aldeburon."

Eagle heard the woman's words and felt a brief moment of hope. She had expected her subordinate to do her dirty work and apparently the man objected. Perhaps for all her bravado she was a little squeamish when it came to torturing prisoners herself. Immediately a coldness settled in his chest. A woman as tough as she had to be to lead these renegades would not hesitate over something so minor as inserting a needle into a prisoner's arm.

"I told you to hook him up," the woman was saying, her voice tense.

"This is a very sensitive procedure," the man answered. "It requires a delicate touch. I thought you would be better suited to make the insertion. Besides, then if anything goes wrong and he dies, I would not be blamed."

Eagle couldn't help but be impressed at the sound of the varied and creative curses—in various languages— the woman was hurling at the blue officer. She had quite a vocabulary. He sobered as she finished her tirade and with one last curse, made her decision.

"*P'fagh!* Very well. Give it to me."

Eagle stiffened again as the helmet was wrenched from his head and he found himself staring into the furious eyes of his captor.

"You can avoid this, you know," she said, her voice harsh. "Just tell us where the child has been taken and you won't have to have your mind scrambled."

He pressed his lips together and raised both brows, then shook his head slightly. "The truth is I don't know where she's been taken."

"Liar. Who took her?"

"I don't know." He didn't know why he should protect Telles, but he'd be damned if he was giving this scum any information. "I thought he was with you."

She muttered a curse that had been banned on two planets that he knew of and turned away. Once again he was taken aback by her tenacity. If he had met her under any other circumstances, he would have sized her up as some government official's daughter bent on making her mark in society. Her poise, her arrogance, the way she carried herself, all pointed to wealth and a classy upbringing. Yet, if you looked more closely, you could see the power hiding inside this woman. Her arms beneath her sleek blue uniform were muscular, taut biceps denoting a warrior's strength. True, her woman's form was amply displayed by the V-neck of the garment, her breasts straining against the material as she moved around him. But she was no woman. She was a soldier cast in a woman's body.

She moved like a bauthah cat, with a slow sensuality that in no way disguised the capability lurking just under the skin. She was a paradox. Her beauty was breathtaking, her body incredible, her ruthlessness unmistakable. Still . . . what in the universe was she doing out here commanding this ragtag bunch of renegades instead of being home with some rich husband, or raking in a pile of credits on some pleasure planet? She turned back to him and all curiosity vanished as his gaze locked on the hypodermic needle in her hand.

"It is unfortunate you won't cooperate," she said, and for a moment Eagle thought he saw a flash of real regret in her eyes. "We don't like to use the ways of the Kalimar, but—"

"But you will," Eagle interrupted. "It's amazing to me how people always seem to decry the tactics of those they hate, until they need to use those same tactics themselves."

"Shut up." Her eyes narrowed and what little compassion he thought he saw mirrored there disappeared as she held the needle aloft. "If I were you, I'd think again about telling us the truth. This is a new experimental mind-probe stolen from one of Zarn's own laboratories. The drug of choice is injected directly into the brain of the subject and the needle left connected throughout the probe. I'm sure it is quite painful, and since we are novices at the actual implementation of the procedure, it is possible we may leave your mind less than whole when we've finished extracting the information we need."

Eagle felt the rage rush over him with the force of an ocean's wave at her unemotional recounting of what was about to take place. He strained against the invisible straps holding him, his fists clenched, his face distorted as he tried in vain to wrench himself free.

"Are you out of your mind?" he said, desperation forcing him to play his trump card. He hated to use his relationship to his father, but there seemed to be no other way to reach these people. "Do you realize what Zarn will do to you if you harm his son?"

A smirk touched the woman's lips and her turquoise eyes turned liquid with feigned seduction. One hand lifted to stroke the side of his face and he glared at her.

"Yes, little space-boy, we know who your big bad daddy is." She leaned closer, her lips scant inches from his. "And we don't give a damn." She jerked back, as if getting too close to him would taint her. She turned to the blue-haired man. "Kell, have you programmed the probe correctly?"

He nodded, his face implacable. "As correctly as I am able, considering I have not been trained to—"

"All right, let's get started. Try to remain still, if you value your mind."

Her hand moved toward him again, this time to press flat against his brow as she used the other hand to hold the needle against his temple. Sweat broke out across his upper lip and across his forehead and drenched his back suddenly beneath him. He ran his tongue across his lips and tasted the salt. He closed his eyes, praying he would not cry out or give these villains any show of weakness. He could feel her fingers moving across his head, as if measuring to find the exact spot for the penetration to take place. Eagle could feel the heat of his body preparing for flight and his pulse was a drum in his head, drowning out the quiet conversation between the woman and her subordinate.

All at once he was no longer in the cargo bay. He was somewhere else entirely. It was a small room, a claustrophobic room filled with equipment and two men. He was small. Or was it that the chair was large? A helmet was being placed on his head and a buzzing began as soon as it connected with his scalp and one of the men flipped a switch beside him. Something else was being placed on his skin at different intervals, little round suctions. They sucked against his pulse points and he began to shake violently.

It was his dream. Ever since Telles's death he'd been plagued with nightmares, nightmares whose details he could never quite grasp, never quite remember. Now he remembered.

"It's all right," a soothing voice said in the back of his memory. "Everything will be all right."

Then blackness, emptiness, a horrible spinning void. Then the same voice again.

"What name do you choose for yourself? What name do you choose?"

"I will administer a numbing shot first," a different voice said, piercing suddenly through the words echoing inside his brain.

Eagle opened his eyes. He hadn't realized he'd had them closed. He stared around the room feeling disoriented, confused. Had she just asked him something about his name? "What?" he said through dry lips. "What did you say?"

She gazed down at him stonily. "Although you don't deserve to be spared any pain, it is hard to insert the probe needle into someone twisting and writhing in agony. This will sedate you somewhat."

Eagle tensed. He didn't know what had just happened to him, but it had to have something to do with the mind-probing. Now she would sedate him and he didn't want to be out of control. The thought of her poking around in his brain was bad enough, but to do it while he was unconscious made his throat tighten with a new fear.

"I don't need your numbing drugs," he said suddenly, jerking away from her touch. "I am the son of Zarn! Your petty attempts to probe my mind will be useless. Don't you realize that I am a superior being, you air-headed bitch?"

Rage blossomed briefly on her face and Eagle swallowed hard.

"Very well, *traugh'fak,*" she cursed at him, "I shall honor that superiority—which I call stupidity—by allowing you to feel the needle pierce your skull and sink into your brain. I look forward to seeing how the great son of Zarn reacts to something that would bring any mortal man to his knees."

"Bring it on, baby," he said recklessly, refusing to take his eyes from hers. "Do your worst."

Her full lips curved up in satisfaction even as a flicker of uncertainty hovered about her eyes. "I intend to."

"Captain—" the man called Kell moved to stand at her side—"I do not think you should use the probe without the anesthetic. It may help to further break down his resistance, and think on it—why would any sane man try to provoke you into denying it to him?"

She nodded and put the large needle down, reaching across his trapped body for something else, her body pressing briefly against his. Eagle saw the woman was sweating too, beads of perspiration glistening on her jawline and across the hollow of her throat. One droplet trickled down the front of her neck, touched the hollow, then moved downward toward the crevice between her breasts. Desire, swift and unexpected, coursed through Eagle's blood and his eyes widened. He was shocked at himself and angry with his body's ridiculous timing.

The brief, crazy surge from his libido died as she held up another hypodermic, this one a modern hypo-spray. She pressed it against his neck and a soft release of air surged out, bringing with it a gentle languor that began to permeate his senses. He fought against it but his natural defenses fell, leaving him helpless. He drifted on a hazy cloud somewhere between wakefulness and sleep, trying to prepare himself for the violation of his mind. Instead, he heard someone screaming. For one groggy moment he thought he had screamed, but it was a woman's cry, wrenched from her soul.

Somehow Eagle dragged his eyelids open, and through a mist, looked up to see his captor standing with both hands pressed to her head, her eyes squeezed shut, her breath coming rapidly as she stumbled against the table on which he lay.

"No!" she screamed, twisting her head from side to side. Her fingers clenched the silver band around her forehead and she seemed to be trying to shove the metallic object more firmly against her brow. "Get out! Get out! I—" She stopped struggling abruptly, her eyes growing wide and round as her movements froze. She collapsed across Eagle, her head turned sideways on his chest, her eyes wide open, staring, unresponsive. She needed help. Eagle tried to move, tried to reach her, but even as he remembered in some still coherent part of his mind that he was shackled and this woman was his enemy, the haze intensified, darkened, and sucked him down.

Chapter Three

Sky found herself suddenly standing in an empty place shrouded with mist. Vast horizons stretched around her and for a moment she could not get her bearings. Where was she? She frowned, trying to remember what had happened. She had been in the cargo hold, about to use the mind-probe on the prisoner when someone had entered her mind, entered swiftly, unexpectedly, circumventing not only the power of the band, but her own mental defenses. She had tried to shore them up and that effort had sent her spinning inward, into her own mind. Now she recognized this place. It was her battle zone, the place she came within her mind when she had to fight against intruders. The emptiness was her own creation. It gave her plenty of room to move about and made anyone approaching an easy target.

And now someone was coming. Sky schooled herself to remain calm. It had been so long since she'd had to fight. The silver deflector had kept her safe for so long. Had it finally failed her? Through the mist a distant figure moved steadily toward her. Sky summoned her strength and shielded herself enough for protection, yet not so much that the intruder would be banished. She wanted to know who had dared to violate her mind. If it was Zarn's son . . .

But no, it was a small form coming nearer—small and slim. Sky caught her breath as the mist cleared and the person was exposed. Mayla. It was Mayla, her little sister, her almost-child. Sky gazed in wonder at the girl approaching. Lavender, almond-shaped eyes stared back at her; soft, silver-blond hair curled around her thin, oval face. And her aura—there was no mistaking her mental aura, the inimitable mental signature, emanating from her.

"Sky—" she called softly, lifting one hand and reaching it toward her. *"I haven't much time. You must listen to me."*

"Mayla!" She couldn't help the shout, nor the quick mental steps forward. How long had it been since she'd seen her, held her in her arms? Three months? Four? Time had meshed together in her frantic search throughout the galaxy. "Where are you? Help me find you! Are you all right?"

"I haven't much time."

Sky took another step forward and stopped. Mayla's figure was wavering, growing hazier by the second. This was not right. When two minds came together, there was as much solidity as in the outer realm of reality. Sky reached out to touch her sister and her hand passed through her.

"Mayla—what's wrong? Where are you?"

It was as though Mayla couldn't hear her. Sky closed her eyes and concentrated, dropping what few natural shields she possessed and calling upon every ounce of strength she had. When she opened her eyes again, Mayla's image was a little stronger, but her voice had grown somehow weaker.

"Listen to me, Sky. This man called Eagle, you must not use the mind-probe upon him. He is not our enemy. He will help you find me if you give him the chance. Do you hear me, my sister?"

Sky was dumbstruck by Mayla's words and it took a second before she could respond.

"Sky—do you hear me?"

"Yes, Mayla, I hear you, but you don't know this man. He's evil—he's Zarn's son! If I don't probe his mind, how will I find you?"

"He doesn't know where I am."

"Do you know where you are?"

The image faltered again.

*"I cannot maintain our connection. Good-bye my sister,
I will contact you again if I am permitted."*

"Permitted? Is someone keeping you from—Mayla—
Mayla, don't go!"

But it was too late. The small form was wavering again
and this time dissipated as though a soft brush had been
washed over her. Her sister was gone, leaving Sky with
new questions and new fears.

Skyra groaned as consciousness returned. A thousand
Dendarian dreamdrums pounded inside her skull and a
haze filtered across her line of vision. She blinked, clearing the last vestiges of confusion away in time to bring
Kell's concerned face into focus. She was in sickbay, lying on the small table where battle wounds were tended.

"Are you all right?" His pale azure hand smoothed a
lock of hair back from her face. "You've been unconscious for an hour."

"No, not unconscious," she murmured.

"What in the world happened? Did your shielding fail?
Did you experience a barrage?"

Sky tried to shake her head but the effort sent a sharp
stab of pain through her temples. A "barrage" was a term
used by telepaths to describe the sensation of many mental voices invading a mind simultaneously. She lifted her
hand to the silver band.

"No," she said, amazed to hear her voice come out in
a weak whisper. "It was Mayla."

Kell blinked twice, then regained his former composure. "Your sister? She contacted you mentally? But
how? The band is designed to keep any thoughts from
yours, even that of telepaths."

"Mayla is not your average telepath." She smiled, the
image of her sister rising unbidden in her mind. "Her
power—" she broke off, her face flushed. She had almost
revealed to Kell the vast extent of Mayla's abilities. As
much as she trusted her second-in-command, that was
something she could never tell him or anyone else. If
Zarn ever found out the power Mayla actually possessed,
killing her would be considered humane compared to

65

what he would likely try to do. She had no doubts that he would attempt somehow to use her for his own evil purposes.

Sky tried to sit up. "I'm fine, really I am. Where is the prisoner?"

"Still in the cargo hold. I left two guards. He's pretty out of it thanks to that shot you gave him, but I'm not sure if there's enough of the drug left in his system to continue with—"

"Release him," she said abruptly, swinging her legs over the side of the bunk and standing. The small cubicle was used for bandaging wounds and doing simple diagnostic work. There was no doctor aboard and none was needed as long as she served as captain. Her ability to heal was nothing compared to Mayla's, but she could handle most situations. She glanced up to see a profound look of surprise on the Altairian's face.

"What did you say?" he asked, his dark blue brows knit together over the paler blue irises below. The expression in their depths said very plainly he thought she had lost her mind. "Release him?"

"I'll explain." Sky stood, rubbing the back of her neck as she walked around the confines of the small room, her thoughts troubled. "Mayla told me not to use the probe against what's-his-name and to release him. She says if we'll give him a chance, he'll help us find her."

"But how did she breach your shield?" Kell insisted. "How?"

"This band"—she gestured to her head—"keeps out any normal person's thought waves that might randomly collide with mine, and it also keeps out the power of telepaths, or at least it has so far. But Mayla is different." She stopped talking and clasped her hands behind her back, pausing to stare into a cabinet containing liquid bandage and tubes filled with painkillers. "She and I share the bond not only of being sisters, but on another, higher level, the bond of being Cezans. I don't know how to explain that except to say that it increases her strength of mind, as far as I am concerned, by one hundredfold."

"Why hasn't she contacted you before?" Kell asked suspiciously. "How do you know this isn't a trick of some kind? Perhaps Zarn's son is a telepath and has violated your mind, convincing you his thoughts are Mayla's so you'll release him."

Sky shook her head, running one finger across the smooth surface of the cabinet door. She spun back around in time to see an odd look cross Kell's face, a look of impatience or irritation. Extremely odd for Kell. He was the most patient of all creatures.

"No, I know Mayla's mental signature. I was startled at first by the sudden intrusion into my mind and it caused me to withdraw into myself, but later I realized who it was. Her essence cannot be duplicated by any means that I am aware of. No, right when I was about to insert the needle into his brain—" she broke off with a slight shudder then straightened her shoulders. "Right at that moment, something happened. I heard someone shout, telling me to stop. I was so startled, so afraid, that I drew inward and prepared to fight the intruder inside my mind. It was there I found Mayla. She told me I was not to probe the colonel, that he was not our enemy, and I was to release him."

The doubt had not left Kell's gaze. "If it was Mayla, why has she not contacted you before now?"

"I don't know. Perhaps she couldn't."

"Did she tell you where she is?"

Sky shook her head, feeling the wave of despair flood over her again. She had been so close to knowing. Why hadn't Mayla told her before she disappeared?

"Remember, Sky, she may be the heir to the throne of Andromeda, but she is still just a child." Kell frowned at her thoughtfully. "Why is she the heir? Why not you? You have the telepathic powers that are the prerequisite, and the healing power as well."

Sky bit her lower lip and hesitated. She hated lying to Kell, after all they'd been through together, but sometimes there was just no way around it.

"The youngest child in the family is the heir," she said, turning so that she wouldn't have to meet his eyes with the lie. "At least, that is our family's custom. At times there have been exceptions, but not now, not when so much is at stake."

"I see. Is it possible her link with you could lead us to her?"

Sky bit her lower lip, shaking her head. "I don't know. Perhaps I could follow the trail left by her thought waves. She was only there for a moment, then she was gone. If she could remain in my mind for a sustained length of time, then perhaps—" She frowned, breaking off the thought. "But if she could do that, she would have contacted me before. My guess would be that she has tried to reach me and has been prevented until now."

"Because of the band?"

"Yes. And perhaps because she is already a great distance away. Even Mayla—" She didn't complete the thought. "If I removed the protective band, perhaps she could reach me more easily."

Kell folded his arms across his chest. "It is also possible your mind would be flooded by a thousand others and send you into telepathic shock."

She nodded, then turned away. "I'm afraid she is being stopped from using her telepathic ability. She said she would contact me again if she was 'permitted.' That sure sounds like someone is holding her against her will. I don't know. In the meantime, release him." Sky placed her hand on the back of her neck and leaned her head back against it. She yawned and Kell gave her a knowing look.

"You need to rest."

"I will—later. Right now, let's take care of our 'guest,' for I suppose that's what he's going to be for the rest of this trip."

"What if he refuses to help us? What if Mayla is wrong?"

Sky moved toward the doorway, a nagging headache beginning between her eyes, right at the pointed apex of the silver band. She touched the spot briefly, willing the pain away before she turned back to Kell.

"Mayla is never wrong," she said. "Well, hardly ever."

"Captain!"

The outcry came over the intercom speaker next to the doorway. Sky slammed the palm of her hand down on the response switch.

"Captain here."

The voice of her security chief blasted back at her. "The prisoner has escaped. I repeat, the prisoner has escaped. He may have killed one of the guards; we aren't sure yet."

A cold wave of anger flooded over her. "What do you mean you aren't sure yet? Is he dead or not?"

"The prisoner has barricaded himself in the hold and is holding both guards hostage. He demands that you come down and speak with him."

"Oh, he demands it, does he?" Sky whirled around. "Kell, get a squad together and arm them with phaser rifles, set on heavy stun."

"What about Mayla's command?" Kell reminded her dryly. "What about your plan to release him?"

Sky narrowed her eyes and curled both hands into tight fists. "Nobody threatens me or my crew on my own *p'flaugking* ship! Nobody!" She stormed out of the sickbay and headed for the cargo hold. If Zarn's son thought she would give in to his terrorist tactics, he had another think coming.

Eagle could barely stand. The anesthetic combined with a day without food and little water was catching up with him. He had been lucky so far—lucky in that the men set to guard him weren't exactly blessed with an abundance of brains, and lucky his pretense of having some kind of seizure had worked. One of the guards had released him from his bonds as he had wrenched and slobbered, and in a matter of minutes, with the training of thirteen years in the Forces on his side, he had subdued both of them, cracking one guard's head a little harder than he'd intended. He hoped the man didn't die because he suspected that little fireball on the bridge would never let him go if he had done serious harm.

His plan was simple. He would tell the woman that if she would release him, he would help her find the child. Then he would send out a coded message to Telles's ship, and if he was anywhere in range he felt sure his old friend would answer if only out of curiosity. He would offer to help Telles, offer to help his captor, and in the end trick them both and bring the little princess back to his father. A picture of the little girl's face hovered in his mind and he pushed it brusquely away. Zarn wouldn't hurt her. He'd make sure of that. The memory of his father's ruthlessness on other worlds sprang to mind. He frowned and checked the charge in the phaser he held. On second thought, maybe the best thing to do would be to take the child to a holding place, a safe place, until he had a chance to talk to his father in more detail about his plans for her.

Zarn would be furious but he wouldn't have much of an alternative. What was he going to do, torture the information out of him? He smiled at the thought. He might not be sure of much in this universe, but one thing he could count on was his father's love for him. They might not always agree, but there was a bond between them that couldn't be broken. Another idea dawned and although he tried to dismiss it, he found he could not.

Even before the battle for Alpha Centauri 7, he had begun to see that his father's way was wrong. People had rights, whether they were Rigelian or not. Telles's feelings about the Kalimar had affected him, he realized that now, and it had been with great reluctance that he accepted the truth: He agreed with his friend. His father should be stopped—but not by more violence. Eagle knew if he could just have the chance, the right chance, to talk to his father, convince him there was a better way to run his little part of the universe, he could make him understand. If Zarn didn't change the way he was ruling his people, he was going to lose everything. Maybe the little girl was the chance he'd been waiting for, the leverage he needed. Blackmail his father into listening? One corner of his mouth lifted. Actually, Zarn would appreciate the tactic. It was worthy of his son.

Wiping his brow with the back of one hand, Eagle felt the too-small uniform he had taken from the still-unconscious guard rip under the arm. He tried once again to pull the two edges of the cloth together in the front and fasten them, but it was no use. His body was exposed to the waist and there was nothing he could do about it. It was immaterial. He abandoned the effort and turned his thoughts to his escape.

He had to get away from these people as quickly as possible, find the child, and take her to a safe place unknown to any of the players in this little drama, then contact his father. Much as he would like to revenge himself upon the silver-haired wench who had tortured him, as much as he would like to hold her at phaser point and do a little torturing himself, the best thing to do was to make his escape, cleanly, coolly, and leave her wondering where in the galaxy he had gone.

"Open this hatch, you son of a Denebian *slumbock*."

As if in response to his thoughts, her voice crackled across the com situated at the side of the cargo hatch, a voice taut with suppressed anger. A half-smile touched his lips as he walked wearily over and leaned against the dense metal. Cargo holds on small cruisers like this weren't graced with invisible energy shields. This one had a good old-fashioned two-foot-thick birellium hatch that could withstand almost any kind of attack against it. The only disadvantage was you couldn't see who was on the other side, but in this case that was a distinct advantage because he was sure the fury blazing in the captain's beautiful eyes might melt him on the spot. He spoke into the unit.

"How lovely to hear your dulcet tones again," he said. "And how courteous of you to arrive so promptly."

"I'm warning you—if that guard dies I will take your head back to your father on a platter!"

Eagle sobered. The guard was stirring now, moaning softly and thrashing from side to side. The other sat beside him, glowering at Eagle, cradling his own injured arm to his side. The wounded men gave him the advantage, and he intended to use it for all it was worth.

"I, too, am concerned about your men, Captain. It seems I hit one of them a little too hard and bounced his head off the inside of this impressive door. He's unconscious." A sudden expletive hurled through that same metal made a smile dart across his face of its own volition. "Temper, temper. And may I say, now that there is a thick hatch between us, Captain, that you have the mouth of a Tantalisian pimp-boy? I must tell you I find it extremely unbecoming in a woman."

"Shut up!" The furious command almost seemed to physically shake the doorway and Eagle chuckled. Perhaps a little revenge would be exacted today after all.

"What's it going to be, Captain? I hate to see men suffer like this. And I'd hate it if one of them died when it could have been avoided with a little help from your sickbay."

Another oath, then muttering between two people, then more outraged cursing. Eagle glanced over at the conscious guard and thought he saw the man's mouth drop open as the cursing intensified, growing more eloquent by the minute. Finally the captain's voice returned to normal and two terse words echoed across the speaker.

"Your terms?"

Eagle smiled. It had been easier than he'd hoped, although he realized he had no way of knowing if she would honor her word once she got the guards back.

"How do I know you'll keep your word?" he said, voicing his doubts.

"How do I know the men are still alive—or are even hurt for that matter?"

Eagle turned and walked over to the man who still clutched his arm. He wasn't seriously injured, just bruised, perhaps a dislocated shoulder and a couple of broken ribs. Eagle's hand closed around the neck of his uniform and jerked him to his feet. The movement itself brought a cry of pain from the man, who then sank back down to the floor, his face as white as a sheet. Eagle pushed aside his niggling conscience and strode back to the com.

"Sorry, I thought I'd bring one of them over to convince you, but I think he passed out again."

"You splay-handed, *dard-mittled*, pox-ridden son of a bitch!"

"Tut, tut, Captain, I don't respond well to that sort of language."

"When I get hold of you—" She broke off. "Your terms—space-boy?"

He leaned against the bulkhead, arms folded across his chest, enjoying her frustration immensely. "And while we're at it, why don't we establish that my rank is colonel. You may call me Colonel Zarn." Eagle grinned as he pictured the irate expression on the woman's face.

"I'll call you a *fark-biddled*—" She broke off again as Kell's deeper voice murmured in the background. Silence. Then an exasperated sigh. "For the last time, what are your terms—*Colonel*?"

Eagle smiled. "Well, now, I don't want much. Just to keep my brain intact, and to be released and given the freedom of the ship. In return, I'll give you your guards back and I'll try to help you find the kid. If we can't find her within, oh, say seven Andromedan days, you release me, no hard feelings."

"Why would you help us find her?"

He shrugged to himself. "Why not? She means nothing to me. I just didn't like being forced to do something that will screw me up with High Command."

"You mean with your father." Her voice was scathing, filled with disgust. "Then you agree to lead us to her?"

"I really don't know where she is, Captain. Your probing of my mind would have been a lesson in futility—and barbarism."

"Yeah, well you should know." Another silence. Whispered mutterings. Her voice once again. "All right, Colonel. You have your terms."

Easier than he'd supposed. Too easy.

"I've got a phaser," he told her. "When I open this hatch I'm going to shoot the first person I see with a weapon drawn. And I don't have it set on stun."

"We understand. I give you my word as the captain of the *Defiant* that no harm will come to you."

"You agree to release me after seven days if we haven't found the child?"

"Yes."

Eagle considered her promise, a phaser in each hand. His captors still had the advantage. If he opened the door they could always overpower him. He had two phasers not fully charged against the complement of the ship. Why should they honor their part of the bargain? He didn't trust her, and yet, for some reason, he believed her to be a person of honor. Besides, what other choice did he have?

"All right. Step back from the door and I'll release it." He reached for the huge manual switch jutting out next to the hatch. He'd disabled the computer-link tying the mechanism into the bridge and auxiliary control. Tucking one phaser into his belt, he pushed upward on the little-used bar and felt it give beneath his hand. Immediately he jumped back from the opening, pulled the weapon from his belt and trained both guns on the empty space being left by the hatch door gliding upward.

She stood on the other side, hands on her hips, blue eyes narrow. Flanked by Kell on one side and a thick-set, burly looking man on the other, he was surprised to see there were no other security personnel in sight.

"We are unarmed," she said, moving her hands apart in a gesture of openness. "Please lower your weapons."

"Not a chance. First let me out of here and show me to a nice cozy room complete with shower, clean clothes, and a hot meal. Then I'll give you the phasers."

Her gaze flickered over his bare chest and Eagle fancied he saw the anger in her eyes falter half a second before it flared back to life. Interesting.

"Lieutenant P'ton will show you to your quarters," she said. The burly man stepped forward, his face dark with anger.

Eagle barely glanced in his direction. "I don't think so. I want the VIP treatment, Captain. You can show me to my quarters."

The tension in her stance was palpable. Her fingers resting on her slim waist tightened and Eagle let a smile flash across his face, enjoying her frustration.

"Sky, I protest, I—" the blue-skinned man began, only

to be cut off by the woman with one long stroke of her hand.

Sky. Eagle almost rolled his eyes. Captain Sky. How eloquent, how droll. He voiced his opinion aloud.

"Captain Sky—how lovely. Brings to mind lazy days in Pernoz back on Andromeda. Couldn't you come up with anything less—fluffy?" He raked his gaze over her. "It doesn't exactly suit you. I would have dubbed you a 'Bodra' or perhaps a 'Henriette,' but 'Sky'?" He shook his head. "Definitely a misnomer."

Her eyes narrowed even more until they were thin slits of rage. Her full lips were pressed tightly together as if to stop the torrent of profanity she wanted to pour upon him. Eagle grinned at her, hoping it would drive her over the edge and he could watch her debase herself with more cursing, but instead her features calmed. The tension faded from her face, the anger from her eyes, and he marveled at her sudden control.

"I will show you to your quarters, Colonel, and I would be honored if you would join me in my cabin for dinner."

Eagle started to laugh, then realized she was serious. What was she up to now? He hesitated, but the challenge in her gaze was impossible to resist.

"I would be delighted," he said, bowing slightly. He waved one phaser toward the three of them. "Lead on, Captain Sky. Your humble servant follows."

She smiled at him, the gesture promising something he couldn't quite define. Revenge? Retribution? He wasn't sure, but he tossed the smile back at her and winked. She spun on her heel and began walking down the corridor, her two cohorts at her side. Eagle watched her go, unable to keep from admiring the way her hips moved sensuously from side to side, her silver-blond hair tossing in exact synchronization with her even strides.

This was going to be interesting, Eagle thought. He stuck one of the phasers in his waistband and hurried after her.

Eagle stood in the center of the cabin he'd been assigned, fighting the urge to throw himself across the bunk and sleep. There was too much to do, too much to figure out. He'd showered, eaten, had his ribs taped and been given a fresh set of clothing that actually fit him. His amusement and interest in his captor's name and backside had vanished as she ushered him into the room and told him coldly that she would expect him at the dinner hour. As the door had closed behind her, the happenings of the last ten hours had begun to sink in.

During his years in the Forces, Eagle had endured many kinds of torture, some while being held prisoner on other worlds, some brought on by his own overactive conscience, but nothing he had ever experienced had prepared him for the bone-chilling panic that had coursed through his veins as he lay waiting for that needle to be plunged into his brain. Eagle let the tense control he'd kept over himself ever since he'd been brought aboard the *Defiant* slip away, and as he did, his legs folded beneath him.

He sank to the gray carpeted floor and brought his hands down, pressing his palms against the flat surface. He bowed his head, allowing himself, just for the moment, the luxury of feeling his fear.

When he'd awakened in the cargo hold, strapped down, the probe beside him, something in him had turned over and inside out. Because all at once he had known how it was going to feel to be put under the power of that machine. All at once he had known the horror of having his natural mental defenses pierced and his mind ravaged by a stranger. In that moment, he had felt helpless, defenseless—violated. It had been as real and as tangible as if he had experienced it all before. He shook the thought away. He'd never been probed. But he'd felt a searing wave of terror as he lay on that table awaiting the needle. A terrible desire to kill the woman doing this to him, to strip her mind from her, to torture her, to violate her as fully as she intended to violate him, had assaulted his mind. The realization had frightened him almost more than the probe. When had he become this vicious, this violent?

His mother had died when he was but a child, and his

upbringing had been solely at the hands of his father. Zarn was a strict disciplinarian but Eagle had found him to be fair in most instances. He remembered when he first joined the Forces wondering about some of the ruthlessness he witnessed, but Zarn had always managed to explain away his concerns. As he had grown and become more experienced as a soldier, he began to understand that when you were fighting a war, the usual rules of life did not apply. When you fought a war, things normally considered wrong, even evil, became necessary devices used to ensure that Rigel would never again be subjugated by another world.

Zarn had taught him, drilled it into him when he was a boy, that in the past Rigel's people had been enslaved by many other worlds and taken to distant parts of the galaxy to serve in subjection and humiliation. He himself had led the uprising of slaves thirty years before, the uprising that had destroyed the invaders then living on Rigel. He had seized the alien technology and within a matter of months, had established a new regime, with equal freedoms for all Rigelians. It hadn't been long before they were attacked by other worlds eager to depose the new government and once again send the Rigelians back into a life of slavery. Zarn had been a natural leader, and his newly developed Forces had beaten off the marauders. That was where it had all begun. Who would have dreamed that within twenty years of that uprising, Rigel would reign in the quadrant, with dozens of other worlds under Zarn's auspicious and protective wings?

Eagle took a deep breath. He had to pull himself together. This maudlin inner dialogue was doing him no good and was delaying him from finding a way off this tub. He pushed himself up from the floor and stumbled to his feet, wincing a little as the muscles around his sore ribs strained with the effort. He moved slowly to the small observation window in the opposite bulkhead. His charcoal-gray uniform—now identical to some of the ones his captors wore—brushed against a small statue sitting on the night table and he caught it just before it smashed to the floor.

He looked down at the object. It fit in the palm of his hand. It was smooth, carved from a piece of black stone in the shape of a Terran cat. It belonged to her. He put it down as the knowledge rushed over him. How he knew, he had no idea, but he knew it, just as he now knew this was her cabin. The captain's cabin. How strangely generous of her—or was it her way of monitoring him at all times, for surely the captain's quarters would have those capabilities.

She certainly didn't allow herself any perks as captain of the *Defiant*, he thought, gazing around at the austere room. Captain Sky. It was too, too absurd. Still . . . He moved back to the bed and finally gave in to his urges, lying back, stretching his aching muscles over the hard, flat surface. He didn't want to think about the indomitable ruler of this ship, but somehow, lying on her bed, in her cabin, it seemed inevitable.

She was an enigma, a beautiful enigma he'd like to unravel slowly from the outside in, beginning with the removal of that masculine uniform she wore. He'd like to find out if the skin beneath her clothing was just as smooth and creamy as the skin exposed at her throat and wrists. He wanted to know if her skin felt like the petals of a flower, if her lips tasted as much like raspberries as they looked. He frowned, frustrated with the direction his mind was taking. Closing his eyes, Eagle tried to turn his thoughts elsewhere but the image of her face, and her body, kept hovering just on the edge of his consciousness.

It was ridiculous. The only reason he was fantasizing about Captain Sky was because he hadn't been with a woman since he'd taken a trip a few months ago to a pleasure planet in the Caldonian system. The experience had ended up being so *un*pleasureable that he had made a decision to remain celibate for a time, at least until he met someone who didn't make him feel soiled by the act. And that someone certainly wasn't Captain Sky Spitfire with the polluted mouth. Not that she made him feel that way. No, she made him feel many things—hot all over, hard as a rock, tight with unreleased desire—but not soiled. He wanted her, and he despised himself for his ridiculous lust.

Or was it lust? Maybe he wanted her because he wanted revenge. Men from the beginning of time had been forcing women to yield their bodies, not to be loved, but to be conquered.

The thought of such a violation immediately sickened him, and Eagle felt relief at the knowledge. Perhaps he wasn't as far gone as he had feared, because it wasn't a forced rendevous he had in mind. When and if he ever removed her clothing, it would be with the slow, soft sensuality of a lover, and if and when he made love to her, she would be in total agreement and respond with the fire and passion he suspected she kept under careful control. To be the one who could make her lower those emotional shields—*that* would be a conquest worth exploring.

With an oath that rivaled some he'd heard from the erstwhile captain, Eagle sat up again and flung his legs over the side of the bed. His feet hit the floor and he leaned his forehead on his hands, staring down at the gray boots he'd been given. The woman had tried to suck his mind from him and he was thinking about seducing her! What was wrong with him? He stood and began pacing with quick, angry strides back and forth across the small cabin, hands clenched into fists at his side.

He crossed the room, idly noting that another, taller statue sat on a low table next to the wall, a rather amateurish attempt at a representation of a woman or a goddess of some sort. Stopping beside it, he fancied he saw a little of Sky in the eyes and cursing, he turned away, pushing thoughts of the woman from his mind.

Eventually these pirates would have to let him go or kill him, and he was willing to bet it would be the former. Even renegades would risk only so much of Zarn's wrath. But he couldn't wait until Captain Sky decided to give him up. Where was Zarn? Did he know about the attack? What would happen when the Kalimar discovered that not only had his new prize been stolen but his son as well? A new apprehension seized him. Zarn could be following them at that moment, just waiting for the right opportunity to attack. He would find them, and Sky and her band of renegades would be taken to one of his infamous prison camps. The thought sent a slight shudder through him, and Eagle paced rapidly across the room and back.

What was wrong with him? Why did the thought of the silver-haired woman being subjected to the worst kind of torture in the universe make him feel sick inside? She'd asked for it and woman or not, she deserved it. You couldn't attack one of Zarn's stations and think you could just walk away from it. She'd known the risks when she attacked. So why had she done it? Why was she even with this little band of rabble? What was the point? Were they part of the rebellion? He stopped pacing. Possibly. But the underground rebellion that had been growing over the past few years was a patient, well-organized lot. They didn't usually attack unless they knew they could win— and this was a no-win situation.

There was a chance Zarn didn't know about the attack yet. If at all possible, Eagle wanted to avoid a big battle between Zarn's forces and Sky's people. Then there was the matter of Telles. He sank down on the bunk and leaned his head in his hands. Telles might no longer be on the right side, but he was still his friend. If Zarn came after them he had no doubt Telles would either be executed or spend the rest of his life in a prison cell.

If I can get a message back to Station One, speak with my people, I'll know where I stand, he thought. And if Zarn doesn't already know about the attack, I'll convince Millon to keep it from him.

Eagle thought it over. Maybe he could get Captain Spitfire to let him make a transmission under the guise of trying to get information. Or he could just find a com unit and make the call without her knowledge. Yes, he definitely liked that idea better.

Galvanized into action, Eagle headed for the doorway. He had plenty of time before his dinner with the captain.

He'd been given the run of the ship, as per their agreement. It still surprised him that she'd honored the deal and hadn't clapped him in irons as soon as he walked out of the cargo hold. Perhaps over dinner he could get a few more answers—like who these people really were and what they had to gain from the risks they were taking. Maybe he'd walk around a bit, get his bearings—find out where the auxiliary control panel was located. It would be a simple matter to send a message from there.

All he had to do was acquaint himself with the ship. After all of his military and intelligence experience, he'd yet to meet a cruiser of this sort that he couldn't take apart blindfolded. He'd find the outgoing com unit or he'd find a way to break into it. Either way, the next step of his plan to escape would be implemented soon, he hoped before the captain had a chance to begin her main course. He smiled and, running one hand through his rumpled hair to give it a semblance of order, headed for the door to the cabin. It slid open and after a quick glance down the corridor, he slipped out.

He wasn't so foolish as to think he wasn't being watched every minute by someone, or something, so he walked casually down the hallway, nodding at one or two crewmen he passed. They stared back at him suspiciously and didn't acknowledge his gesture.

The ship was larger than he'd first thought, and as he walked he began to compare it with other ships he'd served on or fought. A Marovian 286 or a Titanar 3 would be his educated guess. He kept walking, noting that thus far he had not seen anything of real interest and concluded he must be on a deck used primarily to house the crew. If it was one of the two ships he thought it to be, he knew just where to find engineering and the bridge. He began looking for a lift. Once or twice he thought someone was behind him, and he glanced back over one shoulder. No one was there but that meant nothing. She was keeping an eye on him, of that he had no doubt. He wished there was some way he could give her a few dull gray hairs to mix in with that odd silver mane.

He smiled. Maybe he couldn't take the risk of paying Captain Sky back in spades for what she'd tried to do to him, but while he was here, he'd certainly do his best to make her life a living hell.

Chapter Four

"This is insane."

Sky shot her second in command a look that dared him to speak again, and he pressed his lips together tightly, obviously biting back the words he wanted to say. As the captain lifted her hands to the silver band around her brow, he shook his head and laid one pale blue hand on her arm.

"Sky, I beg of you, don't do this."

She lowered her hands and faced him, this time willing herself to smile. "It's all right, Kell. We've taken every precaution and your quarters are more secure than most."

"But we've never tried this before." He released her and turned away, clasping his hands behind his back. "I've never wired anything like this before, and neither has Srad."

"He's the best engineer in the quadrant," Sky replied, sitting down on Kell's bunk. "If anyone could rig up the old helmet deflector apparatus Redar first invented into the ship's internal shielding mechanism correctly, it's Srad."

"I hope so, but there's no guarantee. I don't understand why you don't just torture the information out of the man and be done with it!"

Sky lay back on the bunk, positioning herself for maximum comfort before she began the grand experiment, but something in Kell's voice caused her to turn her thoughts away from the event ahead of her and back to him. She frowned, aware that something was wrong, something she couldn't put her finger on. She raised up on her elbows and found the Altairian staring at her. She had changed out of her uniform into a semisheer caftan in her favorite color of teal-green, in order to free her body as well as her mind. Sky realized belatedly that although Kell was her friend, he was, after all, still a man—a man who had feelings for her that she didn't return. Her flagrant flaunting of her body in front of him was inexcusable and thoughtless, but her robe was back in her quarters and once again she damned the man sleeping there for the trouble he'd caused her. She drew her feet up, arranging the folds of the caftan to conceal herself better.

"Kell, are you all right?" she asked tentatively. "I've never seen you so agitated."

"Agitated?"

She watched as he stiffened, then turned away from her, his back ramrod straight. After a moment he turned back, the irritation she thought she'd seen etched in his features gone.

"Not at all, Captain. I'm just concerned about you."

Sky decided not to pursue the matter. "Mayla said not to hurt him and I must abide by my sister's wishes. I don't understand it either, but I have to honor her commands—she is the heir to the throne even if she is only twelve years old."

"He'll never help us."

One of Sky's brows rose in amusement as she wiggled her toes impatiently. "Of course he won't. That's why this is necessary. If I remove my shielding, it's possible Mayla will be able to reach me, telepathically, and lead us to her location."

"You know the risks you take." To Sky's surprise, Kell sat down on the edge of the bunk and picked up her hand. "Forgive me, Sky, but I'm worried about you."

She laughed uncomfortably and squeezed his hand before gently tugging away from him. "You shouldn't be. I have complete confidence in what you and Srad have done to prepare this for me. With the helmet's capabilities hooked into what usually generates the force field around your quarters, I should be able to remove my band with no ill effects. The shielding from the helmet will be spread out over a much larger area—a room instead of my brain—and shouldn't be strong enough to hinder Mayla's thoughts. It should, however, keep out the rest of the universe. At least, I hope so."

"You hope." Kell shook his head again, rising from the bunk. "I don't like it. The risks are too great."

Sky locked her hands around her knees, searching for words with which to comfort her friend. She found none. "Sometimes risks are necessary, Kell. Now, please leave me."

His eyes widened. "Leave you? Indeed not. What if the shielding doesn't hold? Don't you remember what happened the last time—"

"Yes, I remember," she cut him off. "But I must have complete privacy. Your thoughts alone could interfere, especially in the strange state of mind you seem to be in today! Please, I'll be fine, but if it will make you feel better, I'll stay within reach of the com." She summoned a smile again and forced it to her lips. Sometimes having a close friend could be suffocating—especially when it was a man who felt it his duty to protect her.

"All right," he said, "but I want you to know I'm going along with this under protest."

"Duly noted," Sky wearily acknowledged. "I will contact you later. Set the lock and alarm as you leave, please."

"If I don't hear from you within an hour, I'll be back and I'll come in—whether you like it or not."

Sky bristled, sliding from the bed to her feet in one smooth movement. She stood, hands on her hips, no longer amused at Kell's concern, no longer in the role of friend. Now she was the captain of the *Defiant*, and in complete control of the situation.

"Don't let our friendship fool you into thinking I'll let you cross the line too many times, Lieutenant. I'm still in charge here, and if you enter this cabin before I give my express permission, I will have you arrested and thrown into the brig. Is that understood?" Sky regretted the anger coloring her voice as Kell's fists clenched suddenly at his side. Altairians were very proud and it wasn't a good idea to yell at them too often. He was just worried, that was all, but she grew tired of his hovering and wanted to be left in peace. It was hard enough to face what she was about to do without his doubts adding to her own.

She led him to the door, no longer caring what her thin gown revealed.

"I will lock the door myself," she said, keeping her voice even, "put in my own code. Please leave now, Kell, before we say things we will regret."

Blue eyes locked with turquoise, and for a moment Sky thought she saw fury in the depths of his gaze. Impossible. Kell's emotions were kept under tight control at all times, especially the more volatile ones. She knew his people's history, knew the violent rages that had governed them in the past and the new road of emotional control they had learned to use in an effort to end their civil wars.

Finally, Kell nodded curtly and left the room without another word, without a backward glance. Sky sank back down on the bed with a sigh. She hated to pull rank on her friend, but his stubbornness often left her no other alternative. She was glad he was gone. This was one endeavor she didn't dare risk with him there—or with anyone else, for that matter. Once her shields were down, the mind of anyone inside the cabin would be open to her, and she had to focus, to concentrate on sending out her psychic aura to Mayla. She wasn't just relying on Mayla finding her; she fully intended to use her mental powers to search for her sister.

She couldn't let Kell or anyone else know the extent of her power—and the even more formidable abilities of her sister. The Cezans had learned eons ago never to reveal the complete truth about themselves. If people knew, they usually reacted by deifying them as gods, by trying to kill them, or by trying to steal their powers. Not that there was much to worry about in that area with Kell. He loved her—too much, she was afraid—and would defend her to the death. He would never harm her.

Sky lay back again, her silver hair spreading beneath her in fine waves. She would compose herself for a moment before removing the band, ready herself by strengthening her own mental shields, then once the band was no longer protecting her, she would slowly lower her shields one by one, until either Mayla contacted her or she sensed other minds breaching the integrity of the cabin's shielding. The com was within reach. In spite of Kell's irritating attitude, he had been right about one thing: If the weight of the minds just on the ship alone were to pierce the shielding of the room, she could go into telepathic shock and die.

She smoothed one hand over her abdomen and then down her right leg, feeling the softness of the material beneath her fingers as she began to breathe slowly, rhythmically. She seldom allowed herself the luxury of soft garments. As the captain of the *Defiant* and the protector of Mayla, Sky had no time for gentle clothing or gentle thoughts; she must always be alert, ready for action, ready to fight. She savored the feel of the cloth against her skin, feeling almost guilty for indulging such silly feminine thoughts, but knew the relaxation they brought would enable her to reach down farther into the core of her strength and ready herself for what lay ahead.

When at last she felt she was prepared, she lifted both hands and removed the silver band, holding it above her head like a deposed queen relinquishing her crown. Sky held her breath and squeezed her eyes shut, then opened them warily.

Nothing. No voices, no outside thoughts invading her mind. She released her breath explosively and slowly placed the band on the table next to the bunk, near the com. If the shielding weakened later she could easily grab the band and have it back on before any damage was done. She hoped. Sky closed her eyes again and with both hands curved across her waist, began to send her thoughts out into the universe, searching for her sister.

Eagle hurried around a corner and looking behind him, quickly pried the grid off the endcap of an access tunnel that serviced different parts of the ship. He pulled himself inside the tunnel and replaced the hatch just seconds before the guard tailing him rounded the corner. Eagle froze, watching through the screenlike opening. The man came to a stumbling halt as he realized his quarry wasn't ahead of him any longer, then broke into a run, as Eagle had hoped he would, in an effort to catch up with his assignment. His footsteps pounded off into the distance, and Eagle slipped out of the tunnel and ran in the opposite direction, veering down one adjoining corridor and then another until he was well away from the area the guard would be searching. The man had given himself away about ten minutes after Eagle started his stroll through the *Defiant*.

Looking back over one shoulder to make sure he wasn't being followed again, Eagle turned down another hallway, then stumbled to a stop as he saw the captain's favorite, the blue guy, standing outside a closed doorway. Doing a quick backpace, he cleared a corner and slammed himself against a bulkhead, then stealthily peered around the edge to see what was going on.

Kell hadn't seen him. He obviously had his mind on other things, things that were making him furiously angry. Eagle lifted one dark brow. He hadn't thought the Altairian had that kind of emotion in him. He was frowning at what appeared to be the door to a private cabin. Eagle watched him and, long used to reading faces, even alien ones, realized he was trying to decide something. His fists were clenched at his sides, but suddenly he lifted one hand and punched one finger repeatedly into something—a security alarm pad probably, which were common on ships like this—before turning and walking with rapid strides down the corridor. Eagle waited until he had disappeared before moving quickly to the door.

He smiled. Next to the door was a small sign that read LIEUTENANT COMMANDER KELL R'K'LON.

Well, well, well, the commander's quarters. No doubt the second-highest-ranking officer on the ship would have his own com unit located inside, one strong enough to send subspace messages. And wonder of wonders—

Eagle blinked, not trusting his eyes for a minute. The alarm had been deactivated. Eagle took a step back from the door, instantly alert. He knew how things were on ships like this—the crew might appear to be an all-for-one-and-one-for-all kind of group, but the truth was they generally didn't trust one another. Therefore, not only were alarms standard operating procedure on these vessels, but there was generally a shielding mechanism of some kind, protecting the person when he was inside, or his possessions when he wasn't.

Why, then, had Kell deliberately shut off the alarm and shielding? Eagle had no doubt that was what the man had been debating over and what he had been punching in was a code of some sort that had shut off the alarm to his own quarters. Why? It could be some kind of trap, but what did they hope to gain? Were they trying to lure him into sending a message—a message they could intercept? He smiled grimly. He knew codes they would never be able to decipher.

He hesitated again, then making up his mind, pushed the release switch at the bottom of the alarm panel. The door slid back and he stepped inside, hitting the inside switch that not only locked the door, but turned on the alarm and activated the shielding. He didn't want anyone walking in on him unannounced, that was for sure. The lighting was dim and he squinted, his eyes adjusting to the darker room. As he began to walk toward the com unit sitting on a desk across the room, he stopped abruptly as he saw the inert form of Captain Sky lying in ethereal stillness on Kell's bunk.

He moved closer to the bed and saw that she was breathing shallowly, her chest rising and falling in a slow, gentle rhythm beneath an almost-sheer deep teal green gown. Eagle felt his pulse quicken as he gazed down at the sleeping beauty, unable to keep from staring at the soft curves of her body—a body almost fully exposed to his view. Knowing he should back away and head for the com unit across the room, he tried to move but found he couldn't. He could only gaze down into her face, tracing the soft contours of her lips with his eyes.

Strange how gentle she looked in sleep, how unlike the raging captain who had tried to torture him into revealing the child's whereabouts. Running his tongue across his lips without realizing it, he sank down on the side of the bed. His hand brushed against hers inadvertently and all at once, Eagle felt powerful fingers of thought grab hold of him. They paralyzed him, forcing him to remain at her side as a strong, curious mind reached out and entered his own.

Sky had been drifting silently in her mind, cocooned in the peace of her inner meditation. From time to time she called to her little sister, sending strong mental impulses outward, but mostly she waited, confident Mayla would reach out to her as soon as she sensed Sky's artificial shielding had been lowered.

Sky often thought being a telepath was a curse, the worst thing that could befall a person, but at times she acknowledged the ability had its advantages, like now. When she reached her current level of meditation—unusual in that she seldom had time for it—she could see herself inside her mind. It was like watching an interactive vid, for her mind could create anything, and within its confines she knew a freedom she had never found anywhere else. She flew across a green sky, her arms aloft, the wind pushing beneath her, holding her with the gentleness of a lover's arms. A lover. She smiled and wondered if Mayla would be terribly shocked were she to arrive and find her sister in the throes of a romantic fantasy conjured from the more sensual recesses of her mind. No, she wouldn't subject her innocent sister to such a scene. Still, as Sky lowered herself to the ground, the picture of the perfect man began to form in her mind.

Tall, dark-haired, he would have green eyes the color of the Andromedan sea. He would be muscular, but not in a thick or heavy-set way; rather he would have the fluid lines of a sleek lion, with strength and prowess held under careful control. His jawline would be square, his mouth firm with a tendency to smile, nose aquiline, a slight hook to it; a few tiny wrinkles at the corners of his eyes, dark eyebrows that were thick but not bushy, accenting his resemblance to the ancient Terran jungle cat, and one single dimple on the right side, near his very kissable lips.

Sky stiffened all at once as she sensed she was no longer alone on her battleground. Her imaginary man was there as well. She sensed him before she saw him and allowed his essence to wash over her with a strength that took her breath away, even as his spirit drew her to him. Strange, she didn't usually feel such strong sensations from her mental imaginings. This was silly. She had no time for such nonsense. Concentrating, she shut his image out of her mind, then opened her eyes. He remained, walking slowly, determinedly, toward her. Confused, she watched him approach. She could not see his face, but she began to walk toward him, the pull something she could no longer resist. Then he was there in front of her, but his face was still hazy, blurred, not unusual in a creation of her mind. She reached out one hand to touch his face and immediately a current of desire, passion, need, flowed between them.

Silly. This was completely ridiculous and was taking her away from focusing on finding Mayla. She concentrated again on making him disappear. Instead he took her hand and brought it to his lips, then pulled her closer until they were pressed tightly together. Sky brushed her fingertips against his jaw, tracing a somehow familiar path to his mouth. When she focused on individual aspects of his face, he became clearer. Before she could think, his mouth had covered hers and burned a tantalizing kiss into her, his tongue touching hers slightly, asking entrance that she freely gave.

Sky felt a languidness passing over her, a hot, sultry heaviness flood through her veins and pool down low inside her. She opened her mouth to his and he delved deeper, his hands moving over her body, lulling her into a sweet, sweet peace. She smoothed one hand across his forehead and jerked with reaction. Without warning, thoughts began flowing into hers, thoughts from this dream-man.

Impossible.

An intruder. A horror filled her. This was no fantasy she had created. Someone had entered the room as she lay in her self-induced trance. But who? Although she had taken a personal vow never to enter anyone's mind without permission, Sky did not hesitate. This person had violated her thoughts, and she would not allow him to leave without knowing who had done this, and what his motives were.

She entered his mind, flowing over the outer consciousness, ignoring the random meanderings and delving into the very center of his being. Waves of emotion began hitting her, surged over her, assaulted her with a force too incredible to have been conjured by her mind. Anger, rage, despair—the power of the feelings propelled her back to the edge of his mind.

Her own anger surged, and instead of fleeing the person's mind, she held on against the onslaught of thoughts, looking for a tendril of calm she might hook on to and use as a pathway to the core of the mind. She found it and flung herself against it, riding it through the barrage of intense negative emotions. Gradually she passed the surface tumult and entered the next level of this being's mind. There she found an incredibly complex personality. A man whose mind had been split at a young age in some way she couldn't discern. His original personality and a slightly altered one had merged at some point, she saw, but part of the true self, the original self, was kept hidden away, shielded tightly.

Intrigued, Sky gently rocked herself against the hidden recesses, mentally convincing the shield she was no threat until the barrier lowered and she slipped inside. She wished immediately she had left well enough alone. Inside the hidden core lay the heart of a child, shattered, irreparable. She found grief so overwhelming that she gasped and began to cry, deep, heartbroken sobs. She found anger so intense she thought it would consume her. And she found compassion, soft and soothing.

Who was this man? Who was this person of such sorrow who had dared to invade her privacy? Kell? No, she knew Kell's mental essence from the few times when they had first joined forces and she had accidentally entered his mind, evoking her promise to him that it would never happen again. No, this was someone else. Gently, carefully, she eased out of the depths of the mind, drifting slowly, with unthreatening movement toward the surface, sending her question out as she passed—"Who are you?"

Ranon.

The answer had come swiftly, freely, and Sky felt like a detective who has done a good job of investigation. It was an odd name, one she'd never heard before in all her travels. He was backing away from her, his mind feebly attempting to push her out of his thoughts again. She sensed his weakness and, alarmed, moved quickly upward, through the surface thoughts, breaking the top wave of mental activity like a swimmer. She took a deep breath and opened her eyes. Tears were drying on her cheeks. The man called Eagle sat beside her, his eyes wild, stricken with shock, his body frozen in place.

"You!" she whispered.

But how could it be? His name wasn't Ranon, it was Eagle—a ridiculous Terran bird name. And this man had no dark secrets, no gentle soul. He was Zarn's son and cut from the same cloth of duplicity and murderous greed as his father. But minds didn't lie, and his revealed he was a man of compassion, and perhaps honor. In any case, he definitely wasn't what he appeared to be. Mayla! If she had known she was inside Eagle's mind she could have looked for the information about her sister. Narrowing her eyes at the man who continued to stare at her, features glazed, immobile, she reached out for his mind again. With an anguished cry, Eagle threw himself backward, slamming himself first against the floor, then, stumbling to his feet, he ran into the wall, eyes wide, unseeing, incoherent. He slid to the floor just as Sky reached his side.

Cradling him in her arms, Sky lost no time in seeking to undo the damage she had done. She'd seen this before—mindshock. It happened when a person wasn't prepared for his thoughts to be probed, or when a person resisted violently to such a probe. She shouldn't have probed him, no matter if he had intruded into her privacy. Mindshock was something from which many people never recovered. If he didn't, he would remain in a catatonic state for the rest of his life—and she would have to live with the knowledge that it was her fault.

Sky closed her eyes and reached quickly, cleanly down into Eagle's mind once again, this time not infiltrating his thoughts in the slightest, but sending a soothing calm throughout his mind. As a healer she had an advantage over the general telepath; her thoughts could actually promote the repair of mental and physical damage. She seldom used this part of her power any more unless it was absolutely necessary. Mind healing was too intimate, too risky to the tough shield she kept around her emotions. But this time she had no choice. She flew through Eagle's mind, finding the red-hot areas of fear and pain and distrust, wiping them away with her healing power, until at last she felt the paralyzation begin to leave him and his thought processes edge back toward normal.

Sky opened her eyes and looked down into those of the man she held. For a moment her gaze met that of a boy called Ranon, clear and clean and innocent, then something flickered in the green depths and the innocence disappeared to be replaced first with confusion, then anger, as the man called Eagle returned in full force.

"You mind-stealing bitch," he whispered, just before he passed out completely.

Chapter Five

He sat in a small room, in a huge chair from which wires and tubes protruded. No, the chair wasn't huge; he was small. His arms were bound to the leather by energy strips and his legs were in shackles as well. He screamed, but there was no sound, and he realized the screaming was trapped inside him; he was afraid to let the sound escape. A large helmet glided slowly downward toward him. It settled with a thud around his head, heavy, straining the fragile stem of his neck. Two men stood in the too-bright room, but his eyes were blurred by tears and he couldn't make out their features. A jolt of energy coursed through him, and the screaming stopped inside his head to be replaced by a numbing sensation. The light above him grew brighter and brighter until it encompassed him. Desperately he sought for a lifeline, something to hold on to before the light utterly consumed him.

There was a legendary bird, a noble creature that, it was said, once flew across the skies of Terra. His father had told him stories of how the creature had been used even in Andromedan literature to signify strength, honesty, and pride. Eagle had memorized an ancient quote from one of the books his father had researched. "Rise up, rise up on the wings of an eagle. You shall be weary no longer. You shall fly with courage and strength." It was his favorite of all his father's stories.

The machine balked above him, and suddenly a power unlike anything he could have ever imagined flooded through his body, his mind, his soul, pumped through him, seeking out his memories, his dreams, and his spirit. Sweat poured down his back, pain laced through his brain, and yet he did not cry out. The agony of it seemed to go on

*forever, but at last the machine grew still and the helmet
was lifted slowly from his head. A disembodied voice spoke
to him, asking a familiar question.*

"What name do you choose?"

*He swallowed hard, wishing the dryness from his throat;
blinked, hoping the bright light would be turned from his
eyes soon.*

"Eagle," he whispered.

Eagle awoke in darkness. Lifting one hand to his head,
he groaned aloud with the pain the effort cost him. Every
bone in his body ached; every muscle felt as though it
had been stretched to the limit. He blinked, his eyes focusing slowly in the darkened room. Was he back in the
cargo hold? No, it was a small room and he lay on a hard
bedlike table. Sickbay? Probably. Even small cruisers
had a designated area where they took care of their injured. He sat up. Lights danced in his head and a roaring
sound like an ocean's wave rushed through his ears. He
lay back, gasping a little. Then he remembered. The
dream. God, the dream.

He'd started having the dreams after Telles died—or
after he thought his friend had died. He didn't have a clue
what they meant but figured they must have something
to do with his assignment to Station One. Except the
dreams had started before he ever arrived at the world
and ever witnessed his first mind-probe.

Mind-probe. Sky. She had been in his mind. *She had
been in his mind.* His fists clenched at his side as little by
little the memory returned. He had entered Kell's quarters looking for a com unit. He had found instead the
captain of the ship clad in a diaphanous gown, sleeping.
Drawn to her near-naked figure, he had touched her
hand—and instantly been possessed by her mind.

Slowly, Eagle rolled to one side and propped himself
up on his elbow. Sweat beaded across his forehead, although whether it was from the exertion or the memories, he wasn't sure. She had seduced him first, coercing
him into some depraved fantasy of her own making, and
he had fallen headlong into it. Even now he could recall

the taste of her lips, the feel of her skin, as though the experience had actually happened in the flesh and not just in their minds. It had been delicious, and he grew flushed with heat as he remembered. He had begun to come into some awareness of what was happening when, without warning, everything had changed. She had banished the sensual illusion and like the marauding pirate she was, had penetrated his innermost thoughts and ruthlessly probed his mind. He shivered with the strength of the memory. No wonder she had not pursued the mind-probe—she'd had another method in mind, one that did not rely on Zarn's devices and that usually left the victim alive unless he resisted.

Rage, swift and silent, surged up inside him, and with an oath Eagle sat up, fighting the dizziness and the nausea. Dangling his legs over the side of the bed, he took several deep, strong breaths before trying to stand. Once on his feet, the rush of lights and the roar of the ocean returned, but only for a moment or two. The symptoms ebbed away and left him feeling weak, but able to stand. Could he walk? He took two stumbling steps forward and made it to the doorway. Cautiously, he stuck his hand through the opening, somewhat surprised to find it was not guarded by shielding. She must know his plans concerning the child, Mayla. So why then did he still seem to have the freedom of the ship?

He stuck his head out and looked down the corridor. A solitary guard sat snoring on a stool a few feet from the door, his legs sprawled out in front him, his chest rising and falling rhythmically beneath his crossed arms. Eagle leaned one hand against the doorway for support. He was cold in spite of the long-sleeved uniform he still wore, but he ignored the chill along with all the other discomforts in his body as he evaluated the situation.

No, not quite freedom. He was being guarded. But why hadn't she simply turned on the shielding? Did Sky think him so badly injured he wouldn't be able to leave under his own steam? Possibly. Or perhaps she feared he would rouse and stumble into it blindly, adding a new shock to the one he was still recovering from. She couldn't trade him back to his father if he was dead. Eagle pulled in fresh air, feeling dizzy and spent. Once he'd realized she was inside his mind, he had fought her. Not the smartest thing to do given what he knew about mind-probing and the dangers of resistance, but the reaction had been immediate and uncontrollable.

He ran his hands down the sides of his thighs, the memory of her violation making his palms clammy. Rivulets of perspiration traced faint pathways down the side of his neck. He ran one hand through his hair, his mind racing as he glanced around the sickbay, looking for a weapon. His gaze lit on a hypo-spray lying nearby, and he smiled grimly as he picked it up and read in the little window on its side what medication it contained. Laudax. A heavy-duty sedative. They had probably used it on him to take him out of shock. There was more than half left inside. Nice of the captain to leave him exactly what he needed.

He took the hypo and headed back to the doorway, sagging against it, his arms cradled across his stomach, his face twisted in a paroxysm of agony.

"Guard, guard, help me—for God's sake, help me!"

The guard, startled from sleep, jumped to his feet and ran to the side of the stricken man. Eagle staggered into him, grabbing both his arms and pulling him downward with his weight. They hit the floor, and before the guard even realized what was happening, Eagle pressed the hypo to his neck. The man was out cold within seconds. He dragged the unconscious body into the cubicle and, with effort, placed it on the table he had been lying on, covering him with the light blanket provided. With luck, at a glance someone might think it was Eagle, still asleep.

Pocketing the hypo for possible future use, Eagle moved back to the door and glanced down the hall in either direction before heading for the nearest hatchway. Ladders ran between levels on the ship, encased in round tubes. Once inside he would be hidden from view, but he would also take the risk of meeting crew members crossing from one level to another. He hoped most of the crew used the lift instead. In any case, it was his safest bet. He was heading for the closest communications junction. In most cruisers of this type, it was installed on the fourth deck near engineering. If he couldn't find an open com unit to send his subspace message to Station One, he would have to break in via the junction and boot-leg it into the system.

Eagle winced as the soles of his boots hit each rung of the ladder, the sound echoing down the hatchway. He inched downward, sure that at any moment he would be discovered and taken back in shackles to the cargo hold. But the hatchway remained empty, and he made it to the fourth level unmolested. After making sure the corridor was empty, he slipped stealthily down the length of it. He passed four closed doors without a second glance, but paused beside the fifth, smiling at the sign posted beside it: AUXILIARY CONTROL. Every ship worth its engines had a separate unit for controlling the ship besides the one on the bridge, just in case the bridge was ever inacces-sible.

The hypo ready in the palm of his hand, Eagle tensed to spring as he pressed the release button and the door slid back. Empty. Unguarded. Well, that wasn't uncom-mon on a ship this size. The complement couldn't be more than twenty-five at the most, and he'd only actually seen a total of ten people since his arrival. Besides, the captain thought him well out of the action. Until the guard in sickbay woke up or someone else came to check on him, he had this window of opportunity.

Swiftly he entered the room and closed the door be-hind him, glad to see it had a simple locking mechanism. He didn't want any interruptions, even if a crew member found the locked door and grew suspicious. He sat down at the curved console that ran the width of the room. The console contained a computer linkup to the rest of the ship as well as helm, navigation, phaser, and shielding controls. He could virtually take over the ship from here, if he so chose. It was a thought, but maintaining the con-trol would be the hard part.

On impulse, before he tried to reach Station One, he punched up the subspace frequency he knew Telles's ship would likely be tuned to and entered a complicated series of numbers and symbols that would turn whatever he said afterward into so much gibberish unless the person intercepting the message had the deciphering code. He and Telles had a long-standing system with which to find each other in the galaxy. He entered the last number and flipped a switch, keeping his voice low.

"Tiger's Eye," he said, purposely using Telles's code-name from his Forces days, and his own. "Tiger's Eye, this is Spacehawk. Do you read me? Repeating, Tiger's Eye, this is Spacehawk. Vital that I talk to you. Imperative to your mission. Repeat. Tiger's Eye—" The screen on the console flickered suddenly from darkness to the image of Telles. It still stunned him to know his friend was alive.

"I'm not bringing her back, Colonel," Telles said, his blue eyes narrow beneath the dark brows. "You'll never find us, even if you follow this signal."

"Shut up and listen," Eagle commanded, wincing inwardly as his friend's jaw tightened with anger. "Okay, okay—*please* listen to me for a minute, Telles. I don't want you to bring her back. I want you to meet me somewhere and the two of us will take her to a safe place."

"What about Zarn? What about your orders?" The suspicion in his voice cut through Eagle's defenses more than he liked to admit. He looked away, trying to summon words that would convince the angry man. "Where are you, anyway," Telles went on, "sitting in your office with the Kalimar a few feet away, listening to my every word?"

Eagle cursed eloquently under his breath before turning his gaze once again to the image on the screen. "Listen to me. I've been taken captive by a band of renegades who are after the child. They're the ones who attacked the station when you escaped."

"I thought they were Zarn's men, after me," Telles said thoughtfully.

"They won't stop until they find her. I don't know what their agenda is, but they're being led by a woman who would make Lucreda of Cybord 7 look like a loving mother by comparison. I want to make a deal with you. I'll help you get the child somewhere safe, but you've got to help me get off this barge." He stopped talking, his throat dry after the rush of words had ended. If Telles wouldn't agree to help him, he would have to try to take over the ship himself, or he'd have to get help from his father and abandon his plans to use the little princess as leverage.

Telles leaned a little closer to the screen, his gaze searching Eagle's. "You know I want to believe you," he said softly. "But I can't take a chance on something happening to her. You don't understand. She isn't like you or me. She's special, she's—anointed by some higher power. She is the heir to the Andromedan throne."

"Why is it so important to you? Why the hell do you care so much about Andromeda all of a sudden?"

His blue-gray eyes darkened with an expression Eagle couldn't read. Telles didn't answer his question. "I'm willing to meet with you, only because there are things you need to know, but you must give me your word of honor that you won't bring the Dominion into this."

"I won't. You have my word." And he wouldn't bring his father into it. This was his mission and he would do it his own way.

Telles narrowed his gaze. "Why? Why are you willing to help me hide her?"

"I have my own reasons and I'll discuss them with you when we meet. Do you remember where we spent our last R and R together?" Eagle glanced back over his shoulder toward the door. Things had gone smoothly so far, perhaps too smoothly. It was making him edgy.

Telles frowned. "Yes, I remember. How could I forget you in that—"

"That's where I want you to meet me," he said, cutting him off quickly before he could give any details that might tip off anyone who might, however unlikely, have unscrambled their code and be listening. Surely if his communiqué had been picked up on the bridge, the captain would have already twitched her curvy little behind

101

down there to send another jolt of phaser fire into his system.

Telles shook his head. "I don't know. How do I know you won't double-cross me?"

Eagle spewed out his breath in exasperation. "Have I ever double-crossed you, Telles? Where in the hell is all of this suspicion coming from?"

"You've never had to choose between me and your father before. Besides, I know the rules. Things like treachery and deceit don't apply if they're done in the name of the Dominion."

Eagle rubbed his brow with the tips of his fingers, fighting the aching in the depth of his skull and the lethargy beginning to attack his entire body. He decided to up the ante. "If you don't help me out of this, old buddy, you may not ever have to worry about my loyalties again. They already tried to put me under a mind-probe—one of my father's new handy-dandy improved versions."

Telles lifted one brow and something flashed in the depths of his eyes. "What happened?"

"They didn't go through with it. I guess it was a bluff, and at the last minute, apparently the captain didn't have the guts. I think she has other, more primitive kinds of torture planned to make me talk."

"About what?"

"Where the kid is." Eagle said. "We've made a truce for now. I've agreed to help them find her. Once we reach the rendevous point, I'll lose them and meet you."

"I don't know."

He slammed one hand down flat on the console, exasperated. Once they had vowed to lay down their lives for one another. Now his best friend didn't even trust him. "Damn it, Telles, make up your mind."

Telles stared at him for a long moment. When he finally spoke, Eagle realized he had been holding his breath. "All right," he said, "all right. But if you hurt that little girl"—he lifted one shoulder in a casual shrug—"I'll have to kill you."

Eagle felt awareness dance down his spine. If he

needed any more proof that Telles had changed, those words proved it.

"I give you my word I will not hurt her, nor will I allow her to be harmed in any way." He leaned back in the chair, away from the screen. "Is that good enough?"

"No," Telles said, the shadow of a smile touching his lips. "But I guess it will have to do."

Again Eagle felt the pain of his distrust. He shook it away. The Telles he had known was apparently gone. He would just have to adjust to the new situation. "All right. Meet me there in two days' time—got that? No sooner, no later. Two days' time."

"Affirmative. Out."

Eagle watched the screen darken and closed his eyes, slumping down in his chair. He had to get up now, find his way back to sickbay, or perhaps the bridge to confront the captain, and figure out how he was going to get this tub to the rendevous point. Somehow he couldn't make his body follow the commands his mind was issuing.

"Your old friend doubts you."

Eagle felt his body stiffen, tighten in every tiny muscle; every part of his skin constricted as the sound of the all-too-familiar voice echoed in front of him.

Damn. He'd hoped for more time. Schooling his features, pulling himself inward quickly, he opened his eyes and faced his father's image on the screen. The handsome, rather rugged face smiled at him, but the gesture never reached his green eyes. Not a good sign.

"Hello, Father," he acknowledged with a nod of his head. "It's about time you showed up. I've been stalling Telles for days."

Zarn smiled, the lines carved around his full lips growing deeper, his still-dark brows lifting in amusement. "Yes, so I overheard. Apparently your friend has risen from the dead. Interesting."

So Zarn had broken his code. Had he heard his offer to meet with Telles? No doubt. Well, the game wasn't over yet. Ignoring his last words, Eagle leaned forward slightly.

"If you were listening, you're aware of my situation. I'm glad you're here, because I'm going to need some outside help."

The Kalimar's face grew larger in the screen and Eagle could see the disappointment in his father's eyes.

"And what exactly is the situation? Your old friend apparently has the child you were ordered to bring to me on Rigel. You appeared to be pleading with this same friend to meet with you so that you could spirit the child away to a safe place, away from these renegades—and myself."

Eagle let a small stream of air escape slowly through his parted lips. He hated lying to his father but it was for his own good—and the good of the Dominion.

"Pretty good, eh? I learned from the best. But you're wrong about Telles. He isn't the bad guy in this scenario; it's those renegades."

Something flickered in the depths of the eyes staring back at him, a slight hope, and his stern lips twitched. "That remains to be seen. What happened on Station One?"

"Here's the way it went down. The kid arrived, and as soon as I received your orders, I was suddenly attacked by this band of renegades—hell, the whole station was attacked. They took me captive, demanded to know where the girl was, and when I wouldn't tell them, they beat the hell out of me and took me to their ship. But before the renegades came, Telles had shown up out of the blue—alive—and I told him about the child. When the attack started, he took the initiative to get her to a cruiser and get her off the planet, keeping the pirates from getting her." Eagle leaned back in his chair, still feeling slightly weak and hoping it didn't show. "Now, what I suggest we do is—"

"A moment." Zarn himself leaned away from the screen, steeping his fingers together on his chest as he gazed at his son, his eyes gleaming like two black stars. "If your friend Telles is simply keeping the child safe for me, why did he require a promise that you would not take her, nor harm her?"

Eagle hesitated, then decided on the truth. "He's gotten

kind of attached to her, I admit. She healed him and—"

"She did what?"

Eagle kicked himself mentally as he saw the bloodlust he knew so well fill Zarn's eyes. He hadn't known. Damn it, he really hadn't known.

The green eyes narrowed to slits and the wide mouth curved up, filling his face with a malevolent smile. "So, she does have the powers. I knew it; I could feel it." The big man clenched one fist and brought it down in front of him. "You will bring her to me. The Cabinet is not happy with this turn of events, my son. They blame you." His brows collided above the large, straight nose. "If the child is not returned to me within a few days—a week at the most—they will demand that I send Intelligence after her, and after you. You know what that will mean."

Eagle's fingers tightened against each other. Yes, he knew all too well. He had once been a member of that elite corps of assassins. "Tell me, who's running your empire, now, Garnos? You or the Cabinet?"

Zarn frowned at his use of his first name. "Don't try to use your gift for strategy on me. I need my Cabinet. They help maintain the links between the governments of the worlds under my control. I have placated them by telling them you are in hot pursuit of these rebels and that you will return the child to me within seven solar days."

Eagle leaned toward the screen, letting his frustration show. "Why do you say it like it's a story you've created? What the hell do you think I'm trying to do?"

His father stared at him for a long moment without speaking, and once again Eagle felt the subtle shift in the universe around him. He had felt it first with Telles, now with his father. Things were changing but he couldn't understand how, or why.

"I will be honest with you, Eagle. I am not sure what you are doing. Bring the child to me and then I will be sure."

"I'm amazed that you can't see what your Cabinet is trying to do by casting suspicion on me," he said, carefully keeping his features taut, his gaze never leaving that of Zarn. "You know I have as many enemies as you, as many who would see me defeated and cast from your side. Divide and conquer, isn't that how the subversives work?" Eagle clenched his jaw, lifting his chin arrogantly. His father appreciated arrogance. "The rebellion gains new converts daily. Only by sticking together may we weather the next tide of dissent when it comes."

Zarn inclined his head slightly. "You have created the suspicion with your behavior over the last few months. But I was not worried about it at the time because I had a way to restore you to favor. You would be assigned to Station One and when I found the child—I knew I was very close to discovering her—she would be sent to you. You would deliver her to me and in this way you would receive credit for the capture. All is not lost, however. All you have to do is bring her back." His stern face softened, the lines around his lips easing. "Good luck, my son."

The screen went black and Eagle sagged forward, letting his head rest against the console.

"You back-stabbing, filth-ridden, *zanacle*-plagued *son of a bitch*!"

Eagle spun around to find Captain Sky glaring at him, hands on her shapely hips, her eyes flashing murderously.

"Did you hear him, Kell?" She demanded of the man standing behind her.

"Yes, I heard it all," he said calmly. "As I told you, your sister is still but a child, and her evaluation of human nature is immature at best."

"I can explain—" Eagle began, only to be cut off by the quick downward thrust of Sky's hand.

"Shut up! I'm going to take your worthless hide and—"

A message blared suddenly from the com unit next to the door. "Captain—incoming message. Highest priority."

Sky crossed to the unit. "Incoming message? From where?"

There was a long pause, then T'Varr's voice came back to her, shaken. "From two parsecs away, Captain. But—there's nothing there!"

Sky didn't hesitate further. She snapped into action

and headed through the doorway, tossing orders over her shoulder. "Bring him to the bridge," she ordered. "If Zarn's out there, I'll put a plasma-blaster to his baby boy's head and dare him to fire the first shot."

"There's nothing there, Captain. And the request for communication has not been repeated."

Sky spun the command chair around wearily in the direction of her communications officer, T'Varr. She glanced over at Eagle, standing with his arms folded over his broad chest, his legs squarely apart. He gazed out across the bridge as if he owned it. How could she have ever entertained feelings of guilt over violating his mind? The only thing she regretted now was that she hadn't probed him more completely; she might have been able to find vital information about Mayla. The realization that she had violated another person's mind had made her hesitate, and that, combined with her embarrassment over her fantasy—she shook her head physically as if to dispel the thought and tried to focus on her command, her crew.

She refused—refused—to think about what had happened before she'd realized she was not in one of her own fantasies but in the mind of an intruder. A warm blush stole to her cheeks unbidden as she glanced at Eagle again. This time he met her gaze and she quickly turned away, focusing on the back of T'varr's head and forcing her attention back to the matters at hand. It had to be Zarn. But where was he? They weren't close to any worlds and sensors had picked up no ships in the vicinity. Sky's dormant senses went on instant alert.

"Run another sensor scan of the immediate area and check for ion emissions, trails, anything," she ordered, leaning forward slightly, her fingers clutching the arms of the chair.

"I already did. No one is out there, Captain." T'Varr turned and gestured with one hand to the earmike that allowed him to monitor the communications. "I couldn't even trace where the signal was coming from because it broke off before—Wait." His eyes widened and he looked up at Sky, nodding. "He's back. He demands we answer."

"Who's demanding? Let's see who's so anxious to talk to us. Put it on screen."

The viewscreen, which could be turned off to show real space, or used by the computer to display distant views or visual communications, stretched across the front of the circular bridge, which measured about thirty feet across. Three officers shared the bridge with the captain, each in charge of one of the three main stations—communications/sensor, helm/weapons, and science/navigation. The screen was suddenly illuminated with the four-foot-high image of a man's face, and Sky's palms grew suddenly damp with sweat against the slickness of the chair arm as her worst fears were realized. That face adorned banners and flags in every world in this quadrant: Lord Zarn, ruler of the Dominion. She wasn't in the least surprised.

Intense green eyes, too much like Eagle's, stared back at her, and Sky took a deep breath, her mind racing. The man was undeniably attractive. He was about sixty years old, the lines of experience graven in his face only adding to the overall appearance of a man of power. His nose was prominent, aristocratic, his eyes deep set and long lashed. His lips curved up in a smile that could only be described as charming.

Yeah, charming like a snake. Sky couldn't help the slight shiver that danced down her spine as she noted the glint in the eyes of the man who had murdered her parents. Cruel. This man was cruel, evil, depraved. And his son was just like him. She didn't care what Mayla said or what his own thoughts had revealed. Whoever Ranon was or had been, he was dead now. Dead and buried in Eagle's subconscious mind.

Don't let him see you sweat, she cautioned herself.

"I am Captain Skyra of the *Defiant.* Identify yourself and state your business." She was amazed her voice sounded so cool, so calm, when actually she could feel the sweat forming on the soles of her feet inside her boots and a cold bead of perspiration was making its way slowly down the back of her neck.

"How do you do, Captain Skyra of the *Defiant*." One side of his mouth lifted a little higher and his eyes mocked her as his feigned courtesy continued. "I am Lord Zarn, ruler of this system. I do beg your pardon for detaining you, but I believe you are in possession of a couple of items that belong to me."

Sky ran her tongue over her lips before she realized she had done so, and she saw Zarn's gaze quicken with lust. She gritted her teeth. His thoughts were obvious, even without the aid of a mind-probe.

"I don't know what you're talking about," she said, hating the fear creeping unbidden into her voice. "I'm headed for Canara to take on supplies and give my crew some time off."

"In need of a little recreation, Captain? Excellent. I myself have grown weary of the heavy weight of authority and responsibility I must carry daily. Perhaps we might mutually ease one another's burdens." Zarn's dark brow rose questioningly even as his lips curved up in sardonic assurance.

From the corner of her eye Sky saw Eagle's face darken and he took a step forward before catching himself. Interesting. She tossed Zarn her own arrogant grin. "No thanks. I'm afraid I haven't time. Thanks for calling, drop by if you're ever in the neighborhood, and—"

"Excuse me, Captain, but I believe you still have two items belonging to me."

Sky narrowed her eyes and leaned forward, balancing her forearms on her thighs as she clasped her hands together. "I don't think so, unless you've lost a rather smelly cargo of tanusian root, because that's all we're hauling this time around."

"Please prepare to be boarded."

The transmission ended abruptly and Sky's feet hit the floor. "Ajax—plot a course out of the quadrant!" She turned and shouted at her navigations officer. "Cordo, prepare to get us the hell out of here."

She crossed in front of Eagle, ignoring the way his gaze followed her. There was no denying the strength in the determined set of his jaw. His eyes flashed her a look promising—what? Retribution? Revenge? She'd have her own revenge before this day was over.

"It will take him about five minutes to punch in the commands necessary to punch through your shields," Eagle said. "I suggest we get out of here."

Ignoring him, Sky brushed by him and strode to the navigation console, leaning over the helmsman's shoulder.

"Have you got us ready, Ajax? Weapons armed?"

"Ready as we'll ever be," the double-eared Denebian said, his voice filled with doubt.

"Stand by, Cordo." She straightened and paced the small space between their stations, hands behind her back. "T'Varr, keep your sensors sweeping around us. He's out there somewhere, and I want to know where!"

"You'll never find him," Eagle said, taking a step forward.

"I think it's time for you to get off my bridge, space-boy." Sky glanced back over one shoulder. "Where is Kell? You can rot down in cargo until I can think of a less elegant jail for you."

"You need me up here," he told her.

"Like hell," She turned on her heel, snapping out orders. "Ready aft phasers, Cordo! Keep the shields at maximum." She paced to the other side of the bridge. "Where the *zlaughk* is Kell?"

"Are you out of your mind?" Eagle circled behind the helmsman and grabbed Sky by one arm. He stumbled backward, from weakness or weariness she couldn't tell, but the movement brought her abruptly against him and her arms went around his waist to keep from falling.

Sky felt as though her body were on fire, burning with a delicious heat that warmed her from the outside in, spreading through every nerve ending touching him, across her breasts, over her stomach and down. She looked up into his eyes and realized with a jolt that her foray into his mind had connected them on a psychic level—not deeply enough to read each other's thoughts, but enough to create an abnormal sensitivity between them. He wanted her. Even as he stood there glaring and hating her, he wanted her. She knew it. And she wanted him. The realization sent a shockwave through her veins.

The doors to the bridge swished open behind her and Kell entered, his tall, lanky form moving quickly to Sky's side.

"Let her go at once," he commanded, his hand coming down roughly on Eagle's shoulder.

"Gladly," Eagle said, dropping his arms from her as though he had been the one burned, though his eyes never shifted from her face. He cleared his throat and ran one hand through his dark hair. For an instant, Sky wanted to follow the gesture with her own fingers. She shook herself mentally and turned her attention to her second in command, hands on her hips.

"Where have you been?" she snapped at Kell. "Take this *jardeesh* and put him—"

"Do that and this tub is going to light up the heavens, and us with it," Eagle said.

"Are you threatening me, Colonel?"

His fists were knotted at his side as he met her gaze squarely. For a scant second she remembered feeling as though she might drown in those green, green eyes. She shook away the fleeting memory. It hadn't been real—that was what she had to remember—it hadn't been real, just a fantasy in their minds, nothing more.

"Do you really think you can outrun or outfight him?" he demanded. "He'll squash you like an insignificant speck of protoplasm."

Sky spun away. She stalked over to the command chair and sat down, her face and her thoughts fixed straight ahead. "Not if he thinks I have something he wants, like you. I'm just trying to get some distance so I can put together a plan. I'm wondering—should I offer to give you back simply in return for his promise of a safe escort out of the system, or should I demand a little money as well?" She shot him a derisive look. "You know Daddy best, space-boy. What do you recommend?"

Eagle moved to stand behind her, his hands resting on the back of her chair. He bent down and Sky stiffened as his lips came dangerously close to her ear. He spoke softly. "I recommend you let someone with a little common sense command this barge. Don't you know that Zarn has cloaking capabilities and that some of his transporters can pierce shields now?"

Sky felt the blood drain from her face but she didn't move as she shot her scornful reply back to him. "Are you suggesting your father is able to float unseen through space, wait until his unwary victim appears, then slip through a force field like a ghost—with enough men to take over a ship?"

"I'm not suggesting it, I'm telling you it's a fact. I helped develop both the cloak and the transporter, and if you've got one ounce of intelligence in that pretty little head of yours, you'll listen to me."

"Don't you dare patronize me, Colonel!" Sky shouted. She took a deep breath, bringing her temper under control before turning to face him. He was still too close but she refused to back down. "Why should I believe you? Why would you want to help us?"

"Because I have my own reasons for wanting to keep the child away from Zarn."

Sky gave him a scathing look. "Sure you do. Well, tell me then, what do you suggest we do, surrender? I'm sure that's what you want, Colonel, but I, on the other hand, don't intend to go down without a fight."

Kell took a step forward. "Maybe you should listen to him, Captain. If Zarn can really do the things he says—"

"*P'tosh!*" Sky shouted the curse, swiveling her chair around to face her first officer. "Don't be a fool, Kell. He wants us to believe this nonsense so we'll give up easily." She spun back around. "T'Varr—anything on sensors yet?"

The officer shook his head, dark eyes fixed on the screen in front of him. "Nothing. I can't even pick up an ion trail. No one is out there."

"Oh, he's out there all right," Eagle said, leaning close to her again. "If you want to save your hides, I suggest you take evasive action and warp this tub into maximum."

Sky stood, quickly putting a little distance between

them. She would have almost been willing to go down in a sheet of flame from Zarn's phasers rather than do anything this twisted son of a mind stealer suggested. But he was right. She hesitated only another moment before nodding sharply.

"Cordo, max our warp. Ajax, set our course in an Alpha-Zi pattern and let's get out of here before Daddy dear decides to invite himself to dinner." She glanced back at Eagle, her voice taut. "Any other suggestions, Colonel?"

"There is an asteroid field not too far from these coordinates. Duck inside and you'll lose him. I happen to know Zarn has a fear of asteroid fields."

"How human of him," Sky said, hands on her hips. "I happen to have a few qualms myself. However . . . Ajax?"

"I know the field," the Denebian said, nodding. "I can do it."

"Wonderful." Sky turned and faced her prisoner. He stood on the level just above her command chair and she disliked having to look up at him, but she didn't want to be anywhere near him either, so she held her lesser position. "Kell, you have the bridge. Colonel, you will come with me. You have a great deal of explaining to do."

Eagle's eyes narrowed beneath his dark brows and he folded his arms across his chest, the thick muscles flexing in a defiant kind of body language no one could misinterpret.

"I'm not the only one, *Captain*."

Chapter Six

Eagle sat in the briefing room, anger rolling over him like an ocean's wave. He was fighting to keep his temper, struggling to be in a level frame of mind when the captain and her minions walked through those doors in a moment to listen to his demands. And he was suddenly in a position to make them. He knew Zarn, knew his ships, knew what he would likely do next. If Sky and her renegades wanted to stay alive, they'd better damn well listen to him and they knew it.

He leaned his head against both hands, his elbows propped on the table. He had planned to trick Sky into going to the place he was supposed to meet Telles, or else take the ship and pilot it there himself. Now he had the terrible fear his transmission had given away his friend's position to Zarn. His father might be on his way to find Telles even as Eagle waited for Sky to sashay into the briefing room.

Eagle pushed himself up from the table and began to pace. Zarn had demanded he recapture the child and bring her to him on Rigel. Then he had turned around and attacked the ship before he could make a move. What else had he said? "You have two items that belong to me." Was it possible he believed the child was aboard the *Defiant*?

With the help of her helmsman and navigator, Sky had managed to put some distance between her ship and Zarn's, and with Eagle's direction, the *Defiant* now lay hidden on a chunk of rock in an asteroid belt light-years away from where Zarn had made contact. Did the Kalimar think his son wouldn't make good on his promise, or had it just been his way of stirring things up on board the rebel ship so that Eagle had some sort of advantage? He stopped pacing. He didn't know what his father was up to, but he intended to find out.

The doors slid open and Eagle turned, expecting to see Sky flanked by Kell and her security chief. Instead, she stood alone just inside the doorway, her cool, turquoise eyes meeting his for only a scant millisecond before she walked crisply across the room and took a seat at the long oblong table. Suddenly it all rushed up at him: Her ruthless capture of him, the threat of the mind-probe, the waiting for the needle to pierce his brain, the violation of his mind. No, he wasn't going to tell her anything, not until he gave some kind of vent to the rage tearing him apart inside. Zarn might find them—at the moment he didn't give a damn. This woman had scarred him, and he wanted some kind of payment, some kind of revenge.

"Please, sit down, Colonel," she said, indicating the chair opposite hers.

Her silver-blond hair fell over one shoulder and she tossed it back impatiently, glancing up at him. She wore the silver headband again around her forehead. What was its significance, he wondered? He was struck by her diminutiveness as she sat facing him, her legs crossed, one booted foot twitching up and down. Funny, he'd never thought of the big bad captain as petite, but she certainly was. Her authoritative attitude gave her a psychological "height," he supposed, but as his gaze traveled over her taut body and his eyes shifted to lock with hers, her size became immaterial. Her full lips parted as if she wanted to speak but couldn't. Before he realized what he was doing, Eagle had crossed to her side and now stood towering over her, one side of his mouth lifting derisively as he picked up one long lock of her hair and wrapped it around his fingers.

"Lovely stuff, this," he said softly. "Amazing how solid things can feel inside your head, isn't it? But in real life, it's even better. Everything feels better, don't you think, Sky?" He grazed the side of her face with the back of his knuckles.

Her gaze darted to one side as she jerked her hair from his grasp. When she spoke again, she sounded almost breathless.

"I said, sit down, Colonel. We have much to talk about."

"Yes, we do, don't we?" Eagle knelt down beside her and with one hard shove, sent her chair spinning around to face him. He enjoyed the startled look on her sculptured features as he abruptly stopped the ride, his hands splayed across both her thighs. Today she didn't wear her usual jumpsuit uniform. Today she wore a short turquoise tunic the color of her eyes, the hem barely grazing the top of her thighs. Belted, it rose even higher. He hadn't noticed on the bridge because he'd been so furiously angry. He noticed now. Knee-high boots completed the ensemble, and the sight of her long, slim legs bare beneath the sheer tights she wore made his heart begin to throb. Not to mention other parts of his body.

Easy, he cautioned himself. This little byplay was to intimidate her—not show her how easily she aroused him.

"How dare you!" she sputtered, grabbing his hands and trying to wrench them from her legs. Eagle tightened his fingers and slid them higher, raising his body from the floor, leaning forward until his face was almost touching hers, his arm muscles flexing as he positioned himself over her.

"How dare I? But, sweetheart, how can you say that after all we've meant to each other in the recesses of your wicked little mind? Baby, you left me wanting you. I think you owe me something, don't you?"

He could feel her breath warm on his face, whispering out from her parted lips. Long eyelashes cascaded downward, back up again, revealing the brilliant blue eyes a man could lose his soul in. Unable to control the sudden need to feel her skin against his, Eagle moved his hands to her waist and pulled her roughly forward, crushing her mouth against his, drinking in the richness of her breath, her scent. Running one hand up her side, he caressed her through the cloth even as her mouth opened beneath his and he changed his rough demand to a more gentle embrace. She moaned and Eagle almost toppled the chair beneath them. He had expected her to fight him, to kick him, to scream—and he in turn planned to show her what it meant to be overpowered by a superior strength. He hadn't actually planned to hurt her or violate her physically as she had violated him mentally, but he had wanted to put a hell of a scare into her. Instead, she was melting beneath him, her well-formed arms lifting to hold him, her fingers tangled in the too-long hair at his collar.

He pulled her from the chair and began backing her up until they collided with the wall. Her mouth was his. He plundered it, as she had plundered his mind. He trapped her against the wall, his body pressing into hers, as she had trapped him within her mind. Her arms went around his waist and her body moved beneath him in a sensual movement that was almost his undoing. He wanted her. He didn't want to punish her. He wanted to lay her down right there on the briefing room floor and make slow, passionate love to her. He wanted to lie with her naked and let her long, silver-blond hair trail across his chest as they held one another. He wanted to caress every inch of her skin; he wanted to strip her bare and trace a path over that creamy expanse he knew awaited him beneath her clothing. He wanted her—and he hated her for making him want her. She was his enemy. She had violated his mind and he still didn't know how much of his innermost thoughts she had seen.

Using every ounce of emotional strength he had left, he tore his mouth from hers and pushed himself away. She opened her eyes languidly and gazed up at him, confused by his sudden withdrawal. Invisible fingers gripped him by the throat and he took another step back from her, putting more distance between them.

"There, Captain," he said harshly, "that's how it feels to be left in the lurch. Whether it's in your mind or in real life, it amounts to the same thing—frustration, and when someone else is in control—humiliation."

He forced himself to look at her and was in time to see
the softness fade from her eyes and a rapid series of emotions flash across the turquoise depths: hurt, disbelief,
embarrassment, and finally, raw fury. She straightened
her tunic, pulling the hem back down where it belonged,
hiding the long legs he still longed to caress. He looked
down at the floor, willing the thought away as he waited
for the barrage of profanity—and probable physical violence—to begin. Nothing happened. He glanced back
up at her.

Sky stood pressed against the wall, her hands flat
against the panel, her gaze lowered too, hair cascading
across her face like a silver curtain she hid behind. He
could see even from three feet away that she was trembling, and he felt the cold, hard regret slice through him
again, more deeply. Why he felt such regret he wasn't
sure. She deserved what he had put her through—and
more. But he wasn't that kind of man, that kind of monster—was he? Had all the years of being willing to do
whatever it took as a soldier finally coalesced into this?
A total disregard for human dignity?

But Sky had her own dignity. She pushed away from
the wall and without looking at him, head erect, shoulders square, eyes straight ahead, she walked past Eagle
and out the door. He cursed himself roundly, eloquently,
wishing she had stayed to hear.

Sky made it to her quarters before the shame hit her.
Once inside with the door locked, she let the stark, unfamiliar emotion flood over her, send her to her knees
beside her bed, and she leaned her head against the side
of the bunk, her eyes dry and wide with shock.

How could she have done such a thing? What in the
world was the matter with her? First she tried to seduce
the man in her mind and now she melted into his arms
at the first opportunity in real life—pressed against the
briefing room wall like a whore from a pleasure planet!
Her eyes closed and her face burned as she allowed her
tortured muscles to collapse. She fell to her knees and

stretched out flat across the floor, her hands beneath her face, her eyes clenched shut.

She had never had a man touch her like that before— like she was a desirable woman. She had loved Redar, intensely, totally, but the few times they had made love she felt he was doing it only to appease her, not because he truly desired her. True, he had been ten years older than she, but it hadn't mattered to her as much as it had to him. Or else it was as Kell said, and his only real interest in her was what she could do for his business and his rebel activities. And Kell—he was her friend, her confidant, but in spite of his open adoration of her, she did not feel an attraction to him in the way a woman should. Since she had taken over the *Defiant*, none of the men aboard dared approach her as anything less than the captain—Kell saw to that—and so she had reached the age of twenty-six years with little experience in this area. Was that why she had crumbled like a tooki-cake in Eagle's arms? Was that why she felt as though her heart, her soul, the very core of her being was on fire when he touched her?

She pulled herself up to her knees, and with effort, pulled herself onto the bunk, rolling to her back, one arm flung across her eyes. Of course, that was all it was. She was a grown woman who'd had no time for things of a sexual nature in her life. It was only normal she would experience desire sooner or later. But why with this— this—spawn of Satan? Better she should give herself to Kell than to the son of the man who had killed her own father. What had she been thinking?

She groaned aloud. She hadn't been thinking; that was the problem. She had made herself vulnerable to the enemy and the worst of it was, now they needed him and Eagle knew it. He wouldn't hesitate to gloat about this, use it to embarrass her in front of her crew if he got the opportunity—or to blackmail her. Or would he? She released her breath explosively and sat up, hugging her arms tightly around her. When he had flung himself away from her, he had seemed so harsh, so vindictive, and she had known, suddenly, horrifyingly, that he had been using her to make a point, to say, "In this arena I hold the power." But she had also seen the look in his eyes, had caught a glimmer of regret and his own shame. Or had she imagined it—conjured it in order to save her own pride?

Her fingers moved unconsciously over her body, touching herself lightly, smoothing her hands down the length of her body as his hands had only moments before. She shuddered as she realized she still wanted him—in spite of his parentage, in spite of his arrogance, in spite of it all. And he wanted her too—no matter how he sought to deny it, to himself or to her.

"So where do we go from here?" she wondered aloud, and quickly scolded herself. "Idiot! There is no time for this nonsense! Concentrate on how you're going to get your crew out of this mess and still save Mayla!"

But not right now. Right now she was too tired. How long had it been since she had slept? She didn't know, but the encounter with Eagle had left her shaken and weak. She needed to rest, to rebuild her strength. She pressed the switch on the com next to her bed, activating the link to the bridge.

"Kell, this is the captain. I have decided to speak with the colonel in a few hours. Please take him back to the cargo hold until you hear from me."

Kell's voice came back to her and she could almost see his blue brow lifting in disapproval. "Are you sure that's wise? We shouldn't antagonize him if we want his help."

"I'm not in the mood to argue," she said, lying back on her bunk and hoping the fatigue didn't show in her voice. "Put him in the hold and post a guard and tell him we'll talk later. I doubt he'll give you much argument about it."

"What makes you think so?"

Sky closed her eyes wearily. "Just do it, Kell. Sky out." She reached over and snapped off the link. Now she would sleep. Now she would strengthen her body and her mind for what lay ahead. But sleep did not come easily, and every time she had almost drifted off, the image of herself and Eagle intertwined in each other's arms would send a swift denial through her veins and awaken her. At last she slept from sheer exhaustion, but her dreams were of a handsome man who turned suddenly into a great bird and flew high above her, leaving her with empty, outstretched arms.

Eagle had made up his mind. He had to get off of this ship. He had to find Telles, take the child to safety and plan how he would use her to force Zarn to listen to his ideas about the future of the Dominion. He paced the small confines of the briefing room, remembering with disgust how only a few hours ago he had been seducing a woman he despised. She must have gotten over her embarrassment because Kell had found him and clapped him back in the cargo bay for six long hours until the captain deigned to see him again. He didn't blame her. He clasped his hands behind his back, and pushing the thought from his mind, focused his attention on his situation. Why did she want the kid so badly in the first place?

A memory came rushing back at him: He was lying on the floor of his office on Station One right after Sky had beat the hell out of him. Her words cut through this mind. *We will not waste time with you, Guardian—or should we call you murderer—mindstealer—defiler of children?*

How had he forgotten that? Well, he had been pretty out of it for a while, and then there had been too much else to deal with even to think about everything leading up to how he had gotten here. But now that he thought about it, those words didn't belong to someone who wanted to bring harm to a child like Mayla. Those words belonged to someone who hated Zarn and cared about children. Those words belonged to a rebel.

He sat down abruptly in one of the chairs near the table, trying to think it through. She would be there any minute. Kell had shoved him into the briefing room and told him to wait. No doubt they were planning how they were going to force him to honor his promise to help them. He linked his hands together on top of the table. He had to think. He had to figure this out.

All right, so she hated Zarn, probably. So what? Half the quadrant hated him. So she had made a statement about the children, in defense of them. Again, so what? And so what if she was a rebel? That didn't mean she didn't have her own agenda for Mayla. That didn't mean she wasn't a black-hearted witch who had tried to probe his mind first with a machine and then with her own power. So what would be his stance? His angle? His position when they walked into the room? Clenching his jaws together so tightly they ached, Eagle made up his mind. He didn't know why she wanted the child but he had to reach Telles, and one way or another Captain Sky was going to take him there—but not with a crew of twenty aboard waiting to clap him back in the cargo hold once they arrived. They would leave the bulk of her crew at a designated place, or he would refuse to help her evade Zarn and he sure as hell wouldn't lead her to Mayla. But she must already know that he had no idea where the kid was. She'd been inside his head. She must know everything.

He took a deep breath as the door to the room slid open and Sky, this time accompanied by Kell and the security chief, walked in, one at a time. Eagle deliberately leaned back in the hard chair, feigning an ease he didn't feel as he let his gaze rake over the now demurely clad captain. She wore her regular uniform, this one charcoal gray and as far from sensual as a garment could possibly be. She shot him an answering, appraising glare. He only hoped his own green eyes conveyed the depth of his contempt.

"Captain," he said, inclining his head as she entered. "We meet again in the briefing room. This place is beginning to be filled with fond memories for me." She flushed at his words before slamming back the chair opposite him and taking her place.

"We have been on this rock for almost eight hours, Colonel," Sky said, her voice crisp, professional. "You will help us leave undetected by your father."

Eagle folded his arms across his chest and studied her. He liked the way she sat so erectly, shoulders back, her hair neatly coiled at the nape of her neck. Every inch the captain. Every inch under that long-sleeved gray uniform. Every inch of that smooth creamy skin he had touched not so long ago.

Appalled at himself, Eagle tried to balance the thought by shooting her a cocky look and folding his arms across his chest. He felt an immense pleasure when his next words sent a flame of anger into her turquoise eyes.

"Will I really, Captain?" he said casually. "And why is that?"

She stared at him, stone-faced, and he gave her credit for not wavering even slightly under his gaze. "Because if you don't, I'll kill you."

The side of his mouth twitched. The smile spread across his lips, culminating in a loud burst of laughter that made Kell and the security officer frown. Sky stood, slapped her hands down on the tabletop, and leaned toward him. The movement shook her and the neat chignon at the nape of her neck came loose, her long hair falling over one shoulder. Eagle felt his senses stir and foolishly wanted to reach out and take it between his fingers, wanted to draw her toward him and kiss her until she couldn't speak.

"You think I won't?" she demanded.

Eagle couldn't stop looking at her. Why did the witch have to have such soft, luscious lips? He felt Kell's gaze on him and he quickly pulled himself back to the situation at hand, lifting one brow in a gesture of unconcern.

"Damn right I think you won't. Not if you have any sense, which, granted, is doubtful. I'm the only hope you have of getting away from Zarn, darlin', and I'm the only way you'll ever get your hands on that kid."

"You piffle-warted—"

"Uh-uh." Eagle wagged one finger at her, turning her potential tirade into sputtered curses. "Don't make the man mad or he may not help you."

Sky sat back down in her chair, her shoulders rigid, her hands still splayed on the surface of the table. Eagle found himself noticing how small her hands were, how well manicured. Her nails were short, rounded into smooth half moons. He blinked, wondering if he was losing his mind.

"What do you want, space-boy?" she snapped. "Or should I say, how much do you want to get us away from Daddy and lead us to the child?"

He stared at her, startled. Then she didn't know. She'd been inside his mind, but she didn't know that Mayla's whereabouts were as big a mystery to him as to her. He quickly recovered.

"Didn't you see her location when you rummaged through my brain?" he asked.

"I didn't mean to read your mind," she said, sounding annoyed. "I assure you it was a most unpleasant experience."

"Thank you."

"To read anyone's mind." She drummed her fingers on the desk. "I was . . . resting. You came in and must have touched me." She shot him a derisive look. "My mind is very sensitive for a telepath, and somehow you were pulled into my meditative trance. But to get back to your concerns, reading someone's mind isn't as easy as most people think," she said, sounding annoyed. "There are sections, pockets, nooks, crannies. Finding one particular thought or one bit of information can be extremely difficult. Now, please, how much do you want?"

So she really didn't know. Terrific. It was time to strike a deal. "I don't want your credits."

One of the woman's brows darted upward. "Then what *do* you want?"

For a moment she looked vastly uncomfortable. Eagle frowned, wondering what had caused the change, when he realized she was afraid he would ask for her body in return for his help. A quick grin split his face and he shook his head.

"No, Captain, you can rest easy on that score." He saw Kell dart a sharp look her way, and Eagle wondered again exactly what the relationship between the two really was. "Too rich for my blood. What I want is information."

Sky relaxed visibly, her fingers curling inward as she

brought her hands together. "Information? What kind of information?"

"I want to know why you want the kid. The truth."

Eagle watched her carefully as he made his request and was not surprised to see a shadow dart across her features.

"What does it matter to you?" she asked, averting her eyes.

"It matters. In fact, it matters so much that if you don't tell me, and if I don't believe you, I won't help you."

She shifted her gaze back to his, biting her lower lip in a gesture that was totally endearing. If she had known how vulnerable, how childlike it made her look, she would have been appalled. Eagle drew a deep breath and stilled the lust fighting for dominance inside him. For of course, that was all it was, just animal lust, the kind that was a result of biology, not rationality.

She lifted her chin. "All right," she said, the almost whispered words belying the temerity snapping in her eyes.

"Sky, you can't!" Kell objected, moving forward from his position near the door. He crossed to her side and sank down in the chair beside her, his blue brows knit together in consternation. "You can't trust him with the truth! What in the—"

"Shut up, Kell." Sky stood again, this time with her fingertips barely touching the table yet giving the stark impression they were all that held her erect. "We've got to get away from Zarn, and as much as I hate to admit it, we need this moon snuffer."

"But Sky—"

"I've made up my mind. Besides, what harm can it do?"

Eagle watched as her chest rose beneath the black uniform, pent-up breath held inside her for a moment. He watched as the first officer's and the captain's eyes met for the heartbeat of a moment. He watched as she sat back down at the table. He watched, and knew the next words out of her mouth would be a lie.

"Colonel, I—"

"Forget it." Eagle leaned away from her, one hand still

resting casually on the table. "You don't get it, do you, Captain? I want the truth, not some trumped-up story you think will appease me. You forget—our minds have touched. That gives me a little bit of an edge when it comes to discerning if you're lying to me or not." His hand flexed into a fist. "I don't recommend it."

"Are you threatening her?" Kell asked, his blue eyes narrowing. "And what do you mean your minds have touched?" He looked at Sky, his chin lifting. She ran her tongue over her lips but didn't speak.

"Sky?"

"I'll explain later, Kell," she said, her voice low. She shot Eagle a look that promised a later reckoning.

Eagle smiled. "Yes, do let her explain later, but in the meantime, in answer to your question, yes, I'm threatening her. In fact, I'm threatening this whole damn ship. Either you tell me what's really going on, or this tub is going to go up in the biggest blaze since Tantus went nova, once Zarn finds you."

"You'll go with it!" Sky retorted.

He shrugged. "Oh, I think Daddy dear will perhaps transport me out before the fireworks begin. Now, what's it going to be? Truth—or consequences?"

Sky's face sagged, and in one swift movement her hands came together in a paroxysm of panic. But panic was foreign to the captain of the *Defiant*—wasn't it? Eagle looked into the woman's eyes and knew she was about to tell him the truth. He steeled himself for it and suddenly wished he'd let her lie. After all, he planned to take over the ship anyway as part of the deal. What difference did it make what her reasons were? Her pale lips parted, and he almost stopped her from speaking, but the look in her eyes, the agony he saw mirrored there, prevented him. He leaned forward to catch her whispered words.

"She's my sister," she said.

Eagle sat down before the shock hit him fully. Sky sank back down too and wouldn't meet his eyes. She kept her gaze on her hands, her fingers continuing to twist together in a totally uncaptainish display of emotion.

"She's your *what*?"

"Sister."

If he hadn't been trying to maintain at least a facade of calm, Eagle would have slapped the palm of his hand against his forehead. Of course! What an unobservant idiot he had been! Sky's hair was a silvery blond; Mayla's was a silvery blond. They both had almond-shaped eyes that turned up at the corners. Even their names were similar in their cadence: Skyra and Mayla, such as parents might give two sisters. But their eyes—

"Your eyes are turquoise," he said faintly.

"She is the heir, not I. Only the heir has lavender eyes."

Kell turned to her, his brows making a sharp V in the center of his forehead. "You never told me that." She waved one hand as if to silence him.

"Damn." Eagle had to swallow. He couldn't help it. No wonder she'd been so angry, so determined, so ruthless. If he'd been in her position, he'd have done the same.

"Do you—are you a healer like Mayla?" he asked. "I know you have the telepathic powers."

"I have some healing ability, but not like my sister. She is the heir to the throne. I'm only her guardian." She leaned forward, reaching one hand out to touch his arm. Eagle tensed as her fingers curved against his skin. "All right, no more games. I need your help, Colonel, and I'm not above begging you for it. I know that you know where Mayla is or you know something that will help us find her." Her voice softened. "She's just a little girl. Please—" She broke off and looked quickly away from him, and he knew she was fighting for composure. She didn't want to break down in front of him or let him see how weak she really was where her sister was concerned. When she finally looked back at him and spoke, her voice was steady once again.

"You aren't an evil man, Eagle. I sensed that while I was in your mind. Please help us. Doesn't your father have enough systems under his thumb? Doesn't he have enough power without adding my sister to his list?"

Eagle. It was the first time she'd spoken his name, and the effect it had on his senses was unexpected. He could

hear her, in his mind, saying it with a gentle caress, with
a loving smile, and he turned away from her, pulling his
overactive imagination back in line. But was it his imagination or was it the curious bond that now linked them
together?

"How do I know you're telling the truth?"

"You said it yourself—we have a link now between us.
You'd know if I was telling a lie. You knew I was about
to, before."

"True." Eagle rubbed one hand down his face, weary
beyond measure. He hadn't gotten much sleep since he'd
come aboard this tub, and his confrontations with the
dragon lady always left him drained. But now it seemed
the dragon had been tamed. All the fire was gone from
her and she was asking him—no, she was practically begging him—to help her find her little sister.

"Okay," he said at last, "I'm going to help you, but
you're going to have to be willing to make some conces-
sions, and I can tell you right now you aren't going to
like them."

Sky released his arm and her hand quickly snaked
back to her own side of the table. She held herself stiffly,
as if trying to regain some degree of equilibrium. "What
do you want?"

"I want you to turn this ship over to me."

"What?" Kell came out of his chair, his usual calm face
twisted in outrage. "You must be insane! The captain will
never—"

"Yes, the captain will."

The weary tone of her voice made Eagle frown. Something wasn't right here. Sky was a dynamo, a volcano
waiting to erupt. What had suddenly taken the wind from
her sails, the spark from her engine? Their encounter?
His rough handling? She was, after all, a woman, no matter how tough she might appear to be. Had his "attack"
somehow caused this change? Or was it totally her concern for her sister?

"Then you agree?" he heard himself saying.

"If you will give me your word that you will take me to
my sister and return the ship to me at that time."

He nodded. "I give you my word."

"Pah! What is that worth?" Kell grabbed Sky by the shoulder and jerked her to face him, his face now wreathed in an uncharacteristic fury. "You are betraying Mayla by this action! You are betraying all of us! Tell me what happened between the two of you? Did you bed him? Did you bond with him mentally? Did he satisfy your human lust so well that you would give him the ship just to keep him around for your pleasure?"

Eagle's fists knotted of their own accord, but before he could move, Sky beat him to it. She was on her feet in seconds, trembling with rage as she drew herself up to her full height and glared at the Altairian.

"How dare you? Just who the hell do you think you are?" she demanded. "I could have you thrown into the brig for insubordination, and don't think I won't do it! How dare you?" she repeated, her eyes flashing with outrage.

Kell stood immobile, his own anger fading rapidly from his face. "Captain, I—My apologies. I don't know what came over me. I shall prepare the crew for the change in command."

Sky took a step back, apparently somewhat appeased by his quick turnaround. "I know what I'm doing, Kell, and I'm doing this for Mayla—not for myself! You have a completely wrong conception of what is happening here."

"I'm sure that's true," Kell agreed, his blue face once again taciturn and controlled. "Again, my apologies."

"Accepted. We will talk more later." She took a deep breath and turned to Eagle. "Well, Colonel, if that's all you need. I'd better figure out a way to make the crew accept this. Maybe I could tell them—"

"Wait a minute." Eagle strode quickly across the room to block her way as she moved toward the door. "We aren't through yet."

She sighed loudly and swung back around, hands on her hips. "What is it now?"

"How many people does it take to run this ship?" He waited for her response. He knew quite well that five ex-

129

perienced people could fly a cruiser of this size. But would she lie to him?

"Six. Five if they're really good at it. Why?"

Eagle paced around the small area, hands locked behind him. "So besides the three of us, we'd need two more. Do you have two people you can trust implicitly?"

"I can trust all of my crew. What are you trying to say?"

"We're going to have to dump most of your crew."

Kell turned to face him, his blue eyes empty, devoid of feeling. Eagle wondered exactly what depth of feeling lay behind those eyes. He had a sneaking suspicion the display they'd just seen was the tip of the iceberg.

"I do not believe the crew will take kindly to that proposition, Colonel."

"No, I don't imagine they will. However, if they care about getting the heir to the throne to safety in one piece, they might be willing to do their part."

Sky shook her head. "They don't trust you. They'll think you're holding something over my head, forcing me to do this. You'd be in the cargo hold before you could blink."

"All right, then make up something. Tell them the *Defiant* needs an engine overhaul, new thrusters, whatever. Give them some extended shore leave, except for the two you choose to go with us."

"But why? I assure you I would trust any of my people with my life." The color had returned somewhat to her face, and Eagle admired her ability to roll with the punches.

"Then you're a fool," he said, stopping in his stride and looking pointedly in her direction. He watched her bristle and almost grinned. The spitfire was back. "Never trust anyone."

"What a lovely sentiment, Colonel," Sky drawled. "I'm so glad I don't have your warped view on life."

"You keep your rose-colored one and you may not be around much longer."

Sky shot Eagle a furious look. "P'ton can be trusted. And Cordo and T'Varr. And my engineer, Srad."

"Keep the engineer. Choose one more." He nodded toward Kell, still standing, unspeaking, across the room. "I'm assuming the two of you can handle any aspect of this tub. Captain, Lieutenant, it's time to leave this rock behind and get going." He crossed in front of Kell, then paused, and turned back. "Are you ready, Princess?" he asked softly, holding out his hand. To his astonishment, she took it.

"Yes," she said as her fingers curved over his.

Eagle felt such an overpowering urge to kiss her at that moment that he almost gave in and swept her into his arms. Instead, he squeezed her hand gently before releasing it and bowing toward the doorway.

"After you."

She started forward, but stopped just as the door slid open. The bright lights from the corridor sent her body into stark relief, and his pulse quickened as the smooth curves of her body were suddenly cut in silhouette before his eyes. She looked back at him over one shoulder.

"She's just a child," she said, her low voice husky with feeling. "If you plan to double-cross us, I beg you to remember this. She's just a little girl."

For a moment Eagle couldn't speak; he was too busy struggling with feelings he shouldn't be allowing himself to feel for the woman who had tortured him. Finally he found his voice, and a smile to toss after it.

"Trust me."

She stepped back into the room, the light illuminating her face just in time for him to see the cynical glint return to her eyes as one corner of her mouth lifted in contempt.

"Yeah. Right."

She spun on one heel and stalked through the still-open doorway. Eagle gestured for Kell to follow and headed up the rear, wondering how his hatred of Captain Spitfire had suddenly shifted into something vastly, disturbingly different.

Chapter Seven

"I'm not going to wear it!"

Eagle looked down at the thin dress in his hand, then back up at Sky.

"Why not? It's perfectly respectable."

Her blue eyes flashed with indignation as she stood facing him, hands on her hips, and he couldn't help smiling, which only seemed to infuriate her further.

"Respectable? Sure, if you're a trifling in some *p'flauk*house! You said I was supposed to pose as a trader's wife."

Eagle's grin widened and he tried to hide it, but he had to admit he was enjoying this immensely. Sky was so used to getting her way. He loved taking her down a peg or two.

"It's all I could find, but suit yourself. You can always go back to the ship." Kneeling down, he began pulling clothes out of the bag, ignoring Sky as she began walking around the shuttle, petulantly kicking the side of it. He hoped she didn't break her foot because he wouldn't be around to carry her lovely body to get help. The small shuttle, hardly more than an escape pod, had been scarcely big enough to hold the three of them for their journey down from the cruiser. He was counting on that small fact. Cordo, Srad, and P'ton had been left behind on the *Defiant*, keeping it in orbit, ready for a fast getaway.

"Oh, and don't forget," he said, "if we get separated for any reason, we'll meet at the Domma Domma."

"The what?"

Eagle sighed. "Weren't you even listening during the

132

briefing, Captain? The Domma Domma is a tavern. It's on the edge of the city and makes a good rendezvous point."

They had landed on Barbaros 9 only an hour before, two days after Eagle had successfully piloted them out of the asteroid field and headed the *Defiant* into deep space. Barbaros 9 was a spaceport well known as a hotbed of criminal activity, the perfect place to melt into a crowd and never be seen again. He and Telles had spent their last R & R in this godforsaken place and had barely escaped with their lives if he remembered correctly. His throat tightened. Sky would be at the mercy of the scum of the universe once she reached the city. Maybe . . . He pushed the thought away. Kell would be with her. They'd be fine.

As he had flown the *Defiant* and helped navigation plan their journey to Barbaros 9, another part of Eagle's brain had been working on his problem with Sky. For there was definitely a problem. He had never thought he'd feel this way about a woman. There was no place, no time in his life for such feelings. But he had thought long and hard about it and had come to the conclusion that those feelings were very real—and they didn't matter in the slightest.

Forget the fact that she hated him. Forget the fact that sometimes he hated her. Forget she was a rebel. Maybe they could get past all of that, but there was one thing they'd never get past: He was the son of the man she believed had murdered her parents. No amount of passion or desire could conquer that. He had decided to treat her as kindly as possible, but it was inevitable that he would dump both her and Kell and disappear. He'd never see her again; she'd never see him again. It was simple.

Yeah. Right.

He'd also thought long and hard about what his actions in the next few hours would mean to Sky and her little sister. A muscle in his jaw tightened reflexively. There was a risk to the child, no doubt about it, but she was his only hope of getting Zarn to listen. For over a year Eagle had debated about approaching his father with his thoughts, his ideas for the Dominion. Rigel was a peaceful world now. Its inhabitants had freedom, equality, and justice—all thanks to his father. Why then did the rest of the quadrant have to suffer? Why couldn't all the other planets live in the same peace and harmony? It made no sense to him. And after meeting Sky and Mayla, he was more determined than ever to reach his father somehow and make him listen to reason.

He stuffed some of the clothes back into the bag and pulled himself to his feet. "Are you going to try on this dress or not?" he asked.

"I don't know why you got to be the one to go in and find clothing," she said, moving away from the shuttle and kneeling down at the pile of garments. "You are obviously the last person in the world who should have been buying clothes!"

"I went into the city because I know this world and I knew who to contact. Besides, this isn't a fashion show, Captain," he added dryly.

"Why can't we just wear what you're wearing?"

Eagle glanced down at himself. He'd put together a disguise of sorts by combining different parts of uniforms from the *Defiant* and hiding his dark hair under a nondescript hat Sky had produced from her quarters. It had been a simple matter to find a vendor, but another matter entirely when it came to buying suitable clothing. Apparently such a thing did not exist on this world. He'd done the best he could and returned with a variety of garments in all colors and conditions.

"Because any kind of uniform draws suspicion on this world. I just went to the edge of the city and believe me, I drew stares."

Sky snorted and began pulling pieces of clothing out of the pile. She held each one up for a scant second before tossing it aside.

"Where's Kell?" she asked, pulling out a bright purple shirt and flinging it to the ground with more than her usual vehemence.

"On the com inside the shuttle talking to P'ton. He said

he had a few last instructions to give him about what to do if the ship is ordered to land."

She glanced up. "Is that likely?"

"It's a good idea to take precautions. Barbaros 9 authorities are somewhat unpredictable."

Sky sighed and threw the last piece of clothing to the ground. She stood, brushing the dirt from the legs of her dark blue uniform. Eagle had to look away. The sight of the wind blowing her long hair in wild abandonment around her beautiful, irate face made what he had to do all the harder. Her hair whipped around, slapping her in the face, and, obviously irritated, she pulled it back and knotted it behind her neck. She looked up at him, hands on her hips, eyes reflecting her weariness even if her voice did not.

"Why are we here, Colonel?" Sky demanded. "I'm not willing to go any farther until you tell us."

"We're here to find your sister."

She cocked her head at him. "So you're telling me she's here—on this gutter world?" Her tone said she didn't believe him.

"I can't tell you that for certain, but the person who took her from Station One is here."

Her eyes widened and she took a step toward him. "You mean you know who took her? You said you didn't!"

He shrugged. "I lied."

"You—you—" She sputtered, out of words, and stood blinking at him in amazement. "I can't believe it." Her hands settled on her hips as she lifted her chin, her eyes narrowing. "I can't think of anything bad enough to call you."

Eagle held up a lime-green tunic and frowned at it, then lowered the garment as he glanced her way. "You? Out of words? I can't believe it either."

"But I'll think of a way to pay you back," she added, her voice soft with promise—but not the kind he thought about at night when he tried to sleep.

He tossed the tunic aside and leaned his foot against one of the large rocks that dotted the landscape on this world, resting both arms against his thigh.

"Look, sweetheart, you didn't level with me until last night. Why should I have leveled with you any sooner? We're here, I'm taking you to him. That should be enough."

"Well, it isn't enough. See here, Colonel—"

"Eagle."

She looked at him, startled. "What?"

"We're partners now, sort of, so let's try to put the rather rocky beginnings we had behind us. I'm willing if you are."

Sky laughed sharply. Turning away from him, she strode the few feet back to the shuttle and leaned against it, folding her arms stubbornly across her chest. "I don't know what your game is, Colonel, but let's stick to business. And we are not partners. You have forced me into this position against my will." Her gaze slid back at him, mockingly. "Which is something you seem to be very good at doing."

Eagle shot her an incredulous look. So, she was going to bring it up, was she? She had more courage than he gave her credit for. He moved toward her, keeping her gaze locked with his. When he reached her side, he felt as though she had reached out and snagged his insides, pulling him to her. Similar to the power he had felt from Mayla before, but infinitely different. This heat was the heat of their mutual passion. He saw awareness flicker in her eyes, and she took a step back from him, sliding her body along that of the shuttle.

"That was a mistake," he said, leaning one arm from elbow to wrist against the metallic surface near her head. "Don't you agree?"

She lifted her chin, giving him such a cool look he almost shivered. "Definitely. I'm just not used to having a man force himself on me with so little provocation."

Eagle stared down at her, shaking his head slowly. "You'd like to think that, wouldn't you? You wanted me just as much as I wanted you."

She opened her mouth to deny it. He could see it in her eyes, but she pressed her lips back together tightly.

Because she couldn't. She had wanted him. She still wanted him. Her tongue darted out to wet her lips, and he followed the movement, feeling something in his gut tighten with need.

Sky tossed her head and looked away from him, breaking their connection. "You'd like to think that, wouldn't you? Men use that line of thinking to justify their own kind of violence. You didn't want me," she accused. "You wanted to punish me."

Eagle eased the smile across his face as he tilted his head toward hers and raised both brows. He reached for her and suddenly she was in his arms, her soft, supple body pressed tightly against him. Their lips were very close and he kept his voice soft, very soft.

"Well, let's try it again, Princess, and this time you can 'punish' me."

She leaned toward him and Eagle could almost taste her when pain darted through his foot, his instep, and up his leg as Sky's boot heel came crashing down.

"Damn!" he shouted, jerking away from her and stumbling over to a rock. He sat down and glared up at her. "What was that for?"

"That, my dear Colonel, is just a little reminder for you to keep your hands to yourself. I am not interested in you as anything but a means by which to reach my sister!"

Eagle rose slowly, feeling the anger inside rise along with him. With difficulty, he kept his temper under control as he walked back and stopped only inches away from her. He didn't touch her, but he moved as close as he could, threatening her silently with the heat of his body. She swallowed hard and he watched a small dart of fear flicker through her turquoise eyes.

"Does that go both ways, Captain?" he asked, in a deceptively quiet voice. "And in return will you agree to keep your mind out of my brain? What was all that about anyway? Was your little excursion into my private thoughts just your way of showing me what you're capable of?

"No," she said hotly, "that was an accident." She looked away. "It was a mistake."

"Oh, like my mistake in desiring your lovely body." She shot him a derisive look and he chuckled. "I've heard stories about you Cezans. Crazy with power and not afraid to use it. No wonder my father wants to keep you all under lock and key."

Sky turned on him like a she-cat, one hand raised as if she would strike him. He never flinched. "You're wrong," she hissed, lowering her hand back to her side. Eagle saw the pain in her eyes as she turned away, and it was with difficulty that he kept himself from lifting a hand toward her in sympathy. Instead he shoved both hands into the pocket of the oversized jacket he'd borrowed from P'ton on the *Defiant*.

"Am I? About what?"

"Zarn doesn't want to lock us up—he wants to kill us, like he killed the rest of my family on Andromeda." Her lips curved up as she rested her hands on her hips, her stance cocky, arrogant. "But I'm not like the rest of my family, space-boy, and never make the mistake of thinking that I am. I'm tougher, I'm meaner, and I'm a hell of a lot harder to kill."

"Big words," he said, turning away and kneeling down to open the chest of supplies they had brought along. He pulled out a regular blaster and holster and stood, fastening it around his waist. She watched his movements and he wasn't surprised when she demanded her own weapon. He handed her one complete with holster as he continued.

"My father never killed your family," he said. "Your own people killed them in retaliation for their dealings with the slavers who first invaded this system. If it hadn't been for my father and the Forces, Andromeda would have been stripped of her resources and her people."

"Instead, we were just stripped of our children and our rights as human beings," she said softly.

Eagle heard the pain in her voice and drew in a sharp breath as he felt her despair slice through him. He finished tightening the holster and forced himself not to look up. He tried to keep the sharp edge of anger he'd had a minute ago but couldn't find it. Their connection was already too deep. He couldn't ignore her pain. He glanced up at her and was captured momentarily by the agony in her eyes. He cleared his throat and averted his gaze, using the ploy of checking his blaster's energy level to keep from looking at her again.

"We saved your entire race."

"You don't really believe that stupid story, do you?" she asked, the agony in her words cutting through his defenses. "Zarn arbitrarily attacked our world for our resources and the power my family possessed. There were no slavers."

Eagle shoved the gun in the holster and finally looked at her. She wasn't looking at him. She was staring at the ground, her arms wrapped around herself as if she feared that if she let go, she would fly apart. Faint tears traced a pitiful pattern down her cheeks, and her dark lashes painted a half-moon across her creamy skin. He wanted to reach out and brush the tears away. He wanted to take her in his arms and hold her and tell her he'd never let anything hurt her again. Instead, he summoned the hard control that had kept him alive in the Forces for so many years.

"My family did nothing wrong," she went on, her voice gaining in strength. "My parents ruled Andromeda in benevolence and kindness, just as their parents before them and their parents before them. Your father's troops stormed the palace; they slaughtered my mother and father, my sisters and my brothers. Two of them weren't even five years old." Her grief rushed out to consume him and Eagle closed his eyes against it. A silence stretched between them, broken only by her ragged breathing. She was trying not to cry, he knew.

"Listen," he said, keeping his voice even. "I know that's what you believe happened, but were you there?" She shook her head. He moved a step closer. "Think about this: Isn't it easier to believe the Rigelians destroyed your family than their own people? Of course it is. This is just more of the propaganda the rebels have spread about Zarn."

Sky wiped the tears from her face and turned on him,

her eyes snapping with rage, all trace of weakness gone. "And I suppose the fact that our children are stolen from us, that's just propaganda too! And the mind-probing—that's a lie started by the rebels. Is that what you would have me believe?"

"No, of course not. But those things can change."

"How?" she demanded, turning toward him. "How can it change?"

Eagle slid his gaze back to her. "There is a way. Just believe that for a while, will you?"

"Believe what?" Kell came around the side of the shuttle, his stride purposeful. He glanced from Eagle to Sky and back again. "Is something wrong?"

"Not if you don't mind purple," Eagle said easily, tossing a pile of brightly colored clothing to the man. Kell caught it and looked down at the bundle. One blue brow darted upward in eloquent silence.

Eagle lifted one shoulder apologetically. "Altairians are known for their flamboyance, aren't they?"

"Sure, just as Rigelians are known for their loyalty and compassion," Sky taunted.

Eagle ignored her. Kell continued to stare at him, and at last Eagle cleared his throat. "Okay, so they aren't. Just put them on, will you?"

"And just where am I supposed to do this?" Kell asked, his hands flat beneath the mound of clothing as if he was trying to keep from touching the garments any more than possible.

"How about the shuttle?"

His only answer was silence. The shuttle was too small to do anything in except sit. Eagle was counting on both Kell's and Sky's unwillingness to use it as a changing room.

"Okay, then how about the forest over there. Nice, dark, leafy. I promise no one will intrude on your privacy."

Kell turned and looked where Eagle was pointing. The road leading to the distant city was flanked on either side by a thick, twisted forest. Their shuttle had landed at the top of a small hill and looked down on both the road and the forest, but a few copses of the strange trees with blue-green bark and dull orange and gold leaves grew at the bottom of the hill.

Without another word, Kell turned and headed toward the wooded area closest to them. If Eagle hadn't known better, he'd have sworn the Altairian was muttering to himself.

"You're next, Captain," Eagle called, holding out the dress to her. Would she take it, he wondered, or would she decide to go back to the ship? Ha. He wished he could take bets on that possibility, but the odds would be too ridiculous.

She strode across the short distance and snatched it from his hand, her eyes narrow. "You did this on purpose," she retorted, before turning and marching toward the other side of the same wooded area as Kell.

Eagle threw his own chosen costume of dark trousers and shirt over one shoulder, and just for a moment leaned back against the shuttle door, contemplating the peace surrounding them. Green mountains pushed against the sky on the distant horizon while blue-green grass traced a path up the rolling hillsides nearest the shuttle. Farther away the blue forest looked almost black, and the gold and orange leaves glimmered in the fading sun like some kind of rare metal. The sky was a beautiful pink, and as the red sun sank in the north, the color changed to a deeper rose, then to burgundy. In the opposite direction, the sky was not beautiful and ethereally painted with pastels. A muddy gray haze hovered above the central city of Barbaros 9, a sprawling, filth-ridden metropolis where the only law was the survival of the toughest.

Eagle glanced down the hillside. Sky was disappearing into the blue-green wood. He had purposely landed miles from the metropolitan areas to give Kell and Sky a chance to disguise themselves and make their plans. *His* plans were already made. Whistling, he pulled the hatch on the shuttle open and climbed inside.

* * *

Sky hurried down the dark alleyway, calling herself every name she knew in every language. It was taking her a good deal of time because she spoke at least seven languages fluently. But that was good. Let it take time. The flood of words dancing through her mind were keeping her fears at bay as she rushed down the dismal corridor she had accidentally stumbled into while trying to escape the clutches of a man enamored by her resemblance to a two-credit prostitute.

Damn Eagle! She quickly switched the target of her mental tirade from herself to the man who had done this to her, to the man who had tricked her, lied to her, given her this *p'fauking* excuse for a disguise, taken the rest of the clothing and disappeared, leaving her and Kell with no choice but to head for the city on foot wearing the ridiculous costumes he'd provided. Their only alternative was to wear their uniforms, which would be asking for trouble.

When they had arrived at the city they were exhausted, hungry, and ready to kill Eagle on sight. Barbaroscity had been worse than they expected. An added problem was the discovery that Eagle had taken all of the credits they'd pooled together for their excursion.

She gritted her teeth and kicked her foot out as some small, unidentifiable animal scurried near her. Sky hurried forward, trying to keep her thoughts on what had led her to this dank alleyway.

Once inside the city they had immediately started asking for directions for the Domma Domma tavern on the off chance Eagle had actually intended to meet his contact there. Knowing his devious brain, he would have thrown out the name, then expected them to think he had given them the wrong place, when all the time it was the true rendezvous point. Her outfit had drawn everything from wide-eyed stares to drooling leers to outright propositions and worse. She and Kell had decided to stay together, although Sky had argued they could cover more of the city if they split up. Kell had considered it until a huge bear of a man had tried to drag her into a doorway and force himself on her. Luckily the man had been intoxicated and all her first officer had to do was yank her away.

Her disguise—if it could be called that, since it disguised little—was made from a soft blue material called wessil, and it fit as if it had been painted onto her. Transparent, it revealed every curve, every valley of her body. Too tight, too short, too low in the neckline, it was Eagle's revenge, loud and clear. Her anger against the man surged inside her chest again. He had known what kind of reaction people on this world would have to such a costume, and still he had left her in the predicament! She was glad she hadn't taken any of the ridiculous heat between them seriously. She was glad she had kept her heart completely closed away from the infuriating man.

She hurried on through the alley, her feet crunching down on small, rough objects, some of which cracked like the thin bones of some poor creature. The stench was enough to fell a grown man, and when she stumbled into a refuse can, knocking it over and adding to the horrible aroma assaulting her nostrils, she ground to a halt, pulling back and bending over, trying to catch her breath.

It had been the last lewd proposition that had gotten them into trouble and ended up separating them. The Daltanes were possibly the most repugnant humanoids in the galaxy. Short, squat, with hardly any neck, the five-eyed beings had three tongues, and when one of them saw Sky beside a peddler's cart, he had run up to her and started salivating. Unfortunately, his tongues were on a level with her chest, and when one of the slimy green extensions touched her right breast, Kell had uncharacteristically exploded. His fist had connected with two of the Daltane's eyes and all hell had broken loose. One thing they quickly learned about Barbaros 9—everyone there apparently loved to fight.

She had been pushed out into the streets and jostled into the crowd. She pulled the blaster Eagle had given her from the holster at her side, but it was quickly knocked from her hand. Somehow she'd managed to tear a cloak from someone plunging into the fight. She had veered off from the brawling crowd, wrapping the cloak protectively around herself, when the force of the mob pushed her off the street and into a dark alley. And now someone was following her.

The sound of footsteps around the corner sent her into action, and Sky gathered her muscles for another run for freedom. Then he was there, or at least his shadow was. For a moment she wondered if perhaps he wasn't real at all, just some ghostly vision. Then he grabbed her by both arms and she knew he was very real, very dangerous.

She began fighting him, kicking, gouging, using her nails, her teeth, anything she could to gain some sort of advantage over the tall man. He was strong, and his fingers bit into her arms, not savagely, but firmly. She tried to aim a kick toward his groin, but he spun her around and pinioned her arms to her chest, his arms around her, his body pressed against hers. For the first time in a long time, Sky felt the desperation of fear tighten its grip around her throat. She'd been afraid for her crew in recent months, and afraid for Mayla, but not for herself. She'd been too busy, too focused. And besides, the fear of another ship attacking yours was quite different from the fear of a man assaulting you in a dark alleyway on a planet where no one cared if you lived or died.

He began dragging her down the alley and she continued to struggle, though she knew she struggled in vain. She tried to scream but her throat was too tight. On this world screams permeated the streets. No one paid them any mind. She continued to fight him. Every ploy she used, every defense technique, he countered. Her foot came down on his instep—almost. He moved it just in time. She slammed her elbow into his ribs, but he held her so tightly she couldn't get a good shot into him. She was helpless. The fury welled up inside her like a palpable object, pushing into her chest, choking her. All at once she realized he was pulling her toward a dim, recessed light in the wall of the alley, near the back door of some establishment. She began to fight him in earnest again. If she could get loose, she could run inside that door and perhaps get away.

"Oh, really, I have had enough of this," the man said

flatly. Sky froze. That voice. She knew that voice. With more force than necessary, he slung her against the wall next to the door, the dim light above them finally allowing her to see who her attacker was. A man stood staring down at her, hands gripping her upper arms, entrapping her, his face close to hers. Tall, human, handsome, his golden hair glinted in the pale light and hung down past his shoulders, some of it braided intricately. Two blue-gray eyes bored into hers.

"Hello, Sky," he said softly.

Sky stared up at him, disbelief and rage pounding through her veins, throbbing into her temples.

"You!" she whispered. Of all the people in the world, the last person she expected to see in this horrible place was the man who had betrayed her to Zarn. The man who had betrayed her little sister. The man she had vowed to kill if she ever saw him again.

Telles.

Eagle entered the Camara Tavern and glanced around, taking note of how many other Rigelians were in the place, looking for the telltale insignia that gave them entrance to any business, the best seats in any theater, the best tables in any restaurant. He took a quick survey. Only two that he could see, but the place was so dimly lit it was hard to tell. He took his seat in the booth that the cheery-faced Caldonian directed him to, and told him, in halting Caldonese, what he wanted to drink. He wasn't wearing his own emblem but he was served quickly, the waiter returning almost immediately. He politely placed the drink in front of him, hovering to see if it met with his approval. Eagle tossed it down, welcoming the burning rush of Llimo whiskey to his throat and stomach. He nodded at the waiter, who beamed with two of his three mouths and hurried away. Leaning back, Eagle surveyed the wretched dive where he'd agreed to meet Telles.

The fast-fading daylight of this dark, dark world flickered faintly through a tiny window. The tavern was in poor repair, its interior shabby with dim lights recessed into the low ceiling at six-foot intervals. A long bar stretched the length of the room, which was only about thirty feet wide. Stools of every description and size were strewn in front of it, in differing states of deterioration. Across from the bar, fifteen feet away, were booths, one of which he now occupied. The stools and the space between the bar and the booths was filled with people—or rather, other beings—crowded together, boisterously babbling in a dozen different languages.

Pretty clever of him to tell Sky to meet at the Domma Domma if they got split up. Now she would feel compelled to check it out and that particular bar was on the opposite side of the city. He lifted his glass in a mock salute to himself and took a healthy swig.

"Miss me?" a sultry voice at his ear asked.

Eagle choked on the liquor and slammed the glass down, coming to his feet as he coughed, trying to get his breath.

Sky. Captain Sky. Captain Sky in all her glory and fury. She stood beside the booth, clad in the thin dress he'd cruelly given her to wear, a cloak tied crookedly around her shoulders. Her face was pinched, her brows arched knowingly above her furious turquoise eyes, and in her hand was a Mac57, one of the most lethal blasters in existence. Eagle sank back down in the booth before the power of her gaze—and her gun.

"You knock-kneed, *jax-crotted*, *bic-dytled*, flea-ridden, *pax* eater!" she shouted. A few patrons in the bar turned to see what the commotion was about, then turned back to their drinks, uninterested. Death happened every day on Barbaros 9. It was part of the glamour of the place.

"Don't kill him, Sky. Not yet."

Eagle whirled around and stared at the man on the other side of the booth. They had him cornered. He was almost as tall as Eagle, with long golden hair and wide-set, eloquent blue-gray eyes that were presently staring down at him from beneath dark brown brows. Telles. With Sky. Perfect.

"And I still think you shouldn't have kneed that guy in

the crotch outside and taken his gun. He's going to be waiting for us when we go back out."

"He won't feel like doing any fighting anytime soon," she muttered, keeping the blaster trained on the middle of Eagle's forehead. He opened his mouth to speak but before he could utter a word, Sky grabbed him by the front of his shirt and jerked him to his feet.

"You lied to me," she said, biting off each word, her intensity building as she pressed the weapon right up against his brow. "You double-crossing, devious, dark-witted, son of a mind-probing bastard!!"

Telles moved around the booth to stand beside her, thumbs hooked in the belt around his hips which held his own still-holstered blaster.

"Don't be too hard on him, Sky. He can't help what he's been conditioned to be."

What the hell did that mean? Realizing he was at a distinct disadvantage, Eagle forced a smile and gingerly, with one finger, pushed the muzzle of the blaster away from his head. Sky made an indiscernible noise of disgust and turned away, slamming herself down into the booth he had just unwillingly vacated. Eagle released his pent-up breath and straightened his white, open-necked shirt, hitched his own holster a little higher over the tight black trousers he wore. He stood almost eye to eye with his old friend.

"Hello, Telles." He nodded at Sky as if she hadn't just threatened his life. "Hello, Sky. Well, this is luck. I've been looking for the two of you."

She still held the blaster in her hand and was checking the charge. She looked up at his words and leveled the weapon over her wrist, pointing it directly at his middle.

"Oh, really? Is that why you left me and Kell in the middle of nowhere? Sit down, you poor excuse for a man, before I make your gutlessness a physical reality."

Eagle looked from her furious gaze back to Telles's stone face, and gave them both a big, superficial grin. "Let's all have a drink, shall we?" he asked, spreading his hands apart in supplication. "I'm paying." He snapped his fingers at the three-mouthed waiter. "Three Llimos over here."

"Oh, you bet you're paying," Sky said, her voice not much more than a hiss, "but you'll pay for more than a lousy drink."

Eagle sat down on the opposite side of the booth, and Telles slid in beside Sky. Four eyes reflected back to him his own treachery, and for a moment he felt the way he had during his days in the Intelligence force—disgusted with himself. Then he remembered his goal and the shame melted away.

"All right, I know this looks bad, but I can explain."

"Sure you can," Sky snapped. "You're a master of explanation and prevarication, just like your father. So this is why you contacted your father from my ship. All your fine talk was just that—talk."

"He's been in contact with Zarn? You didn't tell me that," Telles interjected.

"We caught him in the auxiliary control room sending a message," Sky informed him.

"That isn't true." The waiter walked up just then and plunked down three short glasses of Llimo whiskey. Eagle lifted his and bolted it down, glad for the burning excuse not to talk for a moment.

"Really?" Sky leaned forward, her blaster cradled between both hands on the tabletop. "Then you deny talking to Daddy dearest?"

"I deny that I contacted him. I was sending a message to Telles and he intercepted it."

Now Telles leaned forward, elbows on the table, his fingers tense against his own arms. "He broke the code? He unscrambled my message?" Eagle nodded reluctantly. Telles pressed his lips together before picking up the glass in front of him and taking a drink. He set the glass back down with a thud. "Then he knows. He knows I have Mayla; he knows where we are. We've got to get out of here."

"We've got to find Kell first," Sky said, "after we rid the galaxy of one less Zarn." The hatred in her turquoise eyes disturbed Eagle more than he cared to admit, even to himself.

"Wait a minute before you go flying off half-cocked." Eagle twirled the glass between his fingers, his gaze on Sky, his words to Telles. "He doesn't know where we are. He may have unscrambled the code, but we didn't say where we were meeting, remember? I just told you to go to where we took our last R & R."

"And you don't think he knows where that is?" Telles's quiet voice was tense, strained.

"Why should he? I'm telling you, we're safe."

"Unless you told him." Telles drained the last of his whiskey and shoved his glass away.

"Is that what you really think?" Eagle forced himself to meet Telles's steely gaze. "That I would betray you?"

Telles lifted one brow. "Why not? I'm not one of you anymore."

"What happened to you after Alpha Centauri?" Eagle asked, shifting his eyes away from his old friend's, staring down at the glass in his hand. "Who brainwashed you into all this rebel stuff?" He glanced up to see Telles's reaction.

Telles laughed, shortly, loudly, and flung himself back against the booth, his arms moving to rest on the back of the frayed material, one hand grazing the edge of Sky's shoulder. Eagle stiffened and looked away again. What was the matter with him? So another man touched her. So what? Telles always got the girls, always had, always would.

"Look space-boys," Sky said, putting the blaster at last out of sight below the tabletop. "I don't know what your history together is and I don't give a damn. I want to know where my sister is and I want to know now. Telles, you said you would tell me once we found this piece of rat bait, although why we don't drag him into the streets and flay his worthless hide, I—"

"Sky." Telles's calm use of her name quieted her and again Eagle felt a sharp prickle of jealousy. "We need Eagle to recover your sister."

149

"To recover her?" The color left Sky's face. "You mean she's been captured?"

"Well, not exactly."

The blaster came up from its hiding place, this time turned on Telles. "Damn you, Telles! The only reason I let you live is because you told me you rescued Mayla from Station One!"

"It's the truth. Ask Eagle." He darted a look at him and Eagle leaned back against the booth.

"Why should I tell her anything?"

"Because at heart you are still an honest man, in spite of Zarn's indoctrination."

Eagle frowned. "Now there you go again with the innuendoes. What are you talking about?"

"We've got to talk. There's a lot you don't know, Eagle. About the past. About your life."

"I want to know where my sister is!" Sky thrust the blaster between them. "You two can catch up on old times later, but right now I want some answers. What do you mean not exactly?"

Telles put one hand on top of the blaster and closed his fingers around it. He tugged and Sky stubbornly held on to the grip.

"Sky, put the weapon away. No threats are necessary. I'm happy to tell you what I know."

Sky blinked and lowered the blaster, her gaze wary. "All right," she agreed. She gave him another hard look before fitting the weapon into the holster strapped to her side.

"It's really too risky to talk in here," Eagle said, hoping to stall for time. If Telles told her where Mayla was, she wouldn't need him anymore. "We shouldn't even be discussing this at all. Zarn has informers hiding in the carpet for all we know."

"Or at the same table," Sky said. "Shut up and let him talk."

Telles leaned closer, his hands knit together in front of him, dropping his voice to a whisper.

"Mayla had me take her somewhere safe."

"Where?" Sky asked, the word coming out in a rush of

soft air. Eagle felt another dart of conscience, this time sympathy for her obvious worry over her sister. And he was intending to add to that worry.

Get a grip, he ordered himself.

"I don't know," Telles said.

"What do you mean, you don't know?" Sky grabbed Telles by the forearm, forcing him to look at her.

He glanced down at her and Eagle saw the regret in his eyes. Damn. He didn't know. He didn't know where the kid was.

"She made me forget," he said softly.

"What?" Sky almost shouted the word, her fingers tightening on his arm.

"I'm sorry, Sky." His hand covered hers and his blue-gray eyes softened with sympathy. "The truth is, I have no idea where in the universe she could be."

Chapter Eight

Sky stared at Telles, feeling stunned. When she'd realized who was stalking her in the alleyway, she'd wanted to kill him. Telles. The man her sister had nursed back to health. The man who had betrayed them both. But as they stood in the dank, smelly alley, he explained what had happened. How he had been lured next door by the neighbor who had actually turned the child in, and been held there until the soldiers had taken Mayla away. He had escaped and followed, knowing exactly where the child would be taken—to Station One, where his old friend Eagle was in charge. He hadn't realized it was Sky's troops storming the place, he claimed, or he'd have waited and turned Mayla over to her then and there. At least that was what he had said, and he had convinced her. And now he was telling her he didn't know where he himself had taken her sister.

Her voice rose and she rose along with it, her palms pressing down tightly against the tabletop as she towered over him.

"What do you mean she made you forget?"

"Sit down, Sky," Eagle said, staring down into his empty glass.

"I'm not talking to you, space-boy!"

"Sit down and for once in your life, shut up."

Something in the tone of his own quiet voice, in the sudden slump of his posture, the shifting of his gaze toward the entrance of the tavern, made Sky do as he said. She recognized the aura of command settling on the colonel's shoulders; it was the same one she wore when confronted with a situation dangerous to her crew.

152

"What is it?" she said, sitting down and lifting her glass casually to her lips, taking a tiny sip. She put the glass down. Her muscles were tense, her body ready for action. She glanced at Telles and his jaw muscle tightened. Eagle turned his collar up and looked as though he were trying to sink into the dilapidated seat of the booth.

"Damn. Listen, just follow my lead and—"

"Colonel?"

They looked up into the stern, unyielding face of a Dominion soldier. He was dressed in battle gear, wearing the flat-sheeted armor across his chest common to soldiers heading into a war zone. Sky felt her throat contract.

"You must have me confused with someone else," Eagle said, a slight drunken slur to his words. Since his glass was empty, he picked up Sky's drink, saluted the man, and tossed it down.

"Colonel, if you will please come with me, sir." The soldier stood at attention and Eagle sighed as he pushed his glass away. He and Telles exchanged glances and Sky saw a silent signal pass between the two men. She slipped her hand down and curled her fingers around her blaster's grip.

Eagle stumbled to his feet. "Well, if you insist," he mumbled, then lurched against the soldier as though off balance. As the soldier reached out to steady him, Eagle grabbed his arm and Telles came at him from the other side. All three went down, fists flailing, Eagle trying to disarm the soldier while Telles held him down. Sky stood over the three, unable to get a clear shot, feeling unusually helpless in the face of their barroom brawl. In a matter of moments, however, Eagle emerged victorious. He stood and smiled down at the soldier, blaster in hand, all trace of drunkenness gone.

"Sorry," he said, brandishing the weapon. "Guess I'll have to take a raincheck on that little excursion you had in mind."

"Oh, yeah?" The soldier snarled up at him from his position on the floor. Telles had one knee in his chest

153

and his own blaster aimed at the man's head.

"But don't worry, I won't let you take the blame for not bringing me in."

"Oh, yeah?" he said again, a little louder.

The beginning of a grin started at the corner of Eagle's mouth. "I know that you're just doing your job, but—"

"Oh, yeah?"

Eagle shook his head in amusement. "Okay, have it your way. Yeah."

Sky smiled and rolled her eyes, Telles laughed aloud, and for a brief instant she felt a camaraderie between the three of them, a bond. The feeling disappeared as she turned and saw at least twenty Dominion soldiers crowding into the bar. She glanced at Eagle as he turned and faced the flood of men. He didn't betray one iota of alarm—or surprise—as the leader of the group, a tall man also wearing battle armor and carrying a large blaster rifle, strode toward the three. He stopped in front of Eagle and gave him the age-old salute of fist to chest, then arm extended.

"Colonel," the man said, his words loud, with proper military inflection, "you are ordered to surrender your weapon and report to Lord Zarn at once."

Eagle surveyed the man coolly, then handed the blaster toward him butt first. Sky felt the faint hope flickering inside of her die.

"Where is my father?" he asked the man in front of him. Sky looked at him sharply, noting the weariness in his voice.

The soldier gestured behind him and he turned toward the front of the tavern where people were scurrying left and right, leaving a broad path down the middle of the seedy establishment. In its wake strode a tall, distinguished-looking man with gray-streaked hair and an arrogance Sky could feel across the room. A man whose face was known on every planet in the quadrant. It was evident in the very set of his shoulders that he believed himself to be a superior being. Sky shuddered slightly as he strode across the room, his black cape billowing behind him. How dramatic, she thought. How typical. She glared at Eagle and felt the tension in him, though there was no evidence of stress in the rugged contours of his face. Fury rose inside her, coupled with confusion. Whose side was Eagle on?

She glanced at Telles as he rose from his position beside the soldier on the floor, his gaze locked on his old friend. He shot her a look that told her to wait and see how Eagle played this hand of the game. She didn't have to wait long. There was the barest instant of hesitation on Eagle's part, then the tension dissipated from his features and a broad, cocky grin eased across his face. He raised one brow in Zarn's direction, hands on his hips, and Sky shrank away from the man beside her, moving to Telles's side.

A spark of defiance lit Eagle's eyes, giving her a brief hope again—hope that was dashed to pieces seconds later as the colonel nonchalantly folded his arms across his chest and spoke.

"So—what kept you?"

Sky cursed. First she cursed Eagle, eloquently, then Zarn, then the universe at large, and finally herself for ever believing that the son of a thieving, murdering bastard could be any less of a thieving, murdering bastard himself. She paced the small confines of the cell on Zarn's ship and tried to think, tried to form some kind of coherent plan. But she couldn't. The power of Eagle's betrayal had robbed her of all cognizant thought and left a pure, raw rage she could not purge. She wanted to scream, to smash things, to beat her fists against the wall. Instead she fumed, wondered with an aching fear where Kell might be. Had Zarn already picked him up as well? If so, there was no hope at all for them.

She wouldn't even begin to entertain that thought, though. Not yet. She couldn't. Sky kept pacing back and forth until she grew too weary to continue. Stopping at last, she leaned her back against the wall farthest from the doorway. Sliding downward, she wrapped her arms around her doubled-up legs and rested her head on her knees.

What was she doing here? Why had she ever left Mayla alone that day? That had been the start of this nightmare. No, the start had been the day her father had sent her on the diplomatic mission and Zarn's fleet had entered the Andromedan system to begin their murderous assault on their planet.

Quick, hot tears stung behind her eyelids. If Zarn hadn't come and destroyed her parents, her family, their very way of life, Sky would at this moment be sitting in the royal palace, probably indulging her love of painting or sculpting. Wistfully, she thought back to her youth, when she had created childish works of art her father had exclaimed over, calling her his little Nonjeen, the name of a popular artist of the day. Sky lifted her head and stared down at the palms of her hands as a wave of anguish swept over her. Once these hands had created things of beauty—even if they had been the awkward creations of an inexperienced child—but now these same hands destroyed. These hands had killed by pulling the trigger of a blaster. She closed her eyes and leaned her head back against the wall. Once her heart had been filled with childish wonder and a joy for what the future would bring. Now it was cold and dark and filled with hate, and there was no tomorrow.

Her world as a child had been one of culture and beauty, her life one lovely party or gala occasion after another, filled with happy people in bright colors, shaping the future of their world with vision and tolerance. Now Zarn's dark presence had eradicated every ounce of joy, every bright hope the Andromedans had ever had. Tears traced a languid path down Sky's cheeks as memories flooded her mind. Images of her mother and father, brothers and sisters now long dead. Their voices, their lives, echoed in her head until she thought she would go crazy. She lifted her hands to her head, her fingers tangling into her hair, gripping her scalp. Cold metal slid beneath her fingers as she touched the silver band around her temples. An equally cold chill shook her suddenly to the marrow.

Eagle, spawn of hell, would tell Zarn that she was

Mayla's sister. At least he didn't know about the full extent of her power, or the fact that the silver band was the only thing between herself and insanity. She'd never willingly reveal anything she knew to Zarn, of course, but if he sought to probe her mind—She paled. His machines would detect the deflective power of the band and he would take it from her. And since she had no control, no ability to shield her thoughts without it, Zarn could easily probe her mind and destroy her. That was one reason Mayla was the heir to the throne. A Cezan must not just have the power, but be able to control that power as well. Thank the Creator she did not know where Mayla was hidden.

But Telles did. Sky lowered her hands from her temples and felt new fear well up inside of her. Even though he couldn't consciously remember where Mayla was, he must have the actual memory somewhere inside his mind. Surely Eagle would not allow his father to harm the man who had been his friend for twenty years! Another thought: Was Telles part of this too? Had the whole thing been an elaborate ploy to capture her and Mayla—the last of the Cezans—so Zarn could be sure their kind never rose up to take power again? She closed her eyes.

"I don't know who to trust," she said aloud. Laughter echoed around her and Sky jerked her head up toward the sound, stumbling to her feet, fists clenched, feeling the hot flush of anger stain her cheeks.

"Poor, dear child." The voice of Zarn boomed down at her mockingly from somewhere and she searched the room futilely for a hidden com unit. "Trust me."

"What are you going to do to me?" she demanded.

"That is entirely up to you." The smooth, cultured tone in his voice altered abruptly. "Where is your sister?"

So he knew. Eagle had betrayed her again.

"Where you'll never find her," she said, then added silently, *I hope.*

"I think you're wrong, my dear. Your friend with the long golden hair knows exactly where you sister has been hidden."

Had he already probed Telles? Did Zarn know where

Mayla was? The thought of Mayla being at this monster's mercy sent a surge of energy through her weary limbs.

"Go to hell!" she shouted, shaking her fist at the ceiling. She spun around as the door slid suddenly open and two burly Dominion soldiers entered, blasters at their sides, rifles in their hands. The voice spoke again, the soothing tone sliding like a snake's skin across her fearful senses.

"Go with them, Captain. You will be joining me in hell very soon."

Telles lay strapped to a table, tilted at a forty-five-degree angle, as two attendants in pale blue coats attached electrodes to his arms, chest, groin, legs, and face. He stared straight ahead stoically as they readied his naked body. As always, the victim's clothes had been taken, stripped from him ignominiously, leaving him even more vulnerable, more helpless.

Every muscle in Eagle's body buzzed with tension. He was trying to relax, trying not to reveal how much this facade of composure was costing him internally. He'd done it for years; it should have been child's play. But as he watched his friend being hooked up to the monstrous machine that would read his thoughts, Eagle wasn't sure he could maintain the mask of indifference. He leaned against the bulkhead nearest the door, arms folded across his chest, behaving merely as an interested spectator even as his mind explored every possible means of escape.

Eagle's gaze flickered over his friend. If he knew the whereabouts of the heir to the Andromedan throne and told Zarn, it would destroy Eagle's plans to use the child to make his father listen to him. If Telles didn't know where she was, Zarn would probably kill him.

Telles gazed straight ahead, lying as if frozen, his jaw locked—to keep from crying out? Eagle closed his eyes against the sight, his thoughts rushing back to his incarceration on Sky's ship and his own humiliation. Strange, the memory had dimmed against the knowledge that what she had done, she had done for her sister and for the good of Andromeda. Ironically, that was what he had to do now. For Sky, and strangely enough, for his father.

"Now, I believe we are almost ready to begin, except for our audience. We must have an audience." Zarn gestured toward the guard standing in the doorway. The man turned and pressed a series of buttons beside the door, lowering the shield protecting the room.

Eagle knew before the door slid open who would be standing on the other side. She walked through the doorway like a queen, shoulders back, head high, her turquoise eyes snapping with ill-contained fire. Damn, she was beautiful. And brave. And strong. And everything he'd ever wanted in a woman. The realization hit him hard, and it took everything inside of him to keep from reacting outwardly. Then she saw Telles strapped down and sorrow flooded her gaze briefly before the flame returned and she spun to confront him.

"You son of a bitch!" she shouted, crossing the room and slapping him hard across the face before the hand of one of the guards clamped down on her shoulder and dragged her back. "Let him go!"

Eagle rubbed his jaw ruefully. "Glad to see you too, Princess."

"Who is this delightful piece of fluff, Eagle?"

So he didn't know Sky was Mayla's sister? Then maybe he had a chance at least of saving her, although at the moment she looked as if she could certainly hold her own and was anything but fluffy. Even cornered by her enemy, by the man who had killed her family, she stood defiantly, arms tight with contoured muscles, fists clenched at her side, legs braced as if for a blow, or a battle. He regretted now his momentary weakness, the desire to see her in anything besides that plain uniform she wore aboard the *Defiant*, that had led him to buy her the short tunic she wore. Now, sans protective cloak, the garment was almost transparent and her body strained against the too-tight material in all the right places. He felt his own kind of strain as his gaze traveled over the short hemline to the long, sleek legs below. Zarn moved to stand beside his son and chuckled.

"Yes, indeed," the Kalimar said, "one of yours, son? Feel like sharing with your dear old dad?"

Eagle forced a laugh even as he forced himself not to slam his fist into his own father's face.

"She's nobody," he said shortly, dismissing the woman with a wave of his hand. "Telles's latest girlfriend," he added, then cursed himself for a fool. Zarn was looking for his friend's most vulnerable spot. If he thought Sky meant anything to him ... "Or should I say *ex*-girlfriend," he amended. "He dumped her a couple of weeks ago, but she keeps tagging along after him everywhere he goes. She showed up at the bar unexpectedly."

Zarn's gaze locked with his son's for a long moment and, not for the first time in his life, Eagle was glad Zarn was not a telepath. His thoughts at this moment would have had him stretched out beside Telles in a matter of seconds.

"Why are you lying to me?"

Startled, Eagle swallowed hard, but quickly recovered his poise. "I'm not lying. What are you talking about?"

"Do you think I don't know that this is Skyra Cezan? The sister to the heir of Andromeda?" His green eyes narrowed as he stared at his son, and suddenly Eagle knew everything was lost. "I will ask you again, why are you lying to me? Can it be you've joined this disreputable band of renegades?"

Maybe not lost completely. He saw a glimmer of anxiety in Zarn's eyes. Eagle laughed out loud, hands on his hips. "Of course not," he said, not hesitating even an instant. "Let me ask *you* something—why didn't you stick to our original agreement? Why didn't you let me bring the kid to you on Rigel?"

He heard Sky's quick intake of breath and when he glanced her way, the look of raw fury in her eyes was enough to make him take an involuntary step backward.

"Are you trying to tell me that you have lied to me because I arrived on Barbaros 9 unexpectedly?" Zarn demanded, his voice flat, filled with suspicion.

Eagle shrugged. "I haven't lied to you. I didn't know who she really was. I was just repeating what Telles told me." He could feel Sky's fiery gaze boring a hold through him. Damn, damn, damn. He hated sounding like the kind of man who would lie to save himself. If he could only let her know he was lying for all of them. "But I don't like surprises. And I don't like you giving me an assignment and then going behind my back—acting like I can't handle it."

"Or is it that you still have feelings of friendship for a man who is obviously a rebel?" Zarn tapped his index finger thoughtfully against his nose as he walked around the fettered Telles. "And a woman who has, perhaps, enticed you to forget where your loyalties lie?"

"We have no proof that Telles is a rebel," Eagle objected. "I told you, the child healed him and he feels a responsibility toward her. And the woman—" He smiled lewdly in Sky's direction. "All right, I'm no saint, but I've had my fill of her. She means nothing to me."

"Oh, I'm a rebel all right." Telles spoke from the table and Eagle shot him a cautioning look. The man strained against the straps holding him down, his eyes slightly wild. "I'm a rebel and damn proud of it! You think I'm your friend, Eagle?" He laughed, the sound harsh and angry.

"Shut up." Eagle said the words quietly. If Telles confessed to treason, Zarn would have no choice but to kill him. "I don't want to hear this."

"Well, isn't that too damn bad?" He laughed again. "It's time you heard the truth! I've used our connection any way I could. Me, the friend of the son of the great and powerful Lord Zarn." He pushed upward, feverishly allowing the straps to bite into his flesh, faint droplets of blood staining his skin as he did. "I used you. I used you to do whatever I had to do to try to overthrow your father's tyranny."

Eagle turned away, too furious to speak for a moment. Telles had dug his own grave, and if they didn't get out of this somehow, Zarn would bury him in it. In the meantime, he would use his friend's stupidity or ploy, whichever it was, to solidify his shaky position with his father.

"So tell me something I didn't know," he shot back over

one shoulder as he walked away from the man. "You think I didn't know it? You think I didn't have you watched constantly? Why the hell do you think I left you for dead on Alpha Centauri?"

He stopped walking and turned, hands on his hips. Sky was staring at him, the look on her face one of shock and disbelief. Surely she didn't believe what he was saying. Surely she knew he hadn't—that he couldn't—leave his friend on a distant planet to die.

"Enough." Zarn was suddenly at his side. "Get on with the probing. Eagle, you will do the honors."

Eagle blinked. That was the last thing he expected his father to say.

"Me?"

"I'm anxious to see what you've learned since you've been on Station One." Zarn's gaze was hard, unyielding. "Shall we begin?"

Eagle ran his tongue across his dry lips and stepped onto the platform beside Telles. He had been fully trained on Station One in all aspects of the mind-probe. He had just refused to do it. He picked up the helmet and lifted it over his friend's head, sending him a silent message of apology. He was relieved when the blue-gray eyes flickered back a second's understanding.

Suddenly, Telles's face blurred and shifted and Eagle saw not his friend beneath the helmet, but his own face, though younger. He blinked, and for an instant felt as though he might black out, then he saw Telles again, and the dizziness passed.

He cleared his throat and began adjusting the helmet. "You don't have to be put through this you know." He flipped the switch that would apply the tele-lodes beneath the helmet directly over the specific pulse points and cranial locations known to provide entrance to the human mind. "All you have to do is tell us where you stashed the kid."

"I didn't stash her." Telles said, his usually terse lips curved up in a smile. "She stashed herself."

"C'mon, Telles, you can still walk away from this." Eagle drew one long tube from the helmet and inserted it into the probe's central unit. He couldn't stall much longer. "Where is she?"

"I don't know."

"Eagle." Zarn's voice was soft from the corner where he had taken himself to in order to watch the proceedings. He stood, arms folded over his chest, his tall image clothed in black creating its own dark shadow. "Let us begin."

Eagle's hand hovered over the switch that would activate the probe. Telles drew a long, shuddering breath, and Eagle tried not to look his friend in the eye. Telles was scared. He didn't blame him. Hell, he was scared for him. Neither of them had ever been probed.

"What are you doing?" Zarn's voice echoed again from the dark corner and Eagle froze. It was now or never.

"Turn on the lights," Eagle managed to choke out. The room was illuminated and he blinked, adjusting his eyes to the light before he straightened and turned, meeting Zarn's narrow gaze.

"I'm sorry, Father." Eagle said, trying not to blink against the brightness. "I can't do it."

Zarn stepped forward, and for a moment his features appeared almost vulnerable, his eyes registering his shock an instant before rage lit the emerald depths. "What do you mean you can't do it? I order you to do it!"

Eagle swallowed hard, then shook his head. "No."

The explosion caught them unawares. One moment they were standing facing one another, and the next the ship bucked and pitched to one side, throwing everyone to the deck. Klaxons rang out as a deep voice called battle stations over the ship-wide communications system.

"What the hell!" Eagle stumbled to his feet, heading back toward the table where Telles was bound. If there was a chance of letting him go in the confusion, he'd be ready to take it. He barely made it to his friend's side before another ominous explosion shook the ship.

"Someone is attacking the ship!" Zarn shouted from his hands-and-knees position on the floor. He struggled to his feet and spun around, glaring at Telles and Eagle. "Is this one of your rebel tricks? Guards! Stay here and make sure no one leaves this room!" Zarn strode to the doorway, his long cape flapping about his heels.

Eagle quickly pressed the button, deactivating the energy shackles holding Telles captive even as one of the guards hurriedly crossed the room, blaster in hand.

"Hey, you can't do that!"

Telles's blow caught him squarely in the nose, and the man stumbled backward as the other guard left Sky's side and ran forward, his weapon laying down a quick succession of searing red blasts in their general direction. The blasts missed them and sizzled against the bulkhead behind them.

"It's not on stun!" Eagle shouted, pulling Telles back behind the table and down beside him in a crouching position.

"You might as well come out!" The guard shouted. "There's no way out of this room and—Uhhhhh." The sound of a thud, followed by another, cut off the man's ultimatum, and Eagle and Telles looked at each other in confusion, then grinned at the same time.

"Sky," they said in unison, and stood.

The royal princess of the Cezan family stood with one foot on the fallen man's chest, his blaster rifle balanced against her hip. The other guard lay nearby.

"Hello, boys," she said. "Shall we go?"

Sky wasn't exactly sure what had happened back in the inquisition chamber, but she knew Eagle had protected her by not revealing who she really was to Zarn and that he had refused to probe Telles's mind. For those things she was temporarily giving him the benefit of the doubt. Besides, there was no time for explanations, not if they wanted to stay alive. They had paused long enough for Telles to don his clothing, and now were headed for the huge ship's shuttle bay, running at full speed, two blasters from the fallen guards in hand. They had them set on heavy stun at Eagle's insistence.

She had insisted on keeping the weapon she had captured, and Eagle had given the other to Telles, leaving him unarmed. He followed behind them muttering under his breath. Thank the Seekers he knew this ship so well. She didn't trust him, not for a minute, but whatever his motives were in helping them get to the ship's shuttle, she would use his help and deal with him later. She had to live to get off of this ship and find out what Telles had meant when he said that Mayla had erased his knowledge of her whereabouts.

Rounding a corner, they were suddenly confronted by six Dominion soldiers. Cursing herself for being lost in thought instead of ready and primed for action, Sky fired off a series of blasts from her weapon only seconds behind Telles's defense. Two soldiers went down in front of them. Telles and Sky managed to push them back with the sheer audacity of refusing to yield, and continued to move forward, firing constantly, forcing the Dominions back past their fallen comrades. As Sky and Telles covered him, Eagle quickly removed the weapons and power packs from the men and entered the fray himself. Now with four weapons between them, they stepped up the firepower and pushed the remaining four soldiers back until they had reached the corridor leading to the shuttle bay.

Sky gauged the situation with a military mind even as she crouched around the corner. This corridor was shaped like a T, with the Dominions firmly ensconced in the long part of the corridor, in the direction of the shuttle bay. She occupied one side of the T crossing and Eagle and Telles the other. They were lucky, for now they had some slight protection. They could hide around the corners and fire out at the soldiers who had no protection at all. It was a miracle none of the three had been hit, but then blasters weren't known for their accuracy, just their deadliness. A cold bead of sweat broke out across her brow. They had to clear the corridor and reach the docking bay before more soldiers arrived, while they still had a chance.

Sky wiped the sweat from her eyes with the back of one hand and thought of Mayla. Where was she? What was happening to her?

The fear Sky felt for Mayla, somewhere alone, maybe

helpless in spite of her powers, made her reckless. Suddenly she jumped to her feet, screaming at the top of her lungs as she threw herself forward, firing in a frenzy. Telles and Eagle followed her, laying down a line of cover. As she ran, screaming, she felt elated by the looks of sheer terror on the soldiers' faces as they panicked and ran. She dropped the first one. Eagle got the next and Telles the third. One was all that was left between them and the door to the bay. He was running, glancing over one shoulder as the three of them bore down on him. As Sky lifted her blaster for one last shot, the soldier turned and fired. She felt the searing pain enter her shoulder even as Eagle brought the last Dominion down. She stumbled to a halt, fire spreading through her chest and down her arm. She looked down, stunned, and saw she was covered with blood.

"Sky, damn it to hell! What did you think you were doing!" Eagle shouted, running to her side, grabbing her and jerking her around to face him. His eyes widened as he stared at the scarlet liquid staining the blue tunic she still wore.

Sky felt a moment's peace as she saw the terrible fear in his eyes. Telles was at her side then too, and as her eyelids fluttered closed, she felt a second's irritation that it was he who had caught her as she fell, and not Eagle.

Summoning all of her mental ability, she concentrated on the pain, easing it from her body, casting it away as her mother had taught her to do so many years ago. The pain eased. Now the bleeding. She closed her eyes and pictured the pumping blood slowing, the veins healing. She felt herself fading, even as Eagle's choked cry reached her. She barely felt the touch of his hand against her face as she slipped into the darkness.

Chapter Nine

Sky woke in a dimly lit room. She opened her eyes with difficulty and tried to orient herself, but could not at first, because her vision was too blurred. Finally she was able to make out a few shapes in the shadows. A cruiser cabin. How could that be? She was supposed to be on a shuttlecraft. Why was she supposed to be on a shuttlecraft? She blinked as her memory returned. The battle—Zarn and Eagle and Telles—she'd been wounded.

Her hand flew up to her shoulder and encountered the soft surface of a bandage. Glancing down she saw she was naked except for the blanket covering her. Gingerly she touched the surface of the bandage and found there was still a little soreness in the shoulder. Later she would do more to heal the wound, but not now. Now she was too tired and too many questions were bouncing around inside her head. She scanned the room and realized, with surprise, that it was her own cabin. Captain's quarters on the *Defiant*. A sense of relief flooded over her.

The door to the cabin opened and she raised up on her elbows, feeling suddenly vulnerable in her state of undress. When she saw it was Eagle, her wariness increased, but she lowered herself back to the narrow bunk and wrapped her arms protectively across her middle.

"Feeling better?" he asked, his green eyes sweeping over her, pausing at the bare skin exposed above the edge of the blanket.

"What happened?" She pulled the cover more securely around her, tucking it under her arms as best she could with one hand. "How did we get back on the *Defiant*?"

"We had a little unexpected help." Eagle sat down on

167

the edge of the bunk, his tawny brows pressed together, his mouth tight with apprehension.

Once again she felt the connection between them, Something was wrong.

"What is it?" She touched his arm before she thought and quickly snatched her hand away as he lifted his gaze to hers. Why was it that the sight of his dark green eyes always made her feel like warm Tantalisian coa-coa? Why did the mere touch of his skin against hers make her want him—even though she knew, she *knew*, he must be on Zarn's side. Her nakedness beneath the blanket suddenly jumped to the forefront of her mind as her skin became hypersensitive. She moved restlessly beneath the cover and forced the sensations coursing through her to abate. All of this—his help on Zarn's ship, his heroics—had to be an elaborate staging guaranteed to make her trust him and reveal—what? *She* didn't know where Mayla was and Eagle knew that. All right, maybe it had all been for Telles's benefit. He knew where Mayla was. He had to know.

"Could you hand me my robe please?"

Eagle frowned down at her. "Well, I don't know. I rather like you like this, to tell you the truth."

Sky smiled with feigned sweetness. "I'll bet you do. Look inside my closet, Colonel, on the left. It's blue."

"Of course it is," Eagle muttered to himself. Sky hid a smile behind one hand. It was amusing to see the big tough space soldier rummaging through the filmy caftans and gowns she kept for special occasions. He held one beautiful peacock-blue evening dress out and gazed at it for a full minute before putting it away.

"Is Telles all right?" she asked as Eagle turned around, holding her robe.

He lifted one dark brow and handed the thin blue garment to her. "*Telles*"—he emphasized his friend's name—"is fine. Thanks so much for asking. Everything is just fine."

"Then what is it? What's wrong?" She shimmied into the robe, and to give the colonel credit, he turned slightly away to give her a semblance of privacy.

168

"Nothing. Lucky for you that you have the power to heal yourself. Otherwise you'd be dead." His words were flat and Sky felt the lack of emotion over her possible demise like a slap in the face. "Feel like eating something?" he finished.

Sky glared at him. Typical male. Offset deep emotions with questions about dinner. "Yes, but first I would like to know who attacked the ship. How were we able to escape so easily?"

He laughed without humor. "Your idea of easy and mine must be vastly different. But maybe you'd better ask our saviour yourself."

"Our what?"

Eagle moved to the door and pressed the release switch beside it. He stepped out into the corridor. A few seconds later a familiar blue face appeared in the doorway. The tall Altairian entered the cabin as Eagle stood in the doorway, arms folded over his chest, his face unreadable.

"Kell," she said softly. "You saved me."

"Kell, you saved me."

Eagle mimicked the words, throwing himself down on the narrow bunk in the cabin he was sharing with Telles and crossing his arms behind his head. He ordered himself to stop thinking about her. Skyra Cezan was the last thing he should be worrying about. Finding her sister was uppermost in his mind—or should be. Surely Telles knew where he had taken the child. He had just been bluffing before.

Eagle stared up at the ceiling, fighting his anger and frustration, and—if he was honest with himself—his fear. Everything was falling apart. His father thought he was one of the rebels, and his attack against Forces' soldiers—not to mention helping the rebels escape—would be all the proof he needed. He flung his feet over the side of the bed and sat up, too restless simply to lie there. He stood and began to pace.

Surely his father would trust him. Surely he would figure he had a reason, a plan behind his actions. A shadow crossed his thoughts. But what was his plan? To use the heir to the throne as blackmail to make his father listen to him. Not exactly one of the most honorable plots he'd ever conceived, but someone had to take a stand. Someone who had a little power and knew how to use it. He wasn't a rebel, and wouldn't turn against his father. He just knew if he could make Zarn stop and listen, he could convince him that unless he changed the way he ruled, his rule was doomed. In his entire life he'd never opposed his father, until now. And now his father thought he was one of the enemy. He had to find a way to make him understand.

"I will," he said aloud, pushing the disturbing thoughts away. "I will convince him. He'll understand eventually."

He turned his thoughts to the next problem: Sky. Why had it made him so furious when she'd murmured those words to Kell?

Because I saved her, that's why. He felt the anger all over again. *If I hadn't gotten us to the shuttle after disabling the tractor beams and the shields long enough to allow us to take off, we would've ended up in a nice little explosion just off the port bow.*

He rubbed an aching spot in the middle of his forehead with two fingers. Yet, he had to admit she had done her fair share. He was even willing to concede he hadn't saved her at all. They had all saved each other. What a team they had made—Eagle and Sky and Telles. Like a smooth piece of machinery. As if they had fought at each other's sides forever.

Sitting down on the bunk, he realized all at once how exhausted he really was. He lay back, stretching out on the hard surface, glad for just a moment of peace before he had to start fighting again—for he knew once Sky started remembering what had taken place before their escape, she'd be ready to go at it tooth and nail. If only he could convince her that his plans would mean a better life for the Andromedans, for everyone.

He drifted, his mind growing fuzzy with sleep, when a sudden noise made him bolt upright. The door to the room slid open and a young man, about fifteen years old, entered. He carried a helmet in his hands, and as Eagle focused on the object, he recognized it as the device from his father's mind-probe on Station One. The young man had dark hair and looked somehow familiar. His green eyes seemed glazed over, hollow, and as he walked toward Eagle, he began to speak in a monotone.

"What name do you choose? What name do you choose? What name do you choose—"

Eagle sat up in bed, sweat pouring down his back and beneath his arms. He was breathing heavily as if he'd been running and he threw himself out of the bunk, circling the room to find the intruder before he realized it had only been a dream. Another dream. He sank down on the bed and let his head rest against his hands. What did it mean? More guilt from his brief tenure on Station One? He shuddered as he thought back over it. The boy was him of course, with dark hair and green eyes. But why did he keep dreaming of himself as a boy? He lay back on the bunk again, hands behind his head, this time keeping his eyes open.

Before he could puzzle it over any further, the door slid open. Eagle jerked to an upright position, half expecting to see his own image walk in, then relaxed as he saw it was Telles. His friend stopped in the center of the room and stared at Eagle, arms folded across his chest, his blue-gray eyes calm, resigned.

"So how is she?" he asked.

The last thing Eagle wanted right now was to talk to Telles, even though he knew he didn't have much of a choice, given their close quarters. It was inevitable, and he might as well get it over with. Besides, it would take his mind from the dream.

"She's okay. She's going to be fine."

"Good." The silence stretched between them, but Telles made no move to leave the room. He cleared his throat noisily. "Thanks—for what you did on Zarn's ship. About the mind-probe."

Eagle waved his words away. "I couldn't let him do that to you." He glanced over at the man, still standing near the door. "After all, you were once my best friend, before the rebels got hold of you."

171

Telles's eyes had grown cloudy, troubled. He lowered his arms to a less hostile position and took a step forward, then stopped again.

"Eagle, there's someting I've got to tell you."

Eagle stretched both arms above his head and yawned, hoping he'd take the hint. "You know, I'm really beat. Could this wait for a while?"

"No, it can't."

Eagle nodded. "All right. Come in, sit down, let's talk."

Telles walked across the room and stopped at the end of the bunk, his long hair falling over one shoulder, his hands clenched nervously at his side, and all at once Eagle wondered what he was so anxious about. When he spoke, his voice was soft and filled with pain.

"If you hadn't stopped Zarn today, it wouldn't have been the first time I'd been probed."

Eagle pushed the chair sitting beside the bed out with one foot. "Sit down and tell me what the hell you're blathering about. You've never been probed any more than I have. We're Rigelians."

Telles laughed shortly, without humor, tossing his long hair back from his shoulders as he turned the chair around and straddled it. "Funny you should put it in quite those terms." He leaned forward, his gaze intent, and Eagle's guard went up. He knew that look. What the hell was going on?

"This isn't going to be easy for you to hear. Believe me, it wasn't easy for me."

Alarms rang loudly in the depths of Eagle's mind. He swung his legs over the side of the bed and stood, hands on his hips, staring down at the other man. "Back off, Telles. I don't want to hear this. Whatever it is, I don't want to hear it."

"You have to hear it."

"No, I don't." Telles was suddenly beside him, his hands locked around his forearms as he forced Eagle to face him.

"Let go of me," he ordered, feeling the beginnings of a dark, terrible panic form deep inside of him. "Damn it, Telles, let me go or—"

"Listen to me!"

Eagle jerked out of his grasp and turned toward the door. Telles moved to block his way, his hands knotted into fists.

"Am I going to have to fight you?" he demanded. "I'll do it if I have to."

"Get out of the way, Telles."

Telles dropped his fists to his side, his voice low, building with fervent emotion as he began to speak. "You don't want to hear it because already inside of you, your mind is rebelling, your old thoughts are rising up telling you the truth—forcing you to remember that you are not a Rigelian. *You are an Andromedan!*"

He hissed the last words, and for an instant in time Eagle died. He stopped breathing. He stopped thinking. His brain ceased to function. Everything around him ground to a standstill. Telles was speaking but he couldn't hear his voice. Everything blurred and went to black. Then life blared out suddenly again and he could hear, could see, could understand every ridiculous word his friend had just uttered. He began to laugh, but somehow the laughter died in his throat.

"I am an Andromedan," he said, the statement sounding even more incredulous coming from his own lips. "I am not a Rigelian but an Andromedan. Tell me, Telles, does my father know about this? And my poor mother— did she realize she was giving birth to an Andromedan?" A smile twitched around his lips. He didn't know what Telles's game was, but it had to be something clever.

"I'm not Rigelian either," he said. "We're both Andromedans, Eagle. Your mother was called Pelana and your father was a Seeker, Toma N'chal."

"Oh, of course. And what was my name?"

"I—" He looked away. "I don't know. I couldn't remember your name. Somehow it had been totally taken from my mind."

Eagle started to laugh again but the sound died in his throat. He opened and closed his mouth several times but couldn't manage to say anything. He didn't remember what he wanted to say anyway. His throat felt dry. Very dry.

"Get out," he managed at last.

"We were among the first children brought to Station One," Telles said, speaking slowly as if to a small child. "We were the older ones—I guess we were about fifteen years old. We were among the first to be placed under the probe, but Zarn took a fancy to the two of us and decided to try something different than the same old indoctrination. He was experimenting a lot back then, and he decided not only to suppress our memories of our past on Andromeda, but to give us new ones—and not just the usual 'Andromeda attacked Rigelian ships first.'" He shook his head.

"No, he wanted to try something bigger, more grandiose. Instead, he implanted the memories in our minds that we were Rigelians. He particularly liked you. He admired your spunk and the way you had tried to fight the troops when they killed your father and mother. He didn't have an heir, and for some twisted reason it gave him pleasure to think the son of a Seeker would be raised to be his heir apparent. He implanted the belief in your mind that you were his son."

Eagle moved to the chair and clutched the back of it, half-afraid that if he let go he would crumple to the floor, no longer able to stand.

Telles paused and crossed to his side. "Do you understand what I'm saying, Eagle? He was afraid the strength of our friendship would break through and we would remember our true pasts, so he gave us the memory of growing up as childhood friends on Rigel. He gave you the memory of a wonderful childhood, a wonderful mother. He gave me similar ones. He took away the memories of his slaughter of our parents and our brothers and sisters. My father was a Seeker too, Eagle." Telles's gaze dropped. "He killed them in front of us—our mothers, fathers, everyone."

Eagle stared at him, his jaw slack for a moment. Finally he swallowed hard and spoke, his words harsh as though each one was being ripped from his throat.

"Why are you doing this to me?"

Telles looked up, compassion in his eyes. Eagle looked away, unwilling to let him see what he knew must be mirrored in his own. Telles reached out and grabbed him by the arm, his grip reassuring.

"I know it's a lot to take in all at once and I'm sorry I had to tell you so abruptly, but you had to know—before we go any farther."

The man's fingers tightened on his arm and with a sudden sense of panic, Eagle shoved him away. He was dizzy again. Terribly dizzy. He staggered, a terrible sense of unreality flooding over him, confusing him, dragging him toward darkness, a darkness from which he feared he would never return. He had to get out. He began backing toward the door, wishing he had his phaser.

"Eagle," Telles said, voice hushed, brows pressed together. His face was wreathed in concern as he moved slowly toward him. "Hell, don't go. We'll talk this out. We'll get through it."

"Get away from me, Telles." Eagle groped the side of the door for the release switch. The surface behind him slid open and he backed through it into the hallway, feeling as though a giant vortex had just opened beneath him and was pulling him down. He had to get away from Telles. He had to get where he could be alone, where he could think. This was ridiculous. Preposterous. Of course it was. Then why did he feel the screaming beginning, deep inside him? Why did he hear it reverberating inside his skull? He had to get away. He turned, and ran.

"Eagle—damn it to hell—don't go!" Telles shouted after him. "Let me help you!"

As his feet hit the deck in one resounding thud after another, Eagle felt the last shreds of his old life crumble around him.

"Kell, I'm so glad to see you!" Sky motioned for the man to come closer and reached out with her good arm to pull him down beside her.

"I'd rather stand if you don't mind," he said, looking stiff and uncomfortable.

Sky's smile faded. In recent days Kell seemed to be keeping his distance, physically and emotionally. She'd once thought she was the only one who could provoke feeling from the Altairian. Her thoughts flew back to the day they had begun this voyage, how he had knelt beside her and massaged her hands. What had happened to that Kell? She sighed and turned to the business at hand.

"How did you find us? The last thing I knew was we had gotten separated during that fight in Barbaroscity, and after we were captured I didn't—"

"Captain."

Kell's quiet use of her title sobered her abruptly and a quick flush stained her cheeks. Here she'd been babbling like a teenager, but she'd been worried about him. Why couldn't he unbend just for a moment?

"Yes, Commander," she answered, slipping back into her command mode. "I presume you have much to report. Please, sit down."

The pale blue of his skin was a stark contrast to the purple tunic he wore. Sky stifled a smile.

"Er, you're still out of uniform, Commander?"

Kell grimaced. "I haven't had a chance to change. I've been seeing to the engines after having to shift into warp drive so quickly." He pulled the chair next to the bed out and sat down in it stiffly.

"So tell me what you think of our situation. Eagle— that is, the colonel—helped us escape. Should we trust him now?"

"Not in the slightest. The colonel is not on our side, Captain. You must remember this in your dealings with him. He is only pretending in order to find out where your sister is. You must know that in spite of your . . . connection to him."

Sky looked away from the censure in Kell's gaze. The truth was she didn't know what to think of Eagle anymore. "I'm not sure what he's up to," she said with a sigh, leaning back against the pillows behind her. She drew the robe more tightly around her. "He did refuse to probe Telles's mind, though. He stood up to his father."

"It was probably some prearranged performance designed to make you trust him. The only thing you can trust is that the colonel has his own agenda. I did not even want to let him and his cohort aboard the ship, but what choice did I have? They had you and you were injured. I must say I think you are making a mistake by allowing them the run of the ship."

"What else can I do?" Sky took a deep breath and tried to ignore the slight throbbing in her shoulder. "They are the only ones who can lead us to Mayla. And they did help us escape, whatever their underlying reasons may have been." She smoothed one lock of hair back from her face and noted that once again Kell looked uncomfortable in her presence. Did he think that she was crediting Eagle with their rescue? "You were wonderful, Kell," she said quickly. "But I'm curious. How did you manage to fire on a Dominion ship and not be blown out of space? How did you find us? Why did—"

"Captain, you need your rest." Kell's smooth interruption made her frown again. Kell never interrupted. Was the strain telling on him as much as it was her? He went on, as he rose and stood at attention. "I will give you a more detailed report when you are fully recovered. But I must ask you, did you discover where Mayla is hidden?"

"No." Sky sighed and lifted one hand to rest lightly on the bandage at her shoulder. "Telles claims he doesn't know."

"Do you believe him?"

"Well, actually he said that Mayla had caused him to forget where he had taken her."

"Then it might be possible to find that memory, if she only obscured it somehow."

Sky felt a sudden depression sweep over her. She didn't want to think about all of this anymore. She didn't want to try to figure out the enigma of Eagle. She didn't want to think about her little sister, alone, needing her.

"I think I do need to rest for a while, Kell." She yawned and turned slightly away, dismissively, hoping he would take the hint.

"Sky."

At his hesitant tone of voice, she turned back. Kell seldom appeared indecisive, but she sensed this time he was not altogether sure of what he was about to say. He sat back down, his hands spread tensely on either leg as if for support, his blue eyes so dark they were almost black.

"What is it?" she asked, drawing herself up and away from the pillows behind her. Kell was never tense. She didn't like it. She didn't like it at all.

He cleared his throat. "I think the colonel knows where Mayla is, and I think we are being led into a trap."

Sky closed her eyes, shutting out Kell's face. She wished she could as easily shut out her doubts about Eagle.

"You must find out, Captain." Kell's voice was filled with determination. "Either Eagle knows, or Telles. You must use your abilities and read their minds."

Sky opened her eyes and stared at him, smoothing the top of the blanket with both hands distractedly. "Kell, you and I agreed on this after Redar died. I won't use my telepathic powers any more to invade another person's mind—not even for the rebellion. You know what it costs me, emotionally. My one journey into the colonel's mind has already clouded my judgment where he's concerned; you said it yourself. Why would you want me to do it again?"

"It may be the only way you can save your sister." He shook his head. "I don't know what game Zarn and his son are playing, but I am convinced they know where Mayla is. They are setting a trap for you, and you must use whatever weapons you have to fight them."

She leaned back against the pillows. So much had happened in the last two days. She couldn't even remember the last time she'd eaten. She seized on the excuse as a way to get her first officer out of the room.

She allowed a wan smile to flicker across her lips. "You know, I just realized I don't think I've eaten in about thirty-six hours."

"I'll bring you something at once," Kell said, rising hastily from his chair. "I should have had something sent up for you already."

"That's all right. I was asleep until just a few minutes ago."

"Just rest, Sky." Kell was all business now, having been given an order and a way to help his captain. "I'll be back shortly."

Sky watched him leave, keeping her pent-up breath under control until the door slid shut behind him. She released it in a long sigh, then threw the covers back from her body and sat up. Easing herself to the floor, she was surprised to find she felt a little stronger, in spite of what she had told Kell. Moving to her closet, she opened the door and rummaged inside for something comfortable but a little less revealing. She pulled out the short tunic she'd worn the day Eagle had almost seduced her in the briefing room. Staring down at it, she rubbed the material between her fingers for a moment as she remembered what his lips had felt like on hers, hot, burning, demanding. She flushed and threw the garment back inside, not bothering to hang it up again. Angrily, she jerked out a regular one-piece uniform in navy blue and spun away from the closet.

She didn't care what Kell said. She wasn't going to infiltrate Eagle's mind again. There had to be another way to find out where Mayla was—there had to be! Since her first journey into his thoughts, she had become fixated on the man. If she explored his mind again, she knew she would be lost. Quickly she shed the robe and donned the uniform, feeling immediately better, more in control. *Why?* she demanded from herself as she sat back down on the edge of her bunk. She picked up the small cat statue on the nearby table and idly smoothed it with her fingers. *Why is it so necessary to feel in control every minute? You've been injured; give yourself a break.* The answer came to her swiftly.

Because I am afraid. Because I am no longer in control of anything, including Mayla's safety.

The thought pierced her and spurred her to action. She had to question Telles now that she was coherent and back on her feet. A wave of dizziness swept over her. Well, practically back on her feet. She turned to switch

179

on the com unit near her bed and order Kell to bring Telles up when he brought her food. He would argue with her but she couldn't eat a bite until she talked to the man. The door buzzer sounded, indicating someone was outside. Kell? Back so soon? With a sigh, she replaced the little cat on the table. He would scold her for getting out of bed. Sometimes his concern bordered on suffocation. She sat back down on the bunk with a sigh.

"Come."

The door opened but instead of Kell, Telles strode into the room. Startled, Sky jumped to her feet and drew herself up into her usual erect military stance. To her surprise, Telles did the same, standing at attention just inside the door. Something was wrong. She sensed it.

"Telles," she acknowledged, a formal tone in her voice. She realized she didn't know his rank or she would have called him by that. "I was about to send for you. We need to talk."

"Yes," he agreed. "Eagle told me you're a telepath."

She nodded, warily, wondering what else Eagle had told him.

"I want you to help him."

Sky sank back down on the edge of the bunk.

"Help him? What's wrong? Why does he need help?"

"Sky, I've got to tell you something that is going to make you trust me and Eagle even less than you already do, but it can't be helped because I'm afraid for him. I can't let him face this alone."

She shook her head, uncomprehending. "Face what?"

"The knowledge that he is not Zarn's son but the son of an Andromedan, a Seeker."

The blood drained swiftly from her face and Sky reeled with his words, her vision growing blurred, her senses faint.

"What?" she whispered.

Telles moved to her side, pulling a chair closer to the bunk and slamming himself into it. He leaned forward, his arms resting on his thighs, his golden hair like a bright curtain around a face dark with fear.

"Read my mind, Sky. Look inside my head and find the

truth—about me, about Eagle, about Mayla. I freely open myself to you—just believe what I'm telling you. Eagle is not Zarn's son. His true nature, his old memories, are beginning to surface. He is beginning to rebel against Zarn, but unless someone trained—like you or Mayla— helps him, he may lose his mind."

"I don't understand. How do you know all of this?"

"Mayla. She never told you that when I was brought to Bezanti I had been a Forces soldier, did she?" Sky shook her head, shocked. "I was left for dead on Alpha Centauri and found by rebel forces looking for survivors who could give information against Zarn. That's how they get a lot of their recruits, you know. They scour the battle-fields and get the soldiers who are fed up and sick of the carnage of the Kalimar." A shadow touched his face. "But I was dying. They took me to Mayla, who healed my body—"

"Wait a minute. Who took you to Mayla? Why wasn't I told?"

"The leader, Redar I think they called him. He died not too long after that, I heard. Apparently she did this for him all of the time." Telles took her hand as she sat in astonishment, holding it between both of his, his voice fervent. "But do you hear me, Sky? Your sister healed my body; then she healed my mind. You see, Zarn can't really take out the memories without risking damaging the mind, but he can overlay the memories with other, more dominant memories. She saw my real memories and made them the dominant ones."

"She never said a word to me."

"Your little sister is a very forgiving child. Perhaps she wasn't sure you would welcome a Forces soldier into your home so easily."

"But what about the rebels who brought you to me? They never said anything about your being a Forces soldier."

"Same reason. They're used to taking burnt-out soldiers and convincing them to come over to the rebellion. And since I readily gave them information, they were pretty sure about my new loyalties. But they were probably pretty sure you might not feel the same way." He leaned toward her. "Will you do it, Sky? Will you read my mind? We've got to help him. You've got to help him."

"I'll do it," she said, lifting her hand to touch the silver band around her forehead, feeling vastly overwhelmed. The door to the room slid open and Kell walked inside, his blue face taciturn. Sky jerked her head toward Telles.

"He wants me to read his mind, Kell. What do you think?"

The man almost smiled and Sky almost fell off the bed. The first officer caught himself and subdued the emotion, leaving his captain wondering as he turned to Telles and nodded.

"An excellent idea. We must find the princess."

Sky stood and motioned Kell to one side, keeping her voice low. "You get your cabin set up again for me to take off my band. Take Telles there."

"How did you get him to agree?"

Sky started to tell him the whole story, but for some reason hesitated. He wouldn't believe Telles's story and she'd rather have the proof, one way or another, before she went into the whole thing with him. If it wasn't true, she didn't want Kell thinking her a fool for even entertaining the possibility.

"He says he wants to help," she said, in answer to his question. "Maybe he means it."

Kell lifted one blue brow and his eyes told her eloquently what he thought of her statement. "There's only one way to find out."

"Yes." She turned to Telles, who'd been listening to the whole exchange, arms crossed over his broad chest. "Take him down to your room, Kell. I'll be there directly."

"Where are you going?"

Still tired from her ordeal, Sky turned on the officer in irritation. "Am I now to report my every move to you, Lieutenant? You forget yourself."

"My apologies, Captain," Kell said. "We will be waiting for you."

* * *

Sky found Eagle on the small observation deck of the cruiser after searching the bridge and all the living quarters. She had hurried Telles and Kell out of her quarters. Why was she so anxious to find him? Why was she willing to help the man she knew to be her enemy? Because deep down, she didn't really believe he was. It was foolish, crazy even, but nevertheless, ever since she had joined with his mind, on some level she had trusted him, at least where Mayla was concerned. She hadn't admitted it to Kell, of course. But it was true. It was also true that she desired him as she had never desired another man. But that was all secondary.

If Telles was right, if this wasn't some elaborate hoax, then Eagle was not her enemy. And if he wasn't her enemy, if she could help him understand what Zarn had done to him, perhaps he'd be willing to help them rescue Mayla. One thing was certain: If what Telles said was true, she knew when she found him she would find a man whose world had suddenly come crashing in on him. He needed her.

She came to a stop as she rounded the corner leading to the observation deck and saw him standing in front of the curved window. On the *Defiant*, everything was functional. It was a ship designed for hauling cargo—or fighting. The observation deck was a tiny cubbyhole of a room about six feet wide by ten feet long, curved, hidden at the end of a hallway in an alcove that doubled as an auxiliary phaser bank. She watched Eagle silently for a moment. Starlight glimmered outside the window. Since the ship had dropped out of warp a few hours ago, the dim pinpoints of the distant stars were clear and stable, not blurred as they were when viewed while the ship was traveling at the speed of light.

Eagle stood staring up at the stars, his dark hair looking strangely silver in the muted light of the room and the reflection of the glass. She could see a tiny muscle twitching in his jaw. His hands hung at his sides, opening and closing reflexively. His broad shoulders, usually held at careful attention, were slightly bowed and as she watched, he lifted his hands and pressed them flat against the curved window, then leaned his head against the glass too.

"Eagle," she whispered, afraid to move forward for fear he would bolt like a trapped animal.

He spun around, his gaze registering no surprise at her presence, no pleasure either. His hair was disheveled as though he'd been tearing at it with his hands, and his clothing was rumpled, his face haggard, drawn, and pale. He never said a word, but his eyes spoke to her. Green as emeralds, but for once not as hard, his eyes were filled with pain and fear. Sky swallowed hard, realizing how much she had begun to count on Eagle's courage. Eagle wasn't afraid of anything. He couldn't be. His gaze flickered and became hollow, empty. He continued to stare at her for a brief moment, then turned away, back to the stars.

She forced herself to walk toward him, one small step at a time, her voice soothing. "Telles told me. I'm here to help."

"There is no help," he murmured to the window.

"Yes, I can help you, Eagle, if you'll let me."

He turned on her, faint lines that hadn't been there before trailing across his forehead and around his lips. "Why? Why do you want to help me? Do you think your sister's whereabouts lie dormant in my brain?" He gestured to his head. "Here. Come on in, look around." She didn't respond and he turned away, shoving his hands down into his jacket pockets. "Well, don't say I didn't offer."

"I want to help you, Eagle," she repeated. "I know what Telles told you must have been a shock."

He laughed shortly. "You didn't really believe him, did you? How could you of all people fall for such a story?"

"Why would Telles say it if it weren't true?"

"A hundred reasons—no, just one. A plot to make me think I'm an Andromedan so I'll help him save his sweet little goddess."

She took a step toward him, wondering if he could hear the pounding of her heart. To her it seemed to vibrate around the room. "Denying the truth won't make it go away."

"It isn't the truth."

"Let me inside your mind and I'll help you know for certain whether or not it's the truth."

She was watching his reflection in the window but was still unprepared when he spun around and grabbed her by the arm, drawing her close.

"How? By taking your word for it? How do I know you won't go in and plant your own thoughts, your own commands for that matter? How do I know I won't be turned into some kind of mind-slave? I've heard about the Cezans and the power they wielded over the Andromedans."

"It isn't true. Please, Eagle, let me help." Sky hated the quiver she heard in her voice, hated the way her blood heated at the merest touch from this man, hated that at that moment more than she wanted to help him, she wanted him to kiss her, to touch her, to make love to her.

"Please, Eagle," he mimicked. "Oh, how the mighty have fallen. What's wrong, Princess, feeling sorry for me?" He pushed her roughly away from him and Sky fell back against the wall. "Well don't, because it isn't true. I'm Zarn's son. I'm a Rigelian. Nothing can ever change that."

"And you can't change the truth. Let me inside your mind and I promise I'll tell you the truth."

"Why?" He turned away and stared out through the window. "Why should you? I'm the enemy, Sky. Never forget that."

Sky moved up behind him and quite without meaning to, she slid her arms around his waist, bringing her body in direct contact with his back. She heard the quick intake of breath, felt the muscles in his back stiffen, then he slowly turned to face her.

"Are you?" she whispered, her hands moving to his chest. "Are you my enemy?"

Suddenly their reason for being there faded, their conflicts disappeared. Suddenly there was only Eagle and Sky, together in the darkness, beneath a velvet sky filled with stars. She lifted her hand to touch the side of his face and her fingers met the stubble of two days' growth of beard. The roughness of it sent a thrill down her spine. Eagle's hand closed around hers and he brought it to his lips. Sky leaned toward him as his mouth closed around her fingertips, one at a time, his tongue touching her skin with a heat that sent a warm rush of yearning through her soul.

A faint covering of dark hair curled at the V of the uniform he wore, and her hands came up between them, her fingers moving across his chest in a caressing motion. She could feel his heartbeat quicken even as his breathing began to come more rapidly. She could feel the fire between them. His head bent closer to hers and Sky lifted her lips to his—almost. Their breath intermingled, but just before their lips touched, he pulled back and turned away.

Sky shuddered as he withdrew from her, the loss leaving her feeling strangely cold and bereft. His rejection—once again—lit an angry fire in the pit of her stomach, and she lifted her chin as she glared at him.

"Is this some kind of game you play, Colonel? See if you can get the stupid woman to desire you, then reject her? Well, it worked again. Yes, I want you, Colonel, just as you want me. You can deny it all you want, but the truth is there between us and you know it."

She flung the words down like a gauntlet and waited to see if he would pick up the challenge. He stood with his back to her for a long moment. Slowly he turned around. The naked need she saw in his eyes shocked her, and when he took a step toward her, Sky unconsciously took one back.

"Do you want me, Sky? But who am I? The son of Zarn? The son of a Seeker? A man without a name?"

He lifted one hand to her face and moved it upward, tangling his fingers into her hair, stopping when they encountered the silver band around her forehead. His thumbs made lazy circles over her skin, her lips, her chin.

"Whoever you are," she said. "I want whoever you are."

"I don't know who I am," he whispered, moving his lips close to hers.

She started to speak but the words died in her throat as his mouth descended over hers, staking a fiery claim that burned his soul into hers. Cradling her face in his hands, Eagle ravaged her mouth, caressed her mouth, teased and cajoled each lip, then moved to the soft skin at her throat. One hand moved to the small of her back, and gently he pressed her against him, letting her feel the long, hard length of him through his clothing, letting her know his need.

Sky groaned aloud and her hands moved around his waist, clutching his back as he plundered her mouth, her throat, the edge of her collarbone; his mouth dipped lower and found the shadow between her breasts. He found the fastenings in the back of her suit and tugged, forcing the garment from her shoulders and down to the floor, leaving her naked. He stepped back to gaze at her and Sky found herself blushing uncharacteristically. She started to cover herself with her hands, but he caught her wrists and gently moved them apart.

"Let me look at you," he whispered. "After all, I'm no one. I may not even exist. A man without a name can't hurt you."

"I know your name," she said, her voice hushed. She moved toward him and his arms went around her, drawing her close to him. His head lowered to hers again, and she shuddered as his lips brushed against the side of her neck.

"No, no names tonight," he said softly. "Not here. Not now."

His hands moved to barely graze her skin, first down her back, then up her sides, over her breasts. His fingers traced a path that his lips quickly followed and red-hot coals ignited inside her as his mouth painted promises, hot, burning promises she could not resist. He teased and tormented her until Sky sank down to the floor, unable to stand any longer, bringing him with her. She was suddenly reminded of another time they had melted together in passion. This time he would not roll away and leave

187

her wanting. This time Eagle and Sky would fly together. Laughing aloud, she pulled at the fastenings of his uniform and soon his clothing joined hers, flung to the far side of the room.

His hot flesh met hers and she cried out in wonder. They joined in one smooth movement and Sky felt the world explode around her. Then she was melting, she was dying, she was soaring above the clouds, reaching upward even as Eagle's flesh seared into hers; she arched against him, seeking the journey, feeling her soul stretch out, her mind soar beyond the sky. But she wanted more. She wanted to join with his thoughts again and let him join with hers. She wanted to stop him, wanted to tell him that she didn't want just his body, she wanted all of him—the Eagle he was in his innermost thoughts and being, the anguished child she had glimpsed, the man who had no name. Yes, she wanted to take him inside her body, but also inside her soul. She tried to speak but couldn't. She tried to push him away but found herself drawing him closer still. As the stars crashed down around her and within her, spiraling her upward to meet them, at the last moment Sky pulled her emotions back, unwilling to touch the bright ecstasy they offered. Eagle froze, as though he sensed her silent withdrawal.

"Sky?" he whispered, his mouth against her hair.

"I desire more than just your body," she said, her voice hushed with a hurt she had not even realized existed. She wove her fingers through his midnight hair and turned his face to hers, gazing deeply into his troubled eyes. "Will you ever let me truly join with you—with your mind? Will you ever trust me?"

"Just let me make love to you," he said, smoothing her hair back from her face, his touch gentle, loving. "Maybe what you and Telles have told me is true. If it is, I've been living a lie for fifteen years, and I have no name, no past, no soul. But right now, here with you, I don't need a name. Let me possess you, Sky, though I can't let you possess me. Not yet. Maybe never."

His mouth moved over hers and she was lost. The crescendo came all at once for both of them, and the stars, the bright stars exploded inside her, fragmented into her heart, pulsated through her soul, and sent her straight into the heavens. As they glided back to reality together in each other's arms, Sky looked up at the thousand twinkling lights glimmering through the curved glass above them. One tear traced its way down her cheek before she closed her eyes against the distant suns.

Chapter Ten

Eagle donned his uniform and crossed to stand beneath the stars while Sky dressed. There had been no lengthy holding or caressing afterward, yet it hadn't seemed awkward either. He didn't think she had wanted to prolong the aftermath of their ecstasy any more than he had dared. It was too painful. Ecstasy. He grimaced at the window. Oh, he felt sure Sky had enjoyed their lovemaking, but there had been another level, a higher plateau he knew they would never know—the intertwining of their minds. He couldn't help it. He wasn't ready yet to hear the truth and if he let Sky into his mind, he knew it would be forthcoming. The truth.

He spun around in time to catch the vulnerable look on Sky's face as she fastened the last closure on her uniform and rose from their impromptu bed. She masked her features quickly when she realized he was watching her, drawing herself up with the same quiet dignity he remembered from other occasions when she felt herself outmatched or outgunned. She walked silently to the door of the observation room and pressed the control to slide it open. She took a step back as though startled.

"Telles. How did you—Come in."

Eagle rested his hands on his hips as his friend walked in and gave first him the once-over and then Sky. He had no doubt the man's trained eye had taken in every rumpled edge of clothing and every tousled hair on both their heads. He didn't expect the disapproval however, or the disgusted way Telles shook his head and cursed.

"Hell, Eagle, don't you have a clue as to what's going

on? She comes up here to help you find out who you really are, and you—"

"Shut up." Anger, sudden and swift, crowded Eagle's mind. He took a step toward him, fists clenched at his sides. "You don't know what you're talking about, so just shut the hell up."

Telles turned to Sky. "Are you ready to help me now, Sky? And help your sister? You do still want to know where she is, don't you, or has the colonel here knocked that little thought out of your head while he was—"

With a roar, Eagle swung, his fist connecting with Telles's jaw. The two men fell to the floor and rolled, feet flailing, arms swinging.

"Stop it, both of you!" Sky shouted. "This is ridiculous!"

Telles pulled Eagle to his feet with both hands and slammed him against the bulkhead. "You heard the lady," he said, breathing heavily, keeping Eagle's shoulders pinned back.

"She's a captain, not a lady." Eagle spat out the words, then slammed his fist into his stomach. Telles doubled over with a gasp and fell to his knees, arms across his middle. The sound of his breathing was labored as he glared up at Eagle.

"She's more of a lady than you'll ever deserve," Telles said through clenched teeth, unable to stand. "Had enough, Colonel?"

"Yeah, I've had enough," Eagle said. "I've had enough of these games you're playing. This is just some new ploy by you rebels to trick me into opposing my father."

Telles shook his head, his face reflecting his obvious disgust. "You really don't trust anyone, do you?" He shot Sky a look. "Remember that, sweetness, when you're falling into his arms."

"Why don't you both just shut up?" Sky said. "Look, I don't give a *pefarking* damn about trust or tricks or anything. All I care about is finding my sister!"

"Then come on. Leave Eagle to his brooding. There's only one way to find out where Mayla is." Telles pulled her toward the doorway.

Eagle's head snapped up. "You're going to read his mind?"

"Yes. Apparently it's my only chance of finding my sister," she said.

He nodded. "That's good. You should do it then."

Sky bristled. "Well, I don't need your permission, Colonel. Come on, Telles."

Eagle wasn't just angry, he was livid. Why the news she was going to journey inside Telles's mind should send a shimmering wave of outrage through his veins he didn't know, but it danced down his spine and into his fingertips. He knew what an intimate joining it could be, to venture inside someone's mind. He didn't like it. He didn't like it one little bit. But he didn't have any right to say a thing, not even after what they'd just shared. Because he'd just been a world-class jerk—again. The knowledge made him lash out.

"Oh, and of course whatever you come back and tell me you've found in his head I should believe. Just like I should believe that I'm not Zarn's son because he says it's true. Give me a break."

He saw the effect of his words register on her features. Her lower lip trembled the slightest bit; her turquoise eyes flashed, first with pain, then with fire.

"What are you talking about?" she said.

"We have to trust what you say. That's the bottom line in this, isn't it?"

Telles stopped and turned back, one hand moving to rest protectively on her shoulder.

Eagle watched her as she swallowed, hard, before speaking. He hated himself for hurting her. He hated her for making him care.

"Yes, I see what you mean. If you don't trust me, what difference does it make what I tell you I have seen in your minds?"

"Exactly."

Their gazes locked for a space of time that seemed an eternity to Eagle. She broke the contest first, turning away, her back to him, her body trembling. He released his pent-up breath silently when she suddenly spun around, hands on her hips, turquoise eyes filled with fire.

"Don't worry, Colonel. I wouldn't touch your mind with a ten-foot pole, but before Telles and I leave you to grovel in your self-pity, I have a few things I want to say to you."

She turned to Telles, her fury obvious from the top of her head with its mane of sexy tousled hair, to the tips of her still-naked toes. She hadn't managed to get her boots on before Telles interrupted them.

"You should listen to your old friend, Telles. You will have to trust me—have to trust that I'm not pulling some kind of trick in your mind, putting in the very things I'm going to tell you I find. You're making yourself vulnerable, so be warned. But that's something Eagle will never have to worry about, because he'll never open himself to another human being—not his mind, not his soul. Zarn took that ability from him when he took his memories—if in fact he did take them at all. I guess we'll never know the answer to that." She broke off, took two steps forward, and shoved Eagle backward, hard. He slammed against the bulkhead, wishing he was back on Alpha Centauri, or on Station One, or anywhere else but facing Sky's wrath. He deserved it. He deserved more. And yet he couldn't stand any more.

"Sky, don't do this," he said.

"You see, Telles," she went on, thrusting her finger against Eagle's chest, "Zarn took more than his memories, he took his soul too. Isn't that right, Colonel? Didn't you lose your ability to trust, to believe, to *feel*?" She wanted to strike him, he could tell. She knotted up her fist and Eagle hoped she would hit him—anything to relieve the guilt settling in his heart. But she lowered her hand, her voice pitying. "People like him can't trust anyone else," she said softly. "They don't have the guts."

She spun away from him, but not quickly enough to hide her tears. "Take me out of here, Telles," she said. "Let's get down to business."

Telles gathered her into his arms and gave her a tight, hard squeeze. "Sure, angel." He glanced over at Eagle, his blue eyes narrowing to slits. "We'll let you know what we find out, Colonel. That is, if you're interested."

"Sure." One corner of Eagle's mouth curved up derisively. *Make her hate you*, something inside of him said. *Make her hate you and then you won't have to let her in.* "And let me know if she whispers your name too when she's writhing underneath you. Nice touch. Makes you feel almost like you're something special."

"You son of a bitch!" Sky pulled herself out of Telles's arms and crossed the short distance between them. She raised her hand to slap him, and he caught her by the wrist.

Go ahead, he silently told her. *Slap me. I deserve it. I deserve so much worse. It's all a lie, everything I'm saying, but I have to say it. I can't take the chance of letting you get any closer than you have.*

She froze, her arm in midair, her fingers curling inward as the rage ebbed out of her. With a choked cry, she turned and ran into the corridor with Telles close behind. He paused at the doorway and looked back, shaking his head in disgust.

"My mistake, Colonel. You are Zarn's son—the spitting image."

Eagle hated himself. In the space of a few moments, he had destroyed whatever feelings Sky might have had for him as well as his friendship with Telles. He stood in the silence of the deserted corridor and felt the oppression of the silence. It was over. Their brief union as friends, his friendship with Telles, his love for Sky.

Love for Sky?

Yes, he loved her. Loved the way she straightened her shoulders and took charge, loved how she wasn't afraid of anything and could wield a blaster as well as a man in a fight, loved the curve of her cheek and the glow of her eyes, loved her long silver-blond hair against his hands and the softness of her body beneath his. He loved her and it didn't matter, because he didn't know who he was. How could a man without a past love a woman like Sky? Was it true? Was Telles speaking the truth?

TO TOUCH THE STARS

My mistake, Colonel. You are Zarn's son—the spitting image. The cold wave of fear danced around him as Telles's words echoed through his mind. He wrapped his arms around himself as if to stave off the chill, bowing his head as the pain filled him again. He let it rock him, let it squeeze his heart and collide with his soul as he sank to his knees. He let the knowledge sear him, let it taunt him, let it invite him to the edge of the madness.

He was in a small room sitting in a huge chair from which wires and tubes protruded. No, the chair wasn't huge; he was small, skinny, his arms bound to the leather by energy strips and his legs shackled as well. He was screaming but there was no sound, and he realized the screaming was inside him because he was afraid to open his mouth and let the sound escape. A large helmet glided slowly downward toward him. It settled with a thud around his head, heavy, straining the fragile stem of his neck. Someone fastened it under his chin and the eyeholes were too big and too far apart. Two men were in the overly bright room but his eyes were blurred by tears and he couldn't make out their features. Then a jolt of energy coursed through him and the screaming inside his head stopped as the light above him grew brighter and brighter until it encompassed him. Desperately he sought for a lifeline, something to hold on to before the light utterly consumed him.

His father had told him stories of how a legendary creature, more noble than any other, once flew in the skies of Terra. The creature had been used in Andromedan literature as well to signify strength, honesty, and pride. There was an ancient quote from one of the books his father had been researching, and as a child he had memorized it. It began, "Rise up, rise up on the wings of an eagle. You shall be weary no longer. You shall fly with courage and strength." It was his favorite of all his father's stories. He would think of the eagle—he would remember its strength and courage and he would be strong.

The machine balked above him and suddenly a power unlike anything he could have ever imagined flooded

195

through his body, his mind, his soul, pumped through him, seeking out his memories, his dreams, and his spirit. Sweat poured down his back, pain laced through his brain, and yet he did not cry out. The agony of it seemed to go on forever, but at last the machine grew still and the helmet was lifted slowly from his head. A disembodied voice spoke to him, asking a somehow familiar question.

"What name do you choose?"

He swallowed hard, wishing the dryness from his throat; blinked, hoping the bright light would be turned from his eyes soon.

"Eagle," he whispered.

"Eagle," he said aloud. Eagle opened his eyes. He was on his knees in the observation room, tears drying on his cheeks. The dream. But it wasn't a dream at all. It was a memory.

"All right, I'm ready."

The lights in Kell's cabin were dimmed and the shielding firmly in place once again. Sky and Telles sat on the floor, cross-legged—her request—and Kell had already taken himself out of the cabin, begrudgingly.

"Now, this may feel strange at first," she cautioned him. "The important thing is to relax. Don't fight me."

Telles wiped the palms of his hands down the sides of the dark blue trousers he wore. "I'll try not to," he said. "Damn, Sky, I have to tell you this is harder for me than I thought it would be. I keep remembering—"

"Don't." She cut him off, reaching over to squeeze his hand. "This is nothing like what Zarn did to you. There are no machines, no rays, no pain. There is just my mind melding with yours, and I will stop whenever you tell me to do so, all right?"

He nodded but Sky noted a thin bead of sweat trailing down the side of his face. "I'm ready," he said, just the slightest tremor to his words.

Before she could even lift her hands to take off her silver band, a pounding suddenly sounded against the door, followed by loud voices in the corridor.

"What in the—" Telles jumped to his feet and crossed to the door, sending it sliding open.

Eagle and Kell stood nose to nose in the hallway, their brows meeting angrily in the center of their equally irate faces. Sky stepped into the corridor, hands on her hips.

"Call off your watchdog, Sky," Eagle demanded, turning to face her.

"What do you want?" She was rather proud of the haughty tone she managed.

"What I want is—" He broke off, his eyes burning into hers, telling her it wasn't over yet, not by a long shot. Something quickened between them and hope sprang anew in her heart.

Stupid heart, she admonished, lifting her chin a little as she waited for Eagle to continue.

"Yes?" she prodded.

He tore his gaze from hers and shrugged. "I want to come in."

"Out of the question—" Kell began, only to be cut off by Sky.

"Why?"

"Because I—" He stopped talking again and shook his head. "Telles might need me."

Sky arched one brow. Maybe their argument had done some good after all. "I thought you didn't trust Telles anymore. I thought you didn't give a damn."

"I trust him more than anyone else in this universe," he said quietly. He took a deep breath and released it explosively. "I give a damn."

Sky moved toward him. "What happened, Colonel? Did you have a second thought? Not the great Eagle— surely not."

"I thought about what you said. About what Telles said. I don't know what's going on, but I suppose I've got to trust someone. I trust Telles."

"But not me."

Something flickered in the depths of his green eyes. "Sky, I'm sorry. And I do trust you, to an extent. I just believe if it came down to your sister's life or the rest of us, we would all be expendable. And I'm not crazy about the idea of someone else running around in my head—not even you."

"You aren't needed in this experiment, so you don't have to worry."

Eagle leaned against the wall of the corridor, arms folded over his chest. "You aren't going to make this easy for me, are you? Okay, Captain. I want to know the truth, whatever it is. Maybe if I see it in Telles's mind first it won't be so hard to accept it in my own."

Sky pretended to consider. "If you come inside the room, you'll have to be part of the meld. Otherwise you might get pulled in accidentally and that would be dangerous, but then you remember that from our last experience together. But don't worry, Colonel. I won't be going into your mind, just your friend's."

"I understand."

Sky let him sweat for a minute, noting the tension around his lips, then nodded. "All right."

"Sky—Captain—really I must protest!" Kell moved between the two, his back to Eagle, his face only inches from hers. "You would not allow me inside the room while you probed the man's mind. Why should you allow this—this—" He broke off.

Sky opened her mouth and closed it twice before she could gather her thoughts. Why *was* she willing to let him come in?

"He's Telles's best friend."

"Don't let him in on my account," Telles interjected. "He may trust me, but I'm afraid I no longer return the favor."

"You see—even his friend no longer trusts him," Kell said, his eyes wide with anger.

"All right, damn it." She moved toward the open doorway, flinging her words back over her shoulder. "I want him to know I'm telling the truth about what I find in Telles's mind." Sky felt relieved to say it aloud. "If I bring him into the meld, there will be no doubts."

"And what of my doubts?" Kell asked.

Sky spun around, her heart beating a little faster. "You doubt me, Kell?"

His blue face was flushed, something she'd never seen before; purple shadows were evident in his cheeks. "I doubt your ability to withstand the allure of this man! For all you know, he could be a telepath himself, just waiting to get you alone in order to cause some kind of damage to your mind."

The memory of their tryst in the observation room made Sky turn away for a moment to hide the consternation in her eyes. No, Eagle had not wanted to enter her mind then, and he didn't want to now. Suddenly she didn't want him to either. She turned back.

"I don't think that will be a problem. Since he isn't a telepath, I think I can keep him out of my thoughts. I'll still have some protection from the deflector in the internal shielding, you know. I won't enter Eagle's mind and he won't enter mine. I'll just allow him to see what I find in Telles's mind." She caught the relieved look that crossed the colonel's face and felt a small pang in her heart. She ignored it.

"Then include me as well," Kell demanded. "Allow me to go with you."

"No." Telles stepped up beside Sky. "I choose who goes inside my head, and it isn't you, Commander. Sorry."

"I apologize, Telles," Sky said hastily. "I shouldn't have presumed—perhaps you don't want Eagle to come either. It's your call."

Telles turned and faced the colonel. Sky didn't envy Eagle as the man turned the full bore of his gaze upon him. The colonel met his evaluating glare undaunted and after what seemed like an eternity, Telles nodded.

"All right, he can come." He shot Sky a grin. "Sounds like we're planning a journey to a pleasure planet, doesn't it? Tell you what, when this is all over I'll take you to one, okay, Sky?"

"Sure," she said with a smile.

"Sky wouldn't like a place like that." Eagle leaned against the bulkhead, his arms folded across his chest.

He had changed clothes, Sky noticed for the first time.

Instead of his usual plain jumpsuit, he wore sleek black trousers that dipped down at the waist into a V. An equally tight white shirt stretched over his muscles, accentuating his hard, washboard stomach and broad chest. His arms were bare, the muscular contours making her mouth dry with longing. She swallowed hard, then tossed her hair back from one shoulder and folded her arms over her chest.

"Sit down, Colonel. You don't have any idea of what I might like, and aren't likely to find out in the near future. I'm ready, Kell. Please leave us."

"Captain, I—I—" She turned to find Kell sputtering in fury. He shot her a look filled with more anger than she'd ever thought he was capable of feeling, then spun on his heel and stalked out of the room. Sky watched him go, feeling terribly guilty.

Sky slipped the silver band from around her forehead and laid it carefully next to her on the floor. Ah, then it was more than a fashion statement, as he'd suspected all along. Somehow the band was connected with her telepathic power.

"What is that?" he asked bluntly.

Sky glanced up at him, hesitant, then gestured toward the object. "It protects my mind," she admitted. "I am highly sensitive, even for a telepath, and it is . . . difficult at times to keep the thoughts of others out. This device acts as a shield."

Reasonable answer. Whether it was true or not remained to be seen. Eagle sank down next to her and prepared himself for the ordeal to come. And he had no doubt that it would be an ordeal. Even when his and Sky's minds had joined together before when she had tried to contact Mayla, in spite of the gentleness of her psychic touch he had been terrified. Now he knew why. If Telles's accusations were true . . . to have someone in his mind . . . He shuddered involuntarily and Sky glanced over at him, her beautiful face reflecting her curiosity before she turned back to Telles.

"I will begin very slowly," she said, "but in order to

begin we must all touch. To facilitate a better, smoother transition, I will touch your face, Telles, with one of my hands. Eagle, you take my other hand and Telles, take Eagle's free hand."

"I heard about this kind of thing on one of the pleasure planets," Telles quipped, "but I never thought I'd be part of one."

Sky blushed and Eagle watched the way the color flooded into her pale, peach-tinted cheeks, wishing he dared to lift his hand and brush his fingers, then his lips, against her skin. He shook the thought away. In spite of her promises not to delve into his mind, he felt sure she could glean his surface thoughts. Better bring them under control if he didn't want to make a fool of himself. Again.

"Let's begin," she said. Lifting one hand, she placed her fingers delicately on Telles's face, her index finger resting against his brow, thumb against his right cheek, the other three fingers pressing next to his left temple.

Eagle felt the breath leave his body as suddenly the cabin around them disappeared and he was sucked into another world, a vortex of color and silence. He stiffened, his mind rebelling against the sensation of nonreality when a clear, smooth thought dropped into him.

Eagle, it's all right. Trust me. Go with me. Ride the wave.
Immediately the tension left him. Ride the wave. He saw it then—a blue-green sweep of color moving through his mind; he saw Sky as well, beckoning him forward. Cautiously he checked his own thoughts and was satisfied she was keeping her word; she was staying out of his mind.

Come on, Eagle, she urged, *Telles is waiting.*
He swallowed hard. This was why he had come. For Telles. To find the location of the child. He nodded and took a step forward into the melee of color. The wave seized him, drew him in, and suddenly he wasn't just riding the wave, he was the wave, and Sky was the wave. He could feel her inside him and he inside her, and yet there was no exchange of thought. He felt strangely bereft. Now the colors intensified and new ones collided

with the blue-green wave—purple and pink, dashes of red and chartreuse, swirling around them as Sky took them deep, deep, deep into Telles's subconscious. There was no time and yet it seemed to go on forever as they traveled downward, though he knew there was in reality no down. No up. The thought began to shake him and all at once he felt Sky's soothing touch against his fear. He relaxed.

There, she said. *There is where we must go.*

Eagle felt Sky turn him in the right direction and he saw an intense mixture of color, dark, foreboding.

What is it? he thought to her and felt a warm rush of satisfaction in return.

It's all right, she said. *This is the very center of your friend's mind. This is where the secret hidden part of himself lies. This is where we will find Mayla's location, or not.*

Together they moved in toward the whirling maelstrom—for that was what it appeared to Eagle, a swirling mass of colliding molecules, confused, erratic. Eagle drew back and Sky waited for him.

He's a brave man, Eagle murmured back to her. *He's willing to let us see who he really is.*

Yes, Sky agreed. *And that takes the highest kind of courage.*

Eagle noted her pointed remark but refused to dwell on it. Not here. Not now. He took a deep breath. But there was no breath. He pushed the confusing reality thoughts from his mind as all at once he had the sensation of Sky's hand in his. He looked down. He could see himself now and he could see Sky. She smiled at him, her turquoise eyes filled with understanding.

Better? she asked.

He nodded, feeling such great relief he was ashamed.

Then let's go in. She glanced back at him. *And Eagle—it's all right to be afraid. This is new territory for you. Don't fight your fear. Face it.*

He had no answer for her presumptuous remark and instead concentrated on bracing himself for the cachophony of color and confusion they were about to enter. They held hands and walked into it.

Eagle gasped as the kaleidoscope of colors and sounds met him. Sky seemed undaunted and continued to move forward. He clung to her hand feeling like the worst sort of coward.

Do you see the dark colors? she asked. He nodded, too numb to speak. *The darkness denotes trauma or great sorrow.* She shook her head. *Telles has endured both to a large degree. The darkness gathers even deeper ahead in order to protect the core of who he is.*

They walked into the darkness together and Telles met them there. One second there was only the swirling gray, and the next he was in front of them. Incredible. Eagle reached out a hand and touched Telles's arm. Solid as a rock.

Are you ready, Telles? she asked. He nodded and Sky took each of the men by the hand and together they turned and walked into the darkest part of his mind.

Eagle felt completely disoriented for a minute as the gray haze deepened, becoming almost black, spinning around them like smoke wafting from a chimney.

Look, Sky said softly.

All at once forms began to solidify around them. Shapes of people, men, women, children. Telles walked in to stand amidst them.

Who are they? Eagle asked.

These are the people who have most influenced Telles in his life, she answered. She pointed to a tall man clad in a long, dark blue robe. *This is his father, Kalah, one of the Seekers. He shaped Telles's young years.* She turned to the woman beside him. *His mother, Manila—she loved him more than life itself. She was the first of the Seekers' families to die. This man was his father's best friend, Toma N'chal.*

Toma N'chal. Eagle gazed at the kind, strong face and felt a panic unlike any he'd ever experienced seize him. He could feel himself withdrawing, moving back from the images, feel himself being propelled outward, away from the darkness. He couldn't breathe. He had no heartbeat. He couldn't breathe.

Eagle. Sky's voice found him and her mental arms

closed around him. *You mustn't leave me*, she said anxiously. *You are withdrawing from Telles's mind and I can't stop now to take you out. If you let go of my link, you'll be swept away.*

I can't do this, he said.

Yes, you can.

No he couldn't. He was not ready for this. He and Telles had grown up together on Rigel. He and Telles had grown up together on Rigel. He knew his friend's mother and father. He knew them. He became aware of his heartbeat again, felt his chest rise and fall as air entered him again.

Come, Sky said to him, pulling him back toward the darkness. *We'll find Mayla's handiwork.*

This time they did not enter the place where the images stood. Telles rejoined them, silently, and Eagle felt them rise up together, above the dark mist below. They were flying somehow. Flying through Telles's mind. He shivered with the power of it. No wonder his father feared the Cezans. No wonder he had tried to destroy them.

Tried to destroy them? Where had that thought come from? No, his father had done nothing to the Cezans. Nothing. They had destroyed themselves by betraying the Andromedan people.

Shhhhhh. Sky's voice startled him out of his reverie. *Stop thinking, Eagle. Stop trying to figure it all out. Look.*

She pointed downward. Below them was a long line of midnight blue, a streak of color against the gray. Then they were standing beside it, suddenly, magically. It stretched like a river at their feet. Telles knelt down beside it, one knee on the ground, his hands linked together over the other.

This is where Mayla touched Telles's mind, Sky told them.

Eagle glanced at Sky. She had her eyes closed, her hands stretched out toward the river of blue. He followed the path of her fingers and before his eyes the blue river rose, gyrating in front of them, spinning like a cyclone. The gray began to break up around it, to dissipate like smoke, parting like a dismal curtain to let in a beautiful picture hovering behind. Eagle could see a blue sky, the color as deep as a Rigelian ocean. Pink clouds drifted across the broad expanse and below, a beautiful city glimmered, its tall spires and buildings darting upward like ethereal monuments. The shapes were very familiar to Eagle. He'd been given his first medal in the tallest building, at his first Forces awards ceremony. The image sharpened, shifted, and he could see another, older building, large, once magnificent, now half-demolished, dirty, its columns eroded by time.

The palace, he whispered.

The picture changed again, this time giving them an aerial view looking downward on some sort of compound ringed with twisted columns. In the center was a large building, three huge squares built one on top of the other, growing progressively smaller.

The temple, he said.

With a start, Eagle realized what he was looking at. He turned to Sky. Telles rose and crossed to stand beside him.

Andromeda. Eagle made the pronouncement, feeling some sense of relief sweep over him.

That's where my sister is, Sky said, and he heard her own relief, tempered with fear. *Mayla is in one of those places we just saw—either in one of the government buildings, in the old palace of my family, or . . .* She looked directly into Eagle's eyes. *In the temple of the Seekers.*

Chapter Eleven

The *Defiant* entered orbit around Andromeda, and Sky leaned back in the command chair, releasing her pent-up breath in a soft, soundless sigh. She had set course as soon as she had brought herself and Eagle out of Telles's mind. Eagle hadn't said one word of opposition, but neither had he acknowledged what she had shown him in his friend's thoughts. At the moment, she didn't really care. To be on her way at last to her sister—a thousand sons of Zarn could not shake her elation.

She had kept her distance from Eagle since they had started for her homeworld. It had taken three days to reach Andromeda, traveling at top warp, and she had spent most of the first day in her cabin, finishing the healing process she had begun on her shoulder wound, resting for what might lie ahead. The second day she had met with Kell, Telles, Eagle, and P'ton to discuss how they would get by the Forces security system that guarded Andromeda. She had been proud of how cool and aloof she had managed to stay, in spite of Eagle's green eyes burning a hole through her during the entire meeting.

Now they were here, at her homeworld, a place she had not seen in twelve years. Andromeda. Just the name brought back memories so poignantly sweet that tears filled her eyes as she gazed at the viewscreen. It was a blue-green world, covered by pale clouds that kept the planet shrouded in secrecy—until Zarn's forces had ripped away the veil of privacy and contentment. Now the clouds remained, but Andromedans were little more than slaves, and the once-proud people viewed with no greater respect than any of Zarn's conquered empires. But it was all about to change. Sky leaned forward, her hands linked together in front of her.

"Are we ready?" she asked P'ton. He nodded and she settled back against the chair trying not to look at the helmsman's station where Eagle sat.

It had been decided at their meeting the day before that they would attempt to enter Andromedan space by using a code Eagle would provide. Eagle would fly the *Defiant*, and if all went well, the code would bring down the force field protecting the planet long enough to let them slip into the atmosphere. How Telles had managed to circumvent the defense system and bring Mayla to Andromeda—or why—none of them could fathom, and Sky had not been able to discover during her probe into his mind. They had seen no details of his forgotten journey, only the destination.

Once they breached the force field, they wouldn't be able to shield themselves from the Forces' sensors, but they could sure run like hell once they got inside. Eagle said he could do it, could evade the ships and find a safe place to land to begin their search for Mayla. Now if only he was telling the truth . . .

"Prepare to transmit code," she ordered. Kell moved closer to her chair and placed one hand on the high back. She was glad for his presence. Things had been strange between them lately, what with his anger about Eagle and her own tension. After this was over, she would sit down with her friend and they would have a long talk, straighten everything out.

"Transmit."

"Aye, aye, Captain," Eagle said. He glanced back and to her astonishment, winked. For some reason she felt the tension leave her shoulders, and she had the oddest sensation that everything was going to be all right.

Then everything went terribly wrong.

"The shield isn't going down," Eagle said, his fingers flying across the instruments in front of him. "We're going to have to pull up."

"What's wrong?" Sky darted a look at Kell, and he

crossed the bridge to Eagle's side, taking the empty navigation seat beside him. He began punching in a series of commands and after a moment, turned and nodded at Sky.

"It isn't responding. Hard about."

"Hard about, Colonel," she snapped. "Why isn't your code working? Or is this another one of your tricks?"

"It's possible—no, it's probable—that after the fiasco on his ship, my father contacted Andromeda and told them to change the codes."

"Damn." Sky knotted one fist. "Now what?"

"Let me try another angle. I know a few tricks that have been known to fool a shielding program. Maybe I can still get it to lower."

"The dragon?" Telles's voice came from the lift and Sky turned. He moved across the bridge to Eagle and stopped beside him. His friend glanced up and nodded.

"Yeah. It worked on Cantus 5."

"Sure, but that was an old security system. You know Zarn keeps his best defenses around Andromeda and Rigel."

"It's worth a try."

"What is the 'dragon'?" Kell asked, piqued out of his silence by his curiosity.

"Just a program Eagle came up with that keeps a certain part of a shielding system busy while another command sneaks in and orders certain parts to lower. If it works, it'll punch holes in the shield and we'll be able to slip through."

"But won't they still catch us with their sensors?"

Eagle and Telles exchanged glances.

"That's why we call it the dragon," Telles explained. "When we hit the holes in the shield, for an instant our image will waver. In that instant, we'll send a burst to the Forces computer telling it that what it is seeing is a dragon."

Sky stared at him open-mouthed. She shut her lips together abruptly, then shook her head. "A dragon," she repeated. "I might have left your brain more scrambled than I thought."

Telles chuckled. "They'll be trying to figure it out for at least a few minutes, and that will give us time to evaporate—to head for a secluded landing place."

"That Eagle will find for us, no doubt."

He shrugged. "We haven't got a whole lot of choices. Remember, you're the one who was talking about trust."

"Yeah, right. Trust." Sky turned to face two clear green eyes. "What about it, Colonel—can I trust you to help me find my sister?"

Eagle held her gaze without speaking for too long before he finally nodded. "Yes, I'll help you."

"And then what? What happens after we find her?"

He clenched his jaw and looked away, back to the viewscreen displaying Andromeda in all of her glory. A darkness darted like a shadow across his eyes.

"Then?" he said softly. "You get your sister back."

He turned away and Sky felt the bond between them once again, and this time it told her Eagle was hiding something from her, something dangerous, something likely to break the fragile thread of trust between them.

The landing was rough. Eagle switched off the viewscreen computer and for a rare change the bridge window became exactly that: a window. The twisted blue-green vegetation outside the *Defiant* wafted against the window, the large, fanlike leaves almost covering the ship itself. The "dragon" had worked. He had successfully punched holes in the force field and slipped through, convincing the Forces' computer it was seeing a mythological creature, not a space vehicle, confusing the system and buying them the time they needed to dart across the sky and evade the sensors' second sweep of the area.

Eagle had known where to land, just as he had promised Sky, and had settled the ship down in a secluded wilderness area near the temple of the Seekers. He frowned. He didn't like being there, didn't want to explore the ancient ruin, but it was the most logical place for Mayla to have hidden, and he had to help Sky find her. Now, more than ever, he was determined to use Mayla as a means by which to force his father to change.

He thought Sky would understand; still, he couldn't take the chance on her negating his plan under the guise of protecting her sister. He wasn't going to let anything happen to Mayla, but he felt sure there would be no real way to assure Sky of that.

Sky. Their journey together through Telles's mind had shown him again this woman's inner essence, had bound him to her on a deeper level. He was still struggling with her claims of his parentage, still too afraid to let her inside his own mind, but he had finally found the courage to admit, at least to himself, that he loved her. What she felt for him, he hadn't a clue. She stood now, just behind him, staring out at the lush landscape of her homeworld, her fingers biting tensely into the headrest of his chair.

"Where are we?" she whispered, her voice filled with something he couldn't define—fear, awe, trepidation? Or was she just overwhelmed because she was home again, at long last?

"We aren't too far from the Seekers' temple," Telles said, stepping up and peering through the window. "Do you see that large stone?"

Sky leaned forward and squinted her eyes. "Near that big tree? Yes."

"That's a sort of guidepost, a marker, leading to the temple."

"Sky."

Eagle glanced up at the man who had spoken. Kell's blue eyes were like hard shards of glass. He had opposed their coming to Andromeda, sure it was some kind of trick, positive that there was no way Telles could have brought Mayla to a world so well guarded by the Dominion, and lived. Eagle had his doubts too, but he knew what he had seen in his friend's mind. Perhaps they should have allowed Kell to come with them into Telles's mind. Leaving him out of the loop had definitely caused a rift between him and Sky and had obviously heightened his suspicions.

Sky turned to face him, her hesitance obvious. "Yes, Kell?"

"I am asking you again not to do this. This is a trick."

He shot Eagle a furious look, then turned his gaze to Telles. "I don't know how they fooled you but I assure you there is no possible way your sister could have been brought to Andromeda without the Dominion being alerted."

"They haven't been alerted to our presence this time," she countered. "Perhaps Telles used the 'dragon' to gain entrance when he brought her."

"How do you know they haven't been alerted?" Kell said sharply. "Because *he* says so?" He gestured at Eagle with one hand, then folded both behind his back, as if aware he was becoming too emotional. His voice calmed. "Sky, I will not follow you into this trap."

Her chin lifted and her smooth jaw tightened. "Then I will go without you."

Kell held her gaze, his own pointed chin rising, his eyes becoming hooded, wary. "Very well. That is your decision." He spun on his heel and left the bridge, the doors of the lift sliding shut behind him with solid finality. Sky stared impotently after him before striding across the room to the lift. She stopped and looked back at Telles and Eagle. P'ton and Cordo were busy in engineering and for a moment, the camaraderie, the connection, was back between the three of them in full force.

"I'm going to my quarters for a few moments to prepare. Please meet me in the docking bay in fifteen minutes." She pressed the button beside the doors. They parted and she disappeared into the lift.

Eagle watched her stalk into the confines of the elevator, her back ramrod stiff, her shoulders taut, and felt his admiration for the woman flood over him again. What strength, what courage in the face of overwhelming odds. If only he truly was an Andromedan, perhaps . . . He pushed the thought abruptly away. He was not an Andromedan. He refused to accept it. He didn't know why he was experiencing the strange waking dreams, or why Telles insisted on sticking to this bizarre story of Zarn's treachery against him, but he felt, to the core of his spirit, that he was not Andromedan. Wouldn't he feel it, being back on Andromeda? And he had been here many times over the years and never—His thoughts stopped as though they had hit a stone wall.

He had never been to the Seekers' temple. How had he known where to land the ship? He shot a look over at Telles. He had never been here either. How did he know about the stone marker?

"What's going on?" he said, watching his friend's face carefully. "You've never been here before."

Telles turned from looking out the wide window and raised one golden eyebrow. "I beg your pardon? I was born here. My father brought me to the temple twice a week."

Eagle rose from his seat, running one hand through his hair before facing the man with his doubt. "Telles, how do you know that someone hasn't implanted *these* thoughts in your mind?" He saw the barest glimmer of fear dart across the blue-gray eyes and quickly disappear. Eagle moved closer to his friend, ready to press his point.

"What are you talking about?" Telles asked.

Eagle leaned back against the control panel next to him and folded his arms across his chest.

"What if these memories you think you're having about being the son of a Seeker, about my father probing your mind and erasing your memories—what if *those* thoughts are the ones that have been placed in your mind—by the rebels? If Mayla has the kind of power I suspect she has, it would have been simple for her to do that, especially if you were almost dead, too weak to resist her."

Again, the brief flicker of fear. Eagle felt a sad sort of triumph. Telles wasn't as sure about all of this as he purported to be.

"Yes, what you're saying might be true," he said. Eagle couldn't speak for a minute. He'd expected more denials, more arguments, not this careful capitulation. Then Telles continued and he knew he'd been very expertly trapped by his own words, hoisted on his own petard. "But there's only one way to find out."

"And what would that be?"

Telles's gaze shifted from Eagle's to the blue-green jungle outside the *Defiant's* window. "Our answers lie in there, Eagle. In the temple of the Seekers. Now," he folded his own arms in mirrorlike imitation, "the question is, do you have the guts to face the truth? Do you have the courage to find out who the hell you really are?"

Eagle couldn't help the quick glance toward the mammoth stone in the distance, couldn't help the sharp intake of breath. He'd rather face a hundred Centaurian bone-disjointers than walk inside the ancient ruins of the Seekers' temple. Telles was right. It would take courage for him to search their archives and prove to his friend there was no record of his existence on Andromeda.

A cold sweat broke out across the back of his neck and on the palms of his hands. *The archives?* What archives? Everyone knew the writings and records of the Seekers— the great historians and philosophers of Andromeda— had been destroyed by their own people after Zarn's Forces arrived and eradicated the threat of the slavers, placing the world under his protection. All records of Andromedan history were gone. Then why did he know they existed? Why did he have a very clear picture in his mind of exactly where those ancient archives were located?

He staggered a little as the blood rushed away from his head, and Telles held out a steadying hand against his shoulder.

"Eagle, what is it?"

"Nothing. I—" He broke off and shook his head. "Nothing. Sky's waiting. We'd better get going."

"You didn't answer me." Telles's fingers tightened on his shoulder, keeping him from moving. "The answer for both of us lies in the temple of the Seekers. Are you willing to look for the truth, and accept it when we find it?"

"If we find it."

Telles smiled, a grim, tight smile. "We'll find it."

Eagle straightened his shoulders and Telles's hand fell away. "All right," he agreed. "If this is what it takes to make you realize you're the one being duped, then I'll help you search for this so-called proof." He turned and let his gaze sweep over his friend. When this was all over, Zarn would kill Telles unless Eagle could convince him otherwise. "If we don't find it," he said, "you have to come back with me to the Forces."

Telles's mouth lifted in a real smile. "So your father can execute me for treason? I don't think so."

"He won't. I'll see to that."

"You aren't exactly on his A list anymore, bud."

"I'll make things right with my father," Eagle said, emphatically. "Say it, Telles. If we don't find this 'evidence,' you'll come back with me. We'll rejoin the Forces, I'll get a new assignment, and it'll be just like the old days."

"Is that really what you want? The old days?"

Eagle didn't answer.

Telles sighed, toying with one of the scraps of material wound around the end of one long golden braid. "All right," he said. "I can agree because I know what we'll find inside the temple. I know this is true. I am the son of an Andromedan Seeker, and so are you."

Eagle clapped one hand on his friend's shoulder and shook him slightly. "We'll find out, together."

They started toward the lift and Telles stopped, turning and raising one brow. "But I'm not cutting my hair," he said.

Eagle laughed until the doors to the lift shut behind them. His laughter died away as they traveled down to meet Sky in the belly of the ship. He felt pain in his hands and realized he was clenching his fists so tightly at his sides that his nails had broken the skin and his palms were bleeding. He wiped his palms on his trousers.

"Courage," Telles whispered.

Courage, Eagle silently echoed. He was beginning to wonder if he knew the meaning of the word.

Sky leaned back against a tree and watched Telles and Eagle evaluate the denseness of the junglelike terrain stretching before them. After Kell's fit of temper—that was the only way she knew to describe what had happened on the bridge—she had gone to her cabin and paced, weighing his disapproval and his advice. In the end, she knew she had to take the chance, even if it proved to be a trick. But she wasn't walking blindly, innocently into anything. She had donned the tynarium droid suit and as she did, was struck by the irony of the situation.

She had first worn that suit to attack Station One and rescue her sister. There she had met Eagle and her world had been sent spinning into a vortex from which she had still not yet been able to extract herself. Now Eagle was helping her find her sister and she was wearing the suit again for protection. Why Eagle was being so cooperative she couldn't fathom, unless he was beginning to believe Telles's claims they were both Andromedans. Surely it wasn't because he cared anything about her. Her face still burned every time she thought of their tryst beneath the stars. It seemed almost like a dream, as though it had never really happened. As surreal as their first mental touching had been so long ago.

Could it possibly be true Eagle was the son of a Seeker? She lifted her hand unconsciously to touch the silver band around her forehead. If only he would let her inside his mind, she could end this debate. But only for herself, for Eagle didn't trust her. Until Mayla was found and brought to safety, Eagle would always think everything she did and said was tied to saving her sister. She closed her eyes and let the cool breeze of Andromeda brush against her face. How good it was to be home. She hadn't realized until now how much she had missed it. Since coming back had never been an option, she had blocked all dreams of returning to Andromeda, all memories of her happy childhood days there. To remember would be to torture herself with something she could never have. Now she was here with Eagle—and that made her homecoming all the more intense. If only she could know for sure that he was truly on their side. If only she could trust him and he could return that trust. She opened her eyes and her gaze drifted over him where he stood talking to Telles.

He was so handsome. His dark hair had gotten slightly longer in the days they had spent together, and she found the habit he had of raking it back from his face oddly endearing. His face. Had there ever been a face so strong, so filled with determination, so square-jawed with confidence? And yet she had seen the other side of that strength—seen the vulnerable man who needed her, needed to be reassured he still existed. He glanced over at her just then, his eyes as green as some of the fernlike plants around his feet. His gaze quickened when he saw she was looking at him, and a slight smile curved one corner of his mouth before he turned his broad shoulders back toward Telles. She loved him, and the knowledge startled her. She loved him. She loved his square, rough hands, and the way he gestured with them as he talked. She loved the slight crook in the bridge of his nose and the way his mouth hardened into that grim, determined line, but could just as quickly alter into a sensual smile. She loved the faint crinkles at the corners of his eyes. She loved the fact that he was loyal to his father, even if his father was a lying, murdering bastard. She loved that the more he had to face what his father had done to Andromeda, the more he struggled with that same loyalty.

She loved him. With a groan she closed her eyes again and leaned her head back against the huge, rough-barked tree behind her. Footsteps, hurried, pounding, startled her into alertness, and she opened her eyes to find Eagle towering over her, his hands moving to circle her upper arms, his face dark with concern.

"Sky, what is it? Are you all right?"

She stared at him, open mouthed, then found her voice. "I'm fine. What's the matter with you?"

"You groaned and threw your head back. I just thought—" He broke off and dropped his hands from her arms. "You've been through a lot in the last few days, you know. Are you sure you're up to this?"

A smile touched her lips. He was concerned. The man never ceased to amaze her. Shouting at her one minute, caressing her the next.

"I'm really all right. I was just—just yawning," she finished lamely.

Eagle's gaze swept over her, taking in the droid suit, dissproval settling over his features.

"Why in the name of—why are you wearing that contraption? It will just slow us down."

"It gives me the strength of twenty men," she said, unable to look away from his eyes, aware, as always, of the heat between them, even when they weren't touching.

"Yes, I'm quite familiar with what it enables you to do," he said dryly. "The first time I saw you I thought you were an android. Imagine my surprise when you pulled off your head and instead were a beautiful woman."

Sky blinked before laughing self-consciously. "Why, Colonel, I think that's the first nice thing you've ever said to me."

It was his turn to blink now, and a look of sincere regret flashed across his features. "Is it?" he said softly, lifting one hand to lightly touch the side of her face. "That's a shame. There are so many nice things I want to say to you, Sky. So many nice things I want to do to you."

"Ahem."

Sky felt both frustrated and relieved by Telles's not-so-subtle interruption. *You can't trust him,* her inner voice screamed. And at the same time, another, stronger voice whispered, *But you love him. Would you—could you— love a murderer? Maybe Telles is right. Maybe he's not his father's son.*

"Ready?" Telles asked, his tone flat but somewhat amused. He held something at his side, something long and sharp.

"What's that?" Sky stared as he held out the weapon for her inspection. It had a wooden handle and a huge, curved metal blade. "Where in the world did you get that?"

"It's a packing splitter," he explained. "Pretty ancient actually, but I found it in your cargo hold. You must have an antiques collector among your crew."

She nodded. "Srad, my engineer. He collects old things." Sky smiled, imagining Srad's face once he discovered something from his precious collection was missing. "I'd put that back if I were you," she advised. "You wouldn't like to see Srad get angry."

"We need it to cut our way through this jungle." He

217

waved his hand toward the dense vegetation in front of them.

"Let's cut through it with phasers. Wouldn't that be faster?"

"We can't," Eagle explained. "We can't risk the noise or the heat. Sensors would pick them up."

"Then are we ready?" Telles asked again. "We've got to reach the temple before dark."

Sky glanced upward. It was only an hour or so after sunrise. They had plenty of time, as long as the Dominion Forces didn't discover their presence.

"Yes, let's go."

Telles took the lead, chopping the thick brush and long, stiff-limbed branches that wound over what he said was once a road leading to the temple. She and Eagle followed in silence, stopping now and then to help him clear the hewn limbs from their path. To her surprise, as they walked, Eagle started another conversation.

"Did you come here often as a child?" he asked.

"Can you believe that I've never been to this particular part of Andromeda in my life?" Sky admitted. "I never really knew much about the Seekers. My mother loved history and insisted on teaching me of Andromedan history herself, instead of using a Seeker as a teacher, as the Cezans usually did." She smiled, picturing her mother's face for a moment. She'd been beautiful, but more than that, she'd been a wonderful mother.

"I think now that perhaps she sensed what was going to happen in the future and wanted the time with me. I was her only daughter, then. She died only days after Mayla was born." Tears glazed her eyes and she blinked them back hurriedly. This was no time for morbid recollections. "But why did the Seekers build their temple in such a remote, unapproachable area?"

"It wasn't so remote or unapproachable fifteen years ago," Telles said as he hacked through another patch of blue-green bramble. "The Seekers liked their privacy, and it was a sanctuary where they could study in peace without the distractions of the outside world. But over the years the road has fallen into disuse and the jungle has grown up around it. Even the Forces won't come out here. They're afraid of the place."

"Afraid?" Eagle helped him pull a large branch from the path. "Of what?"

Telles glanced back over one shoulder and shrugged. "It's said that the ghosts of the Seekers who were slain by Zarn walk the halls of the temple. Who knows, maybe we'll run into our fathers."

Eagle fell silent and Sky felt a sudden compassion surge through her. She reached over and took his hand. He looked up in surprise, then squeezed her fingers tightly in his, pulling her closer to his side. They walked in companionable silence for what seemed like hours when Telles finally stopped walking, his arm hanging limp at his side as though broken.

"Need a break?" Eagle asked, grinning. "You Andromedans always were weaker than Rigelians."

Telles glared at him, hot, sweaty, and obviously in no mood for banter, especially on that subject.

"You think you can do better? Have at it."

"Wait a minute," Sky said, moving to stand between the two tall men. "Let me cut the path. All I have to do is connect the energy ports on my suit and I'll have the strength of twenty men. I can plow a road through here in no time. I don't know why I didn't think of it sooner."

Telles handed her the blade, but before she could even curl her fingers around the broad handle, Eagle plucked it out of her grasp.

"I'll cut the path," he said.

"Why?" she demanded. "Because I'm a woman? With this suit I'm stronger than both of you."

"Not because you're a woman," he said, sliding his hand down the front of his shirt, splitting the closures. He pulled the cloth apart and the harsh invectives Sky had been prepared to hurl at him died in her throat.

"Then what?" she said, her gaze glued to the thick swirl of dark hair across the broad, sculptured chest. She ran her tongue unconsciously over her lower lip as he tied the shirt around his waist.

"You should save the energy in that thing for a time

when it might be really necessary—life or death. I can handle this."

"Uh, sure," she heard herself saying as he turned and began attacking the undergrowth. "I think you're right." He shot her a look of surprise over one shoulder, then shrugged and lifted the blade above his head, bringing it down with a resounding whack.

She followed him, Telles behind her. It was good for him to do something physical like this, she reasoned, trying to keep her mind off the sudden curious aching inside of her, the yearning she wanted desperately to ignore. She shook her head, wishing she could shake the slow burn from her veins. Yes, chopping through a jungle would take his mind off what might possibly lie ahead, what they might discover. In the meantime, what could possibly take her mind from the thought of making love to this man? She knew she must look like a love-sick schoolgirl, drooling over the sleek, well-honed muscles rippling through his arms as he swung the blade through the undergrowth, but she couldn't help it. She couldn't help but admire the slope of his back, the narrowness of his waist in contrast to the broad shoulders. Once or twice she had to restrain herself from walking up and wrapping her arms around him, pressing her lips against the bare, hot flesh of his back. When those urges came upon her, she thought desperately of Mayla, of her parents, of anything but Eagle. Or she tried.

At midday they took a break, sitting down and opening the container P'ton had filled with food for them. Sky leaned back against a tree, grateful she no longer had the temptation of Eagle bare to the waist in front of her. Her relief was short lived. He came strolling up just then and plopped down beside her, cross-legged. She groaned inwardly and closed her eyes, trying to ignore the pulsating fire pumping through her body.

"Berry?"

She opened her eyes and Eagle was only inches away from her, holding a *mekalb* berry to her lips. Unable to speak, she opened her mouth and allowed him to place the fruit on her tongue. Juice dribbled down her chin, and he wiped it away with his finger, then stuck his finger back in his own mouth. Sky blinked, then scrambled to her feet.

"I need to—need to—I'll be back in a minute." Walking quickly, she plunged into a dense part of the forest surrounding them and stood, trembling for a full minute. What was the man trying to do? No, she knew the answer to that—he was trying to seduce her again. But why? She had nothing he could possibly want, no secrets to entice from her, no information. She refused to entertain the thought that he might simply want her for herself.

As she stood there, trying to gather the shreds of her poise, something suddenly registered within her mind, within the deep, telepathic part of her mind. She felt it, as though a piece of information had just been dropped into her brain. Intrigued, Sky turned inward, searching for what had touched her. She found it. It was a subconscious knowledge, a telepathic insight. Mayla was not here. Sky drew in a quick breath. Mayla was not on Andromeda. She felt it to the fiber of her being. Of course there was no way to know for certain, not without removing her deflector band, or unless Mayla contacted her again. But she had learned over the years to trust her telepathic instincts. If Mayla wasn't on Andromeda—then what were they doing here? Was it a trick? But she had seen the information in Telles's mind. Making up her mind, she marched out of the forest toward the two men. They both looked up as she approached and she stopped, hands on hips, glaring down at them.

Eagle was still munching a bunch of *mekalb* berries and gazing up at the dense foliage above them.

"How much farther?" she demanded, turning to Telles.

"I'm not sure."

Eagle tossed one of the berries he held up into the air, caught it in his mouth, and crunched it as he remarked cheerfully, "Not much farther. There's another stone up ahead and that's the one-mile marker that—" He stopped speaking, his breath catching in his throat, his fingers crushing the berries in his hand. The juice ran down his fingers, blood-red. He stared at the stain, then lifted his horrified gaze to hers.

For a moment Sky forgot her suspicions, for the look on Eagle's suddenly ashen face affected her more than she wanted to admit.

"Eagle," she began, kneeling beside him and placing one hand on his arm. "Let me——"

Without warning, he jerked away from her and jumped to his feet. Throwing the crushed fruit to the ground, he began pushing his way through the jungle, the blade forgotten and abandoned. Sky followed quickly behind, never losing sight of him. He moved like a man possessed, his fingers digging into the twisted, heavy growth, bloody welts rising on his hands as he tore through the vegetation, bloody strips appearing on his arms as flexible limbs snapped and flailed him. He ignored them, pushing forward like a madman, sweat glistening on his body, until at last he came to a stop beside a large flat stone stuck in the ground like an ancient signpost. Sky stumbled up to his side just as he slid to the ground beside the rock.

"I've never been here," he said to himself, his eyes glazed. "I've never been here."

"Eagle," she said softly, kneeling down beside him. "You can't do this alone. Let me help you."

He looked at her, his face fierce, forbidding, closed. She trembled a little at the strength she saw in that face. The determination. Then she found her own courage and lifted one hand to touch his stiff jaw.

"Let me help you," she repeated softly.

With a groan, Eagle pulled her into his arms. She felt the tension of those strong arms as they wrapped around her and crushed her against his hard body. His mouth sought hers with a savage desperation and Sky was there, opening beneath his rough demand, allowing his need to possess her for the moment. He ravaged her mouth, holding her so tightly she thought her ribs might crack, then suddenly his hands slid to her waist, cradling her gently, his lips softening, moving to caress her neck, the hollow of her throat, the edge of her collarbone with infinite care.

"Eagle," she whispered, her arms around him, "you can handle this. We can handle it. Whatever lies ahead for you—for all of us—we can handle together."

"Why?" he said, his voice ragged, his breath rushing over her mouth, his hand cupping her face. "Why should you? If Telles is wrong and I am Zarn's son, and if what you believe is true, then my father killed your people. Why would you want to help me?"

"Because I believe Telles is right."

"Then that leaves me as a nameless, mindless—"

"No!" Her fingers covered his mouth to stop the terrible words, and he captured them with his lips, then moved his mouth back to hers, his need burning into her, his fear, his denial. She broke the embrace and threw her head back as she gazed up into his pain-filled eyes. "You aren't nameless—or mindless! You have a name." Sky hesitated. Should she tell Eagle of the name she had seen in his mind—Ranon? She was afraid, afraid if she told him it could trigger a violent reaction. She cleared her throat. And your mind—your mind can be healed, Eagle, if you'll only let me try."

Something connected them in that instant as Eagle's green eyes seemed to engulf her soul. Something inside of both of them. She knew it, she could feel it. Then it was gone. He had shut it down, sealed it off, denied it. He was shutting her out again. Carefully, he set her away from him, and Sky steeled herself not to feel the pain of this gentle rejection.

"I'm sorry. Forgive me, Sky," he said, reaching out and tucking one long strand of hair behind her ear. "Let's get to the temple." Hands on his hips, he glanced back at Telles, who was slowly approaching.

"Are you all right?" he asked, tossing Eagle his shirt.

Eagle nodded and used the garment to blot the sweat from his face before he slipped his arms into the sleeves. He left it open and Sky turned away, unwilling to let herself be tantalized again. She couldn't bear this anymore. Every time she reached out to him, he caressed her in return, devoured her senses and sensibilities, then left her wanting and angry. He was messed up—his brain probably so skewed, so twisted there was no telling who or what he might really be. And no way to find out. She had to pull back, protect herself, before it was too late.

Telles stood beside her, frowning. "What about you, Sky? You okay?" She nodded, unable to speak for a minute. "Maybe your sister will be waiting for you inside. Don't give up hope."

Hope. She almost laughed aloud. Her hope for her sister was quickly dying. Her hope for herself had already dissolved as Eagle gently disentangled himself from her arms, and her life.

"Maybe," she said, her voice little more than a whisper. But it wasn't true. Mayla wasn't here, she knew it, felt it in the pit of her stomach. So why were they here? She glanced at Eagle. Was all of this poignant struggle with the "truth" part of a well-orchestrated show? Was Kell right and she was walking into a trap? If so, she wasn't walking in blind, not anymore. And she wasn't walking in defenseless. The suit she wore gave her strength. Now she needed a weapon.

"Before we go any farther, I think we should break out the blasters from our supplies," she said. "Telles, you were in charge of that."

"I think we should wait until—"

"Now, Telles." Her command voice usually got results. This time was no different as Telles slung the pack off his back and opened it. He took out two small phasers and one slightly larger blaster. He kept the blaster for himself and handed the others to Eagle and Sky. She stared down at the small weapon.

"This is it?" She gestured toward the small gun with the other hand. "This is my weapon? Am I supposed to use it to shoot someone or to manicure my nails?" She glared at Telles, her suspicions igniting once more.

"That's all I could fit in the pack. You said to carry light. Don't worry; it can still kill a man at ten feet. If we get into a fight, it will likely be in close quarters."

"Of course," she muttered. She stuffed the small

weapon into a pocket in the droid suit and leaned down to pick up the wilderness-carving blade on the ground.

"I'll do it, Sky," Eagle said.

Sky slashed the blade down between them, effectively stopping Eagle's offer to continue chopping through the jungle. He didn't move a muscle as the weapon sliced through the air, burying itself in the ground next to his foot. She pulled the blade free, shooting Eagle a look that dared him to challenge her.

"I don't know what's going on," she said, "but I am taking command of this mission, boys. Now shape up, or I'll leave you behind."

"Sky, what in the world is the matter with you?" Eagle asked, rubbing the back of his neck with one hand. "I thought—" She cut him off.

"I'm beginning to think Kell was right and I've been played for a fool. If that's true, I promise the two of you will be very sorry." She pulled the small phaser from her pocket and pointed it at Telles. "Ten feet, eh? Give me the blaster." Without a word he handed it to her. She activated the larger weapon and turned it on Eagle. "Now you."

With a snort of disgust Eagle tossed it over.

"Now, Colonel, you're so eager to cut the way through—go ahead. Telles, you help him." She gestured with the blaster. "I'm tired of both your games. Get us to the temple. I know Mayla isn't there, but I intend to find out what's going on—and what the two of you have to do with it."

"What do you mean, you know Mayla isn't here?" Eagle asked, his dark brows colliding as he took the blade from her hand. She took a step back from him to put a little distance between them. He grimaced at her movement. "You think I'm going to cut you in half, I suppose? If I'd wanted to kill you, baby, I could have done it a dozen times over." His mouth tightened. "And you'd have never known what hit you." He shook his head in disgust and released his pent-up breath in one long rush. "Women!"

"Shut up," Sky ordered. "No more talking. No more nice little stories about erased memories. The two of you are going to walk in front of me and clear the way to the temple. Once we get there, if I can't find a reason why

Mayla might have sent us here, we're returning to the ship and getting the hell out of here."

"But Sky—"

"Shut up, Colonel!" She tossed her long hair back from her shoulders, the blaster trained carefully on Eagle's chest. "Just start swinging that blade and carve us a way through the jungle."

He looked away, his fingers tightening around the handle of the ancient machete. "Fine. But this is the end of the line for me. I'm not going back to the ship with you if we don't find her. You agreed on seven days." He shot her a look, his green eyes glittering with suppressed anger. "My time is up."

She nodded, feeling that familiar rage course through her again as he stared haughtily at her, arrogance written in every handsome feature.

"Yes, space-boy, your time is up. But maybe not in quite the way you figured. Start chopping and start walking."

Eagle's face closed and he turned toward the tangled growth in front of him. Telles moved beside him, and together the two men started clearing the ancient path to the Seekers' temple.

Sky followed, feeling as though the wide, sharp blade was coming down, stroke for stroke, into the very center of her heart.

Chapter Twelve

Eagle hacked through the underbrush, mad enough to tear the forest apart with his bare hands. He wasn't angry at Sky, but at himself. What was wrong with him? First he had made love to her, feeling a passion and desire he'd never thought possible; then he'd abandoned her, fearful of her power. She had weathered his cruelty, offering her trust, her understanding, back on the ship, a second time, and again he had rejected her. He'd gathered his shreds of courage about him and gone with her into Telles's mind, but once the light had been turned to his own part in things, his own past, the questions he couldn't answer, he had run back inside himself like a scared little boy and deserted her again.

He glanced back over his shoulder. She was trailing behind Telles, and because she didn't know he was looking at her, the haughty, tough mask had dropped from her porcelain features. She looked tired, infinitely sad, and discouraged. He longed to take her in his arms again and this time promise her the world, promise her sister's return, promise her forever. He couldn't. He couldn't promise her anything. All he could promise was pain, and he refused to be the bearer of that gift anymore.

Eagle sliced through a particularly tough patch of brush, feeling his muscles strain with the effort. He didn't care. He welcomed the pain. Deserved the pain. Where was the man who had fought so many battles he couldn't even number them or recall their names? Where was the man who had cold-bloodedly chosen men to die in the name of the Dominion—who had callously defended his father's actions for so many years? Where was Benjakar Zarn? Where was Eagle?

He had disappeared and in his place was this mewling, weak imitation of a man, a man he despised. A man who whimpered on a woman's shoulder and was too afraid to face a fictitious story about his past. A man who was too weak to risk himself for love. He slammed the blade into the ground, and using his hands, pulled two thick vines apart, wrenching them back, sweat pouring down his shoulders, tiny scratches causing blood to spot across his skin. He bent over, catching his breath, hands resting on his thighs, then heard the quick intake of breath behind him. Looking up, he straightened slowly, stunned at the sight before him. He heard Sky's awestruck voice from behind.

"Is that it, Telles?" she was whispering. "Is that the temple?"

"Yes. Isn't it magnificent?"

Eagle's eyes slid shut, but they did not block out the glorious image in front of him. The picture was burned forever in his mind, and had been for a very long time. He was only just now remembering it.

No. You aren't remembering it, he shouted inside. *I don't know how you know this, but you are not remembering.*

High, smooth walls of deep, jade green stretched toward the sky, at least three stories, each level smaller than the last, resembling a huge, tiered cake. Round columns adorned each corner of the structure, reaching even higher than the walls, ending in twisted, swirling points. There were no doors, no windows, no openings of any kind, but Eagle knew exactly how to gain entrance. He took a deep breath as knowledge burned into his soul and a floodgate somewhere deep inside his mind opened. He did not stop the outpouring, though he suspected he could. He did not stop the flood of thoughts and memories, though he knew by allowing it, he was welcoming his own doom. His hands flew to his head, his fingers tightening against his scalp.

He knew. He knew everything about this place. The

Seekers temple was built from beautiful blocks of a green stone called malachite. Legend had it that the stone had been brought from the mythological world of Terra, although when, or how, only the Seekers were said to know for certain. That had been before the first Cezans, during the dark times when the future of Andromeda looked dim and uncertain. The Seekers had been established by the first ruling Cezan in order to preserve the history of Andromeda, her people, and its beliefs—as well as the knowledge of where those beliefs originated.

"Well, magnificent isn't exactly the word I'd use to describe it," she said. "More like mossy and moldy. I guess no one has been able to take care of the place over the years."

Eagle glanced at Sky and frowned. What was she talking about? The temple was beautiful. It was—before his eyes, the structure began to shift, to change, to corrode from the proud emblem of Andromedan culture to a crumbled ruin of a building, gray, and as Sky had said, moss-covered. He staggered.

"Eagle?"

He heard his name but he couldn't respond. Swirling colors converged inside his head, pulsating against the back of his eyes. He had to pull back. He had to stop the flow. It was too much. This had to be some kind of trick. This place was somehow shooting these images into his mind. But if that was so, why couldn't Sky see it? The colors surged again, and instinctively he was hit by the knowledge like a flood of water and imagined a dam, blocking the flow, halting the wave of liquid facts threatening to drown him, dancing down his synapses, prodding him for entrance. He felt Sky's touch on his arm. Slowly he lowered his hands from his head. Taking a slow, shuddering breath, he opened his eyes. The glory had returned.

"Follow me," he said. He moved toward the shining green stone, wondering if the old Eagle would ever return from its depths or if he was doomed, once he stepped inside, to being sucked down into the spinning black hole opening inside his mind.

"There aren't any doors," Sky said as they approached the huge building.

"Yes, there are." Eagle pushed ahead of her. Huge blue-green ferns tinged with violet grew around the base of the temple, some affixed to vines climbing up the side of the smooth jade mountain.

"You're remembering," Telles said, his voice hushed as he moved to Eagle's side. He grabbed him by one arm, forcing him around. "What else do you remember?"

Eagle pulled away, gesturing in front of him. "I don't know what you're talking about. You lead the way," he said.

Telles shook his head. "Nope. You're leading us, buddy. How do we get inside?" His blue-gray eyes were filled with such hope that Eagle could hardly bear to look at him. He moved toward the monolithic structure, his hands on his hips, coming to a stop only inches away from the first round pillar.

"We think ourselves in."

"What?" Sky walked around, confronting him face to face, blaster still in her hand. "Are you crazy? What is that supposed to mean?"

"Give him a chance," Telles said.

"Sure, I'll give him a chance." She lifted the gun and pressed it into the center of his chest. "What do you mean?" she repeated, talking slowly, as if to a child.

Eagle pushed the barrel of the weapon aside. "I mean, that there is a door here, it's just hidden."

"Hidden?" She glanced around. "By a plant?"

"No, it's hidden from our minds. The temple must transmit a signal that tells all who approach there is no door, just as it tells all who approach that it is a dilapidated old ruin. It isn't. Don't look at it with your eyes. Look at it with your mind. This should be child's play for you, Sky."

She stared at him while Telles's face was split by a totally uninhibited grin. "You're remembering," he whispered again. Eagle ignored him, concentrating on the wonder on Sky's face.

Tentatively she reached out a hand to touch the rough

rock and jerked it back as if she'd been burned. "It looks rough but it's really smooth. What does it really look like, Eagle?" she asked. "What are you seeing?"

"Smooth green stone, the color of the leaves and vines around us except deeper. It's called malachite. It came from Terra."

Sky spun around, her mouth open. She snapped it shut as Telles laughed out loud joyfully. "Terra?" she said on a breath. "Terra is only a legend. Surely you aren't suggesting—"

"Can't you see the real temple?" he said, unable to resist the temptation of goading her. Was it possible he could use his mind in a way that Skyra Cezan could not? "Come on, Sky, just concentrate."

She glared at him, then turned her narrow gaze toward the temple. After a moment he heard her sigh with pleasure. The sound sent a sharp pang through him. Not too long ago he had been causing those sighs. Now there was no chance for them—or wouldn't be, once they found her sister.

"I see it!" she shouted, throwing her arms wide. "I see the temple! It's beautiful!"

Eagle couldn't help smiling. "Can you see the door? I couldn't see it at first either."

She paused, then pointed toward a corner of the structure. "Yes! There it is—a small door, barely taller than I am."

Telles shot Eagle a curious look. "You seem to be taking this rather better than you were before."

Eagle shrugged and tried to keep his tone nonchalant. "Go with the flow, I always say." Flow, hell. He didn't believe this for a minute. It was some kind of trick, some kind of setup Telles or the rebels or someone had engineered to convince him. He had to believe that. He had to believe it was a ruse. Because if he believed it was just a ploy on the part of the rebels, he could handle it. He could do what he had to do.

"Let's go in," Sky said. "Maybe we'll find the evidence you're looking for, Telles, and you can prove your theory to Mr. Hardhead."

He raised one golden brow. "And to you?"

The joy she'd expressed over the beauty of the temple faded, along with her eager tone of voice. "Yes, and to me."

"Aren't you interested in finding Mayla?"

A shadow touched her face. "Mayla isn't here, Telles." She glanced at Eagle. "You both know that."

Telles shook his head. "No, I don't know it at all. What makes you say this?"

"If she was here I would feel it, I would sense it. I am a Cezan and so is she—we know when a member of our family is nearby."

"I'm sorry, Sky," he said. "But I don't understand why you say that Eagle and I knew this. We didn't." He shot Eagle a look that spoke volumes. "At least, I didn't know."

"She doesn't trust us anymore." Eagle said the words flatly. "She thinks this is some kind of a trap because she senses Mayla isn't here. You said yourself she could be any number of places."

"But she's not on Andromeda," she said, her voice tight. "Come on, boys." She gestured with the blaster. "I still want to see what's inside this rock. Let's go explore Andromeda's past, shall we?"

"Not until you put that thing away," Telles said in disgust, hands on his hips, blue-gray eyes flashing with rare anger. "We're all in this together. I let you inside my mind, Sky. Surely that entitles me to a little of your respect, if not your trust."

Eagle watched the exchange and felt a sharp stab of jealousy. It flared into outright pain when Sky nodded and lowered the weapon.

"You're right. I'll put it away, but I'm sorry, Telles, I can't give you my trust again just yet."

"I understand."

Eagle turned away from the two and ducked under an overhanging branch, ignoring his desire to punch Telles in the nose. Telles was much more suited to Sky than he could ever be. Maybe that was the way to get over her—encourage his best friend to become her lover. His hands tightened into fists and he had to turn his thoughts quickly away from the mental picture of Sky and Telles together before he did damage to something or someone. He stopped in front of the hidden opening and concentrated on getting into the temple. Telles and Sky followed close behind him.

The door was small, the height of it barely clearing Sky's head. It was made from the same smooth stone and seemed to be sealed shut with no obvious way to open it. The three stood staring at the impenetrable surface it presented, then looked at each other.

"Do you remember how to get in?" Telles asked. He leaned one hand flat against the door, hooking the other over his hipbone.

"No, I don't remember," Eagle said, growing progressively more irritated with this game Telles was playing. He placed his own hand flat against the smooth surface next to the doorway. "But I know how." He flexed his fingers three times against the stone and the door parted from an invisible seam, splitting down the middle.

Telles caught himself in time to keep from plunging through, his grin getting broader every minute. "This is fantastic," he murmured. "It's all coming back to you, even without Sky's help."

Eagle snorted and ducked under the low opening, once again heading the expedition. Maybe Mayla wasn't here, but he intended to get to the bottom of this inexplicable stream of knowledge pulsating into his brain. And he meant what he had told them—he would not return to the *Defiant*. He'd strike out cross country if he had to and make it to the city. If he couldn't find the child, he would have to make things right with his father and find another way to convince him his regime was doomed.

He straightened inside the doorway and stopped in his tracks. As pristine and lovely as the outside of the building was, he found the inside even more beautiful. Everything was made from wood, from the paneling covering the walls to the sculpture in the center of the large room that reached almost to the twenty-foot ceiling. There were shelves everywhere—empty, filled with dust and cobwebs, as well as a dozen long wooden tables and benches scattered in disarray, as though their occupants had pushed them back hurriedly, had shoved them aside in a panic.

Eagle pushed the thought away and concentrated on the reality of what he was viewing. He crossed to the wooden sculpture, his footsteps stirring the inches-deep dust on the floor. He touched the wood reverently with one hand, feeling the smooth texture against his palm. He knew about this too. The abstract artwork represented Knowledge. It twisted intricately around, forming knots within knots, and yet was so simplistic it seemed anyone could have carved it. Legend had it that the first Seeker had carved it, many years ago, to show that knowledge was simple and available to all who sought it, but was also complex, and understanding hard won. His fingers traveled over the curved surface until they reached a dark spot about three inches wide and eight inches long, the color there a deep, dark reddish-brown, totally out of synch with the rest of the sculpture. Eagle looked at it more closely, running one finger over its surface. There was something about this. Something familiar. A weight came down suddenly on his shoulder, and he jerked before realizing it was Telles.

"Maybe we should look around some more," his friend said, hand firmly on his shoulder. His voice sounded strained, nervous. "If Sky is certain Mayla isn't here, then we can at least look for proof of who we are."

Eagle found himself nodding. "The archives," he said.

"What archives?" Sky asked, moving to stand beside him and the sculpture. His gaze was still fixed on the smooth carving. He didn't answer her, and at last Telles began to speak.

"When the Forces attacked Andromeda, they came to this temple and wiped out all of the ancient writings the Seekers had accumulated for centuries. Books, scrolls, discs, artwork—it was all destroyed by Zarn's soldiers." He glanced at Eagle, who was purposely ignoring him. "Or so they thought. Zarn didn't know there was a secret archive where the originals were kept. All those on display in the upper chambers were merely copies."

"What kind of information do these writings contain?"

"Everything from the history of Andromeda to the Seekers' own personal histories. Once a Seeker was accepted into the organization, he or she was expected to write a work that included the story not only of his life, but that of his family and his ancestors. In this way, the Seekers had countless corroborations of different stories, from different viewpoints." Telles moved to the other side of the sculpture, facing Eagle. "That's what made them so dangerous to Zarn. They dealt in the truth. So how about it, Colonel? Are you ready to fight the real battle?"

Eagle glanced up from the stained wood into his friend's eyes. For the first time in a long time, he saw the old bond between them reflected in those blue-gray irises. Telles was still his brother, in spite of everything that had happened. All he had to do was go along with this charade and prove to him they were both being duped by the rebels, by lovely Skyra Cezan and her mysterious sister. It didn't matter what they found in the archives. What mattered was what he knew in his heart, in his spirit. He was Garnos Zarn's son and nothing would ever change that. Not Sky, not Telles, not any ancient, crumbling piece of parchment scrawled on by some forgotten philosopher.

"Sure," he said, without emotion. "Let's get to it."

Sky followed the two men down a narrow stairway behind a door whose doorway had been hidden in the wall. Eagle had walked right up to it and tripped a secret switch in the wood, opening a panel that slid back, exposing the door behind. Telles had explained that while the mechanism that opened the door could be triggered to allow someone to enter, once a person was in the chamber and the door shut, there was no way to leave until someone else activated the device. The activation was caused by pressure against one of the stones near the doorway. Because the Seekers had kept someone perpetually in the archives, changing shifts every four hours or so, this way of keeping their chamber secret worked very well.

The stairway led in a twisting, writhing pathway downward into the very bowels of the planet it seemed. The steps had been carved from a rough kind of stone, not like the beautiful green stone on the outside, and appeared to be much, much older than the rest of the temple. Perhaps the underground part had been built first, years before the rest?

The toe of her boot caught just then on a crevice in one of the steps and she pitched forward. Telles caught her, his hands around her waist. He steadied her and smiled before turning back to follow Eagle. Eagle had already turned back to the dark stairway but not before she saw the flash of anger and jealousy in his eyes. She couldn't help smiling into the darkness. She stumbled again, but this time it wasn't the stairway tripping her, but a soft, sweet signal resounding deep inside her mind.

Sky.

Mayla.

Her sister was trying to contact her again. She froze, one hand to the silver band around her forehead. Should she take it off? Could she take the chance of discarding the only protection she had against the thousands of mental voices on Andromeda? True, they were far away from any large city or village, but distance wasn't always a sufficient deterrent. She hesitated and her sister's voice came suddenly, clearly, loudly into her mind.

Take off the band. You will be safe. Your power will be needed.

Sky hesitated no longer. She slipped the silver deflector band off her head and stood for a moment on the stairs, expecting a flood of voices, a barrage that might send her spiraling into unconsciousness. But Mayla had said she would be safe.

"Sky, what are you doing?" Telles was looking up at her, his brows knit together in concern. "Why are you taking off your band?"

"Mayla told me to," she whispered.

Eagle moved back up the stairs and wedged his form

between the two of them. "Mayla? Then she's here?"

Sky shook her head, her gaze fixed above them. Mayla was trying to tell her something, something important.

"Can you read our minds?" Telles asked. Eagle stiffened at his words and Sky shifted her eyes to him.

"No, something strange is happening. I know I could go inside your minds if I chose, but there is no outpouring, no unguarded flood of thoughts from you like I would usually experience without my band."

"How?" Eagle's hand closed around hers and Sky felt suddenly very safe, very protected. How foolish.

"I don't know. It could be Mayla's doing, but to exercise power of such magnitude she would have to be on this planet, and I just don't sense her presence." She stood there for another moment, then shook herself mentally. "She isn't there now. Let's go on. Let's make the most of our time."

They reached the bottom of the long stairwell and stepped into total darkness. Sky put her hand out in front of her and came in contact with a hard, broad back. There was a movement and suddenly she was touching soft hair that curled against a hard muscular chest. Her fingers spread unconsciously for a scant second before she snatched her hand away. She gasped as her own chest was explored in turn, by a large, gentle hand.

"Oh, is that you, Sky? Sorry, I couldn't see." Eagle chuckled as she slapped his hand away from her breast and kicked him solidly in the shin. The cursing that followed was music to her ears.

"Oh, dear," she said sweetly, "was that you? Sorry, I couldn't see."

"If both of you are quite finished," Telles drawled, "I'd like to turn on the light."

"What's stopping you?" Eagle asked.

"I didn't want to embarrass myself. I wasn't sure what position I'd find the two of you in."

"The only position you'll find me in is straddling this big lummox with my blaster up his nose!" Sky shoved Eagle aside and felt her way to Telles's side, feeling completely humiliated. "Turn on the *p'faugking* light!"

A humming sound filled the darkness, followed by faint traces of illumination high above them on the ceiling. Dim lights seemed to hover in midair. They flickered once or twice, then bloomed into full, brilliant light.

"By the great Cezan," Telles whispered.

Sky silently echoed his reverent epitaph as she gazed around the huge chamber in which she found herself. From the floor to the thirty-foot-high ceiling, the walls, made to form a hexagon, were covered with shelves filled to overflowing with ancient books, rolled-up scrolls, containers of computer discs, maps, huge volumes, tiny pocket-sized manuscripts. Every nook and cranny was filled. In each corner of the room stood large, chestlike pieces of furniture, and in the center was another sculpture, this one a large piece of violet crystalline about two feet wide and four feet tall, mounted on a wooden pedestal.

"I wonder if this crystal has anything to do with the mental projections we experienced outside." Eagle moved to the object and let his hands hover inches away from it, never touching. "You can feel the energy. Crystals are often used as energy sources. Many of our own ships are powered by Kyron crystals. The Seekers must have found a way to project subliminal programming using the power source."

Sky stepped up beside him and held her hand out. He was right. She could feel the power throbbing from the center of the crystal's core. "Amazing." A memory pierced her thoughts. A crystal, small, slim, this same color of purple, hanging from her mother's throat. She'd worn it all her life. One just like it had been given to Mayla when her position as the heir had been established.

"So where do we look first?" Telles asked, spreading his hands apart. "We could look in here for a century and still not have seen everything."

"What are those?" Sky pointed at one of the large chests in the far west corner of the room. "There's one in each corner. They seem significant." She crossed to it and ran one hand over the smooth, golden wood. It was about three feet tall, two feet wide, and four feet long. The sides were flat but the top was rounded, curved unevenly, almost like an ocean's wave. "That's funny. There are no seam, no hinges, no opening. Again."

She smiled and closed her eyes, opening her telepathic portals. How wonderful it was to use them again without the fear of being assaulted. How had Mayla done this? She had kept the minds of others from her while they lived on Bezanti with great effort and it had weakened her. How was she possibly preventing it here on Andromeda, possibly light years away from wherever she was? Or was it the crystal? Was it somehow helping her?

Images formed in her mind of families: fathers, mothers, brothers, and sisters. More images: animals she had never seen before, a rush of stories, names, places that did not exist on any world she knew.

"They are in here," she said, the wood feeling almost alive beneath her fingers.

"Who?"

She felt Eagle at her side. She reached for his hand and placed it on the chest beside hers. "The Seekers. Their families."

Sky opened her eyes and found Eagle staring down at her. His long lashes swept downward as if to hide the honest emotion she saw shimmering in his green gaze.

"How do we open them?" Telles asked, coming up behind them. Sky turned away from Eagle's hooded features and took a deep breath.

"I'm not sure. Come here, Telles. Put your hands on here too." He complied and soon the three of them were standing side by side, their fingers spread atop the chest. "Now, concentrate on the Seekers, on Andromeda. Think about why we are here."

Sky slid Eagle a sidelong glance and caught the hesitation on his face before he closed his eyes and knit his dark brows together. What happened next was truly startling. Sky felt the wood under her hands begin to move, almost as though it were alive.

"What the—" Eagle said, dropping his hands away. Sky caught them and put them back on the wood.

"No, no," she said hastily, "keep your hands on the chest. It's opening!"

The chest moved again, a movement like a gentle sigh. The curved top bucked just a little beneath their fingers, then four drawers, one on each side, slid out of the chest. In the drawers were dozens of small, multi-colored balls.

"Great," Eagle said in disgust. "We found where the Seekers keep their marbles."

"Don't be absurd," Sky snapped, scooping up one of the orbs carefully in her hand. "These are almost alive. I can feel them vibrate into my soul."

"Recordings of some kind?" Eagle suggested, dropping his sarcasm and picking up a pale green ball. It fit perfectly in the palm of his hand.

Telles nodded and moved to take one for himself. "That would make sense. Now, how would one go about hearing or reading what was recorded?"

"Look around," Sky said. "Maybe there's a device they fit into."

"Let's search the other chests first."

They placed the orbs back into the drawer and in short order had opened the other three chests. Inside they found more of the same.

"It could be anywhere—whatever it is," Eagle said, gesturing upward. "On one of those shelves, maybe."

"Or—" Sky picked up a dark blue orb and held it out in front of her, moving toward the crystal in the center of the room. As she got closer, the orb began to glow with a translucent, irridescent quality. "I can feel it," she whispered. "It's vibrating as though it's alive."

"It is alive," Telles said. "Alive with memories." He shot Eagle an arch look that the other man ignored. Sky had reached the pedestal now and held the orb toward the shimmering crystal.

"I am Nabom." A voice boomed out of nowhere. "I am a Seeker."

Sky was so startled she almost dropped the orb, but as the voice spoke the object vibrated violently in her hand. "It's the orb," she called to the men. "The crystal activated it."

They crossed to her side and stood gazing down at the shimmering globe. The voice continued.

"My father was Malkigh and my mother Neara. I was born under the Polii moon in the month of Kanu."

The voice went on, documenting every fact about this Seeker's family and life until at last the sound began to fade and the orb stopped glowing and fell silent.

"Wow." Sky put the orb back in the drawer reverently. So much knowledge! Such incredible stories. But how could they possibly search through all of them? They couldn't. There just wasn't time.

"There's no way we can listen to all of these," Telles said, echoing her thoughts. "Eagle, what do you—" He stopped abruptly and Sky turned. Eagle was standing across the room in front of one of the other chests, staring down into its depths.

Sky glanced at Telles questioningly. He shrugged and shook his head but began to move toward his friend. Sky followed. There was a magic to this place, a mystery. Ever since they'd arrived, Eagle had acted strangely, as though he was affected somehow simply by being here. Could it be that the hidden memories Telles claimed were in his mind were somehow being awakened?

Eagle had one of the orbs in his hand. It was a beautiful deep amber color. He didn't even look up as Sky and Telles flanked him, both looking anxiously into his glazed eyes.

"Eagle?" Sky pulled on his arm, trying to get his attention. He continued to stare down at the object in his hand. He held it as though it was a precious treasure.

"It's here," he said softly, cradling the orb. "It's here."

"What's here?" Telles asked, his eyes filled with hope.

Eagle took a deep breath and released the air slowly, as though he were trying to somehow gain the time he needed before he answered.

"What?" Sky demanded, too anxious to wait. "What are you talking about?"

Eagle lifted his gaze to hers and Sky took a step back. Emerald-green eyes reflected a pain so deep she could not bear to look at him, and yet she sensed that beneath

241

the pain was joy almost too wondrous to be borne. He smiled and Sky moved closer again.

"Tell me, Eagle," she said. "What is here?"

"My life," he whispered.

Chapter Thirteen

Eagle stared down at the glowing orb. Quite without his consent, his feet began to take him toward the crystal in the center of the room. Telles and Sky hung back, and he was only aware of their presence in a hazy, subconscious kind of way. He held the dark amber gently, as if it held fragile, precious secrets, for he knew that it did. The closer he got to the crystal, the more terrified he became, and yet he was drawn closer, pulled by a power he could not understand, a power inside himself, a power demanding to be heard.

The orb in his hand began to glow. He could feel it come to life against his palm, but he still was not prepared for the quiet, familiar voice that came dancing down around him as he stopped directly in front of the pedestal.

"I am Toma N'chal, a Seeker, husband of Pelana, father of Keela, Mok, Zanik, and Ranon, my little eagle." Eagle felt a surge of adrenaline rush through his veins, felt the blood just as quickly rush away from his head. He staggered and caught himself against the side of the pedestal as the voice continued. "I am the son of Konak, grandson of Saxin, great-grandson of Meinak, all Seekers, all bound by the philosophy of total brotherhood passed down to us from our forebears on Terra. My wife has been the perfect helpmate and her own story may be found in our archives. I could not be more proud of my children. My oldest daughter will follow in my footsteps, as will my youngest son, Ranon."

He went on to tell that each child had been given the opportunity to choose a favorite story to be placed in their family archive. Eagle stood in stony silence, listening intently until he came to the one chosen by Ranon, the youngest son.

"Ranon's favorite story is an ancient Terran tale of a flying creature that once soared across the skies of our mother planet. 'Once there was a man whose fear ruled his life until one day he turned his vision to the skies. There he saw a great and glorious bird spreading his wings, sailing upon the winds of fortune, and he heard the voice of the Creator say to him, "Rise up, rise up on the wings of an eagle. You shall be weary no longer. You shall fly with courage and strength.'" There was a soft chuckle. "My son, Ranon, sees himself in that great bird, that great eagle. I am pleased."

By the time the voice had reached the last sentence of the story, Eagle was saying the words along with him. And by the time the last words of his father faded away, he suddenly knew what the stain on the wooden sculpture upstairs really meant. He took a step back from the pedestal and registered, somewhere in his thoughts, that Sky was beside him. Without looking, he handed her the amber orb, then turned and ran across the room, heading for the twisted stairway.

"Eagle, wait!"

He heard Sky's frantic call but could not have stopped if the galaxy had been on fire. Images crowded into his brain, superimposing one on top of the other, dancing across his thought processes, twisting rational thought into fragmented questions without answers. He took the steps two at a time, stumbling twice and falling, sliding down three steps, then pulling himself to his feet and lunging upward, his hands clawing for purchase. He reached the top at last and plunged into the room upstairs, staggering to a stop beside the beautiful carved work of art in the center. He searched the wood until he found what he was looking for: the stain. His fingers touched the blemish carefully, gently, before curling back into his palm. He felt the knowledge crash in on him, and this time there was nothing he could do to stop it. There were no dams strong enough to hold it back, no walls thick enough to halt the onslaught.

They had taken refuge here, on that long-ago night. His family, among others who had at last believed the incredible stories that Andromeda was under attack from outside forces, their king and queen murdered, their world conquered. The Seekers had brought their wives or their husbands, their children and grandchildren to the temple. The children had been sent below to the hidden chamber, but the spouses of the Seekers and those children who had attained adulthood had elected to remain above in the meditation room, to defend the rest.

Eagle had not been a child; he had been a young man almost fifteen years old when his father had calmly led him into the place where the two of them had spent many a long hour in serious conversation. As the youngest of his father's children, he was the only one of his family designated to remain below, in spite of his fervent pleadings to stay with them. When the Forces came, Eagle was hovering at the top of the stairs, his best friend Telles beside him. They both heard the shots ring out in the temple and immediately plunged through the opening leading into the great chamber above. Fortunately the chaos going on inside the hall was enough that the two boys were quickly able to seal the door closed behind them before the soldiers saw the entrance to the secret room. They stumbled out into the battle and stood for a moment, stunned, too shocked at first to realize what was happening.

They had nothing to fight with, but it didn't matter. The fight was over almost before it had begun. Eagle had stared around at the bodies tangled together in various paroxysms of death on the floor and had felt something inside him die as well. Telles's father and mother, his older brother, lay prostrate on the floor in one another's arms, covered with blood. His friend fell to his knees, retching at the sight, sobbing broken-heartedly. Eagle couldn't move, couldn't comfort his friend.

"Little eagle . . ." He had turned glazed eyes toward the whispered entreaty. His father leaned against the great wooden sculpture, half his left arm torn away, a gaping hole in his chest. Eagle ran to him, catching him as he fell. He died before he could speak again, as Eagle sank to the floor holding him in his arms. His mother and the rest of his family were already there, lying in their own blood. As Eagle stared down into his father's sightless eyes, he had felt a grief so intense, so all consuming, he thought his mind would explode. He sat back on his heels, rocking back and forth, his father clasped to his chest, his own tears trapped inside him. He could not cry. He could not scream the agony he felt. For if he did, if he gave in to the grief, he would go insane. And first— first he had to kill whoever was responsible.

The soldiers spotted him and began shouting. Eagle gently laid his father beside his mother and stood, reaching a bloody hand out to balance himself. His fingers had closed around one smooth section of the sculpture and left a crimson stain. He had pushed himself away and straightening, walked through the dead and dying, toward one of the soldiers, vengeance in his heart, death in his eyes. The man had lifted his blaster rifle to his shoulder and fixed him in his sights. Eagle had tensed but kept walking, determined to take one of them with him when he died.

"Wait." A voice had come from behind the soldier. Eagle grimaced against the memory. The man had strode up with such purpose, such confidence. "Don't kill him." The man wore a long black cape enveloping his form, snapping around his ankles. His face was handsome, his hair dark, wavy, tinged with silver at the temples. Eagle had no idea who the man was, but he felt himself being weighed by the blue eyes sweeping over him. When the exam was finished, he felt soiled, dirtied, and knew with a sinking heart it was only the beginning.

"Yes," the man said. "He may be just what I'm looking for." His eyes moved to focus on Telles, still doubled over on the floor. "Bring that one too, then take these rebel bodies out and burn them. Search the rest of the building. The others have to be nearby." He turned and with a swirl of black was gone, leaving Eagle and Telles behind in the temple of the damned.

The burly soldier grabbed him and Telles and shoved them out of the temple and into a shuttlecraft, where they were shackled and thrown into the hold. He had struggled to a sitting position, trying to support the grief-stricken Telles with his weight. "I will stay alive," he had said aloud, tossing his dark hair back from his face, his heart cold, his thoughts crystal clear. "And one day, one day soon, I will avenge my family."

Eagle slipped his fingers away from the stain on the smooth wood and let the muscles in his legs collapse. He fell soundlessly to the floor, to his knees, his hands clasped in front of him, his head thrown back. The children hidden in the chamber below had not been discovered, and the room had remained untouched. But eventually they had been forced to come out to seek food and water. Miraculously, or perhaps protected by some unknown technology, the chamber below had not been found, the door never spotted. Eventually, however, each and every child was captured and taken to Station One by Zarn's men to have their minds altered.

He could not move, could not speak, could not breathe. He heard the sharp intake of breath and the sob that followed but didn't realize it came from his own throat. He was Ranon. He was his father's little eagle. His father had been a Seeker, an Andromedan. He had planned to follow in his footsteps and become a Seeker too. His mother—how he had loved his mother, and his older brothers and sister. Forgotten. Lost until this moment. Stripped from his mind by evil incarnate.

The keening started low inside him, swelled upward to catch in his throat before the heart cry, the grief he could not acknowledge all those years ago, was wrenched from him and sent echoing through the temple. He let it come. He could not have stopped it if his life had depended on it, which perhaps it did, for how could he live with the knowledge of such grief, such agony, such despair? For fifteen years he had lived a lie. For fifteen years he had given his allegiance to the man who had murdered his real parents and destroyed Andromeda and her children.

Eagle began to tremble all over as the sound inside him rose and vibrated through his skull. He wailed as the memories assaulted him. He moaned as fifteen years of grief crashed within him. He screamed as he saw his father's and mother's faces again, open eyes staring without vision, without life. He rocked against the onslaught, his arms wrapped around himself. Then two other arms wrapped around him. Gentle, caring arms, arms that cradled him like a child. Eagle opened his eyes and saw a woman, silver-haired, her turquoise eyes brimming with tears, moisture flooding her face.

"Eagle," she whispered. "The orb—then it's true. You are one of us. Zarn destroyed your world, your life, as he destroyed mine. Oh, my darling—"

Eagle pulled her against him, his hands moving to her hair, then her face as he possessed her mouth savagely at first, then more gently. He held her against him, as if her warmth, her willing body could absolve him from the past. How many had he killed in the name of Zarn? How many Andromedan children had he allowed to be mentally altered during his short stay on Station One? What had he done?

"No." He took her caressing hands between his and pulled away.

He had done enough to hurt her. When he thought of how he had planned to take her sister from her, it sickened him. She had pegged him right from the start. He was a bastard. He would not hurt her any longer. He would not assuage his need with her body, nor would he confess the love he felt for her, when he knew he was a dead man. He had no doubt whatsoever he would be able to kill Zarn. He also knew there was no doubt whatsoever that he would not be alive after their confrontation. But Sky pressed herself against him, her mouth doing wonderful, terrible things to him as she moved her lips up the side of his neck to his jaw and up to his temple. He groaned and released her hands. They flew to his face and her mouth captured his lower lip, her fingers weaving through his hair, her long legs straddling his lap as she sealed herself against him.

"Sky, no—you don't know what you're doing," he said, breaking away from her tantalizing mouth. She ignored him and moved lower, leaving a trail of warmth from his lips to the center of his chest. "Telles—"

"Telles is in the archives, looking for his own past. I left a stone in the doorway, keeping it open so that we'll be able to get back into the chamber below without disturbing him." She raised her head from his chest and Eagle saw a flicker of hesitation in her eyes. "I'm sorry. I didn't mean to be so presumptuous. I—I guess I wanted to comfort you. And I wanted to—to make it up to you."

Eagle shook his head. "Make what up to me?"

Sky looked down at her hands. If he hadn't known better, hadn't known that Sky was too tough, too bold, too strong to be embarrassed, he'd have sworn she was blushing. She *was* blushing. Eagle raised both brows and let his lips twist into the semblance of a smile.

"All the terrible things I called you," she said. "I mean, some of those curses are banned, you know."

Eagle lifted one hand to tilt her face up to his. "I know. Luckily I couldn't understand most of them. Although I got the gist of what you meant."

Sky's blush deepened. "I'm sorry. If I'd known who you really were—"

"You mean if you'd known I was an Andromedan and not Zarn's son? But I'm still that man, Sky," he whispered. Then, unable to keep looking at her, he turned away. "I'm still the man who fought for Zarn on a dozen different worlds. I'm still the man who killed for him. I'm still the man who didn't lift a finger to help the kids on Station One."

"But you would have," Sky said, moving closer again. "I know that you would have."

"Maybe. I like to think so."

"I didn't really hate you," she said.

Eagle laughed shortly. "You could have fooled me, darlin'."

"No, it was the fact that you were his son. I was actually attracted to you all along. And now that I know the truth—it isn't that I expect you to be a different person, as in a different personality, but of course this has to change your opinion of Zarn—and that was all truly keeping us apart."

"Really?" He turned back to her, shifting to his knees. "That was all?"

"That and your fear."

He nodded. "I'm not afraid anymore, Sky. I'm sorry I wouldn't let you in before. I realize now I must have been reacting subconsciously to the buried memory of my mind-probing."

Sky touched his cheek with her fingertips, her eyes so filled with tenderness he thought he would break into a million pieces. "I'm so sorry, Eagle. I'm so sorry for what you've gone through, what I've put you through."

He lifted both hands to her face and slid his fingers into her hair at her temples. His lips lowered to hers, stopping mere centimeters away as he spoke again. "There's no need. You've done nothing wrong. When I think about what I've done for the last fifteen years—what I've believed—"

"Shhh." She silenced him, her fingers over his lips. "Don't think, Eagle. Don't think at all."

"Help me, Sky. Help me not to think."

Sky lifted her face slightly and ran her tongue across his lower lip as her hands began to massage his chest through his shirt. As their mouths joined, she ripped the closures of his shirt apart and pulled it from his shoulders, down his arms, over his hands. She pushed him backward until he was lying flat on his back and stretched atop him, straddling his hips. She grinned down at him.

"Does this remind you of anything, space-boy?"

Eagle felt an odd sense of déjà vu. She was still wearing the silver droid suit, but this time everything was vastly, vastly different.

"Sky, I have to tell you something."

"Later." As he watched, she began to slide one hand

down the front of her suit. She had not connected the energy posts and so it was a simple matter to open the seamless fastenings down the center of her chest and let the upper part of the suit slide off onto the floor.

"Sky." Eagle's breath caught in his throat and he couldn't manage the words he'd been about to say—the warning that whatever they had together couldn't last, that he was bound and determined to have his revenge and he didn't expect to return from the encounter alive. He didn't say them because he was too busy memorizing her beauty, engraving it upon his memory.

She was beautiful. She sat astride him like a goddess who had deigned to come down from the stars to join with a mortal man. Her cream-colored skin was as soft as he'd remembered, her body lush and tempting. She left him abruptly, but only to shed the rest of the heavy ensemble; then she was beside him, tugging his clothes from him. This time when they connected it was skin to skin, fire to fire, and the burn was so intense, so consuming that Eagle feared it. She closed her eyes as he touched her, and all at once he knew there was no longer any reason to be afraid. He and Sky were no longer enemies. They were Andromedans—he the son of a Seeker, she the daughter of a Cezan. They were not star-crossed lovers but well suited to one another, they were allies now.

Eagle drew her down to him and with one deft move, rolled her to her back and covered her with his body. She offered her lips to him and he took them. She touched him, running her hands across his back, and he thought he would melt with desire. But as he returned his ministrations to her throat and she leaned her head back to allow him access, he murmured a request against her soft, soft skin. Sky lifted startled eyes to his. Her lips parted, trembled as her tongue darted out and moistened the suddenly dry surface. Tears glistened in her eyes and Eagle felt a deep and wonderful ache inside. How had he ever deserved this woman? How could he make love to her when he would soon be leaving her ultimately alone? How could he *not* make love to her when he loved her and he knew that she loved him? He owed her this much, didn't he? The ultimate joining?

"Well?" he whispered. "Will you?"

She took his face between her hands and kissed him, the kind of kiss he had once imagined a wife would give her husband: warm with love, hot with passion, fervent with loyalty.

"Yes," she whispered. "If you're sure. Oh, Eagle, this time the stars are truly ours."

Her mind rushed out to his like a vibrant wind, met him, and with the sound of joyous laughter whirled him into her arms and into the vast corridors of their minds. They rode the swirling colors and Sky opened herself to him—took him into her memories of Andromeda, of her childhood, of the first terrible years on Bezanti. She showed him her love for Redar and her grief over his death. She showed him her abhorrence for the things she had to do to keep herself and Mayla alive, but she let him see the side of her that also enjoyed the danger and the cynical bravado that came with being a pirate. Sky let him see her vulnerabilities and her flaws, her strengths and her weaknesses, her need and her ability to give.

In return Eagle let her journey into his innermost thoughts. Together they explored the dim recesses where the forgotten memories had been stored. She helped him open the sealed tombs and let his past soar free once again. She turned what could have been more trauma into delight as she drifted with him through the years, laughed with him over his family's closeness, cried with him again at their deaths. He let her see the person he had become after Zarn had altered his memories, and she did not recoil from him. He hid nothing from her, not even the fact that he had planned to take Mayla and use her to force Zarn to listen to him.

"Eagle . . ."

The pale blue mist encompassed them as the thoughts and pathways they had so earnestly explored faded away, leaving the two of them alone with their love. They touched and with a rush that superseded the one that had taken them inside themselves, Eagle found himself quite physically back on Andromeda again, Sky beneath him on the hard stone floor of the temple of the Seekers. There were no words. There was no need for words. Eagle began to caress her, to move within her with a gentleness that began in the depths of his heart and spread like a fire between them. All was exposed now. All was open. There were no secrets, there were no dark places, no shadows. There was only brilliant, glorious light and freedom.

Eagle made love to Sky, and with every touch he made promises, promises he knew he would never keep. He kissed her ears and promised to be there to listen. He kissed her throat and promised to be there to hear what she had to say. He kissed her gently, oh, so gently between her breasts, just over her heart, and promised to never break that heart. He kissed her lips and promised her forever. But there would be no forever. And he would break her heart, for there would be no chance to keep these promises. He was as good as dead. There was only now, and it would have to be enough.

It is enough.

Sky's voice echoed through his mind and he stopped his caresses, arching back from her, an incredulous smile on his face.

Yes, she said to him. *Now we are truly joined, in every way.*

Eagle bent to take her mouth, and the heat quickened anew between them. Suddenly he was inside of Sky's active, loving thoughts as well as her body, and the knowledge made him throb with power and with some strange, sweet fire he couldn't keep to himself. He kissed her, ravaged her lips, caressed her body, the hidden places, the exposed places; he filled her body and she filled his soul. He catapulted the two of them upward, pushing them into the heavens, into the galaxies, higher and farther, until Eagle and Sky touched the distant stars—touched them and held them and took them for their own, before together they shattered into a million particles of light, a million sparkling pieces of silver, before drifting softly, sweetly in each other's arms, back to the cold floor of the Seekers' temple.

Sky awoke in darkness. For a moment she didn't know where she was and stretched her hand out in front of her, only to meet with warm human flesh.

"I'm having a very curious dream," a deep voice said from beside her. "I'm being groped in the dark by a woman whose face I cannot see. Wonder what the symbolism of that would be?"

"Perhaps that love is blind?" Sky quipped, reaching out to massage the thick muscles across his back, running her hands down to his waist. She bent and kissed the small of his back and he rolled over, folding her into his arms, holding her against his chest.

"I wonder what's happened to Telles?" he said, rubbing one hand up and down her arm. "Is it too much to hope that he actually had the sensitivity to leave us alone?"

"Telles is much more sensitive than you give him credit for," Sky said, sighing like a cat as he continued to smooth his hand across her skin. "He—" She stopped speaking as a shimmer of light danced across the room and landed in front of them. It began as a faint flicker the size of a candle flame, then grew until it was four or five feet high.

"Do you see that?" Eagle whispered.

Sky could only nod beside him as she brushed her long hair back from her face, her eyes fixed on the glowing object silhouetted against the darkness. The image filled, broadened, until it took on the shape of a person. A small person.

Mayla.

Sky sat up, then quickly flattened herself to the floor as she realized she was still completely naked. Of all the embarrassing, humiliating—

"Here," Eagle said, shoving something soft into her hands. His shirt, discarded during their first round of lovemaking. She slipped it on, her back to the image of her sister, and buttoned it with trembling fingers.

Of course! She was no longer wearing her deflector

band and Mayla could easily reach her! Covered as modestly as was possible, Sky turned to face her sister, a broad smile on her face. The smile faded as she saw the solemn expression Mayla wore.

"Mayla! What is it? Where are you? Why did you send us here if you weren't going to be here?" The questions tumbled out before she could stop them, and her sister listened patiently before holding up one small hand. Her lips didn't move but Sky could hear her perfectly, and from the look on Eagle's face, her telepathic speech was reaching him as well.

"Skyra, please listen. I sent you here because it was necessary—for Eagle, and for Telles, but also for you. Only in this place was it truly safe for you to take off the deflector band. The crystal in the chamber below acts as a natural deflector shield—that is how the Seekers were able to keep this place from Zarn. I knew your power would be needed when Eagle faced the truth of his past."

"But I didn't even use my telepathic healing," she said, clutching the front of the shirt more tightly.

"No, you found an even greater power." Mayla giggled slightly and Sky felt her face burning with shame. *"Don't be embarrassed, sister. There is nothing shameful about love."*

"All right, I understand why you brought us here—kind of—but why are you here now? What's wrong?"

Her pale face sagged, and her lavender eyes clouded. *"Zarn is here,"* she said, her words sending a shiver down Sky's spine. *"I did not expect him to learn of your whereabouts, and now you are in grave danger."*

"What should we do?" Sky stood and took a step toward the shimmering apparition. "And where are you, Mayla? I'm tired of this game. I'm your sister and your guardian, and I demand that you tell me where you are!"

"Yes, it is time." She lifted her chin with a dignity that never failed to amaze Sky. *"I am on our homeworld."*

Sky frowned. "But you aren't on Andromeda. I would have sensed your presence."

"No, not Andromeda. On our true homeworld of Nandafar."

Sky ran her tongue across her lips and wished Eagle would stand beside her. In a matter of seconds he was there, smiling down at her.

"Remember," he whispered, "we are joined in more ways than one now."

She reached for his hand and found comfort in the fact that his large one completely engulfed her smaller one. She also took comfort in the fact that he had put his trousers back on before standing up.

"Mayla, what are you talking about? Nandafar is not our homeworld."

"Yes, Sky, it is. It is the world where the Cezans originated, where others are even now being trained to take their places in the universe. I am there, awaiting my coming-of-age ritual, which will take place very shortly. Come to me, Sky. Leave Andromeda and fly to me. But be careful, for someone in your camp is a spy for Zarn."

Her image flickered, dimmed, and disappeared entirely. At the same moment Sky felt a cold chill creep over her, starting at her fingers and inching its way upward to her throat. She whirled around and the sound of deep laughter rang out around them. She remembered that laugh just as she remembered the voice that followed it.

"So. That's where she is. Nandafar. And to think we always avoided that little planet—so devoid of beauty or resources. How foolish we were."

Zarn.

Sky felt her breath leave her body and at the same instant her heart seemed to stop beating. Her fingers bit into Eagle's arm as he slowly pushed her behind him, his thoughts coming fast and furious into her own mind. He wanted to give himself room to attack the man who had called himself his father. Sky felt at a vast disadvantage clad as she was in his shirt. The silver droid suit—her insurance against attack—lay in a heap three feet away from her. She inched backward toward the heavy clothing.

"I don't advise you to do that," Zarn told her.

"Hello, Father," Eagle said, his voice strangely calm.

Sky gave him a startled glance. Father? After all he had

just gone through—after all he had just remembered? She pressed deeper against his mind, but he warned her back and she felt another chill grab her by the throat.

She could hear Zarn's footsteps coming nearer. Why didn't he turn on a light? Or was there a light? When they had arrived in the temple it had been daylight and there had been no need to find artificial illumination. The footsteps stopped very near them.

"Eagle, my son," the voice said, sounding genuinely sad and weary. "So you have betrayed me at last. The council said it would come, but I would not believe them."

"I don't know what you're talking about."

A circle of light appeared on the floor, then lifted toward them. A handheld torch. He focused the sheet of light in their faces and Sky held up one hand to protect herself. As if anything could protect them from Zarn. The man moved closer and he flipped the light upward, illuminating all three of their faces.

"Walking down memory lane, son?" Zarn asked, his green eyes hard, his lips twisted in a bitter line. "Listening to the lies of a renegade and a rebel?" He turned his furious gaze toward Sky. She shivered as he looked her up and down, his eyes darkening at the sight of her long, bare legs and her obvious dishevelment. His gaze shifted back to her face and she saw his expression change, a look of tentative hope spring into his eyes. "Or just enjoying yourself at her expense?"

"Can you blame me?" Eagle said, chuckling a little.

Sky turned and sought his mind with hers. He was trying to fool Zarn into thinking he was still on his side. It wouldn't work. Zarn was too smart to be taken in a second time.

"No," Zarn admitted. "In fact, I think I will partake of the princess right now. After all, fathers and sons share everything." He reached for Sky and she gasped as Eagle's hard, muscled forearm darted out to block his hand. Zarn chuckled, but there was no amusement in the sound. "So it is true."

Eagle pushed her back again and she resisted the urge

to thump him in the ribs. She was no fragile flower to be protected from the big bad man. She could hold her own against any adversary—but she held her tongue for once in her life and stayed behind him, for this, she knew, was Eagle's moment. She would not have taken it from him for the world.

"What's true?" Eagle demanded, his voice dangerously soft. "You mean the fact that my mind was stolen from me when I was fifteen years old? You mean the truth that you killed my real parents and my siblings, then took some twisted delight in taking the son of a Seeker and turning him not only into one of your murderers, but claiming him as your own son?"

The chamber was suddenly filled with light and Sky blinked against the sudden intrusion. A dozen Dominion soldiers ringed the room.

"And even that wasn't enough," Eagle went on, circling the Kalimar, his eyes never leaving his face. "You had to take my past from me, create a new one for me. Did that give you godlike feelings, Zarn? Did it make you feel omnipotent to take a boy and erase who he was, replacing him with someone of your own choosing?"

Zarn sighed, the sound surprising Sky more than anything she'd seen or heard so far this night. His handsome face sagged and she was struck by the haggardness of his features, the circles under his eyes. Was it possible Garnos Zarn truly cared about the man he had stolen for his son? No, it had to be a trick.

"I did not steal who you were, Eagle," he said.

"Don't call me that!" Eagle snapped. "You don't have the right. You couldn't even leave me my name. Even my nickname you had to twist into something of yours instead of my real father's endearment to me. Bastard." He took a step toward the man and every soldier in the room snapped a blaster rifle into position. He stopped, his hands flexing impotently into fists.

"I did not steal who you were," Zarn said again, slowly, as if he were choosing his words with care. "I liked who you were. You had courage, spunk, all those marvelous attributes any man would want to find in a son." He began to walk, his hands clasped behind him. Eagle stood still but his eyes followed the man's movements. "Yes, I admit, at first I thought it a great joke against the Andromedans and particularly the Seekers, that I should take one of their own and make him mine." He stopped in front of Eagle, their gazes even. "But soon I began to respect you, to admire you. And when you were placed under the mind-probe on Station One with the rest of the Andromedan children we had captured, I wanted to erase all the horror from your mind and give you happy memories."

"Like you did all the other children," Eagle said, and only Sky knew how tightly he was keeping his temper in check. "How benevolent of you to erase the memory that you murdered their parents. Unfortunately for you, something inside of me wanted me to remember—it drove me to remember who I really was."

"I truly wanted you to be my son," Zarn said, extending both hands in a fervent gesture. "I had no one! No heir, no wife, no family! The tortures I endured as a slave before I freed Rigel left me sterile! What did it matter if I ruled half a quadrant if there was no one to share it with?" He took a step toward Eagle, his hands still outstretched. "I saw in you, Eagle, a little of me—"

"No!" Eagle took a step forward and shoved the man back, sending him sprawling to the floor. One of the soldiers ran forward and slammed the butt of his gun into Eagle's jaw.

"Eagle!" Sky screamed. She turned on the soldier and punched the flat of her foot into his midsection. He doubled over and two more soldiers took his place as Zarn staggered to his feet.

"Stop!" Zarn shouted. "Leave them alone."

Eagle cradled his swelling jaw as he forced himself back up from the floor. "Let's get one thing straight—I am nothing like you. I was never anything like you. Whatever you saw of yourself in me was there because you planted it there."

"I'm sure it's easier for you to think so. I'll even help you. You may be wondering about our similar eye color."

He smiled and spread his hands apart. "Colored lenses. It was luck that our hair color was the same, as well as having the tendency to wave. But the internal Eagle—no, I left that alone. You may have received altered memories, but I left your personality alone. So if you consider yourself a murderer, you must take responsibility for that yourself."

"Don't listen to him, Eagle," Sky said, tossing her head and lifting her chin with haughty disdain. "He conditioned you to be one of his soldiers, just as all Andromedan children are conditioned. It's part of the process, isn't it, Zarn? They grow up believing it is their duty to serve the great Zarn. How much more would the so-called son of Zarn feel the calling?" Hands on her hips, she looked him up and down, relishing the anger that flashed into his "green" eyes. "The responsibility is yours, Zarn, and no one else's."

"I wanted a son!" Zarn insisted, raising both hands, curling them into fists above his head and bringing them down with finality. "I wanted you for my son, and that is the truth, whether you believe it or not. But it really doesn't matter, because I am the Kalimar, Lord Zarn, and son or not, your treason cannot be tolerated."

Sky was amazed at the look of real regret that seemed to center in Zarn's gaze as he looked at Eagle. He pressed his lips together and shook his head as if he wanted to speak but did not trust himself; he turned away as though he could not bear to look at his "son" any longer. His voice was choked, harsh.

"You will be executed as the ultimate example of how low my tolerance is for rebels. Even my own son is not above my law. Your death will strike a note of terror through the hearts of every planet under the Dominion's rule." He sighed and clasped his hands together in front of him. "I only wish it did not have to be."

"How touching," Sky said dryly. "And what are your plans for the rest of us, as if I didn't know?"

Zarn turned, the weariness etched into his face deepening as he looked at her. "We will all travel to Nandafar, now that your little sister has so graciously revealed her whereabouts. Once there I will take steps to insure that the galaxy is never again polluted by the vile genetic pool of your kind. But do not worry. The four of you started this little excursion together; it seems only fitting that the four of you should finish it together."

"Four of us?" Sky frowned.

"You, Telles, Eagle, and of course, Mayla." Zarn's evil smile broadend. "But now, we must go. After all, we don't want to keep your sister waiting, do we?" He jerked his head toward two of his men and they ran forward, skidding to a halt in front of her and Eagle, rifles at the ready.

Sky grabbed the silver band she had tossed aside during her passionate lovemaking with Eagle and lifted it to her head. Zarn crossed to her side in two swift strides and seized her, his fingers biting into her wrist. He jerked her against him and she shuddered as his evil, handsome face bent close to hers.

"No, no, my dear. You'll have no need of that any longer." Sky stared at him as Zarn took the band from her fingers and handed it to a soldier standing nearby. "Oh, did you think I didn't know?" His lips slid like liquid into an oily smile. "I know everything about you."

Sky tossed her head back and glared up at the man. "So now what? You kill me? You kill my sister? Can you kill everyone in the universe, Zarn?"

Zarn's left arm wound around her waist and he pressed his whole length against her. She was determined not to let him see fear in her eyes, but as his hand moved down to caress her buttocks, her bravado faltered.

"Leave her alone!" Eagle shouted.

Sky jerked her head in his direction, willing him not to speak again. She sent him a swift thought saying exactly that and he fell silent, though a muscle in his jaw twitched dangerously. She turned back to Zarn, blessing the crystal for keeping her safe. But once aboard Zarn's ship . . . The man pulled her closer and slid his hand up her back, over her shoulder to seize her face roughly.

"No, I cannot kill everyone in the universe, my dear," he whispered, "nor do I intend to kill you. Well, not for a while in any case. You are too sweet, too desirable, and since my *son* desires you—" He lifted his gaze to Eagle and Sky suddenly knew that as preposterous as it sounded, Zarn had been truly hurt by Eagle's rejection of him. "—Then you become all the more desirable to me." He rubbed his thumb against her cheek with a languid motion, and Sky closed her eyes, afraid that if she continued to face him, he would see the absolute terror in her gaze. His lips drew nearer. "But your sister, ah, that is another matter entirely."

Sky's eyes flew open and she cried out as Zarn's mouth came down over hers, brutally, in a punishing kiss. She struggled against him and could see Eagle fighting his guards. One of them brought the butt of his gun down against his head. Eagle slid to the floor. Sky wrenched free of Zarn and, doubling up her fist, slammed it into his face, the sound of flesh and bone colliding very satisfying. With a roar of outrage, Zarn backhanded her across the face, sending her sprawling to the floor a few feet away from Eagle. He had already rallied from the glancing blow and was kneeling, his breath coming hard. He glanced over at her and his mind pierced hers:

Use your powers, Sky.

Sky sent him a startled look. *What?*

You are a Cezan. Look at what you were able to do inside my mind, in Telles's mind. Zarn is just a man. Use your power against him. Remember how the temple appeared as something else? Make him believe he is seeing something else besides you.

But I don't know how.

Yes, you do. It's like our dragon ploy, but with your mind. It's within you, Sky. The heritage of the Cezans. I know it. I feel it whenever I touch you. Use it.

Zarn wiped the back of his hand across his bloodied lip and glared down at her, his face almost apoplectic with rage.

"Take them," he said, his voice little more than a hiss. He turned away toward his men. "Put them in the brig in separate cells."

In the brief moment that Zarn's attention was off her,

Sky shrank back into the shadows and began to concentrate very hard. Maybe Eagle was right. Maybe she was more of a Cezan than she gave herself credit for being. She had used variations of the trick coming to mind at different times in her privateering. It was worth a shot. Maybe she could use her power to influence his mind, to convince him that she wasn't there. She delved deep within her mind, finding the center of herself, of her power, and then turned that power outward, toward Zarn and his men.

She has disappeared. She sent the thought straight into his mind. *She is nowhere to be found.*

Zarn turned back from giving his orders and his eyes widened as he stared directly at Sky.

"Fools!" he shouted. "Where did she go? Why did you not stop her?"

The soldiers gaped in bewilderment, staring at the now-unseen Sky before they spread out to search the entire room. She was expending a great deal of energy keeping the image of her disappearance uppermost in their minds, but Sky still managed to use the confusion to move quickly to the side of the soldier holding her deflector band. She stuck her foot out as he rushed by and he sprawled to the floor, the band bouncing into a corner, unnoticed by Zarn as he roared orders at his men. Quickly she scooped it up, adding its disappearance to her subliminal control of the situation.

"This place still has power," one of the soldiers whispered, as they returned to the center of the room to report Skyra Cezan was nowhere to be found. He was a young Teener, Sky surmised, just assigned from one of the Stations. His voice shook. "I remember hearing stories about it—how the spirits of the people who were killed here still roam about."

"Silence!" Zarn shouted, his gaze falling on the boy who had dared to voice his fears. He advanced on the youth, his eyes glittering with violence, and as he berated the young man, Sky headed across the room, but stumbled to a stop as she saw a soldier lean against the wall next to the hidden door. Wincing, she heard the mech-

anism click and the door swung open next to the aston-
ished guard.

"Sir, sir!" he shouted, interrupting Zarn's tirade. "I've
discovered a doorway in the wall!"

Sky pressed one fist to her lips to keep from crying out.
She saw Eagle's green eyes flash with fear as two of the
soldiers wrenched the door open and a contingent of
men began to file down the stairway, their boots pounding on the stones. Zarn crossed to stand at the top of the
stairs, his eyes gleaming with triumph.

"Secure the area and then I will come down," Zarn
said. "No doubt this is where our little princess escaped
to."

Sky bit her lower lip so hard she drew blood. No, the
little "princess" hadn't had enough sense to slip through
the doorway and alert Telles below. She glanced at Eagle
to find he was gesturing for her to leave. He was right.
She had to get out of the temple and somehow find a
ship, find a way to get to Nandafar before them. Kell.
Kell was waiting back at the *Defiant!* If Zarn hadn't gotten to him first—

She ran to Eagle's side. Two soldiers flanked him and
she slipped up to carefully plant a gentle kiss on his lips.
He didn't betray any reaction to her touch, but he gazed
down at her—his eyes conveying the depth of his love for
her. She knew what he planned to do to his father if he
got the chance. She knew he would not survive afterward. This might be their last farewell. Throwing her
arms around him, pressing her body close to his, Sky
kissed him again, then choking back a sob, turned and
ran out of the temple of the Seekers.

Chapter Fourteen

Nandafar. Legendary world of mystery. Eagle stared around in awe as he and Telles were shoved down a narrow path in front of two burly guards, their hands shackled behind them with energy bands. One tall, husky soldier led the way. Now that his memory had returned, Eagle remembered the stories his real father had once told him about the world of Nandafar, where supposedly strange and mystical creatures lived. There had never been any connection to the Cezans, but now that he knew how powerful Sky and her sister were, he wouldn't doubt that the "strange and mystical creatures" had been ruling Andromeda for centuries.

As he walked down the path, his attention was once more drawn to the landscape around him. He'd been to many worlds in his travels, but never one such as this. Curling lavender vines covered the tops of trees, and they writhed with the movement of the wind—or was it really the wind?

Eagle felt only the faintest touch of breeze and yet the vines moved as though a gale blew across the planet's surface. The trees themselves had narrow pale pink trunks and they also swayed from time to time. As Eagle trudged down the obviously little-used path, he realized that while the trunks' movements took them back and forth, the vines on the top of the trees moved up and down. No, not even that—they curled like snakes. Understanding hit him. These plants were alive—not alive in the sense of being living, growing things, but in the sense of being sentient.

265

He turned his thoughts back to more important matters—like survival. Sky had escaped, or at least he hoped she had made it past the outside guards and back to their ship secreted in the forest. It was possible, of course, that Zarn's men had found the ship before Sky reached it and she had been captured.

He hoped like hell she was all right. Their thoughts had touched again as she pressed her lips to his, and he'd wanted nothing more than to stop her, to hold her in his arms and keep her safe. But she wasn't safe with him. She had tossed the thought to him as she left that she was going to find Kell. He frowned as he trudged along. If Sky had made it to the ship and was no longer in danger, he found it hard to believe Kell would be willing to let her risk herself to save the man he seemed to scorn above all others. Then again, he had always obeyed Sky's orders, only voicing his objections now and then. To be fair, she had given Kell the option of coming to the temple or not, and he had exercised that option. He actually hoped the first officer would refuse to help her, would stop her from pulling some damned fool rescue operation that would endanger her life.

Eagle stopped the direction his thoughts were taking. It did no good to dwell on his fears, but did a lot toward paralyzing his thinking ability. The thing disturbing him the most was the fact that since Sky had left him, Eagle had felt no mental contact with her—which could be good news. She might already be off-world and safe with Kell. Or she could be wearing her deflector band again. Still, he missed her sweet presence in his mind. He turned and glanced back at Telles to see how he was doing.

After Sky sneaked out of the temple, Zarn's men had dragged Telles up the stairs from the chamber below, quite a bit worse for wear. Zarn had descended and Eagle had held his breath, sure that he would order the destruction of all of the orbs and the precious archives below. But instead, he had returned to the upper level, bringing, for some unfathomable reason, the huge crystal with him, carried between two husky soldiers. Why? To destroy it so that the orbs could no longer be activated? Probably. Eagle had never felt such helpless frustration in his life as he watched Zarn load that precious piece of Andromedan heritage into the shuttlecraft that would take it to his ship.

"Halt." The sound of a soldier's harshly snapped command brought him back to the present. He looked up to find the leader of their group had stopped and was conferring with another soldier ahead on the trail.

Telles stumbled to a stop beside Eagle, breathing hard. "We could make a run for it," he muttered.

"And where would we go? We have no idea what's out there in that undergrowth, although if those vines are any indication, I don't think the plant life here is exactly like what you'd find in my Aunt Fosey's garden."

The corner of Telles's mouth lifted up. "You don't have an Aunt Fosey." He lowered his voice even more until Eagle could barely hear him. "Any thoughts from Sky—any communication at all?"

Eagle shook his head, his chest tightening with apprehension. "I'm hoping she reached the ship without interference from Zarn."

"I'm sure she did. She's very resourceful."

He watched the two soldiers talking. They were Special Forces, their blue uniforms indicating their assignment to that rough-and-tumble battalion. The Forces had been his life for so many years—how would it be never to wear his uniform again, never fulfill another mission? Eagle shook his head, feeling the disbelief settle over him.

"How could I have bought it all these years?" Eagle asked. "Why didn't my true memory ever push through? What kind of man am I to play the fool for so long?"

"You aren't a fool, Eagle," Telles said. "You're a victim of Zarn's quest for power, just like the rest of us."

"And what are we doing here?" Eagle's gaze was fixed on the growing number of soldiers at the end of the path. "Why didn't he just kill us all back on Andromeda and then come to Nandafar on his own to capture Mayla? What does he need us for?"

Telles shrugged. "Your father always liked an audience."

"Don't call him that," Eagle said sharply. "Don't ever call him that to me again. He isn't my father." His throat tightened. "Not anymore. Not ever again."

Telles glanced up at the pale lavender sky and nodded. "You know, though, in spite of everything, I believe he genuinely cared for you. He did raise you as his son, his heir."

"For his own twisted kind of vengeance." Eagle sighed, keeping his head bowed, his gaze on the gray dirt beneath his feet. "But either way, I've lost two fathers this day—one I never knew I had, and the other, the only one I've ever known."

Telles nodded wordlessly. Eagle felt again the dark despair threatening to engulf him and he beat it back, focusing on the knowledge that it was still up to him to save Sky's sister and get them out of this mess. His head snapped back up. He could lick his wounds and grieve over his lost life later when they were safe. Or perhaps he would never get the chance to grieve at all before he joined his real family in death. If that was his destiny, so be it, but one thing was for certain: Zarn would be leaving this plane of existence too—although Eagle doubted he would end up in the same afterworld as the Andromedans.

He smiled grimly. How wonderful it was to even be able to believe in an afterlife. Before this day, he had always held to the Rigelian belief there was no life beyond the death of the body. No wonder Zarn sought power—this life was all he had.

The soldier in charge nodded his head, then perked up as someone pushed his way through the crowd of men. Telles was saying something to Eagle about Sky's ability with a blaster but he never heard the end of the sentence, for the man pushing his way through the armed group of men looked very, very familiar. Eagle straightened, alarm ringing through him. P'ton. Sky's security chief from the *Defiant*. What was he doing here? Zarn must have reached the *Defiant* then—but why was a captive being allowed to roam free?

P'ton stopped in the middle of the path and addressed the men surrounding him. "We are nearing the place of ritual," he said. "You soldiers are allowed no farther than this. You two will come with me." His hand came from behind his back. A plasma-blaster fit firmly in his grip and he pointed it directly at Telles and Eagle, a grim smile playing around his fat lips. "Remember this weapon, boys? Don't make me use it on you. Lord Zarn would be very unhappy if you had to miss the festivities."

"What the hell is going on?" Eagle demanded. "What are you doing here spouting off orders like you're part of this?"

The small eyes narrowed. "I am part of this. You should know better than anyone how many spies Lord Zarn has planted all over the galaxy. I'm just one of them. When I heard about a woman with silver hair who needed help finding her kidnapped sister, something rang a bell. I'd just received the information from Lord Zarn that the Cezan child had been found and arrested. Luckily, I had a contact aboard the *Defiant,* someone the captain trusted implicitly."

Suddenly Eagle remembered Mayla's words to Sky: *Someone in your camp is a spy for Zarn.* He felt the chill begin at the base of his spine. It shot up to burn at the nape of his neck as realization struck him. "Kell."

P'ton nodded, unsmiling. "Very astute, Colonel. He recommended me."

"But surely he wouldn't betray Sky—he was like a brother to her."

One corner of the thick-set man's mouth lifted. "Perhaps Kell was not interested in being a 'brother' to the captain."

"Hell, even I knew he was in love with her," Telles said. "And I wasn't around the two of them for long."

Eagle shook his head. "But if he loved her—"

P'ton shrugged. "Altairians are actually very passionate people. Their adherence to logic is a relatively new philosophy that doesn't always overcome their true natures."

"And what about you? Sky used to brag about your loyalty to her."

"My loyalties lie with the Kalimar, and he alone. I am Rigelian to the core of my soul. I will never forget how your father brought us from the brink of doom, to become the strongest world in the quadrant."

"He isn't my father."

P'ton gestured with the gun, his face altering into a scowl. "That is your loss, Colonel. Now, if you please, march in front of me, single file."

Eagle didn't move. "Why doesn't he just kill us all and be done with it?"

"The heir to the Andromedan throne is about to receive the full measure of her power. Your father intends for you to be there when that phenomenon takes place."

"Why?"

P'ton stuck the barrel of the blaster into Eagle's side. "Move," he said, shoving him forward with his other hand, then gesturing to Telles. "And while Lord Zarn would be disappointed, it would give me great pleasure to tell him you were both killed while trying to escape."

Eagle began to walk in the direction P'ton shoved him, his mind racing desperately for an idea, a strategy, a way out of this living nightmare. They walked for another fifteen minutes until they reached a small rise where P'ton called out for them to stop. Eagle stood, legs apart, hands still shackled behind him, gazing down at a sight that made his blood run cold. Zarn stood in full battle uniform, cape flapping about his ankles in the slight breeze. Beyond him were at least two hundred men, clad in Forces uniforms, armed to the teeth.

Invasion.

He had seen too many of them, been part of too many to mistake it as anything less. He squinted against the fast-fading sun of this world and realized Zarn was not just conversing with his soldiers, but with a group of men and women clad in pale blue robes. He started down the incline, oblivious to P'ton's orders to stop. He was drawn up short by a guard before he reached Zarn, but got close enough to understand what was going on.

The Kalimar stood surrounded by a small group of what appeared to be dignitaries who had come out to greet them. They were all bowing in front of him, and as Eagle noted their silver hair, their blue and lavender eyes, he understood. The Cezans. As he gazed at their pleasant, calm faces, he was startled. They seemed not in the least concerned about the troops of soldiers roaming across their planet's strange and twisted surface. Had Zarn tricked them into letting him in? Had he somehow already managed to mind-probe these beings and condition this gentle takeover?

"Do they know who you are?" he called out. Zarn snapped his head around to face him, then smiled slowly, the gesture splitting the stoniness of his face.

"Of course. They know I am the Great Kalimar and that I am here to help them."

The members of the delegation from Nandafar were still talking quietly amongst themselves, and they glanced up as Eagle was dragged back from Zarn's side by two soldiers. Their gazes flickered over him curiously, but they were unconcerned. One of them even laughed at something another said. Completely lighthearted and guileless. Like children. Didn't they have a clue as to how much danger they were in?

Eagle jerked out of the grip of one of the soldiers, determined to make the most of this chance.

"My name is Ranon. I am the son of an Andromedan Seeker, murdered by this man. His troops mean you and all of your people harm, and especially the one called Mayla who is under your protection." He searched the gazes of the seven people looking back at him. Four men, three women. They all had the classic Cezan features: silver-blond hair, turquoise-blue eyes. One, a woman who seemed ageless, had lavender eyes like Mayla. Her face was smooth, flawless except for a few tiny lines at the corners of her eyes. Somehow she looked familiar, as if he had met her before, but of course that was impossible. She stepped forward and placed one hand on Eagle's arm in a comforting gesture.

"Do not concern yourself," she said warmly. "There is no danger."

Eagle glanced at Zarn and his anger grew as he saw the smug, complacent look on his face. "You don't understand—"

"Of course we do. We are so glad to finally meet you. We have heard much of you from Mayla."

Eagle drew in a quick breath, his need to make them understand suddenly overshadowed by his need to make sure Sky's sister was unharmed.

"Where is she? Is she all right?"

The woman laughed softly and patted her arm. "She is fine. Do not be concerned. You are all under our care, Colonel."

"Shahala, may I introduce you to my son, called Eagle. He has suffered a head injury and believes himself to be the son of an Andromedan Seeker." He shook his head in feigned sorrow. "You can see I have had to restrain both him and his friend, who is also delusional."

The woman now identified as Shahala shot him a look of astonishment and laughed aloud, the sound like a string of bells being run simultaneously. She met his frowning gaze squarely.

"Nonsense," she said at last. "Come, it is not long until the ritual begins. I know you do not want to miss Mayla's entrance into adulthood, Lord Zarn." She turned and started down the narrow path.

Eagle glanced at Zarn and for the first time saw uncertainty flash in his eyes. Good. He was realizing he might not be able to trick these seemingly simple people so easily. Or was it good? In the past when Zarn felt himself losing control, he saw it as an excuse for unleashing a reign of violence and destruction.

"That bitch will soon learn not to laugh at me," Zarn muttered under his breath. "They are not as all-powerful as they would like us to think, not for long anyhow." He spun around and faced Eagle, one corner of his mouth taut, smug. "Anxious to see your lover's sister? You will, soon enough. And that little tramp you love as well."

"I know about Kell," he said. "And Sky is no fool. She'll figure it out."

"But not in time." He nodded at the guard next to him and Eagle felt himself once more being shoved along, down a path that cut through the heart of what seemed a wilderness of pinks and blues and lavenders. Strange, strange world. Strange people so unconcerned. Or was it that they had no reason to be concerned? Was their power that great? Could it stand against Zarn's army? If so, then why had they not saved Andromeda from his grasp?

Eagle looked up to find Shahala next to him. Zarn was several yards ahead, and how she could have slipped past him he didn't understand. He turned and found his guard was nowhere to be seen.

"It was the time of Mon Ser-iah and we could not reach them."

Eagle stared. "You're reading my mind."

"Yes, my child. Do you object?"

"Yes, strenuously."

"I apologize." She inclined her head. "All of your questions will be answered, in time." She turned to go.

"Wait. What did you say? What is the—the Mon—"

"The Mon Ser-iah is a time of renewal, when all Cezans must, in a sense, shut down their powers and allow the Creator to restore them. They expend so much energy throughout their lifetimes that once every year they must have a time of rest. Unfortunately, at this time they are vulnerable to attack."

Eagle considered her words for a long moment, his gaze on the ground. "Then Zarn must have known—but how could he?"

"No, I doubt Zarn knew. He was just extremely lucky in his timing." Shahala sighed and smoothed one silvery strand of hair back from her face. "If there is such a thing as luck in our universe. Or perhaps he did know, for his timing is, once again, unfortunate."

"You mean it's time for this Mon Ser-iah. When?"

"Before the next sunrise."

"Tomorrow?" Eagle stared at her, aghast. Zarn's words echoed through his mind: *They are not as all-powerful as they would like us to think, not for long anyhow.* He strained against the energy shackles, feeling the frustration mounting inside of him. "Shahala, I warn you not to underestimate Zarn. I think he does know—and I'm not sure you are aware of what he is capable."

Her lavender eyes turned toward him. "I am aware, last of the Seekers. He killed my sister, Pelana."

Understanding bloomed inside Eagle's mind. No wonder she looked familiar to him. "Sky's mother—she was your sister. Then where have you been? Why haven't you helped Sky?"

She held up one hand. "All will be explained. All has come about as it was intended."

"Soldier!"

Eagle glanced away from Shahala to the furious face of the leader of the prisoners, who was striding toward him, hands balled into fists. Eagle turned back to warn Shahala, but she was gone, the guard standing in her place looking stunned and dizzy.

"What seems to be the problem, soldier?"

The man opened and shut his mouth several times before shaking his head wordlessly.

"Then come along," he ordered. "And no fraternizing with the prisoners."

Eagle didn't resist this time as the guard pushed him forward. There was more to this planet than met the eye, and, he believed, more to the Cezans than what the gentle people would have them understand. But whatever their powers, if tomorrow they entered their "time of rest," then that was when Zarn would strike, and the Cezans could kiss their utopia on Nandafar good-bye forever.

"Kell, you've got to help me," Sky said to her first officer. They stood on the bridge, the first place she had headed after she had arrived at the ship and been brought back aboard. Sky had known the odds were slim that the Dominion goons hadn't already found the *Defiant* in its sheltered landing place, and it was with some trepidation that she had approached the ship where it hovered just above the ground. Eagle had expertly piloted the ship into a clearing in the middle of the forest, then he and Telles had rigged their dragon image again, to be triggered when and if the ship detected its surface being probed by sensors.

She had hidden behind a bush and observed the ship, keeping a sharp lookout for soldiers or any indication Zarn and his men had been in the area. She searched for footprints, broken plants, but as far as she could tell the perimeter around the ship was just as they had left it, and finally she decided to approach. Kell had his sensors sweeping the area constantly and had immediately identified her and brought her aboard. Still clad only in Eagle's shirt, she immediately headed for her quarters, ignoring the questions in Kell's gaze.

"Where are your new friends?" Kell said, pacing across the bridge and back. "Why do you not ask them for help?"

Sky had dismissed the other remaining crew members so she could talk to him privately. She noted the dark purplish shadows under his eyes and the way those same blue eyes darted furtively to the side every time she spoke to him. Something was wrong. She could feel it. Was he sick? Angry? What was going on? His words were filled with petulance, totally unlike the Altairian.

She moved to block his next pass across the bridge and he stopped, again not meeting her gaze but shifting his line of vision to the left of her head.

"Kell, what is wrong? You look terrible. Are you sick?"

"No, Captain, I am quite well."

"Come on, it's just us. You can drop the 'captain' for now." She moved toward him, frowning with concern. She placed one hand on his arm and he stiffened beneath her touch and moved back a step, allowing her hand to fall away from him. "You're still angry with me, because I followed them to the temple. But Kell, we found out so much!"

For the first time he looked directly at her and one dark blue brow lifted in the old, familiar way. "Did you find Mayla?" he asked.

"No, but she found me."

"Indeed."

She laughed self-consciously, feeling progressively more uncomfortable in his presence. He held himself so stiffly, so unnaturally. Kell on his most pompous day had never acted like this.

"Yes, she appeared to me in the temple and warned me that Zarn was on the planet. We were very lucky he didn't find the *Defiant*."

"Fortunate," Kell agreed, his voice a monotone. "Did Mayla say where she was?"

"Yes, on the world of Nandafar. But Zarn heard too and he captured Telles and Eagle, and now he's on his way there. We have to reach Mayla before he does."

"Eagle is his son."

Sky shook her head, still feeling the amazement of what she knew. "No, he isn't. What Telles told us was true. Eagle is an Andromedan, mentally conditioned by Zarn to believe he was his son."

Kell turned and began walking slowly around the bridge, his feet thumping methodically as he circled behind the chairs at each empty station. His fingers trailed across their backs. He seemed tired, distracted.

"And how did you find this out?"

Sky hesitated, but knew there was no way around the answer. "He allowed me inside his mind."

"Ah. So, the truth comes at last," he said mildly. "And Zarn's reaction?"

"He plans to make an example of Eagle to the rest of the quadrant. He figures if he shows them that he'll execute his own son for being a rebel, it will help deter the uprising."

He nodded, coming to a stop behind the command chair, moving his arms to rest on its high back, his eyes downcast. "And you want me to help you save the man you love." He glanced up at her. "You do love the Colonel, do you not?"

Sky bit her lower lip so hard she tasted blood. She didn't want to hurt him but it was inevitable that he know. "Yes," she admitted. "I love him, Kell. I'm going after them with or without you, but I'll have a better chance with you along."

He didn't answer. He kept his gaze steadily on her and she met his eyes with difficulty. At last he spoke.

"Then of course I must go with you, Sky. After all, I am your friend."

Sky felt the relief rush over her. "Of course you are," she said, hurrying over and impulsively hugging him. He didn't respond except to pat her back almost absent-mindedly. She drew away from him.

"Kell, are you sure you're all right?"

"Of course, Captain." He pulled his attention back to her for a brief moment and his mouth curved up slightly as he lifted one hand to her face. His thumb smoothed her cheek just for a second and his blue eyes kindled with something like their old concern before he moved away from her again. He turned and walked toward the helm. "Shall I program navigation?"

"Yes," Sky said, taking her place in the captain's chair. "And call the rest of the crew to the bridge."

"Of course."

In just a few minutes, the crew was in place and Kell was finishing his computations. As he punched in the last of his equations, Sky suddenly realized he had not seemed surprised by her announcement that Mayla was on the mythical, heretofore imaginary world of Nanda-far. He had not asked for coordinates, nor any kind of details on how to locate the planet. Sky sat back in her chair, puzzled, as he turned and calmly spoke.

"Coordinates locked in, Captain. Warp?"

"Five," she answered. "Push it as hard as it will go."

Her crew turned to their duties and Sky leaned forward, linking her hands together, her gaze fixed on her first officer. Kell was not himself, that much was certain, but the question was, when it came down to it, when her neck and that of Mayla and the others were on the line, would he come through? Would Kell still be loyal to his captain in spite of his personal feelings?

"Locked in, Captain."

Sky pushed herself back in the chair and felt the familiar mantle of command settle around her shoulders.

It felt good, like a comfortable old pair of boots or a well-worn uniform.

"Hit it, Lieutenant," she ordered, and closed her eyes as they jumped to a speed faster than light.

The path ended at a large structure that resembled nothing so much as an upended bowl. As they grew closer to the building, Eagle noticed more of the silver-haired people. Their features were unmistakable—it was like looking at variations of Sky and Mayla.

The guards stopped them several feet away from where Zarn and the representatives of Nandafar were gathered. His father—Eagle stopped the thought, feeling a quick rush of pain gather in his chest as he corrected the words in his mind—the Kalimar turned and began walking toward him, gesturing for the woman beside him to follow.

He took out a small triangular piece of metal and passed it over Eagle's and Telles's hands. The energy shackles popped, then shut down, and the two men were free.

"Shahala is about to explain what will take place during the ritual tonight," Zarn said companionably. "I thought you might find it interesting."

"Why?" Eagle demanded, keeping his gaze on the silver-haired woman beside him.

"So that you will know why we are here."

Eagle fought the old reflex to speak to Zarn as his father. Instead he kept his voice cold, impersonal.

"I know why *you* are here. To take over this world and subjugate these people." He shifted his eyes toward the man, allowing himself a brief, burning glance. "Remember, I used to lead the landing parties, the reconnaissance troops."

A silence fell between them and the woman looked from one man to the other, then spread her hands apart. "Please, if you will all come with me, we will share the evening meal. Once we are in the great hall, I shall explain the ritual"—she glanced back at Eagle—"and other things as well."

Eagle and Telles looked at one another and silently

shared the same sentiment. This was an odd group of people, willing to break bread with the man who was sending a battalion of soldiers streaming over their world in every direction. Eagle began to walk, following the procession in front of him, wondering who this Shahala was and why she seemed so unconcerned. But then, the others with her, obviously Cezans with their silver hair and pale blue robes, seemed equally at ease in the company of soldiers and the monarch of the quadrant known for his torturous practices. Strange, very strange.

It didn't take long for them to reach what Shahala had referred to as the great hall, and Eagle was vastly relieved. He was exhausted and hungry, which wasn't good when you were about to have to fight for your life and the lives of those you loved. The great hall was the bowl-like building, all one level, built entirely of small, white stones, none of them bigger than a man's clenched fist. Windows stretched across the entire surface of the building, each one six feet long, with a space of no more than two feet between each one.

A door made from pale ivory-colored wood led inside, and Eagle and Telles were pushed through it into a corridor that stretched farther than seemed possible. The hallway was adorned with wooden carvings and sculptures reminiscent of the one he'd seen in Sky's cabin. Each was set in a recessed niche in the wall.

"Telles," he whispered as they continued, "there's something very odd about this place."

"What do you mean?" Telles said, his long hair snapping against his back, the braids whipping against his shoulders.

"I don't know. Just keep alert."

They reached the end of the hallway just then and ducked through a low portal. When they straightened, they stood at last in a huge, circular room whose ceiling seemed to stretch up to the sky. "What the—this building wasn't this tall when we were outside."

"Things are not always what they appear to be, son of N'chal."

Eagle spun around at the use of his true father's name

and found himself face to face with a man about the same age as Zarn, but whose lavender eyes looked centuries older. The silver-haired man smiled at him.

"Remember that in the time to come."

The man moved past him and Eagle watched him go, then turned his attention to the room beyond. There must have been more than a hundred people there, all silver-blond haired, all talking cheerfully at the small, round wooden tables dotting the room. In the very center of the hall the woman Shahala was seated at a larger table. Zarn sat beside her and as Eagle and Telles moved between the tables, the Kalimar stood and gestured to their guards.

"Bring them over here."

Eagle and Telles took their places beside each other on the smooth wooden benches at Zarn's table. As soon as they were seated, Shahala clapped her hands and a dozen young men and women appeared from the doorways, bearing great platters filled with wooden bowls containing some kind of liquid. Eagle sniffed at the creamy white mixture in his bowl, then quickly picked up the wooden spoon and began to eat. It was delicious, reminding him of a soup his mother used to make back when he was a child on Andromeda and—

He stopped and put the spoon down. He'd had a mother. His memories from Zarn had not included a mother past the age of three. But in truth, he'd had a mother who had loved him and protected him—until she had died at the hand of the man sitting across from him. The man who had stolen his life. Hate flooded through him, killing his desire for food, but he forced himself to finish the nourishment. He would need his strength before this night was over. Still, there was one thing he had to know before he finished his meal.

"Where is Sky's sister?" he asked.

Shahala wiped her mouth carefully with the folded cloth from her lap, but did not answer. Instead she gazed around the table, her eyes seeming to measure each person, weighing them individually. When her lavender eyes stopped at him, Eagle felt a prickle of apprehension on the back of his neck. Her lips curved upward and all at once he realized she was probably reading his mind, could read all of their minds. Wasn't Zarn aware of this? She smiled as Eagle frowned, and moved on, skipping over her own people and finally arriving at Zarn. The lavender hue of her irises darkened perceptibly as she gazed at the man and he returned her stare undaunted. She smiled then and turned back to Eagle.

"You shall have the answers to your questions, all in good time."

"Where is Mayla?" he insisted.

"You forget yourself, son," Zarn said in a steely voice. "You are in no position to demand a thing."

Eagle turned to Shahala. "I confess I am confused, madame. Is not the child Mayla one of you? A Cezan?"

She nodded.

"And is this man not your enemy? Are you not aware of the fact that he wiped out the entire ruling family of Andromeda except for two?"

Shahala looked down at her bowl of soup, and when she lifted her gaze again, Eagle saw the shadow of pain in the depths of her eyes. "I am aware," she said.

Zarn stood, pushing his chair back so hard that it fell over. "Enough." He gestured to one of his men standing near the door. "Take these two men out of here. They will not receive food again until I give the order. I want three guards with them at all times."

The man ran forward and jerked Eagle to his feet. Eagle smiled smugly at the Kalimar. "What's wrong, *Dad*?" he said, a sneer in his voice. "Did I hit too close to home? Afraid I might tip your hand? But these people know about you. Hell, they know what you're thinking. Do you imagine they'll just sit here and let you do whatever you want? They have power—power you can't even begin to comprehend."

"Why do you think I'm here?" Zarn said, his lips curling back from his teeth as he leaned toward the younger man, his hands flat on the table between them.

"Did he tell you he brought the crystal from the temple of the Seekers?" Eagle blurted out as the guard seized him by the arm and jerked him away from the table. He resisted, leaning toward Shahala. "I'm sure he thinks it has something to do with your power, though what he intends to do with it is a secret inside his warped brain."

"Silence!" Zarn clenched his fist and raised it, trembling in front of his face. "You will be silent!"

"Gentlemen." Shahala's voice sent a wave of calm between the two of them and Eagle felt his tension immediately lessen. "Please. If you wish to hear of the ritual, you must both sit down and cease your hositilies. Otherwise, I shall retire until the evening."

"Take him out."

"Eagle must remain or I shall retire," Shahala said lightly.

Eagle cocked one brow at Zarn. "Well, *Dad*? What'll it be?"

The Kalimar spewed his breath out in frustration then jerked his head at the soldier holding Eagle. He released his prisoner and hurried away. Eagle resumed his seat, never taking his eyes from Zarn, the two sitting down simultaneously as Shahala began to speak.

"We have guarded our secrets zealously until now," she began. "Our origins stretch back into antiquity, and I will not bore you with stories of our travails until we reached our current place in this universe. Suffice it to say that we have attained a certain degree of understanding and, yes, power, which we as a people decided long ago to use only for good. A Cezan must never take another life. A Cezan must never use his or her power for evil."

"What if someone is trying to kill you?" Telles asked. "Can't you even defend yourselves?"

"All things happen for a reason," Shahala said. "Therefore we must weigh such a decision. We must ask ourselves, is this happening to teach us something as a people? Is this happening because we have grown too arrogant or have misused our power? If so, then we must be prepared to take the consequences without taking other lives."

"But what if you haven't?" Eagle interjected. "What if you are innocent?"

Shahala shook her head ruefully and picked up her spoon. She dipped it down into the bowl and lifted the smooth mixture to her lips, tasting it delicately before she answered.

"No one is innocent, my friend, except children. And some of those are wise beyond their years."

"Like Mayla. What will happen to her tonight in the ritual?"

Shahala lowered the spoon back to her bowl and stared down into its depths for a long moment. At last she lifted her head. "The ritual is the culmination of a Cezan's first thirteen years, and is when she or he receives the full endowment of power from the Creator. We all receive differing levels of that power; however, some are blessed with greater abilities. Mayla is one of these. She will be a great leader." She shifted her gaze to Zarn. "She will rule this galaxy."

Zarn laughed but his eyes did not reflect any amusement. He pushed his own bowl away and the liquid sloshed over the side and dribbled onto the tabletop. "A child? But my dear, how can this be? She will need an army to conquer mine, for I assure you I will not lay down my control voluntarily or easily."

Shahala lowered her gaze, then glanced back up at him. "You shall," she said. "And very soon."

Zarn laughed again. "Of course, of course," he said benevolently. "I will be happy to turn what I have worked so hard to attain over to a thirteen-year-old child."

"During the ritual, Mayla's crystal will be joined with the crystal that belonged to her mother," Shahala said. "Our Creator will use the power that binds this universe together, and transfer its energy into the crystals, empowering Mayla with a strength and ability beyond even most Cezans."

Zarn stared at her, his hands still on the table in front of him as he leaned forward. Eagle saw the jubilation in his eyes. "But I have the crystal that belonged to her mother."

Shahala's eyes shifted to his and Eagle saw her pain again.

"Yes," she whispered, "I know." A sad smile eased across her lips. "Why do you think you are here? We could not hold the ritual without both crystals."

"Are you trying to tell me that you people have *caused* me to be here?" Zarn said. He linked his hands together and shook his head. "I came here to find the secret of the Cezans and their power."

"And so you shall," she said softly.

"What about the big crystal?" Telles asked. "Does it have anything to do with this?"

"Yes."

She motioned to one of the servers walking by and the bowls around their table were quickly removed and plates of fruit replaced them. Eagle was no longer hungry. His curiosity, on the other hand, was insatiable.

"During the ritual," she continued, "the large crystal will be placed on the tall hill that lies across from this facility."

"You mean the one that has that odd arch on the top of it?" Telles asked.

She nodded. "We call it the Arch of Transformation. That ancient arch, combined with the two crystals, will take the power from the universe and feed it into the large crystal, then back to Mayla." Her lashes swept downward and Eagle was struck by her beauty even though she seemed quite old. No, on second thought, she seemed ageless. "Mayla is very special. We have not had a Cezan with her potential in a very long time."

"What will be my part in the ritual?" Zarn asked, barely able to contain his excitement. Eagle looked at him in disgust.

"Your part?" Shahala shook her head. "The ritual is for Cezans only."

Zarn leaned back in his chair and hooked one foot over his knee. Eagle saw the subtle play of arrogance in his features and in that moment, hated the man more than he'd thought possible.

"Now, that's where you are wrong, madame. I possess the other crystal. I possess the large crystal. You will not have your 'ritual' without my help."

Shahala lifted both silver brows. "Really," she said. The word was a statement, not a question.

His fingers clenched and unclenched in a nervous rhythm in his lap as he continued to challenge her. "Isn't it true that the person who holds the other crystal receives a portion of that power?" he said.

"Yes." Shahala looked around the table again, her gaze lighting on Eagle. "But that honor is given to the child's mother or father. Or in lieu of them, their closest kin."

"Sky," Eagle said, tensing as he once again wondered where she was. "It should be Sky."

"But the lovely Sky isn't here." Zarn's smile was smug. "Therefore, I will take her place, since I possess the crystal."

Shahala shook her head. "You do not know what you are saying, Lord Zarn. This power is not to be trifled with."

"I do not intend to trifle with it." His lips curved up with malicious pleasure. "I intend to possess it and to use it."

"For evil. For your own wicked purposes."

Zarn lifted both dark brows and spread his hands apart. "Surely the great Cezans are not saying that an insignificant human like myself could be of any concern to such powerful beings?"

"I caution you against this action," Shahala said, rising from the table, her lavender eyes cool, steady.

"Will you stop me?" he asked.

She hesitated and Eagle's heart began to pound more rapidly as she shook her head slowly.

"No, Lord Zarn. We shall not stop you."

"Good. Then I have one more little favor to ask." Zarn stood and for a moment the two were opposite each other, their gazes locked in silent combat until he spoke again. "I suggest that the ritual will not take place tonight. You will wait until tomorrow night."

"No," Eagle said, rising. "You go too far, Garnos."

Zarn shrugged. "How else does a great man attain more greatness? He must be willing to gamble, to risk everything."

"It isn't your risk." He turned to Shahala. "I can't believe you would allow him to do this. Your people have the power to stop him—do it! Do it before Mayla gets hurt or innocent people—your people—are killed. You know what will happen if you wait until tomorrow—and he knows too!"

Zarn's laughter filled the great hall and the Cezans stopped eating and looked up at him, their placid faces reflecting curiosity, not fear. Eagle found their passivity incredible.

"Of course I know," he said. "The first time was a fluke, luck. I didn't expect them to go down without a fight. Pelana told me about the Mon Ser-iah."

Shahala paled. "My sister Pelana? I cannot imagine her sharing that knowledge with you."

His mouth twisted into a smirk. "Even a Cezan will talk if you promise to spare her child."

Shoving his chair back, Eagle circled the table and grabbed Zarn by the throat before anyone could stop him. He felt the soft flesh of the man's neck beneath his fingers and tightened the pressure, bringing him to his knees. His false green eyes grew round, grew panicked as his air was cut off; his hands flailed at Eagle's, trying to free himself, trying desperately to break his grip. The sound of booted men running did not deter Eagle, but in a matter of seconds a dozen soldiers had him surrounded and two had pulled him off of their leader, who now sat on his knees, gasping on the floor.

He lifted a shaking finger and pointed it at Eagle. "Out!" He managed to choke the word out half-coherently. The soldiers dragged him away toward the door and Eagle didn't even struggle.

"This isn't over!" he shouted across the great hall. "If the Cezans won't stop you—I will!"

Zarn staggered to his feet, one hand to his throat. He stumbled after the men, his face red with anger. "Big words from the son of a mealy-mouthed Seeker who couldn't even find the guts to defend his family!" he shouted after him.

The soldiers almost had him to the door when Eagle

slammed his head into the first one's stomach and sent a right uppercut to the other one's jaw. He turned and headed back across the hall as soldiers scrambled to grab him before he reached the Kalimar. But they were too late. Eagle hit the man squarely in the jaw, then followed up with a gut punch that left Zarn doubled up on the floor.

"That," he said with a large amount of satisfaction, "was for my father."

Two soldiers snapped their rifles into place and prepared to fire as Eagle had known they would.

"No!" The cry came from Zarn. He staggered to his feet and with difficulty straightened to face the man he had raised as his son. "He's mine," he whispered, "and nothing so simple as a phaser's blast will end his worthless life."

Chapter Fifteen

"All right, keep this orbit stable," Sky ordered Cordo, rising from the command chair and moving to a panel at the science station. "Send out that dragon message Eagle and Telles rigged and maybe it will buy us a little time."

"Lord Zarn's ship is in a lower orbit," Cordo said, examining the sensor relay. "However, it is only a matter of time before his sensors find us."

"Then we'd better hurry."

"Captain." Sky turned to find Kell behind her, arms folded across his narrow chest. "How do you intend to infiltrate this place? They will see our shuttlecraft immediately with their sensors."

Sky glanced down at the schematics on the panel in front of her. There appeared to be a large settlement in the middle of an otherwise empty area. She was willing to bet that was where she would find Mayla and the rest. She lifted one hand to the silver band once more in place around her forehead, then looked back up at her first officer.

"I'm going to use the transport."

A startled look flashed across Kell's face, which was rapidly masked as he crossed the bridge to her side and spoke in a low voice.

"Captain, you know as well as I that the transport mechanism on this vessel is, shall we say, less than reliable. We don't have the power on this small ship to beam large objects. We usually only use it to transport inanimate things."

Sky glanced up at him and nodded. "Usually, Lieutenant. But today you're going to beam down a bigger package—me. They won't expect me just to materialize in the middle of the camp or town or whatever—though we'll try to pick a spot that won't be so obvious—and maybe I can sneak up on them."

"All by yourself," Kell said flatly. "You intend to conquer Zarn's army all by yourself."

Sky took a deep breath and released it, smiling ruefully. "No. I intend to protect my sister or die trying." She turned and strode across the bridge. "However, this ship is capable of blasting the hell out of Zarn's troops, and I plan to get in a few shots before it's all over."

"What about the Cezans?"

She stopped walking but did not turn back. "Yes, I know." She glanced back at him over one shoulder. "I'll take a portable communicator and try and relay back to you exact coordinates where the blasts will do the most harm with the fewest casualties. I'll be in my quarters, Kell, preparing."

Sky entered the lift and as soon as the doors closed, sagged against the wall of the tiny room. What she was about to do was crazy, totally foolhardy, but it was her only chance. If she took the shuttle, she'd most likely be shot down by Zarn's ship or at the very least captured. The transport beam was unreliable, that was true, but it was her one chance to slip into Zarn's stronghold without being detected first. She hoped she'd be able to do some damage before they caught her. And she'd be able to see Eagle and Mayla before she died.

The door opened and she hurried down the corridor to her room. She'd been forced to leave her tynarium droid suit on Andromeda and so did not have that recourse, that protection; therefore she had to find an alternative. She punched in the alarm code that released the door to her quarters and almost ran inside, heading straight for her closet. She had one of Redar's old uniforms that he'd rigged with special sensors. The sensors reflected back the image of anything it came in contact with, making the wearer practically invisible. It needed repairs, its functions sporadic at best, but she had no other choice. She would put it on and requisition one of the plasma-blasters—that should at least throw a scare into the first few Dominion soldiers she ran into—and head for the small transport bay.

The door to her room slid open and Sky turned in surprise. Kell stood in the doorway for a moment before crossing to her side. He took the sensor uniform from her and tossed it aside.

"You'll have no need of that," he said softly, a great sadness mirrored in his blue eyes.

Sky opened and closed her mouth a couple of times before she could speak. "Kell—" she laughed uncomfortably—"what are you doing?"

"You aren't going to use the transport to beam down to the planet."

Relief flooded over her. He was worried about her. So this was what his odd behavior was about. She patted his arm and bent down to retrieve the suit.

"Don't worry! It will be fine. With you at the controls, I'm sure that—"

"You don't understand, Sky." He knelt beside her and his hands closed around her upper arms. He stood, bringing her slowly with him, his fingers biting into her flesh.

She lifted startled eyes to his. "Kell." Sky let his name fall from her lips with old familiarity even though she knew nothing would ever be the same between the two of them again. "Kell," she said again, this time her voice hardening over the syllable, "what's going on?"

He pulled her closer to him and she saw, in an instant, the real Kell who had lain hidden all of these months, the man who was an emotional being, the man he had tried to deny.

"Did you think I had no honor, Captain?" he asked. "Did you think I would simply accept your rejection of my love? First I had to stand by and watch your simpering adulation of that fool Redar. It was convenient that he died when he did or I would have been forced to kill him. But that man—Eagle—he was by far the greater threat. I knew the moment I saw him that he would take you from me. I had heard gossip about the Eagle, about his loyalties being under suspicion, and so I contacted the Kalimar. He convinced me I would be very well rewarded if I found anything that would either exonerate or implicate his son of dealing with rebels. But from the beginning I sought to destroy him."

"I can't believe it," Sky said, shaking her head, feeling the shock and anguish tighten around her heart. "I trusted you. I thought you were my friend."

"I didn't intend to betray you at first—just him." His blue eyes were fervent as they gazed down into hers. "I thought after he had been executed that you would forget him, and everything would be as it had been, except you would realize I was the better man."

"And when did you change your mind—about me?" she whispered.

Kell let his hands slide down her arms to her hands. He held them for a moment, staring down at their entwined fingers, then released her abruptly, his voice hardening as he spun away from her.

"I didn't realize at the time that your desire for the man would so alter the feelings I had for you, leaving me with this strange and overwhelming need for revenge." He glanced back at her. "Altairians have a great sense of honor, and when it is callously besmirched, only through revenge may it be regained."

"But the Altairians have given up the old ways," she protested, backing away from him, trying to edge toward the door. "You believe in peace, nonviolence whenever possible. You believe in controlling your emotions."

Kell moved to block her from the doorway, and Sky silently cursed as he began walking toward her, the force of his presence pushing her back toward the bunk.

"I tried to believe," he said. "But my own passion—my passion for you—was too strong. And then later, my hate."

Sky stopped moving, her throat tightening with fear. "You hate me, Kell? After all we've been through together?"

"Especially after all we've been through together. For

that should have convinced you, Skyra Cezan, that I was the best choice for you."

Sky thought quickly. Her only contact with an Altairian had been Kell, after he had adhered to the new beliefs. She had no idea how to deal with one who had re-embraced the old ways, the old violence, but she had to try. She took a step toward him. "Kell, I am asking you, for the sake of my little sister, a little girl who never caused you any harm, to let me go and help her."

"You care nothing for your sister."

The words were like a slap in the face. She shook her head. "What? What are you saying? Of course I care for my sister. Why do you think I'm willing to risk my life by using our *befarking* transport? I'm trying to save her from Zarn!"

"You're trying to save your lover."

Kell's usually calm face was twisted now, his features so distorted by his hate that Sky scarcely recognized him. This was no one with whom she could bargain or negotiate. Nothing would make him let her go.

"You hate me so much," she whispered. "How do you plan to kill me, Kell?"

He didn't answer. Pain crossed his face briefly, but the smile, when it came, was malicious, bitter, more frightening than that of any enemy she had ever faced. For this was her friend, her comrade, her compatriot. This was Kell. But it wasn't, not the Kell she had known and loved. Sky ducked her head as hot tears stung her eyes. How was it possible? She took a deep breath and turned away, refusing to let him see how deeply his betrayal had hurt her. She fought back the tears and after a moment, turned back to him, lifting her gaze.

"Was I to pretend that I felt something for you that I didn't?" she asked softly. "Was I obligated to return your love?"

"I loved you and you used me, took advantage of our friendship." His lips curled back over the word. "I thought if I gave you time, you would realize—but then *he* came and you proved yourself to be the trifling woman I feared you truly were."

"I never meant to hurt you," she said, moving a step closer. They were only a few feet from the doorway. Kell's hand moved to his waist and for the first time Sky noticed he had a phaser strapped there. A small but lethal variation on their usual defense phaser, this one was capable of complete disintegration.

"So you're going to kill me now?" Sky asked as he held the phaser and turned it toward her. She ran her tongue over her dry lips, thinking quickly. Her escape from Zarn had been possible because she'd been free from the restraint of her deflector band but had been protected by the crystal. If she took the band off now, Kell's thoughts and that of the crew would overwhelm her. If she didn't take off the band, she couldn't send a telepathic thought that would convince him she was invisible or no longer in the room. She'd have to find another way. She crossed abruptly away from the door.

"Not quite yet," he said solemnly, "but soon. Lord Zarn wants you down on the planet for the ritual."

"So it's 'Lord' Zarn now, is it?" she said, sitting down on the edge of the bunk. "Have you stopped to think how he is using you, Kell?"

One corner of his mouth lifted derisively. "It's use or be used. Kill or be killed. Wasn't that your wonderful Redar's philosophy? I have used Zarn as much as he has used me. I found it an equitable trade."

"What did he promise you if you helped him get the goods on Eagle?"

Both corners of his lips turned up. "To watch him die."

The coldblooded way he said the words sent a chill through Sky's body, but she forced herself to laugh. She lay back across the bunk and stretched her arms over her head, feigning a casualness she was far from feeling.

"Do you really think he's going to kill the man who has been his son all of these years? Don't be ridiculous. He'll just stick him in a mind-probe and alter his thoughts like he did before."

Kell moved toward the bed and Sky could see out of her half-closed eyes that her words had sent a fragment of doubt into his mind. She also saw the raw desire in his eyes as he watched her stretch. Her uniform might not be provocative, but she knew her movements were.

"Not after his betrayal," Kell said, standing only a few inches away from the bed now, staring down at her. "Not after fighting Forces troops and rescuing rebels. After all, Zarn has to answer to his Cabinet."

Sky yawned and stretched again, arching her back against the drab olive coverlet. "You know, Kell, part of the reason I never entertained the thought of you and me—at least not seriously—was because you were so reserved, so restrained." She sat up, rolling upward from the bunk like a cat, her silver hair cascading behind her. She kept her eyes hooded, sultry. "I didn't really know you felt that way about me. I thought you were locked into that Altairian logic thing, the no-emotion thing, you know?" She smoothed the cloth on the bed with one hand, her fingers caressing the material in a sensual movement as she spoke. "To make love without emotion—that sort of thing never really appealed to me."

She sighed and slid one arm outward, lowering her body back to the bed. She watched him through her lashes and felt a quick rush of adrenaline as he took the bait and sat down beside her, the phaser still in his hand, but lowered, seemingly forgotten for the moment.

"The Kalimar also promised me . . . you." Sky felt a sudden panic, but forced herself to lie there. She concentrated on the thought of Mayla, and Eagle. She had to do this for them, for all of Andromeda. He laid one hand tentatively on her arm and she immediately covered it with her own, moving her other hand to curl around his neck, pulling him down to her, to the warmth she offered.

Kell groaned and gathered her into his arms, his lips grinding roughly against hers, stealing her breath. She fought the urge to push him away. It was obvious to her the way his mouth, his hands, tore at her body that he meant to satisfy himself at her expense and cared nothing for her. Yet he claimed to love her. Or was this the revenge he had spoken of? Who was this man? This wild, angry person who had been apparently lurking beneath the surface of his mild-mannered demeanor? Now she felt no sense of guilt for tricking him. He was acting little better than an animal in the way he was trying to rip her uniform from her, and Sky knew if she didn't act quickly, she would be unable to stop him. He had dropped the phaser in his passion and it lay beside them, discarded. It was time to act.

She pushed him back roughly, smiling at his questioning look, then rose to her knees and began to undress him, opening the closures down the front of his uniform, forcing herself to touch his bare, pale-blue chest. He closed his eyes at the touch of her fingers against his skin and in that instant, Sky grabbed the phaser and fired.

The look of outrage on his features was something she would remember for the rest of her life, she knew. She had prepared herself for it. But what she hadn't prepared for was the fact that the phaser was not set on stun, but destroy.

Kell screamed soundlessly in front her, his eyes bulging in terror. She cried out, falling backward off the bed, away from the pulsating energy surrounding him, tearing at him as it shimmered through his body and finally sent his molecules shattering into oblivion.

Darkness came swiftly to Nandafar. One moment it was daylight, and the next a blackness had fallen that was so dense that Eagle could barely see Telles next to him as they sat shackled near the Arch of Transformation, a wide, curved-metal structure, which stood over six feet tall. Three guards sat nearby playing a game of piddles, a betting game. After his little scuffle with Zarn, Eagle had been summarily ushered out of the Cezans' great hall and back into the jungle surrounding the bowl-like building, where his guards had beaten the hell out of him for about fifteen minutes before returning him to his friend's side. This time he knew his rib was broken because he'd heard and felt it crack right in two. Every breath he took now pierced his side with pain. But that was really of little concern since he knew Zarn planned to kill him as soon as the ritual was over.

The ritual. Telles had kept his ears open after Eagle

had been dragged away and had overheard a conversation between Shahala and Zarn. The Mon Ser-iah began at moonrise this night. With his troops backing him up, and the fact that he had the crystals needed for the ceremony, Zarn had forced Shahala and the other Cezans to agree to postponing the ritual until just before moonrise. In this way, Mayla would still be able to receive her power, and in turn, Zarn would receive his. But directly afterward, all of the Cezans would be unable to fight the troops that would then overrun their world. If they had any intention of fighting at all, which Eagle doubted. Telles said he got the impression even Shahala hadn't expected this turn of events.

He leaned his head back against a vine as thick as a tree, then sat up straighter as he saw a row of lights moving up the side of the small hill on which the arch rested. As they drew nearer, Eagle saw the lights—flickering blue flames—were contained in small bowls, each held by a Cezan. They moved to the arch, paying no attention to the two men bound together, and Eagle closed his eyes, wishing he knew what had happened to Sky. Had she made it back to the ship? Had she discovered Kell's treachery?

The thought of Sky alone with Kell sent a hot flash of rage mixed with fear through his veins and he took a deep breath, then gasped as pain laced through his side. He waited until the pain ebbed, then brought his breathing back to a shallow rhythm.

Surely Kell wouldn't harm her. He loved her, so of course he wouldn't want to hurt her. Or would he? Altairians had once been one of the proudest warrior people in the galaxy, and the most ruthless. If he was reverting to form—

Eagle pushed the thought away. No. Kell wouldn't hurt Sky. He couldn't. And Sky could take care of herself. Hadn't she proved that to him over and over again? He shifted against the trunk of the vine and winced as another bruise made itself known. He leaned his head back again. Then where was she? If she was all right, where was she?

"Telles," he said softly so as not to alert the guards. "They're about to start the ritual I think."

"Hmm?" Telles opened his eyes halfway then closed them again. "Not until moonrise. You might as well rest until then, because I have a feeling that things are going to start sizzling around here soon after."

"If Zarn receives part of Mayla's power—"

"He won't. The Cezans won't allow it."

"What makes you think so? They haven't lifted a hand yet to stop him."

"Hey! You two pipe down!" one of the soldiers shouted over at them.

"Yeah? Why don't you come over here and make us?" Telles shouted back. The tall, husky man tossed down his cards and stood, a smile on his face.

"Or not!" Eagle hastily interjected. "Hate to break up your card game just when you were about to win. The arch must be sending special luck your way. We'll shut up."

The soldier looked at him dully for a moment, then sat back down and picked up his cards.

"What the hell were you trying to do?" he hissed to Telles. "Haven't I had enough bones in my body broken today?"

"If we don't get at least one of them over here, how are we going to get a weapon and escape?"

"As we sit here shackled, our hands useless. Forget that plan. Bad plan."

"I suppose you've got a better one."

"Maybe. It all depends on how much my dear old daddy still cares."

Telles sat up a little straighter. "What have you got in mind?"

The people of Nandafar gathered at the foot of the hill, each carrying a small bowl filled with the curious blue flame. They formed a double line and began walking up the hillside with Garnos Zarn at the end of the line, his dark head towering over the shorter Cezans. Eagle and Telles stood in their shadowed alcove among the foliage, watching the procession. The two men had managed, through acrobatic gyration, to pull their hands beneath them and move their shackled fists in front of them. So far the guards hadn't noticed.

"Can you see Mayla?" Telles asked as two by two the people walked up the hill, the blue light held carefully in front of them.

Eagle shook his head. "No, and it's almost moonrise. I've been thinking. Suppose we do something to delay the ritual? Wonder what happens if she doesn't do this before the Mon Ser-iah? Will she lose her chance forever of receiving her power?"

"Maybe she'd be better off," his friend said softly, his eyes shadowed.

Something in his voice alerted Eagle. "What do you mean?"

He shrugged and leaned against the thick vine that had supported them through most of the evening. Eagle joined him and a smaller, tiny vine curled around, winding itself across his chest. Impatiently, he pushed the little plant aside. "The plant life around here is getting too aggressive."

Telles grinned. "I've been noticing those little fellas all over the place. They're sort of alive, I think."

"As long as they're small and vegetarian, I don't care. Now what were you saying, about Mayla?"

"I don't know, I just got the impression when she was with me that this leadership thing weighs pretty heavily on her." He turned to Eagle, his tawny brows knit together, his mouth pulled back in a scowl. "I mean, she's thirteen years old—what's wrong with just being a kid instead of training to rule galaxies?"

"Did you give her your humble opinion of her family heritage?"

"I tried to, but she just stared at me like I was insane." He shook his head and lowered his gaze to the ground as if he was trying to puzzle out her strange attitude.

Eagle laughed softly, darting a glance at the soldiers who had abandoned their game and now stood at attention with the rest, watching the procession. "It's her destiny, Telles. Would you want someone to come and change yours?"

Telles lifted his gaze from the ground, dark lashes sweeping upward to reveal blue-gray eyes filled with pain. "Someone did, Eagle. I didn't like it." He nodded, almost to himself. "Yes, I understand what you're saying. This is Mayla's destiny whether I like it or not."

"Getting a little attached, are we pal?"

The bare trace of a smile touched his lips. "You can't look into her eyes and not get attached. I told you a long time ago, she's special. She's very, very special."

"Apparently all the Cezans agree," Eagle said. "Look."

At the bottom of the hill, now standing next to Zarn, was a young girl on the threshold of puberty. She wore a pale blue gown much like the other Cezans', except hers was made from a flowing, supple material that moved with her like an ocean's waves. Purple and blue flowers were woven in a crown around her head and her silver-blonde hair curled around her porcelain face in charming disarray. Large lavender eyes fringed with dark lashes gazed at the people now assembled on either side of the trail leading up the hill, and Eagle suddenly understood what Telles had been talking about. These were not the eyes of a child. These were the eyes of a very mature, very wise woman.

Come the dawn.

Now he understood. Mayla, in many ways, was an adult woman trapped in a child's body. Was it possible that Telles was not just attached to the girl, but had deeper emotions?

"I see what you mean," Eagle said. "She isn't really a child at all, is she?"

"Only chronologically. If you could just talk to her for a few minutes, you'd see she's brilliant, she's witty, she's smart, she's mature—"

"And she's thirteen years old," Eagle reminded him.

"And she's thirteen years old," Telles repeated. "Don't you think that's a fact I constantly remind myself about? I feel like some kind of dirty pervert who preys on children. It isn't like that at all, I promise. Sex isn't even part of the equation. I just care about her. She's such an incredible person."

"She won't always be thirteen years old, Telles."

He smiled ruefully. "Right. When she's twenty-one, I'll be thirty-six years old. Forget it, pal. Some things aren't meant to be. Shh, listen, it's beginning." He cast his friend a questioning look. "Do you really think your plan is going to work?"

"No," he admitted, "but I don't know what else to try."

"Maybe we should just jump one of the guards."

"This worked on Sky's ship," he said, "or a variation. I wouldn't be the first person in the world to flip out after too many mind-probes and too many phaser burns."

"He won't believe it." Telles leaned back against the vine, keeping a wary eye on their guards, who seemed to be mesmerized by the scene in front of them. Eagle turned and followed their line of vision. Mayla. They were watching the girl, and not with any kind of lecherous intent. There was only admiration in their beady little eyes. Amazing. Maybe Telles was right. Maybe she was more special than anyone realized.

The procession had arrived at the top of the hill. Lord Zarn stood next to Mayla underneath the arch, with Shahala on her other side. The blue flames of the Cezans lent an eerie, surrealistic air to the proceedings. Shahala moved to stand between the two, raising her hands toward the sky, and as she did, as if on cue, the moon rose behind her in all its glory.

Eagle caught his breath. He'd seen many moonrises in his journeys, had visited worlds that had two or even three. He'd seen moons whose natural color rivaled rainbows. But the size of this moon, and the brilliant light it cast down, far outweighed anything he'd ever witnessed. It rose behind the arch, as large as the hill itself, as blue as Sky's eyes.

Sky. He wished he could see her before he died. Somehow he knew he was not going to make it off this hill alive. Call it a premonition or a hunch, but he felt it in the innermost fiber of his being.

"Hey," he said softly to Telles, "tell Sky that I love her, will you?"

Telles shot him a sharp look. "Tell her yourself."

"Tell her for me."

The moon filled the sky, illuminating their faces as Telles nodded and the two men reached a silent understanding. Telles stood and Eagle followed. For a moment the two watched, along with everyone else, the incredible picture of the blue moon rising behind the hill and the arch, looking as though it was balanced on the edge of the world, a fitting backdrop for the drama below.

"While you were recovering from your little encounter with the guards, Shahala told me that this entire ceremony is conducted without words," Telles said. "The Cezans communicate telepathically, so at least Zarn won't be able to be involved in that part of the ritual."

"For what that's worth," Eagle muttered. Zarn was clad all in black—his uniform, his cloak, his gloves, his boots. How befitting the lord of the psychological darkness that surrounded the galaxy. He took off his gloves and handed them to one of his lackeys standing nearby before reaching into a pocket of his uniform and taking out an object about four inches long. Eagle and Telles moved forward as far as they dared without drawing the attention of the guards and saw that he held a crystal. It had no color, no sparkle. It lay in the palm of his hand, dull and lifeless. Shahala gestured to him and he stretched it toward Mayla

Mayla held her own crystal, her small face solemn as the tall man forcing his way into her sacred ceremony thrust the lifeless stone toward her. She touched his crystal with one finger, barely grazing the surface, and the crystal leaped to life, color dancing across its beveled edges, energy lighting it from within.

"I think it's now or never, old buddy," Telles whispered.

"What if this keeps Mayla from obtaining her power?"

"At least it will keep Zarn from his," Telles reminded him.

"I hate to mess up such a pretty picture," Eagle said, feigning a sigh. "But here goes nothing."

Sky hurried down the corridor of the *Defiant* fighting waves of grief and guilt. She hadn't meant to kill him.

TESS MALLORY

She hadn't meant to kill him! But now she had to get to the transport bay and figure the coordinates of a safe place she could beam to, within the perimeter of the Cezan settlement below. She had hoped Kell would help her with the computations but—A sob choked her and she had to stop and lean against the wall of the hallway until she could breathe again. He was a double agent, a spy, her enemy. But he had been her friend, and now he was gone. She had killed him.

She slid to the floor and let the tears come for a moment, allowing their healing flow to let at least a little of the pain drain from her heart. Then she gulped in air and pushed herself back to her feet. No time for this, she told herself. No time. Wiping the last of the tears from her face, Sky hurried on, thankful that with such a skeleton crew aboard, it was unlikely she would meet anyone. There was no longer any way of knowing who among her crew she could trust. As much as she needed the power of the *Defiant*, she couldn't take the chance of confiding in her remaining crew and having them finish the job Kell had started.

She reached the teleport bay unscathed and locked the door behind her before moving to the control panel. Curved in a semicircle, it faced the transport pad, a small round platform about five feet in diameter. Above it hung the technological wizardry that enabled it to work.

As Kell had said, the teleport was primarily used to bring cargo aboard, not to send human beings back and forth, but it could be done. Sky remembered Redar using it once in a desperate situation that had occurred when they attacked a weapons dump on the third moon of Malo. A desperate situation. Sky's fingers suddenly started flying across the keyboard of the controls. Redar had always left copious notes, data entries, accounts of things he did. That was one of the things that had made her transition to captain so much easier.

She punched up Redar's personal code, which she knew by heart after all these months, and breathed a sigh of relief as a directory of his files appeared. Scanning

302

them quickly, she frowned as one row after another rolled by. There were hundreds of entries and it would take—She stopped the scroll of words and focused the marker on one line that read: "Moon Transport." Holding her breath Sky brought up the file and quickly scanned its contents.

Yes, she nodded to herself, this would work. Redar gave the computations he'd used to figure the coordinates to beam himself within a very small space. He'd had to beam down into a tiny room where one of his men was being held. He'd made it. She could make it too.

Quickly she called up the equation Redar had used and began to punch in the information she had concerning the planet below. She reviewed the sensor readings and discovered that over three hundred people were presently gathered around a hill in the center of the village below. Knowledge hit her with the force of a phaser's blast as she stared at the computer screen.

Mayla's coming of age. Of course. Each Cezan came of age at thirteen, receiving his or her full measure of power at that time, which prepared them for their place in the universe. This was why Mayla was here on this strange and unfamiliar world. The Cezans had brought her here for her ritual. Sky had experienced her own coming-of-age ritual on Andromeda, and her telepathic and healing powers had increased after that day. When Cezans received full power, it was usually with the help of their closest kin. When Sky had her ritual, she had worn the ancient crystal—the one that had been given to Mayla when it was established that she was the heir—and her mother had worn another. Both crystals were used in the ceremony, and when she received her portion of power from the Creator, she remembered her mother telling her that she had also received a strengthening of her own abilities.

But the crystal her mother had been wearing had been destroyed in the fire that had gutted the palace after the family was slain. Or had it?

Zarn. He'd been there with the troops that had stormed the palace. Could it be possible that he had taken the crystal from her mother? A cold rush of understanding coursed through her. This was why Zarn was here too. This was why he was so desperate to find Mayla. He could have had the crystal all these years just waiting for his chance to steal power from the very people he had murdered.

"No . . ." she whispered.

She checked the sensors again. The gathering around the hill must mean they were getting ready for the ritual. There was a full moon this night, and that was also traditional. The computer came back into focus, and Sky quickly punched new information into the equation. She had planned to beam down to a sheltered, hidden place and plan her strategy, but there wasn't time. Mayla would be at the top of that hill—and so would Zarn. Moonrise was the time most Cezans held their ritual and—A warning rang out suddenly in the depths of her mind and she tuned into it quickly. Some kind of reminder she had placed there herself, a date that was important . . .

"Damn." Tomorrow was Mon Ser-iah. Tonight after the moonrise, all of the Cezans would be rendered practically powerless, and Zarn would kill every one of them. But not if she could help it.

She finished her computations and entered the data, waiting impatiently as the coordinates for the hilltop came up. Sky entered the new information into the transport computer, then took a deep breath. She'd never transported before. The thought of her molecules being broken down into particles, then being shot across the vastness of space to another location to be pieced together again, made her feel sick to her stomach. But there was no other choice. She had to stop Zarn, and the only way to do it was to beam down to the top of the hill and murder the bastard, just the way he had murdered her mother all those years ago. She reached into her pocket and brought out the phaser she'd had the presence of mind to take with her after she'd—after Kell had—

She sighed as she checked the charge on the weapon

and as she did, a memory, once deeply submerged in her subconscious, came bounding suddenly to the forefront of her mind. It was her mother's voice, cautioning her lovingly.

"We do not harm others, my darling child. No, not even if it means we will lose our own lives. We would die to protect who we are rather than fight and in so fighting, change who—and what—we are."

Sky squeezed her eyes shut but she could not shut out the echoing refrain of her mother's voice: *We would die . . . we would die . . . we would die . . .*

She opened her eyes. "And you did die," she said softly. "But I am no longer one of you, Mother—and I *will* kill to keep Zarn from destroying any more of our people, especially my little sister."

Punching in the final number, she rounded the control panel in two quick strides and bounded onto the platform. The automatic setting kicked in seconds later, and Sky gasped as the transporter beam surged through her. Her vision blurred and every fiber in her body felt as though it were being wrenched apart. She was flying. She was enflamed. She was everything. She was nothing. She exploded into a million pieces. She died and was resurrected.

She stood on the edge of a forest of tall, fernlike vegetation near the top of a hill lit by glowing blue flames. There wasn't time to recover from the trembling aftermath of the transport. She had to reach Mayla. A large group of people were on the small mountain, with soldiers patrolling the perimeter. Sky darted back into the edge of the forest, using the cover to sneak closer. It didn't take long to reach the top, but once there, she watched from the protection of the lush bramble, drawing the small phaser from her pocket. She stared down at the weapon for a long moment, then, with a sigh, set the power on stun. As much as she wanted to evaporate Zarn from the face of the universe, she could not cold-bloodedly murder him, in spite of his crimes against her family. Perhaps there was still a little Cezan left inside her after all.

A large metal arch sat squarely in the center of the hill, and Zarn stood beneath it with Mayla. Relief rushed over her so intensely that she felt her knees buckle. Her sister was alive. She hadn't arrived too late. Another woman stood next to Mayla, her hair silvery blonde, her eyes lavender. Sky frowned. She looked so familiar—and not just because their coloring was so much the same. Sky knew this woman. She turned her attention back to what was happening. Zarn was handing Mayla something—a crystal! Mayla touched it and it sprang to life, then drew her hand back, fear darting in her eyes. Sky tensed. She'd never seen Mayla afraid of anything, though she agreed the thought of Zarn with Cezan power was a terrifying thought.

Something moved somewhere nearby and she ducked down within the ferns and vines curling around her. A man passed her, a man who held himself with the dignity and courage of a prince, his dark hair brushing the collar of his shirt, his broad shoulders held stiffly.

Eagle.

Her fears lessened as she saw him. Thank the Creator, he was alive too. But what was he up to? He stopped directly between her and Zarn and she cursed beneath her breath. Now she didn't have a clear shot at the Kalimar. She tried to inch to the right for an unobstructed view, but she was unable to move. Something had her by the foot. She looked down in terror and found that a thick vine had wrapped itself around her ankle and was gently tugging. She kicked at it with her other foot but it was as solid as a rock. As soon as it had her securely, it stopped pulling, as though content to have her in its grasp.

"Son of a *p'faugking tesseract*," she cursed under her breath.

"Sky?"

The whispered word came from beyond the thick vines around her and she froze, squatting down and trying to disappear into the foliage. She squinted up through the fernlike branches over her and saw someone thrust his head into the forest. The man had long golden hair braided intricately and—

"Telles!" she said in a hushed shout. "Over here."

He disappeared from her line of vision but she could still hear him.

"I can't. Under guard," he whispered back.

"Eagle has to move," she said. "He's in my line of fire and I can't move to readjust. My—my foot's stuck."

"He's pretending he's insane," Telles said. "Trying to keep Zarn from gaining part of your sister's power. The Kalimar has the crystal that was your mother's."

"Yes, I guessed as much. But if Eagle stops the ritual, Mayla won't receive her power either."

"That was a risk we had to take. Can you imagine what Zarn will do if he succeeds?"

She felt the blood leave her face and, propelled into action, began to struggle against the living plant that held her so securely away from her goal.

Eagle stood in front of Zarn, his face carefully masked to hide his churning emotions. Shahala had stopped what he supposed was the beginning of the ceremony as he approached, her lavender eyes wide with apprehension. Mayla looked up at him with identical eyes, but hers were filled with relief.

Soldiers thundered up to the peak, rifles drawn, but Zarn held up one hand, his frowning gaze on the man before him.

"Let it go, Eagle," he said, the weariness evident in his voice. "You are outnumbered. You will never survive. There's no point in dying for these people who won't even lift a hand—or a mind—to defend themselves."

Eagle acted as though he didn't hear him. "Dad," he said softly. "Dad, what's going on? Why are we here?" He let his eyes wander over the arch and the people gathered beneath it, his voice becoming more childlike every moment. "Who are these people? Are we going home soon? I told mother we'd be home soon, you know." He moved closer to Zarn and smiled.

Confusion and indecision darted across the Kalimar's

face and he took a step back from Eagle. He stared at the man he had called son, conflicting emotions showing in his features before settling into a hardness Eagle knew well. Zarn wasn't going to buy it.

"Is this the best you can do?" he said disparagingly. "Get away from me, boy. We shall proceed with the ritual. We must finish before the moon reaches its apex." He turned back to Shahala. "Tell me what comes next or I swear I shall level this place and all of you with it."

"The crystals must touch," Shahala whispered. "Yours and Mayla's."

Zarn thrust the now-living crystal out toward the girl as Eagle held his position in front of them. With a trembling hand, Mayla extended her own.

"I'm not going to let you do it," Eagle said, reaching one hand toward the crystal. "Even if I have to die to stop you."

"Get away, son," Zarn ordered, his dark eyes earnest and determined. "I don't want you to die. You can still be saved, your mind reprogrammed—all can be as it was before. Do you hear me? You don't have to die, Eagle. You can live and rule the galaxy with me. Just walk away."

Eagle felt the moment freeze in time as the huge moon rose behind them, and he looked into his father's eyes one last time.

"No," he whispered, placing both his shackled hands over the crystals and tightening his fingers around them. He felt their heat, their power, but he didn't let go, not even when Zarn roared his outrage and with his free hand, shoved Eagle to his knees.

It was the chance Sky had been waiting for. She didn't hesitate. Her aim was swift and true, but as the searing red light surged from the phaser, engulfing Zarn with its terrible power, she realized, too late, that she had made a terrible mistake.

Eagle, Zarn, and Mayla were all touching the crystals just as the phaser's blast coursed through Zarn, and as the energy sizzled through him and into the other two, the power of the crystals was activated.

Shahala fell backward as an incredible, shimmering light encompassed the three. Then, bursting forth around them, it shot upward and reflected off the arch, filling the air with undulating waves of color and energy that slammed the onlookers to the ground. The vine curling around Sky's ankle shrank quickly away as the tremor hit. Shahala cried out in horror. Sky struggled to her knees even as the next wave of power swept over her. Sky clung to a thick vine beside her as she watched the two people she loved most in the world trapped in the throes of a cataclysmic Armageddon that she had caused. She saw Eagle buffeted by the storm, saw him shake and his face contort with agony. Crying out, Sky made it to her feet and started forward. She heard Telles call out for her to stop as she pushed against the power surging from the sacred hill, as she fought to join her sister and her love. She was almost to the arch when she saw Eagle go down, his eyes rolling back in his head as he hit the ground.

Then everything went completely still.

Sky jolted to a stop, her legs trembling with exertion before they collapsed beneath her, sending her to her knees just a few feet away from where both Eagle and Zarn now lay motionless. Miraculously, Mayla was still standing, a shimmering aura surrounding her, filling her with light. The expression on her face was ethereal, stunned, but she seemed all right. Sky struggled back to her feet. She made the few steps to the arch and fell beside Eagle, her fingers pressing against his throat as she tried desperately to find a pulse point. There was none.

She gazed down at his face, feeling as though she'd been slammed into a wall of stone. It was impossible. Eagle couldn't be dead. She lifted him into her arms and brushed his dark hair back from his face. Dark lashes brushed against the tanned rugged contours of his face, and she waited for him to open them. She smoothed her hand over his rough jawline.

"He needs to shave," she said softly. Then the agony

hit her. She sat back on her heels, clutching him to her bosom as she threw her head back, sending out a cry from her heart, from the depths of her spirit. The keening seemed to go on forever, but when she finally opened her eyes and gasped for breath, Telles was kneeling beside her. He was looking behind her, and Sky turned to find Mayla on her knees, the shimmering aura still glowing around her.

She didn't speak a word but held out her arms. Sky moved to let her take Eagle, though the weight of his body bowed her down. Telles moved to help her and she glanced up at him and smiled. As Sky watched, she began to understand, in some unexplainable way, that she was in the presence not only of her sister, but of some great power, some great entity, connected to Mayla in a way she could not fathom. Mayla held Eagle, her left arm beneath him. Telles had moved behind her and added his support, his arm beneath hers, his face solemn as he gazed down at the silver-blonde head near his.

Sky acknowledged in some distant part of her mind that Telles loved her sister, but that fact was unimportant. Eagle was dead. She continued to watch dully as Mayla held him, moving her right hand over his body in a rhythmic motion, never touching him, a shimmer of light hovering in the wake of each pass she made over his body. Sky watched the movement, her own hands knotted into fists, her teeth coming down into her lower lip so hard that blood poured into her mouth, bitter, metallic. Eagle was dead. He was *dead*, so what was Mayla doing? Did she possibly imagine she could bring him back? Even a Cezan could not do that.

But Mayla was special. Sky had always known it, even when her sister had been just a baby. That was why her father had fled with her instead of staying behind to protect his family. He knew the power that Mayla would someday be capable of, though he had not expected the coldblooded slaughter of those he left behind on Andromeda.

Then Eagle's right eyelid moved. Sky had shifted away from Telles and Mayla to give them room, but now she threw herself back at his side, unwilling even to hope. Mayla glanced up at her and sent her a reassuring smile. Her hands continued to move over his body as Sky hovered next to him, and after what seemed like an eternity, Eagle's chest rose as he drew in oxygen, and he opened his eyes.

With tears streaming down her cheeks, Sky gave a joyful cry as Eagle drew in several lungfuls of air and shakily sat up. His eyes lit up as he looked at her groggily, then moved his gaze to include Telles and Mayla. "What's everyone crying about?" he asked. Sky couldn't move for a moment; she was too overwhelmed as she watched him stand, slowly, and reach one hand down to her where she still sat balanced on her knees. "Sky," he said softly, "thank the Creator you're all right."

Sky jumped to her feet and threw herself into his arms, sobbing, laughing, hugging him tightly and kissing him ecstatically over and over again before she could settle down into some semblance of speech.

"Thank the Creator *I'm* all right?" she said joyfully. "You've just been brought back from the dead, my love!"

Eagle frowned down at her. "I've just been what?"

"Brought back from the dead. My phaser blast apparently activated the crystals, and you and Zarn got hit with not only their power but the power of—" She stopped as Eagle stiffened at her words and turned away. Her heart clenched with sympathy as he moved toward the prostrate form of Garnos Zarn, the Kalimar, ruler of Rigel, the Dominion, and a dozen systems. Even though Kell had been the cause of so much pain, she had loved him and his death had been difficult to accept. She knew, then, that Eagle was feeling a mass of mixed emotions—relief, sorrow, anger, triumph.

He stopped and knelt down beside the body of the man who had taken so much from all of them, and with a trembling hand brushed one lock of dark hair back from his forehead. Mayla moved to his side and smiled down at him. His mouth curved up slightly and he stood, holding out his hand to her.

"Hello, Mayla. I'm Eagle."

TESS MALLORY

She nodded and took his hand. She gestured to Zarn and he looked to Sky questioningly.

"Can't she speak anymore?" he said. "Did the new power somehow steal her ability to talk?"

Sky crossed to his side, wrapping her arms around him, still not quite sure everything that had happened was real. "Mayla never talks; not as we do. All of her communication is done mentally. She knows you don't like that and is respecting your decision."

"I never realized she wasn't speaking aloud," Telles said, his gaze lighting on the girl. Mayla flashed him a smile and he grinned, nodding back at her. "Okay, I see. Sure, I understand."

Eagle turned to Mayla. "But you can speak to me in my mind, too, Mayla. It's all right now. After all, didn't you just save my life?"

Joy bloomed within her lavender eyes and Sky heard her thought, swift and sure, imparted to all of them.

Do you want me to bring him back too?

Sky looked at her sister, startled, then at the man lying dead on the ground. Eagle knelt back down beside Zarn and Sky watched the pain dart into his eyes. He bowed his head for a long moment, then stood. Sky knew what it cost him to turn back to Mayla and speak.

"I must leave that decision to you and your people," he said softly. "It is not mine to make."

Epilogue

"Now perhaps you understand why we could not interfere," Shahala said as she stood with Eagle in the shade of a large fern tree. "We firmly believe that all things happen for a reason and must not be altered by our attempts to 'set things aright.' "

Eagle shook his head, one corner of his mouth turning up in amusement. "But we did interfere," he said. "Me and Telles and Sky. If we hadn't, Zarn would have the Cezans' power now."

"And instead, he has become a convert to our way of life. The Creator has a way of working everything out." Shahala gestured toward two men walking down the path to the great hall. Zarn's dark head was bent as he listened patiently to the elderly, silver-haired man beside him. "It was all meant to be."

Eagle watched the two for a moment, then turned away, his chest tightening with tension. "Well, I don't understand your philosophy, but I respect it. Still, I worry about the Cezans' decision to let him stay here. How do you know he isn't gathering information from all of you in order to try to seize your power again?"

"You forget that when Mayla restored him he was willing to open his mind to us and keep it open for the duration of his stay. He is a changed man, Eagle, and is the first of what we hope will be many disciples who will come here to learn the ways of the ancients," her lips curved up and she inclined her head toward him, "of the Seekers."

Eagle blinked, ran his tongue across his lips, then

blinked again. "Are you telling me Garnos Zarn is learning to be a Seeker?"

Shahala's gaze softened and she reached out and patted his arm. "Yes, Eagle, son of N'chal, it is his desire."

"It's hard for me to believe. He has to have a motive, a selfish reason."

"Or perhaps his experience in dying convinced him that there was a better way to live," Shahala suggested. She waved at the two men and Zarn's face split with a beatific smile as he waved back. His gaze shifted to Eagle and his eyes mirrored a sadness, a regret, as he inclined his head toward him. Eagle couldn't say he didn't care at all about the man, and perhaps that was why he had kept his distance since Zarn's resurrection. He didn't respond to the man's gesture, and the one-time ruler of half the galaxy at last turned away, his shoulders bowed in defeat.

"Ready to say good-bye?"

Eagle turned in relief at the sound of Sky's voice. She moved beside him and he put his arm around her waist, drawing her close to him. Telles and Mayla stood behind her and he smiled at the two of them.

"Yes," he said in answer to her question, "I am quite ready to say good-bye to this world—no offense, Shahala."

She bowed toward him. "None taken. Your destiny still awaits you, my friend. May the Creator smile upon you in all that you do." She bowed again and with one last lingering glance at Sky, walked away.

Sky watched her go, her own eyes filled with longing, and Eagle's hand tightened around her shoulder. She no longer wore the silver band that had so long been a part of her life, for Shalala had given her a crystal much like Mayla's that would allow her to use her telepathic powers while protecting her from the minds of others. When they had asked her why she hadn't contacted Sky before now, she would only tell them, in her enigmatic way, "All has happened as was intended."

"I feel terrible, but I have just had a hard time accepting her decision to stay away from me after my mother died," Sky said with a sigh. "How could it have been for the best? I needed my family and I thought they were all dead. If I had known—"

"You would have gone to live with her, here on Nandafar, and we'd have never met. None of this would have ever happened."

Sky lifted startled eyes to his. "Yes, you're right. But then Kell would still be alive too."

Telles reached out and squeezed her arm sympathetically. "Don't feel guilty, Sky. It was an accident. And the universe is well rid of him."

"I know," she said softly. "I just keep remembering him . . . before."

"Let's turn our energies to things we can change," Eagle said. "Are you ready to leave this paradise and help me dismantle the Stations?"

Unconsciously, he reached inside his jacket pocket and touched the signed orders from Zarn, giving him the right to take all the children incarcerated on the Stations back to their families on Andromeda. He also had orders that would send the Forces back to Rigel. The fact that the Kalimar had given them so freely still puzzled him. He frowned and turned his attention back to Sky. In honor of the occasion, she wore a silky gown the color of her eyes that whirled around her with as much movement as some of the crazy plants on Nandafar.

"What's wrong?" she asked, lifting one hand to his face. "Of course I'm going with you. You don't think I'd let a space-boy like you handle something this important without me, do you?"

Telles laughed and Eagle pretended to glare at him. "At least she's cleaned up her vocabulary a little," his friend said. "For the moment."

"Just wait until I get him alone," she retorted, slipping both arms around his waist and hugging him tightly. "I have three choice words for him, whenever he's ready to hear them."

"He's ready, any time," he said lovingly, planting a quick kiss on her forehead. "But what about the two of you?" The humor faded from his eyes. "Are you both prepared for what may await you on Andromeda? You know, just because Zarn is supposedly throwing in the towel, that doesn't mean someone else beneath him won't seize his abandoned power and simply step into his shoes. And there's still the Rigelian Cabinet that must be dealt with."

"We know," Telles said. "That's why the Cezans approved her request for me to go along as her Chief Advisor. With my military experience, I can help her—and the Cezan Council that's going with us—negotiate with these people."

Mayla laid one hand on Eagle's arm and once again he was momentarily mesmerized by the warmth and energy he felt at her touch. She smiled up at him, her lavender eyes bright with joy.

Everything will be all right, Colonel Eagle, she said telepathically. *Thank you for all you have done for me, and especially for my sister. You've really helped her loosen up. She's always been much too serious.* She winked at Sky and her sister sputtered with laughter and outrage.

"I beg your pardon!" Sky said, pulling away from Eagle and putting her hands on her hips. "If I've been serious it's been because—"

"Shut up, space-girl." Eagle swung her around into his arms and effectively silenced her with a long, passionate kiss.

Telles laughed loud and long and as Eagle broke the embrace at last, he saw Mayla looking up at her protector in rapt adoration. Telles stopped laughing all at once and returned her gaze, the same quick admiration in his eyes.

Eagle relaxed a little. He had worried how Sky would handle being apart from her sister for several months, maybe longer, but now he knew he could reassure her that Telles would take care of her. His love for the girl was obvious, and perhaps that, coupled with her incredible power, would help them through the difficult months ahead.

Sky sputtered worldlessly for a moment. "Now, are you quite finished?" he asked.

"No, I am not, I—"

He kissed her again, his mouth teasing hers, the warmth of his lips melding into hers. He pulled away, wondering how she could not be as moved as he now felt, but she still glared up at him.

"Are you finished now?"

"Eagle, I—"

He bent his head to hers again, this time for several burning minutes as he determined to melt her feigned resistance. At last he felt her stiff body relax and her fingers curl into his hair. When he finally came up for air, she was smiling up at him, her turquoise eyes languid with desire.

"Yes, Eagle," she said softly, "I'm quite finished now."

Her silver-blond hair cascaded down her back, and as he moved to kiss her again, oblivious to Telles's laughter and Mayla's giggles, he almost wished their little adventure wasn't over.

She stopped his kiss this time before it started, her fingers pressed against his mouth. He drew back, frowning down at her in mock severity.

So you think the adventure is over, do you? she whispered to his mind.

His dark brows lifted and one corner of his mouth followed suit. He gathered her into his arms, hardly noticing as Telles and Mayla slipped away, glancing back over their shoulders as they headed for their own destinies.

Isn't it? he asked as their minds intertwined and a warm rush of contentment pulsated through his veins.

Sky reached up and smoothed one dark lock of hair back from Eagle's face, tucking it carefully behind his ear before she answered, her turquoise eyes shining with the brilliance of every star in the heavens.

No, my love, it is only just beginning.

Midsummer Night's Magic

Four of Love Spell's hottest authors, four times the charm!

EMMA CRAIG
"MacBroom Sweeps Clean"

Stuck in an arranged marriage to a Scottish lord, Lily wonders if she'll ever find true love—until a wee Broonie decides to teach the couple a thing or two about Highland magic.

TESS MALLORY
"The Fairy Bride"

Visiting Ireland with her stuffy fiancé, Erin dreams she'll be swept into a handsome stranger's enchanted world—and soon long to be his fairy bride.

AMY ELIZABETH SAUNDERS
"Whatever You Wish"

A trip through time into the arms of an English lord might just be enough to convince Meredyth that maybe, just maybe, wishes do come true.

PAM McCUTCHEON
"The Trouble With Fairies"

Fun-loving Nick and straight-laced Kate have a marriage destined for trouble, until the fateful night Nick hires a family of Irish brownies to clean up his house—and his love life.

___52209-8 $5.50 US/$6.50 CAN

Dorchester Publishing Co., Inc.
P.O. Box 6640
Wayne, PA 19087-8640

Please add $1.75 for shipping and handling for the first book and $.50 for each book thereafter. NY, NYC, and PA residents, please add appropriate sales tax. No cash, stamps, or C.O.D.s. All orders shipped within 6 weeks via postal service book rate. Canadian orders require $2.00 extra postage and must be paid in U.S. dollars through a U.S. banking facility.

Name_____
Address_____
City_____ State_____ Zip_____
I have enclosed $_____ in payment for the checked book(s).
Payment <u>must</u> accompany all orders. ❏ Please send a free catalog.

Futuristic Romance

Love in another time, another place.

Firestar by Kathleen Morgan. Sheltered and innocent, Meriel is loath to mate with the virile alien captive her mother has chosen, for she never expects Gage Bardwin's tender caress to awaken her passion. But during the night of lovemaking their souls touch, and when devious forces threaten to separate them, Gage and Meriel set out on a quest that will take them across the universe and back to save their love.

___52218-7 $5.50 US/$6.50 CAN

Somewhere My Love by Karen Fox. As an officer of the Alliance, Sha'Nara has been trained to destroy the psychics who seek galactic domination. But abducted by Tristan—the most dazzlingly sensual man she's ever encountered—she finds he's not the monster she was prepared for. And soon she realizes that as surely as her body is Tristan's hostage, so is her heart.

___52210-1 $4.99 US/$5.99 CAN

Dorchester Publishing Co., Inc.
P.O. Box 6640
Wayne, PA 19087-8640

Please add $1.75 for shipping and handling for the first book and $.50 for each book thereafter. NY, NYC, and PA residents, please add appropriate sales tax. No cash, stamps, or C.O.D.s. All orders shipped within 6 weeks via postal service book rate. Canadian orders require $2.00 extra postage and must be paid in U.S. dollars through a U.S. banking facility.

Name_____
Address_____
City_____State_____Zip_____
I have enclosed $_____ in payment for the checked book(s).
Payment **must** accompany all orders. ❑ Please send a free catalog.